BESTIES

Look for:

Friend Me

Includes

Mates, Dates, and Inflatable Bras

Mates, Dates, and Cosmic Kisses

Mates, Dates, and Designer Divas

Other books by Cathy Hopkins:

Mates, Dates series

Mates, Dates, and Sequin Smiles

Mates, Dates, and Tempting Trouble

Mates, Dates, and Great Escapes

Mates, Dates, and Chocolate Cheats

*Mates, Dates Guide to Life, Love,
and Looking Luscious*

Truth or Dare series

Truth or Dare

All Mates Together

Love Lottery

The Princess of Pop

Teen Queens and Has-Beens

From Simon Pulse

BESTIES

**Includes books 4–6
of the Mates, Dates series:**

Mates, Dates, and Sleepover Secrets

Mates, Dates, and Sole Survivors

Mates, Dates, and Mad Mistakes

cathy hopkins

simon pulse

New York   London   Toronto   Sydney

SIMON PULSE

An imprint of Simon & Schuster Children's Publishing Division

1230 Avenue of the Americas, New York, NY 10020

Mates, Dates, and Sleepover Secrets copyright © 2002 by Cathy Hopkins

Mates, Dates, and Sole Survivors copyright © 2002 by Cathy Hopkins

Mates, Dates, and Mad Mistakes copyright © 2003 by Cathy Hopkins

These titles were originally published individually in

Great Britain in 2001 by Piccadilly Press Ltd.

All rights reserved, including the right of reproduction

in whole or in part in any form.

SIMON PULSE and colophon are registered

trademarks of Simon & Schuster, Inc.

Designed by Tom Daly

The text of this book was set in Fairfield, Cyne, and Gotham.

Manufactured in the United States of America

This Simon Pulse paperback edition August 2009

2 4 6 8 10 9 7 5 3 1

Library of Congress Control Number 2008930205

ISBN: 978-1-4169-7837-4

Contents

Mates, Dates, and
SLEEPOVER SECRETS

For Rachel

(And thanks to Rachel, Grace, Natalie, Emily, Isobel, and Laura for letting me know what's hot and what's not. And thanks to Jude and Brenda at Piccadilly for their input and for giving me a chance to be fourteen again. And last but not least, thanks to the lovely Rosemary Bromley.)

Noola the Alien Girl

"'We are the champions, *we are the champions,*'" sang some Stupid Boy outside the window of the girls' locker room.

"How sad is that?" asked Melanie Jones as she rubbed strawberry-scented body lotion onto her legs. "We beat them three weeks running and they win *once* and think they're it."

"Yeah," I said as I pulled my hair back and plaited it. "Today," I said, raising my voice so that Stupid Boy could hear outside, "was a mere blip in our team's otherwise excellent performance."

"Yay," chorused the rest of our team, who were in various states of undress after the soccer match.

"You woz rubbish," shouted Stupid Boy.

I shoved my stuff into my sports bag and stepped out-side into the dazzling June sunshine. There was Stupid Boy—namely Will Evans, goalie from the boys' team.

"You talking to me?" I asked.

Will tried to square up to me, which was difficult, seeing as I'm five feet seven and he's a squirt at five feet four.

"Yeah," he said to my nose.

"In that case, would you mind using the correct grammar? It's you *were* rubbish, not you *woz*."

Will went red as the group of guys around him snig-gered.

He stuck his tongue out at me.

"Oh," I yawned. "Like I'm *really* scared now."

By now, most of the girls' team had finished changing and had come out to see what was happening. It was always the same. Every Saturday, after the match, the games continued off the pitch—often with the girls bombing the boys with balloons swollen with water from the locker room taps.

I picked up my bag to go home. I'd got bored with it all in the last few weeks. I was sure there had to be a better way to get a boy's attention than splattering him with water.

Anyway, it was Saturday and that meant lunch with Mum and Dad. Dad insists that we eat together as "a family" on the rare occasions that he's not working. What family? I think. It's not like I have hundreds of brothers and sisters. Only Marie who's twenty-six and left home to live in Southampton years ago and Paul who's twenty-one and been away studying in Bristol.

"Oi, Watts," called Will.

"The name's T. J., actually," I said, turning back.

"T. J.? What kind of name is that?" sniggered Mark, one of the other boys on the team. "T. J. *T. J.*"

I tried to think of something clever to say. "It's *my* kind of name," I said, for want of anything better.

I didn't want to get into the real reason. I'd never hear the end of it. My full name is Theresa Joanne Watts. Like, yeah. How dull and girlie is that? But Paul has called me T.J. since I was a baby and it stuck. Much better than Theresa Joanne. But I wasn't going to explain all this to the nerdie boys from St Joseph's High. If they knew I hated my real name, then that's what I'd be called for ever.

"Okay then, *T. J.* You and me," said Will, pointing at a picnic table by the football pitch. "Over there. Arm wrestling."

Now this was tempting. Arm wrestling was my major talent.

I took a quick look at my watch. I had time.

"Okay, Evans. Prepare to die."

We took up our positions opposite each other at the table and both put our arms out, elbows down. A small crowd soon gathered round as we grasped hands.

"Ready," said Mark, "steady, GO."

I strained to keep my lower arm upright as we began to arm-wrestle.

"Come *on*, T. J.," cried the girls.

"Come *on*, Will," cried the boys.

"Hey, T. J., there's a guy looking for you outside the boys' locker room," said Dave, the boys' team captain as he came out to join us.

"Nice try," I said, not looking up. I wasn't going to break my concentration for the oldest trick in the book. Plus, Dave was A Bit Of A Hunk and I usually said or did something stupid when one of his super species was around. I made myself focus. The crowd around was beginning to get excited as I kept my arm firm and Will's started to weaken.

"Show him, T. J.," said one of the girls.

I could feel my strength wavering as Will fought back

and my arm wobbled. Then I summoned every ounce of energy and *slam*, Will's arm was on the table.

"Hurrah," cheered the girls, then they began singing. "*We* are the champions. *We* are the champions. Champions, the champions, champions of Europe."

"*Stupid* girls," said Will, rubbing his hand and going to unlock his bike. "Anyway, we won the footie and that's what really counts. So there."

"Oh, grow up," I called as I walked away.

"There really is someone looking for you, T. J.," said Dave, catching up with me and putting his hand on my shoulder.

As I turned and looked into his denim-blue eyes, my stomach went all fluttery.

"I didn't say it to distract you. Over there, see?" he continued. "Hippie guy with dark hair and an earring."

I looked to where he pointed and there was my brother, Paul, a short distance away.

"*Nihingyah*," I said to Dave, who looked at me quizzically.

I shrugged and turned back toward my brother, who gave me a wave. No point in explaining, I thought, as I made my way over to Paul. Dave would never understand how I get taken over by Noola the Alien Girl when confronted by Boy Babes. She doesn't know many words. Mainly ones like *uhyuh, yunewee,* and *nihingyah,* which I think means, "oh, yeah," and "thanks," in alien-speak.

"Hey, T. J.," said Paul, giving me a hug.

"Hey," I said, and hugged him back.

"Bit old for you, isn't he?" taunted Will as he rode past on his bike.

"Get a life, you perv," I said as I linked arms with Paul and drew him away from the crowds. "He's my *brother.*"

Paul grinned and looked back at Will. "Looks like I'm interrupting something."

"As if."

"Come on, you can tell me. Someone special?"

"Only the local pond-life," I said. "You home for lunch?"

"Yeah," sighed Paul, and ran his fingers through his hair. "Bad vibes. Thought I'd escape awhile and come and find you."

"Scary Dad still mad with you?"

Paul nodded. "And some. The way he goes on, any-one would think I'd committed a murder rather than dropped out of university. But you know how he is."

Boy, did I know! Night and day, me and Mum had to listen to him going on . . . and on: Paul has ruined his life. Paul has spoiled the opportunity of a lifetime. Paul has wasted his talent. If only Paul were more like Marie. He was always a dreamer. He had it too easy. What's to become of him? Where did we go wrong?

On and on and *on*.

See, Dad's a bigwig hospital consultant. Mum's a GP. Even my sister, Marie, is a doctor. Plan was, Paul was to join the club, follow in the family footsteps sort of thing. Only he never wanted to. He wanted to be a musician. He went along with the doctor bit. Got good grades. Got into medical school. Did a year. Did a self-awareness type weekend in London. Saw the light or something. Dropped out of college. Grew his hair. Started spouting self-help jargon. Got into alternative medicine and rejected pretty much everything Dad stands for. Oops.

Dad mad.

Mum sad.

Me, though, I'm glad. Not that he's having a hard time, of course. I feel sorry for him getting all the stick from Dad, but Dad's got me lined up to be a doctor as well. Ew, no thanks. Way too much blood. I want to be a writer, so I'm hoping all this with Paul will pave the way for my eventual fall from grace.

"Seriously though. Looks like you had a lot of admirers there," said Paul, pointing back to the football pitch.

"Nah," I said. "Boys are never interested in me."

"Looked to me like they were *very* interested."

"Only because I'm the arm wrestling champ," I grinned. "I had to show them what's what after we lost at footie this morning."

Paul gave me a look and sighed. "T. J., you're impossible. Wake up and smell the hormones, kiddo. You're easily the prettiest girl on the team."

"Me, pretty? Yeah, right. Get real."

"I am," he said and pulled on my plait.

"You're only saying that because you're my brother."

"No," he said. "You're always doing yourself down. Like you can't see that you're gorgeous."

"Now I know you're kidding. I couldn't get a boy if I tried."

"Have you tried?"

I shrugged. "Er, dunno. Not really. But . . . it's like, I either talk alien or go into my Miss Strop bossy act and start correcting their grammar. I mean. D'oh. How flirty is that? Or else, I terrify them with my superhuman strength. You know, humiliate them by winning at arm wrestling. Very girlie. Not. It just never seems to come out right."

"It will, T. J.," said Paul gently.

"But *when*? Most girls in my year have sore lips from snogging. Me? The only sore bits I've got are bruises from where some boy has kicked me in a soccer game. I'm hopeless. Hannah was so good at the boy thing. They used to really like her."

Paul looked at me with concern. "Sorry about Hannah. Mum told me. When did she go?"

"Fortnight ago," I said as my eyes stung with tears. I was still feeling raw about her leaving, but I was determined not to cry like a baby in front of Paul. Hannah was my best friend. And she'd just gone to live in South Africa. Yeah, in South Africa. Not exactly the kind of place you can hop on a bus to when you fancy a chat. I was missing her like mad.

"You'll soon find new friends," said Paul.

Arghhh. If another person says that to me, I think I will scream. In fact if Paul wasn't my brother, I'd have socked him. People don't understand. *You'll soon find other friends,* like you can go out and buy one in the supermarket.

"I don't *want* new friends," I said. "I want Hannah back."

Hannah was a riot. A real laugh. I knew I'd never meet anyone like her ever again. It was her that came up with the nickname Scary Dad for my father. And with her around, boys never noticed I was tongue-tied or awkward—she babbled enough for both of us. I could hide behind her and they never realized that my cool was actually frozen shy.

As we turned into our road, we almost ran into Mr. Kershaw on the pavement in front of us. He was walking his dog, Drule. Or rather Drule was walking him. Drule is a big black Alsatian and Mr. Kershaw was having a hard time holding on to the lead.

"He can't wait to get to the park." He grinned as Drule yanked him forward.

I laughed and turned to go in our gate but Paul stopped me.

"Actually, T. J., don't go in yet. I didn't just come to walk you home. I've got something to tell you."

"What?"

As he shifted about on his feet, something told me that I wasn't going to like what he had to say.

2

Giggling Girlies

"Hey, T. J.," called Scott Harris from his bedroom window. "Hang on, I'm coming down."

Before I could answer, his head disappeared and the window closed, so I sat on the front step outside our house and waited for him. The Harris family has lived next door to us ever since we moved here when I was seven, so Scott is the next best thing I have to a brother besides Paul. Scott's two years older than me and lately has discovered girls. Or rather, girls have discovered him. He's cute in a boy band kind of way and there's often a group of giggling girlies outside his gate. Scott liked to talk his latest conquests over with me and no doubt that's what he wanted to do now.

"T. J.," called Mum from inside. "Lunch'll be on the table in five minutes."

"Coming," I called back. "Just got to see Scott for a mo."

I was glad Scott was coming over, as I badly needed someone to talk to. I was hoping he'd distract me from the sinking feeling in the pit of my stomach. Paul had just told me that he was going traveling with his girlfriend, Saskia. For a year, maybe two. Starting with Goa, then maybe Australia and Tahiti. First Hannah, now Paul. What was going on? My two favorite people disappearing out of my life in less than ten days.

"Where've you been?" said Scott, appearing round the rhododendron bush in our front garden.

I opened my mouth to say "football," but he was off again before I had time.

"Been looking everywhere for you."

"Good," I said. "Because *I* want to talk to you."

"Why? What's happening?"

"Oh, everything," I began. "You know Paul dropped out and everything, well, now he's off traveling. Hannah's gone. I—"

"Really? Cool," said Scott, looking at his watch.

D'oh? I thought. No. Not cool. "Scott, are you listening?"

"Yeah. Course. But I need to ask a favor first."

I sighed. "What?"

"Hot date," said Scott, with a grin. "I need to borrow a fiver. Just for today. I'll give it back to you next week when I get my allowance."

Yeah, I thought, you said that last week when I lent you two quid. But then I didn't want him to think I was a cheapskate. No one likes a cheapskate. I was sure he'd give it back to me in the end.

I rummaged around in my sports bag, found my purse, and pulled out the fiver pocket money that Mum had given me that morning.

"Thanks," said Scott. "You're a pal."

"So who's the sad victim this afternoon?" I asked.

"Jessica Hartley. She's from your school."

I nodded. I knew Jessica all right. She was hard to miss. Just Scott's type, glam and girlie with long blond hair.

"Yeah. She's in the year above me. In Year Ten. Anyway, as I was saying, Paul's leaving tomorrow, Hannah's gone and it feels like . . ."

"Actually," interrupted Scott, "talking about your school. Do you know Nesta Williams?"

"Yes," I said. "She's in my class."

Scott looked as though he'd won the lottery. "Wow.

You're kidding. How *fantastic*. She's like, a five-star babe. Could you put in a word for me?"

For some reason this irked me. Who did he think I was? First the bank that likes to say yes, now a dating agency?

"What about Jessica?" I asked.

"What about Jessica?"

"Well, if she's your girlfriend, would she like you asking about Nesta?"

"Hey. Not my fault," said Scott with a wide smile. "So many girls, only one me."

My jaw dropped open, but then I realized he was joking. At least, I *think* he was joking. Sometimes he acted as though he believed he really was God's gift to women.

"Oh, poor you having to share yourself around us miserable impoverished girls," I said.

Scott laughed. "You know, you're really cool, T. J. You're so easy to talk to. Like one of the boys."

"Thanks," I said, feeling chuffed with the compliment. Easy to talk to? Maybe that was it. I didn't need to worry about being tongue-tied or saying the wrong thing. I don't need to talk, only listen. Maybe there was hope for me after all.

"Anyway—Nesta. What's she like?"

It was out before I could stop myself. "Oh—a complete airhead."

I felt a bit rotten saying that, as I don't really know Nesta beyond the fact that she's the prettiest girl in the whole school. I've never spent any time with her.

"Airhead's okay," grinned Scott. "It's not like I want her to *talk* to."

"Yeah, right," I said, suddenly feeling miffed. Maybe it *wasn't* such a compliment that I was easy to talk to? Oh, I don't know. Boys. They confuse me.

"Wanna arm wrestle?" I asked.

Scott looked at me as if I was out of my mind. *"What?"*

"Arm . . . oh, nothing," I said as I saw Jessica tottering up the road in strappy high heels. "Your date's here."

Jessica appeared at the gate and looked surprised to see me. She looked fantastic in a tiny white tank top and white jeans with diamante bits sewn up the seams.

"Hey," said Scott, leaping up and going over to her. "You look good."

Jessica was staring at me as though I'd just crawled out from under a stone.

"Thanks," she said and jerked her thumb at me. "Sister?"

"Next-door neighbor," said Scott. "You know each other from school, right?"

I smiled at Jessica, but she didn't smile back. "Can't say I've noticed her," she said. Then, flicking her hair as if dismissing me, she turned away.

"See you later," winked Scott. He put his arm round Jessica, snuggled into her and whispered something in her ear.

Jessica giggled and they disappeared off down the road.

"Er . . . nice to meet you, too," I called after them.

Huh, I thought. You can act as superior as you like, Jessica Hartley, but I know Scott's got his eye on someone else. One week and you'll be history. So there. Stick that in your diet yogurt and eat it.

I sat out for a bit longer. So much for my heart-to-heart with Scott. Paul was leaving and I felt miserable. Who could I talk to? Scott was a waste of time.

"T. J.," called Mum's voice. "Lunch. On the table. *Now*."

As I got up to go in, I saw Mr. Kershaw and Drule go past again. Mr. Kershaw was jabbering away to Drule and the dog was looking up at him as if he understood every word.

That's it, I thought. I'm going to ask Mum for a dog. She said I could have a pet ages ago. A best friend of the furry kind. One who won't leave the country.

Why didn't I think of it before?

---

e-mail: Outbox (1)
From: goody2shoes@psnet.co.uk
To: hannahnutter@fastmail.com
Date: 9 June
Subject: Norf London blues

Hi Hannah

Miss you loads.

  Idea: Why don't we run away to L.A.? I can write film scripts and you can be a dancer?

  Bad news: Our team lost at footie. But then, you were our best player so I guess it's to be expected. Don't your parents realize the devastation it has caused nationally by removing you from the country?

  My bro, Paul, is leaving. Off to Goa. With Saskia.

  Ag. Agh. *Agherama*. I'm losing all my friends.

  Scary Dad is in v bad mood. It's not *my* fault Paul wants to play the bass guitar and be a hippie instead of being a doctor. Atmosphere at home awful.

  Good news: Beat that scab Evans at arm wrestling. Hahahaha.

  Mum says I can have a dog. Suggest you get one too if your mum will allow until you settle in at school. Dog—man's best friend etc, etc. We're going to go next weekend to look for one.

  Paul is staying the night. Hurrah. And for Sunday lunch. After that he's off and I will be All On My Own.

⊃

And guess what? Jessica Hartley from Year Ten is going out with Scott. But he fancies Nesta Williams. Hahahaha.

If another person says, "You'll soon make new friends," I vill 'ave to keell them.

I am starting a collection of made-up books by made-up authors. For example:

Medical Hosiery by Serge Icklestockings

Modern Giants by Hugh Mungous

Please send contributions.

Tata for now

T. J.

PS: Confucius say: Man with no front garden look forlorn.

e-mail: Inbox (1)
From: hannahnutter@fastmail.com
To: goody2shoes@psnet.co.uk
Date: 9 June
Subject: Cape cool

Hasta banana baby

Miss you too, megalooney.

Keep your chinola up. It's hard for me too. Everything's so differentio here. It's supposed to be winter but it's hot hot HOT. Cape Town is mega. You must come and visit. So far been up Table Mountain. Pretty cool. Though hot. Haha. And to the beach. Pretty hot though cool. Haha. There are loads of beaches here, everyone hangs out there. Boys here look more healthy than back home. All suntans and white teeth. Still stupid though if the one next door is anything to go by. His name's Mark. He's okay but he asked me to a barbie at his house and he eats with his mouth open and you can see all his food. Ew. Gross. He'll never get off with anyone if he doesn't learn to eat properly.

Book titles. Hmmm. Let me think.

Okay.

Pain In the Neck by Lauren Gitis

Hahahahahaha.

Chow bambino

Love you muchomucho

Hannah

Confucius say: Who say I say all those things they say I say?

Arf. Arf.

3

The Wrinklies

"Stand close," said Mum as she pointed the camera at us in the back garden. "Put your hand on Paul's shoulder, Richard. And *try* and look as though you like him a bit."

Dad shuffled about behind us then finally put his hand on Paul's shoulder. "Might be more appropriate if Paul put *his* hand in *my* pocket," he muttered.

"Oh, for heaven's sake," said Mum. "Enough now. You made your point over lunch. This is our last day together as a family before Paul leaves for Goa. Try and act like a grown-up."

Paul and I tried not to laugh as Dad looked at the lawn like a naughty schoolboy. Quite an achievement seeing as he's in his sixties, but Mum can be Scary Mum to his

Scary Dad when she likes. She gets a look in her eye and you know she's not to be messed with. Hannah used to call my parents the Wrinklies because they're so ancient. Mum had me when she was forty-five and Dad was fifty-three. They thought they'd finished having children with Paul. Then seven years later, along came yours truly. I think I was what is commonly known in birth terms as A Surprise. Or A Mistake. Whatever. All I know is that I have the oldest parents of anyone in school. I used to get embarrassed when there'd be all these young mums in T-shirts and jeans waiting after school, then along would come my mum or dad in their "comfy clothes" looking more like my grandparents. I started telling people that Mum and Dad were actually the same age as normal parents but they'd been captured by aliens one summer and kept as an experiment on their space-ship for two days. The trauma made their hair grow white and they grew old before their time. One girl in my class actually believed me.

Mum took her picture and Dad headed for the car.

So much for our last day together as a family before Paul's trip, I thought, as I watched Dad reverse his Mercedes down the driveway and zoom off toward his golf club.

The rest of us trooped back inside, and Paul and I began to clear the table. Lunch had been a strained affair with Dad giving me a lecture about "the importance of qualifications" and "a good career meaning a good start in life." It was so obvious it was aimed at Paul, but I tried to look as if I agreed with everything Dad said. Anything to keep the peace.

Then he started on about how much Paul going to college had cost him. What a waste it all was.

"I will pay you back," said Paul. "I really will."

"It's not the money," said Dad. "I want you to be happy."

"I will be," said Paul. "I *am*. I want to see the world. Experience life. It's going to be brilliant."

"Well, at least let me give you some decent medical supplies for the journey," said Dad.

Paul sighed. "It's sorted, Dad. Don't worry."

Dad didn't look convinced and, for a moment, I felt sorry for him. He doesn't normally look his age, but today he did. He looked sad and a touch weary. Sometimes he can't accept that people have their own plans for their lives. He's so used to people obeying his every word at the hospital, he thinks it's going to be the same at home. Poor Scary Dad. I think he means well.

* * *

After loading the dishwasher, Mum went to water the pots on the patio and Paul and I went through to the living room. Paul flopped on the sofa and began flicking through the Sunday papers. At the bottom of the pile was our school newspaper, which he began to read.

"There are loads of things you can do in here," he said after a while. "Art, drama, choir. Getting a hobby would be a good way of making new friends."

"You sound like Dad," I said, sitting next to him and stretching my legs out onto the coffee table, "organizing my life. Anyway, I have loads of hobbies. Tennis. Football. Karate."

"Sounds like you'll meet lots of boys doing that stuff, not girls."

"Don't be sexist. Girls do all that stuff as well."

"Oh, *sorry*. Didn't realize you're a feminist," he teased.

"I'm not. I just believe women are the superior sex," I teased back.

"Oh, look, there's you," pointed Paul as he came across our class photo. "And Hannah."

"It was taken just after Easter," I said, looking over his shoulder. "I look awful."

"No, you don't. What are the other girls like?"

"Oh, God. All sorts." I pointed to some of the girls in the photo. "That's Melanie and Lottie. I get on okay with them. They were at footie yesterday. Those three are the brainboxes, those two are the computer nerds, Jade and Candice are the bad girls that like to bunk off, Mary and Emma are the sporty girls, Wendy's a bit of a pain."

"So, who do you hang with?"

"Well, Hannah before she went, obviously. And now I suppose Melanie and Lottie a bit, but they're a two-some really. I'm lumped in with the brainboxes seeing as I'm usually first in the class at everything. Except math. I hate math."

Paul continued to study the photo.

"Now, she looks nice," he said. "Who's she?"

"God, typical," I said when I saw who he was pointing at. "She's Nesta Williams. Only the best-looking girl in our school."

"She looks like Beyoncé."

"Yeah."

"So who are her friends?"

I pointed out Lucy Lovering and Izzie Foster.

"They look like fun. Tell me about them."

"Not much to tell. I don't know them that well out-

side school. They don't do football or any of the stuff I
do. Inside school, they're sort of in the middle. Popular.
Not too swotty, not too disruptive, though Izzie does
ask a lot of questions in class sometimes. One teacher
called her Izzie 'Why?' Foster. But *everyone* fancies
Nesta, that I *do* know. Even Scott next door. She's in
the drama group and I think she wants to be an actress.
She's probably completely self-obsessed. Anyone as
gorgeous as her has to be."

"Not necessarily," grinned Paul. "I'm gorgeous and
I'm not self-obsessed."

"And *I'm* gorgeous and I'm not self-obsessed," said
Mum, coming back in with a bunch of white roses
she'd cut. "So why don't you get in with this crowd?"

"Oh, you don't understand, Mum. They hang by
themselves. They'd never let anyone as boring as me in
with them."

"You're not boring," said Mum, taking the newspaper
from Paul and scanning the back page.

"Don't bother to read that," I said. "It's completely
out of touch and dull."

"Well, here's your chance to change it," said Mum,
handing it back to me.

"What do you mean?"

"There, back page. I saw it the other day when I had a look through. I thought you might be interested. It says that they're looking for a new editor, seeing as the old one will be moving on at the end of the year. And they want to make it more of a magazine than a newspaper. Applications open to everyone from Year Nine upward. You only have to do eight pages or so as an example."

"Not interested," I said, putting the newspaper back on the pile of papers.

"But you want to be a writer," said Paul. "You should go for it. It would be good practice."

"Nah, people think I'm a swot as it is. If I went for that, they'd only hate me more."

"Suit yourself," said Mum and began to root around in the cupboards for a vase. "But I see that Sam Denham is doing a talk for all those interested."

"Sam Denham? Where does it say that?"

"Ah, so suddenly it's not so boring." Mum picked up the newspaper and read from the back. "Monday, eleven June, four thirty in the main assembly hall. That's tomorrow. He's going to talk about journalism. It says he got started on his school magazine."

Sam Denham is a celebrity journalist and though he's old, at least in his thirties, he's still cute. They always have him on the news when they want an opinion about anything. He always has something interesting or funny to say.

And he's coming to our school?

"Maybe I *will* go to the talk," I said. "But only to listen."

e-mail: Outbox (1)
From: goody2shoes@psnet.co.uk
To: hannahnutter@fastmail.com
Date: 10 June
Subject: Night night

Hi Hannah

Feeling mis. Bro Paul gone. He and Saskia are booked on the overnight flight to Goa tomorrow. Boo hoo. Everyone I care about is going away.
    Gotta go, school a.m.

    T. J.

By the way, our crapola newspaper is looking for a new editor, and Sam Denham is coming to school tomorrow to do a talk. Apparently he got started on his school mag.

e-mail: Inbox (1)
From: hannahnutter@fastmail.com
To: goody2shoes@psnet.co.uk
Date: 10 June
Subject: Sam the Man

WAAAAKE UP.

Exscooth me? Did you say Sam Denham as in Sam Denham from the telly? He's a top babe. V V jealous. Wish never left U.K. Be sure to wear something short that reveals your legs as they are one of your best features. And sit in the front row.

T. J., you *must* go for editor. You'd be brilliant at it. And it would take your mind off missing me and Paul. I've read all about this kind of thing in Mum's mags. The agony aunts are always telling people to "keep busy" and "throw yourself into your work." I think this is a godsend. Your destiny.

And you think you're miserablahblah? Try being me. In a new country. With no friends at all. Not even Melanie and Lottie. No, young lady, you don't know you're born, as Dad would say.

Yours truly,
Your Agony Aunt Hannah

P.S. Few more for the book collection
Over the Cliff by Hugo First
The Cat's Revenge by Claude Bottom
Arf arf arf arf arf arf!

4

A Lonely
Little Petunia

"I'm just a lonely little petunia in an onion patch, an onion patch, an onion patch," sang the record in my head. It was going round and round, louder and louder, as I sat eating my lunch in the school playground the next day.

I was on my own because Melanie suffers from awful hay fever and thought that sitting outside would make it worse. Course Lottie had to stay in with her to keep her company and hand her tissues. I was going to explain that as pollen is airborne, it could get anywhere, so it wouldn't make much difference where she was, but I didn't want her to think I was a Norma Know-It-All. Too many people thought that already. In fact lately I've found myself holding back when I know the answers to things in class. Let someone else be the one who always gets it right. It doesn't win you any prizes in the popularity stakes.

Perhaps I should have stayed in with them, I wondered, as I looked around at all the groups of friends. It is definitely possible to feel lonelier in the middle of a crowd than when on your own.

Most of the school was out making the most of the heat wave. Everyone in pairs of threes or fours. All busy talking, laughing, having a good time. I always used to sit with Hannah at lunch, and I felt really self-conscious sitting on my tod. Like, everyone must be staring, going, "Oh, poor T. J., she's got no mates."

I continued munching my peanut-butter-and-honey sandwich like I didn't care, but I did care. I didn't like this feeling of being the odd one out.

"Hey, T. J.," called a voice near the bike shed.

I turned round to see Wendy Roberts. "Hey."

"You heard from Hannah?" she asked as she perched herself on the bench next to me and lowered the straps of her top so the sun could get to her.

I nodded. "Yeah. I've had a few e-mails. I think she's missing England."

"You must miss her, too," she said.

"Yeah, I do," I replied, wondering what was going on.

Wendy never normally gave me the time of day, so why this sudden interest in Hannah? Sensitive and caring are not words that come to mind when I think of Wendy. Mean and self-centered more like. But no one else had asked about Hannah or how I was, so maybe I'd got her wrong.

"You going to the talk tonight?" she asked. "Sam Denham?"

I nodded.

"He is gorgeous, isn't he? I saw him on morning telly last week. He was so funny. I wonder if he's got a girl-friend. Are you going to go for editor?"

I shook my head. I wasn't going to tell her, but Hannah's e-mail had made me think. Maybe I *should* go for editor. It would be perfect to take my mind off things, plus, as Paul had said, good practice for when I'm older. But I didn't want to tell Wendy. I didn't want her thinking I was getting ideas above my station, and anyway, I might not even get the job.

Wendy got out her mirror and applied some lipstick from her bag. "Great color, isn't it?" she said. "Natural with a hint of gloss. Good for us brunettes. Want to try some?"

"No, thanks." Us *brunettes*? What is all this matey,

let's-bond-over-a-lipstick act, I wondered. What *does* she want?

"Er, T. J. . . ."

"Yeah . . ."

"You know that exercise we had to do for math . . . ?"

Ah. So that was it. I felt my face drop. I couldn't help it. For a split second I thought someone was being friendly because they might have cared about me. Obviously not.

"Well I meant to . . . ," Wendy continued.

"You want to copy my homework?" I interrupted.

"Oh, T. J., *could* I? You'd be doing me the most *enormous* favor and you know what Mr. Potts can be like if anyone hasn't done it. . . ."

"Actually math isn't my best subject . . ."

Wendy stiffened. "It comes so easily to you but if you're going to be precious . . ."

"I'm not. Here take it," I said and got my book out of my bag. I couldn't be bothered arguing. Math didn't come easily. I had to really work at it and the last bit of homework had taken hours after lunch yesterday and I still wasn't sure I'd got it right. But I wanted friends not enemies, and Wendy could be really nasty when she wanted to be.

Just at that moment I caught Izzie Foster watching me from the bench to my right. She raised her eyebrows and half-smiled at me.

"Thanks. You're a doll, T. J.," said Wendy, grabbing my math book out of my hand. Off she went, leaving me sitting on my own again.

Izzie was still staring. She was sitting with her mates Lucy and Nesta and, like most of the other groups of girls dotted around the playground, they looked like they were having a good time, just relaxing in the sun. Nesta was at one end of the bench rubbing lotion onto her legs and Lucy was at the other with her skirt hiked high and her legs stretched out to get the sun. Izzie said something to them and they both looked over, then Izzie got up and came to join me.

"Hey, T. J. I was just thinking. You heard from Hannah?"

"Wendy's already borrowed my homework," I said.

"What homework?" asked Izzie, looking puzzled. "I saw you sitting on your own and suddenly remembered that Hannah'd gone. I wondered how you were doing?"

So people *had* noticed me sitting on my own. Well, I didn't need anyone's pity.

"I'm fine," I said, getting up and putting my half-eaten sandwich in the litter bin. "Got to go."

I was going to go and sit and read in a cubicle in the loo for the rest of the lunch break. That way no one would see me on my own and feel sorry for me.

"So, to sum up," said Sam Denham from the stage later that day, "you've got five main rules, and if you stick to them, you won't go wrong."

I turned the page of my book to write more notes.

"Rule one," he said. "Your job is to stop people just flicking through the magazine. You have to draw them in to actually read what's on the page. You do this by having hooks on the page. These are pictures, titles, words under the picture that give an idea what the feature is about, a quote and the picture captions. Now, if people scan your page, they can quickly access what it's about. So, the title and the captions should be . . . what?"

He looked around as a few hands went up in the hall, including Nesta Williams' who was sitting next to me. Sam pointed at her to answer.

"*Interesting*," she said, and gave him a flirty smile.

"Right," said Sam, flashing a big smile back at her and keeping his eyes on her for a few moments.

"*Interesting*. Or funny. These hooks are as important, if not more so, than the copy."

I was scribbling furiously to get it all down when I noticed Nesta hadn't written a thing. "Do you need paper?" I whispered to her, ready to rip out a page for her.

She grinned and shook her head. "No, thanks. I'm just here for the view."

You and half the school, I thought. I don't think a talk had ever been so well attended, not only by the girls but also by the teachers. But then, most of the teachers are aspiring writers, according to Hannah's mum. She was a headteacher before she left for South Africa. She told us that half her staff were secretly working on novels and planning to get out of teaching.

"Rule two," Sam continued. "Make sure your picture or photograph is appropriate to the copy. You don't want a big smiley picture of someone next to a tragic piece. Rule three. Use your pictures and captions in a creative way. For instance, you're doing a sports page and have a feature about tennis coaching. Any ideas?"

Wendy Roberts put up her hand. "You could have a photo of some kids playing, with the caption *Learn to play tennis*."

Sam nodded. "You could. It's apt, but not very inspiring. Any other ideas?"

I had one, but I didn't want to look a prat in front of everyone. Wendy was blushing like mad after Sam had squashed her idea. I went over in my mind what I'd say if I could only pluck up the courage.

Sam pointed at a girl at the back.

It was Izzie Foster. "How about a picture of Pete Sampras in full flight going after a ball, saying something like, 'Are you the next Sampras?'"

"Now we're cooking," said Sam. "That's more like it. Only it might be a bit intimidating, as most people know they'll *never* be the next Sampras. So, it might put them off going. But, good idea. Any more?"

Me *me*, I thought, trying to summon up the courage to put my hand up.

"Come on," said Sam, looking round at the rows of silent girls. "Part of being a pro is throwing ideas into the pot and not feeling bad when someone knocks them down. It doesn't matter. We learn as much by our mistakes as our successes, if not more. Come on, who's going to stick their neck out?"

I could feel myself going red as I put my hand up, but I was bursting to see what he thought of my idea.

"You," said Sam, looking in my direction. "Lara Croft on the front row."

I looked behind me. He couldn't mean me, could he? *Lara Croft?* But no one else had their hand up.

He pointed at me again. "You. Come on. Girl with the plait?"

Oh, he *did* mean me! I could feel myself going redder than ever. I took a deep breath. "What if you use a picture of, say, last year's Wimbledon winner," I finally managed to get out, "on his backside with the ball bouncing past and a caption saying something like, 'Even the best need a little extra help'?"

"Love it," beamed Sam. "It may not make you want to play tennis, but it will make you stop long enough to read what's going on."

"Well done, Lara," whispered Nesta as the red from my face spread to the tips of my ears.

"Rule four. Never be afraid to try new things. Rule five. In your layout, make sure the reader always knows where to go next. And make sure the information is accessible, especially in a magazine. Know your market. And not too many long paragraphs. Break some of it up. You know, ten tips about this, five ways to do that, and so on. . . ."

At the end, he took some questions from the floor, but I hardly took in what was going on. I spent the last ten minutes of his talk in a daze at having spoken to him. I was well chuffed that he'd liked my idea. Loved it, in fact. I couldn't wait to tell Hannah later.

As everyone got up to leave, I noticed Sam making his way over to where I was sitting. I froze to the chair. Ohmigod. He was coming over to speak to me. I could feel myself going red again and breathless as I planned what I'd say. I tried my best to look natural and smile as he approached, but I had a feeling I looked like a grinning hyena, I was so thrilled.

As he reached the front row, he knelt down next to me and turned his back.

"So, did you enjoy the talk?" he asked Nesta.

"Oh, yes," beamed Nesta. "Fascinating."

That wiped the smile off my face. Literally. *Fool*, I thought, you utter *utter* fool. He had no intention of coming to talk to you.

I had a quick look round and prayed that no one had witnessed it, but too late, I noticed Lucy Lovering hovering at the side. She'd seen it all. Me perking up with a stupid grin, then Sam turning his back on me to talk to Nesta. God, how humiliating.

I looked away from Lucy and got up to walk out the back door. Sam slipped into my vacant chair as though I'd never been there and continued chatting to Nesta.

"Hey, T. J.," called Lucy, as I reached the school gates and turned into the street. "Wait up."

Oh, no. I wanted to get out. Get home and hide. What did she want? I pretended I hadn't heard and carried on walking.

"T. J.," said Lucy, catching up.

"Yeah?"

"That was a great answer you gave in there."

"Thanks," I muttered and carried on walking. It didn't feel so great anymore. "Bye, Lucy."

"What bus you getting?" she persisted.

"102."

"Me too. We can go together."

"Aren't you going to wait for Nesta and Izzie?"

"Nah. Izzie's gone off to band practice. And Nesta. Well . . ."

"Probably hoping she'll get a ride from Sam Denham," I said bitterly. I couldn't help it. I felt miffed. Nesta wasn't even interested in writing or going for editor and yet she was the one Sam had picked out for special attention afterward.

"A ride from Sam?" Lucy giggled. "That I'd like to see. He came on a bike."

"Really? I thought he'd come in a flash car or something."

"I know," said Lucy. "But it *is* a flash bike. I saw him arrive on it in a helmet and clips and everything." Then she added, "People aren't always how you think they are."

I felt awkward then and a bit rotten about what I'd thought about Nesta. She can't help being a man magnet.

We stood in silence for a few minutes, then Lucy turned to me. "I hope you don't mind me saying, but . . . back there, I saw . . . you know . . ."

I shrugged and tried to pretend I didn't care. "Well, Nesta *is* gorgeous. She has everything any boy could ever want."

"What? A hairy chest and big muscles?" asked Lucy.

I burst out laughing. "I thought he was coming to talk to me. Or both of us at least."

"I know," said Lucy gently. "I saw."

"I felt a right idiot. Like I was invisible or something."

"I've been there, believe me. I used to feel like that a *lot* when Nesta first arrived," said Lucy. "I mean, I know she's my mate, but she is stunning, so people always look at her before anyone else. And she's funny, so people like her. It's easy to feel left out sometimes. I thought she was going to steal Izzie from me when she first began to hang out with us. I thought she didn't want to be my friend, only Izzie's. It was like I wasn't even there. So, yeah, I know *all* about feeling invisible."

"What did you do?"

"Oh, took a very grown-up approach. Sulked. Acted like a baby. Felt *very* sorry for myself. *Hated* Nesta. Then I got to know her. And discovered that she's really nice. In fact she had been feeling the same way. She thought *I* hated *her* and didn't want to be her friend."

Just at that moment, Sam Denham cycled past on his bike and jolted as he went over a bump in the road.

"If you think about it," said Lucy with a wicked grin, "men really ought to ride sidesaddle."

I burst out laughing as I watched Sam wobble down the road and disappear round a corner.

"And he did call you Lara Croft," said Lucy.

"Yeah, he did, didn't he?" I said. I'd forgotten that. "I thought he meant someone else at first. I guess it's because of my plait."

"Maybe. But you do have a look of her. So, yeah," teased Lucy. "T. J. Watts—invisible? Hardly. Only mistaken for the most sexy woman in cyberspace."

"Yeah," I said. "Don't mess with me. . . ."

I liked Lucy. She was a laugh, like Hannah. She had a way of turning things round and making it all seem okay.

Somehow it didn't seem to matter anymore that Sam Denham had snubbed me. He probably didn't even realize he'd done it.

The rest of the journey home flew by as Lucy and I chatted away. As I let myself into the house later, I realized it was the first time in weeks that I'd actually felt happy.

Things were looking up.

e-mail:	Outbox (1)
From:	goody2shoes@psnet.co.uk
To:	hannahnutter@fastmail.com
Date:	11 June
Subject:	Wham Bam thanku Sam

Hi H

Excellent talk by Sam Denham. He fancied Nesta, he made a beeline straight for her after the talk.

I am definitely going to go for editor. Hurrah. And thx for the advice.

Got bus home with Lucy Lovering. She's a real laugh and easy to talk to. She has invited me to her house after school on Friday. Brill. Can't wait.

Scott came over to borrow my *Buffy* DVD. He wants to show it to Jessica. He sends his love. He seems to have forgotten he said he'd give me back the money I lent him. I know I should say something, but I can't face it. . . .

⟳

Got piles of hwk so better go.
Miss you loads
Spik soon

Love,
T. J.

e-mail: Inbox (1)
From: hannahnutter@fastmail.com
To: goody2shoes@psnet.co.uk
Date: 11 June
Subject: School

T. J.

Help. Am mis. Don't like it here. I WANNA come HOME. And
now you're going to be best friends with Lucy Lovering and
you'll forget me. Started school today. Lots of geeky boys in our
class. They have their own language over here. And accent. Like
if someone's invited somewhere they say, "Like, yah, rock up
when you like man." Or "I rocked up to Jine ee's (Janie's) about
farve (five)." And they say "och shame" a lot. And a girlfriend is
called a "cherry." It's going to take me ages to learn it all.
   Gudnight ma cherry
   Spik spox spooooon

   Your v sad friend Hannah. Och shame Hannah.

Mark next door has some book titles for you. As he is a boy,
they are all rude or stupid.
   Rusty Bedsprings by I. P. Nightly
   Chicken Dishes by Nora Drumstick
   And *The Revelations of St. John* by Armageddin Outtahere

5

For Real

"Make yourself at home," said Lucy, flinging her bag down and opening the fridge.

I pulled a chair out at one end of the pine dining table that took up half the kitchen. Before I could sit, I was accosted by a golden Labrador who appeared from under the table. He put his paws up on my chest and began to lick my face with great enthusiasm.

"*Down*, Jerry," said Lucy as another dog appeared next to him and joined in the let's-wash-the-guest's-face game.

"How many are there?" I asked, wiping my face with my sleeve.

"Two," said Lucy, opening the French doors. "Ben! Jerry!" she called as she ran out into the garden. The dogs jumped down and ran after her, tails wagging. Once they were out, Lucy stepped back inside and shut the door. The two dogs looked in through the glass with bemused faces as if to say, "That was a *really* mean trick."

"I didn't mind them," I said. "I like dogs."

"So do I. They're my best friends as much as Iz and Nesta, but they can be a bit much sometimes," said Lucy, then added with a grin, "And so can the dogs."

She held up two cartons of juice. "Cranberry or apple?"

"Cranberry, please," I said, settling into my chair. I liked Lucy's house immediately. It looked like the kind of place you could relax in. "Lived in," as my mum would say. Every surface was covered with books, papers, and magazines, the walls were plastered with paintings and drawings, and there was a lovely old dresser against one wall with colorful bits of mismatched crockery.

"Hi," I said to the boy who was sitting at the other end of the table and reading the latest John Irving novel.

"Uh," he said. Or, at least, that's what it sounded like.

"Steve, this is T. J. T. J., this is my charmer of a brother."

Steve barely looked up. He only grimaced at what his sister had said.

"Oh, hi, T. J.," said Lucy. "I'm Steve. So *pleased* to meet you. I *would* look at you, but then you are my *younger* sister's friend, so why bother? You're too young for me and probably stupid. Nothing you have to say will be of the slightest interest to me. I am your superior in every respect, and everything I say—no, *think*—will be over your head."

Steve's mouth twitched. He almost laughed.

"Good book that," I said, pointing at what he was reading. "I've read all of his, but I liked *The World According to Garp* best."

Then he did look at me. A strange look as though he was considering something unsavory that a cat might have brought in. I met his gaze and tried to look friendly.

"New, are you?" he asked.

"Ohmigod, it speaks," said Lucy, putting a glass of juice beside me. "Sorry about the juice. It's organic, but it tastes okay when you get used to it. My parents are both health freaks, so . . ."

"We have to go out of the house to keep our toxin levels up," said Steve.

"In answer to your question, no, I'm not new," I said. "New here, I guess. But I've been in the same class as Lucy since we began secondary."

"T. J.'s a brainbox like you," said Lucy. "She's going to go for editor of our school newspaper."

"Really," said Steve, looking totally unimpressed.

A brainbox? Was that really how people saw me? How boring.

It got worse.

"She's arm wrestling champion as well," continued Lucy, who was oblivious to the fact that I was squirming in my seat. D'oh. Thanks for the great introduction, Lucy, I thought. Like hi, I'm T. J. Watts, brainbox with muscles. How sexy is that? Not.

Steve put down his book and did what all boys did when my arm wrestling talent was mentioned. He put his hand out.

At that moment, the back door opened and another boy burst in and flung his bag on the table. Blond like Lucy, he looked younger than Steve, maybe fifteen or so, whereas Steve looked like he was in sixth form.

"Excellent," said the boy, plonking himself down next to me. "Arm wrestling. I'll play the winner."

"T. J., other brother, Lal," said Lucy.

We nodded at each other as Steve and I locked hands and put our elbows down. Steve tried to test my strength before we began. I let my hand go limp in his, so he'd think I was weak. This was going to be easy.

"Ready, steady, GO," said Lal.

It was all over in two seconds.

"I wasn't ready," objected Steve, as his lower arm hit the table. "You called GO too soon."

"Rubbish," said Lal, pushing Steve out of his chair and sitting in his place. "You're a puny weakling. Right. Now me."

We locked hands and this time Steve called.

"Ready, steady, GO."

Lal was more of a challenge. Ten seconds.

"Wow. You're pretty good for a girl. Do anything else this well?" he said, picking up my hand and this time stroking it and looking at my mouth with what I can only describe as longing.

Lucy whacked the back of his head. "Take no notice, T. J. Lal thinks he's Casanova."

Lal dropped my hand and Steve did a kind of smirk. "Don't suppose you can mend computers as well as you arm wrestle, can you?"

"Maybe . . . ," I said.

* * *

The rest of the evening went brilliantly.

I fixed Steve's computer no problem. He had one the same make as mine, complete with same operating system. He was well impressed when I pressed a few keys and, hey presto, it worked. He dropped his superior act after that and we got chatting about books. The shelves in his half of the bedroom were heavy with them.

"So who's your favorite author?" he asked.

"God, so many. Can I do top three?"

He nodded.

"Okay, I know that they're kids' books but I still love the Narnia books by C. S. Lewis."

"Yeah. They're cool," he said.

"And I like Bill Bryson."

"Yeah," said Steve, pointing to his shelf. "I've got all of his."

"And I loved *Alias Grace* by Margaret Atwood."

"How's the computer?" called Lucy from the corridor.

"Mended," Steve called back.

"Then stop hogging T. J. She's *my* friend," said Lucy, bursting in the door. "Come and look at my bedroom."

I got up to follow her, feeling well chuffed. She'd

called me her friend. I hoped I would be. Steve and Lal, too. They were all really easy to be with and, for once, I hadn't been tongue-tied when meeting boys.

"Wow," I said as Lucy opened the door to her room. "It's like a princess's room. An Indian princess."

"Thanks," said Lucy, looking pleased. "Me and Mum did it last year. The curtain material is from a sari. I got it in the East End."

On one of her walls were cut-outs of people from magazines. Not the usual pop bands and actors—I didn't recognize any of them.

"Who are all these?"

"Dress designers. Gaultier. Armani. Stella McCartney. I want to do design when I leave school."

"Well, I can see already that you have a good eye for color, Lucy. This blue, lilac, and silver looks gorgeous. I wish you'd come and do my room. It's so boring. I think the paint Mum used was called Death by Magnolia."

"I'll show you some clothes I've made," said Lucy, opening the wardrobe and pulling out a selection of skirts and tops.

She held some of them up against her and they looked good, even to me, someone who doesn't know a lot about clothes.

"Maybe you could do a fashion piece for my news-paper. Like, what's in for the summer."

"Sort of five top tips?"

"Yeah. Summer sizzlers," I laughed.

"Love to," said Lucy. "And are you going to change the name of the newspaper? *Freemont News* sounds *sooo* boring."

"Exactly what I thought. I *was* going to change it. What do you think of calling it *For Real*?"

"Brilliant," said Lucy, "because that's exactly what it isn't at the moment and it's *exactly* what everyone wants. You're going to be so good at this, T. J. I can tell already that you're going to win."

I shrugged. "I'll give it a go. But I was amazed to find out how many others are going for it after Sam's talk."

"I know," said Lucy. "Even stinky Wendy Roberts, though she was mega-miffed after Sam didn't go for her answer. I saw her face at the back. She was livid. Even more so when he loved yours."

"She's even more angry with me today. She borrowed my math homework and I'd got most of it wrong. Not my fault if it's my worst subject."

"Serves her right," said Lucy as the doorbell rang downstairs. "Don't worry, one of the boys will get it.

Probably Nesta, she said she'd come over."

Sure enough, Nesta appeared moments later.

"Hey," she smiled at both of us and flopped on the bed. She looked slightly surprised that I was there, but not unduly bothered. The whole evening was going so well. Maybe I could be friends with her too?

"We were just discussing the newspaper," said Lucy.

"Cool," said Nesta. "So, you going to go for it?"

I nodded. "And Lucy's agreed to do a fashion piece."

"Excellent," said Nesta. "And I tell you what readers like more than *anything*. A makeover. You know, before-and-after sort of thing."

"Good idea," said Lucy.

Nesta was staring at me. "And you know who we should do?"

I shook my head.

"*You,* of course. You could look *fabulous* if you wanted to."

Lucy looked shocked. "Nesta. T. J. *does* look fabulous. Honestly, you and your big mouth. You don't think before you open it, do you?"

"What? *What?*" said Nesta, looking flustered. "I didn't mean anything. . . . I only meant . . ."

I tried to smile but I wanted to die. She thought I looked awful. I knew I didn't wear all the latest fashions, but she didn't have to rub it in. I got up to leave.

"Oh, don't go, T. J.," said Lucy.

I looked at my watch and made for the door. "I have karate at seven and it's the last one before the summer hols, so I can't miss it. Honest, really, it's okay." I did my best to look cheerful, but Lucy didn't look convinced.

"T. J., I hope I didn't . . . ," started Nesta. "Oh, hell. I mean . . . I was only trying to say, I don't think you make . . ."

"Nesta. Button it," said Lucy, linking my arm. "Come on, I'll show you out."

When we got to the front door, Lucy made me promise I'd come again. "You sure you're okay?" she asked.

I nodded. I wanted to get away. And I did have karate that night, not that I was in the mood anymore. I really wanted to go home and talk to Hannah on e-mail.

I looked back at Lucy's house after she shut the front door. No way was I going to go there again for Nesta to point out how awful I look. It's all right for her, she'd look fab in a trash bag.

e-mail: Outbox (2)
From: goody2shoes@psnet.co.uk
To: hannahnutter@fastmail.com
Date: 15 June
Subject: Best friends

To Hannahnutter

I was so wrong about thinking I could be mates with Lucy. Not in a million years. Not while she's friends with Nesta Williams. You won't *believe* what she just said . . . that I need a makeover. So everyone at school pities me. And thinks I'm a swot. And ugly. Everything over here is awful.

I called Scott to ask if he could think of anything I could do to improve my appearance. He laughed and said, you could wear blue more often, it will go with your veins. He thought it was really funny. I said I was upset and needed cheering up and he said he'd phone me back after watching a repeat of *Friends*. He hasn't phoned back yet.

I miss you loooooaaaaads. Spik spoon.

T. J.

From: goody2shoes@psnet.co.uk
To: hannahnutter@fastmail.com
Date: 15 June
Subject: Where are you?

Hannah. *Where* are you?

   Even Scott hasn't phoned me back and he promised.

   And Paul will be on the other side of the world now. Probably on some amazing island like in *The Beach*.

   I feel so alone.

   Love, T. J.

Oh, I met Lucy's bros tonight. They're sweet and the eldest one Steve is okay when he drops his snotty act. He gave me some brill book titles and suggested I put them at the back of the school magazine as a sort of silly fun page.

Bubbles in the Bath by Ivor Windybottom

A Stitch in Time by Justin Case

Chest Pain Remedies by I Coffedalot

Skin Rash Remedies by Ivan Offleitch

WHERE ARE YOU? I have to go to sleep now as it's late.

6

Furry Friends

I woke up the next morning feeling better. It was the weekend and Mum had promised to take me to Battersea Dogs' Home. Who needed girlfriends? I was going to get my new best friend of the furry kind.

I got dressed and hurtled down the stairs. Nobody in the kitchen. No one in Dad's study. No one in the living room.

"Where's Mum?" I asked, on finding Dad sitting out on the patio reading the paper and having a cup of coffee.

"She got called out on a case. Good morning, T. J."

"Oh, yeah. Morning. Good. When will she be back?"

"She couldn't say. . . ."

"Oh, *no!*" I wailed. "We were going to go to the dogs' home. And I have football this afternoon . . . We won't have time if she's not back soon."

"I've got the day off," said Dad. "Ready when you are."

"School all right?" asked Dad, as he drove down Edgware Road toward Hyde Park.

"Yeah."

"Not long until the summer holidays?"

"No. Not long."

"Feeling all right?"

"Yeah. You, Dad?"

"Yes. Fine, thank you."

I could see that he was trying, but I wasn't in the mood for telling him how I was really feeling. He'd never understand how much I missed Paul and Hannah and what it was like to be the only girl in Year Nine without a best friend. Plus, I didn't want to get him started on Paul and how he's wasted his opportunities. The last thing I wanted was a lecture on how I must focus on school and my career and get good grades.

I felt relieved when he gave up and switched the radio on, even if it was to listen to classical music. He means well, Dad does, but sometimes, he's so busy offering his solutions that he doesn't realize that he hasn't really listened to the problem. It's much easier to talk to Mum. She understands better that sometimes people don't want to be told what to do, they just want someone to listen and give a bit of sympathy.

I spent the rest of the journey looking out of the window as we drove down Park Lane, toward Victoria then over the Chelsea Bridge.

"I've always wanted to come here," said Dad as we parked the car near Battersea Park. "I've been wanting a dog for *ages*."

"Really?" I said as we got out and walked round the corner to the home. "I never knew that. Have you ever had a dog before?"

Dad nodded. "When I was a lad. Best friend I ever had. Being an only child, he was my constant companion."

"What was his name?"

"Rex."

"What happened to him?"

"He died after I left for university. I was heartbroken. I thought it was my fault, you know, because I'd gone away and left him. But my mother said it wasn't like that. She said it was his time to go and that he'd waited until I'd gone so as not to upset me."

We walked into the reception area at the home and I watched Dad as he found his wallet to pay our entrance fee. I swear his eyes misted over when he'd talked about Rex. It made me see him in a new light. Dad clearly had a soft side when it came to animals.

"Pound for you," said the lady behind a counter. "And fifty pence for the young lady. Have you come to look or to buy a dog or cat?"

"Buy a dog," I said.

"Then you need to have an interview with a Rehomer first. Follow the red paws on the ground and someone will come and talk to you. See what sort you want and so on. Then you follow the blue paws and go and have a look."

I couldn't wait and felt really excited. I could see Dad did as well. He'd turned from Scary Dad into Smiley Dad.

We followed the red paws and went to sit in the waiting room with a group of other people. A sign on the wall told us that it cost £70 for a dog and £40 for a cat. After a short wait, a man in a red tracksuit came out and called us into a room where he asked loads of questions about where we lived and whether there were other children or cats and if was there a garden.

It was funny because he was stern like a headmaster and Dad had to really sell the fact that we would be good owners.

"Our chief concern," said the man, finally relaxing, "is that the dogs go to a permanent home where they will be happy and well cared for—for the rest of their lives. Hence the interrogation. Many of our dogs are here because their previous owners couldn't or wouldn't care for them. Last thing we want is for a dog to have another bad experience."

"Quite right," said Dad. "I can assure you that we'll take very good care of whomever we get today."

"Okay, then. Let's go and look at the dogs," said the man.

Dad looked at me and winked as we followed the man along the path of blue paws through a courtyard to a building at the back.

Inside it was like a hospital with long sloping corridors leading up to different floors. Each corridor had a different name: Oxford Street on the ground floor where the clinic was; Bond Street and Bow Street on the first floor where the dogs were kept; Regent Street and Baker Street on the second with dogs and cats and a private floor, Fleet Street and Pall Mall on the top.

"Here we go," said our Rehomer, opening a door to a side ward. "I'll leave you to look around. Take your time, then, when you've decided, we'll bring the dog to you for an introduction and see if you get on. Takes about fifteen minutes. Then, if all parties are happy, you can go."

Two things hit us as soon as we entered the ward. The sound of barking. And the smell. Not a bad smell, but distinctive nonetheless. Like wet hay mixed with dog food.

"*Phworr,*" I said.

"Aromatherapy of the canine kind," laughed Dad as we looked in to see the first hopeful face looking out at us from behind bars.

"It's like they're in a prison cell," I said as a Jack Russell poked a paw through at us and barked in friendly greeting.

We spent the next hour walking through all the wards on every floor. We must have seen about fifty dogs. Each one had a little room in which was a blanket, water, a toy, and outside access to a corridor at the back.

There were all sorts of characters to choose from. Collies, beagles, Jack Russells, muts of every color, even a Samoyed, which Dad told me was a rare breed. He looked like a big white teddy. At the side of each cage was a report with the dog's details: the breed, name, age, history, and whether they liked cats or children. Whether they needed an experienced owner and whether they were destructive or not!

At the end of their report was a comment as though written by the dog. "I make a good companion." Or "I need commitment." Or one big dog whose comment said, "I am a majestic individual!"

"That one sounds like you, Dad," I said, pointing at the last one. With his tall stature and silver-white hair, Dad did have a majestic air.

"I don't know what you mean," he laughed, then pointed at one that said, "And there's one that sounds like you: 'I have a strong will and need a lot of training.'"

On one ward, a black mut called Woodie was doing everything he could to get people's attention. All sorts of mad antics—bouncing off the walls, paws up against the bars. It was as though he was saying "pick me, *pick me*, look what I can *do* . . . back flips, jumping, bouncing!!!! Pick me. *Pick me.*"

Another old brown-and-white collie sat looking at us with pleading eyes. She looked as though she had a bad wig on.

"This is heartbreaking," said Dad, reading her report. "She's called Kiki. She's thirteen."

Kiki put her paw through the cage and even though there was a big sign saying not to touch the dogs, Dad took her paw and stroked it. "Hello, girl." Then he turned to me and I swear his eyes were misting over again. "Poor thing. At her age, she's probably here because her owner died or something. She looks as though she's been well looked after though. Shame, because a lot of people come here and only want the young dogs. They see 'thirteen years' and see the expense of vet's bills."

I was finding it excruciatingly difficult. I wanted all of them. Every ward we went into, the dogs would perk up and start wagging their tails as though Dad and I were their best and oldest friends. So pleased to see us. It was like they were saying, "Oh *there* you are, hold on a mo, I'll just get my stuff and we can go." Then, as we walked past their cages, their faces would fall and their tails would go down as if thinking, "Come back. Hey, where are you going? I thought we were outta here?"

"Can't we hire a coach, Dad, and come back with it and say right, everyone in? And then go and buy a big house in the country . . ."

"I wish," said Dad. "But, sadly, we can only have one. Have you made up your mind?"

I shook my head. I'd fallen in love with about six of them. Woodie and the Samoyed and Kiki the old collie, a mut that looked like an old teddy, a beautiful black Alsatian, and a cheeky Jack Russell.

Some had to be overlooked as it said clearly on their report that they could be destructive and didn't like children, even teens. Others, I knew, were too big, like the Alsatian. Arm wrestling champion that I am, I knew I wouldn't be able to keep him on a lead.

It was then that I turned a corner and saw Mojo. He was sitting quietly in his room, a medium-size black dog with a white patch over one eye. He gazed up at us with the saddest eyes I've ever seen. You look how I felt last night, I thought. Sad, lonely, and badly in need of a friend. "Mojo is four years old and a stray," said his report. "He has a very gentle nature and likes people. He is very distressed at finding himself here and would like a good home as soon as possible."

Mojo looked up at me with hopeful eyes.

I glanced over at Dad.

"He's The One, isn't he?" said Dad.

I nodded.

Dad and I didn't stop talking all the way home. He told me all about how he had wanted to be a vet, but didn't think he could cope with having to put people's pets down as you sometimes had to do.

We even talked about Paul.

"At least this fella won't get on a plane and leave us," said Dad, looking at Mojo, who was sitting happily in the back, looking out the window. "Unlike some people I could mention."

"Paul, you mean?"

Dad nodded. "I hope he's all right, wherever he's got to. He may be grown-up, but you never stop worrying. And I know you and Mum think I go on, but I know my own son and he can be naive at the best of times. Even as a young lad, he was a dreamer, too trusting of people. . . . You have to have your wits about you when you're traveling."

"He'll be okay," I said. "He's with Saskia."

"Hmmmph," said Dad. "And she's as daft as he is. Still, I guess he's not alone. You're right."

I was glad it had been Dad who'd come with me to

the home. I felt I'd got to know him better. And discovered he was missing Paul as much as I was.

When we got home, Mojo ran around sniffing everything. Tail wagging happily, he seemed more than pleased when Dad opened the French doors to the garden. He ran out and sniffed the air as if he couldn't get enough of it.

"I think he likes it here," said Mum, watching him from the kitchen. As he ran about familiarizing himself with the smells, the phone rang.

"Oh, that will be someone called Lucy again. She's phoned a few times since I've been back and so has someone called Nesta."

I went to answer the call. Mum was right. It was Lucy.

"About Nesta last night," she said. "She really didn't mean to upset you. What she meant to say was that with your potential you could look totally amazing. She wasn't saying you looked awful or anything."

I'd forgotten all about the incident the night before. And it didn't seem so bad in the light of a new day.

"I suppose I *was* being a bit oversensitive," I admitted. "Overreacted a bit."

"We all have days like that," said Lucy. "Like my mum says, only the wearer of the shoe knows where it rubs. You know, sometimes we don't know where each other's sensitive spots are and tread on them by mistake. Nesta treads on people's sensitive spots with hobnailed boots on. But she doesn't mean to. We all want to be friends. Honest. We all agreed. That's why Nesta came to sit next to you at Sam's talk the other afternoon."

"Really? I thought that was just coincidence."

"No. It was so you had someone to sit with."

"Really?"

We chatted on for about ten minutes and I told her my news about Mojo. She wants to come over on Monday to meet him.

After I put the phone down, I had plenty to think about. It looked like I had misjudged the whole situation and I decided I should give Nesta another chance. I watched Mojo as he ran about. He looked a different dog already. His tail was wagging madly, his tongue out.

Mum had her radio on in the kitchen and an old song was blasting out. How true, I thought, as I listened to the lyrics. "What a difference a day makes, twenty-four little hours . . ."

We're all going to be good friends, I thought, going out into the garden to Mojo and doing what I'd wanted to do ever since I'd set eyes on him.

I gave him a big hug.

---

e-mail: Inbox (1)
From: hannahnutter@fastmail.com
To: goody2shoes@psnet.co.uk
Date: 16 June
Subject: Asta la vista

Ola bamboo baby.

Me velly sollee no e-mail back last night.

Sollee you had bad time. Wish I was there to make it all better. Confucius, he say all things will pass. Particularly if you eat plennee fiber. Arf, arf.

Had brill time. Went for a grand beano feast and drinky drunky woos at a girl from school's. She's new like me only she's come here from Johannesburg (known over here as Jo'burg). I think we might be friends. Her name's Rachel.

Am getting bronzed and beautiful. It may be okay here after all.

She has two book titles for you. Bit rude.
Poo on the Wall by Hoo Flung Dung
Dog Bites by R. Stornaway

Love you loads,
Hannah

e-mail: Outbox (1)
From: goody2shoes@psnet.com
To: hannahnutter@fastmail.com
Date: 16 June
Subject: Illo mysterio of lifeio

Great to hear from you. All changed from last night. V happy.
Have new furry friend called Mojo. He's adorable and Mum says
he can sleep in my room. I think Dad is jealous. He was so sweet
today at the dogs' home. I realized I don't know my dad as well as
I thought. He's v worried because Paul said he'd call when he got
to Goa but nothing so far. Hope he's okay. I think it's just Paul and
he'll call when he remembers.

Also, Lucy called and apologized about Nesta. May be okay
after all, but no one will ever replace you. I am glad you met this
new girl though as I don't want you to be lonely. Lucy said her
bro Steve liked me and thought it was unusual to meet a girl
who had half a brain and was good to talk to. Not sure if this is a
good thing as boys seem to view me as "one of the lads" and I
would like to have a boyfriend some day. Maybe Nesta was right.
Maybe I do need a makeover. Anyway, I told Mum I want to
change my appearance and maybe try and look a bit more like a
girl. She was v pleased and said I can have a new dress.

Scott came over to meet Mojo. He has ditched Jessica already.
He was looking mucho cute and was very sweet with Mojo.

Funny business, life, isn't it? Just when you think everything's
rotten and life stinks, it can all change.

Love you.

T. J.

Books:
   Rhythm of the Night by Mark Time
   Bad Falls by Eileen Dover

e-mail: Inbox (1)
From: paulwatts@worldnet.com
To: goody2shoes@psnet.co.uk
Date: 17 June
Subject: Goa

Hey T. J.

In Goa, it's awesome. We sleep under the stars and look out over the sea. We met some amazing people (travelers mostly—Brits and Irish and a large number of Dutchies) and the locals here are very kind. I have bought an amazing crystal, and every time I hold it, it is like there are enormous beams of light pulsating through my head via my temples, brow and crown chakra, but it gives Saskia a headache. I have been having real funky lucid dreams lately and been feeling like a million dollars with this quartz.

Rock on.

Paul

P.S. Please let Ma and Pa know I am okay. Tried to ring but lost wallet soon after we arrived. Have got job in a bar though. So all okay. Please ask Ma to send some dosh. Tell her I'll pay her back, promise, promise. Don't mention to Dad. Saskia got some nasty insect bites. Please ask Ma to send some more homeopathic stuff—arnica and apis and citronella and lavender oil.

7

Dog of the Week

Our class was in a mad mood the next week at school. I think the heat wave had affected everyone's brain.

It started in science, when Mr. Dixon asked if anyone knew the formula for water.

Gabby Jones put her hand up. "HIJKLMNO," she said proudly.

"Er, can you tell me why?" he asked.

"Yesterday, sir," said Gabby, "you said H to O was the formula for water."

"H *two* O." He sighed, then wrote on the board. "H two, as in the *number*, O. Okay, last question about water. What can we do to save water in a water shortage?"

"Put less in the kettle, sir," said Lucy.

"Excellent. Anyone else?"

"Don't use the hose," I said.

"Another good one. Any others to help our water supply go further?"

Jade Wilcocks' hand shot up. "Dilute it, sir," she said.

Mr. Dixon shook his head, but I could see he was trying not to laugh.

Then it was into the school hall for a film about the cosmos and all the planets and stars. Afterward, Miss Watkins asked us questions to see if we'd been paying attention, as I think some girls used the hour in the dark as an excuse to have a kip.

"What is a comet?" asked Miss Watkins.

I knew the answer to this and put my hand up.

"Star with a tail, miss."

"Correct. And can anyone name one?"

Candice Carter, who was one of those I saw nodding off, stuck her hand up. "Mickey Mouse, miss," she said as everyone cracked up.

But the best was in RE. Again, it was poor Miss Watkins taking the class and she asked if anyone knew what God's name was.

This time it was Mo Harrison who put her hand up.

"Andy, miss."

"Andy? Why on earth would Andy be the name of God?"

"It's in all the hymns, miss," said Mo. "Andy walks with me. Andy talks with me . . . There are loads of examples."

"No, Mo," Miss Watkins said, turning to Nesta who was crying with laughter. "Nesta Williams, seeing as you clearly find it so funny. What do *you* think the name of God might be?"

"Er, not sure," said Nesta, looking caught out. "What do you think?"

"I don't think," said Miss Watkins. "I *know*."

"I don't think I know either," giggled Nesta.

The whole class got detention, but it was worth it. I felt like I'd spent the whole morning laughing my head off.

We never did get to know what God's name was.

"How are you getting on with the mag?" asked Izzie as we sat doing our lines in detention in the lunch break.

"So-so. I've got some ideas, but need to get them down on paper," I replied.

"Come over to ours at the weekend," said Lucy. "I'm

sure Steve would like to see you again, and he can help. And so could me and Izzie and Nesta."

The offer of help was tempting. Less than two weeks to go until the entries were due in and there was going to be a lot of competition. Intense discussions and hushed conversations were going on everywhere.

"I could do a horoscope page for you, if you like," said Izzie.

"That would be brilliant," I said. "And I may do a piece about Battersea Dogs' Home."

I showed Lucy and Izzie the Polaroids of Mojo. Soon, everyone wanted to look, so they got passed round the class. Everyone ooed and aahed until it got to Wendy Roberts.

"Arrr, *sweet*," she said loudly. "T. J.'s new boyfriend. Hey, T. J. Is this *all* you can pull? He needs a bit of a shave."

A few girls giggled half-heartedly, but as though they felt they had to rather than because they thought Wendy was hilarious. Why was she being so horrid to me? Was it because Sam had liked my answer and not hers? Or because she'd got a low mark after copying my homework? It wasn't my fault I was crapola at math. I racked my brains for something funny to say back so it would look like I didn't care, but I couldn't think of anything quick enough. Bummer and bananas, as Hannah used to say. Why can I never come up with the right words when I need them?

After detention, we all trooped out to the playground for the last ten minutes of lunch. I ate my sandwiches and stretched out in the sun, but I couldn't help but notice that some girls were passing a piece of paper round, then staring at me and giggling in a nervous way.

Oh, what now? I thought as Izzie came out to join me on the bench.

"What's going on?" I asked.

"Oh, Wendy. You know she's running for editor as well. She's just jealous. . . ."

"Take no notice," said Lucy, coming to join us. "You don't need to know, T. J. She's a sad cow and you should ignore her."

"No, I want to see," I said, and got up and went over to a group of girls who were standing round Wendy looking at the piece of paper. I glanced over Wendy's shoulder. There was a picture of a dog with its head cut out and mine stuck on instead. She'd cut out the photo of me from the group shot in last month's newspaper. Underneath Wendy had written "Dog of the Week."

"What do you think, T. J.?" giggled Wendy. "You getting your dog gave me the idea. Each month in the newspaper, we pick someone to be Dog of the Week. What do you think?"

As I searched for the right put-down, a voice behind me got in first. "I think, Wendy, that if you were any more stupid, you'd have to be watered."

I turned round and there was Nesta. She looked mad.

She took the paper and, much to Wendy's astonishment, she ripped it up. "This is not remotely funny, Wendy. And you know it's not. It's not journalism. It's just nastiness. Come on, T. J. Don't lower yourself by breathing the same air as this lowlife."

I was as gobsmacked as Wendy, but I turned away with Nesta and followed her to a bench where Lucy and Izzie were sitting.

"Thanks, Nesta," I said, "but I was okay. I can handle Wendy Roberts."

"I know. But I've been waiting for a chance to show you that I'm on your side. I'm sorry about the other day. Sometimes words come out the wrong way."

"Not just then," I grinned. "That was brilliant. I wish I could come out with stuff like that. I always think of good things to say later, like when I'm falling asleep or something. . . ."

"Nesta's special talent is fighting for her mates," teased Lucy. "Her special downfall is her big gob."

"Well, I know what it's like to have some saddo like Wendy have it in for you," said Nesta.

"I don't know why. I never did anything to her."

"With her sort you don't have to," said Nesta. "She's probably jealous."

"Of me? Don't be mad."

"Looks and brains," said Nesta. "Lethal combination."

I felt really chuffed. Maybe she didn't think I looked too bad after all.

Then I looked over at Wendy who was glowering at us from the other side of the playground. I hoped this wasn't going to be the start of something.

Then I looked at Lucy, Izzie, and Nesta glowering back at her like they were my best mates. And I hoped that this *was* going to be the start of something.

---

e-mail: Outbox (1)
From: goody2shoes@psnet.co.uk
To: hannahnutter@fastmail.com
Date: 18 June
Subject: notalot

Dear H

Weather is lovely. Wish you were here.

T. J.

e-mail: Inbox (2)
From: hannahnutter@fastmail.com
To: goody2shoes@psnet.co.uk
Date: 18 June
Subject: notalot either

Dear T. J.

Weather is here. Wish you were lovely. Arf arf. Must dash. Going to movie, i.e., Drive-in. Bigola hugs and heeheehasta la vista baby.

Hannah

Book title:
 Chest Complaints by Ivor Tickliecoff

From: nestahotbabe@retro.co.uk
To: goody2shoes@psnet.co.uk
Date: 18 June
Subject: Friday night

Hey, Lara Croft

Wanna come to a sleepover Friday night? Iz and Lucy are coming. About 7?

Nesta

8

Sleepover Secrets

"T. J.! T. J.!" called Mum excitedly as she came in the door. "Where are you?"

"Here," I called from upstairs, where I was straining to get started on some ideas for the school magazine. So far, I'd written one word. Aggh.

It was Friday night and I was going to the sleepover at Nesta's in half an hour. An evening of culture had been planned. *The Simpsons, EastEnders, Friends,* and *South Park.*

Mum came in carrying a large carrier bag and plonked herself on the bed. She looked *very* pleased with herself.

"I couldn't resist," she said, getting something wrapped in tissue out of the bag. She pulled out a calf-length dress with swirly rust, maroon, and orange-colored flowers on it.

"What do you think?" she asked.

The word *disgusting* came to mind, though I suppose it was pretty in that cottage-chintzy-curtain-fabric way.

"Not your *usual* taste, Mum," I said, thinking I was being diplomatic. Mum isn't fashion-conscious at the best of times, but her style is more plain than flowery. Jaeger and Country Casuals for work and sloppy tracksuits for the weekend. And her idea of making an effort to dress up is to wear a blue glass bead necklace. Even if it's with the tracksuit.

"Not for me, silly," said Mum. "It's for *you*."

Whaaat? Aggggh. No. *Buuuut it's horrid*, I thought.

"It's lovely, isn't it? I saw it in a little boutique opposite the surgery and remembered what you'd said about wanting to look more like a girl. Perfect, I thought. I described you to the lady in the shop, said you had dark hair and hazel eyes and she said you'd be an Autumn according to her Color Me Beautiful chart and would suit the brown rusty colors," said Mum, not drawing breath. "Cost a fortune but we won't tell Dad. It's about time you had something nice. So what do you think?"

She was so delighted with her purchase that I didn't have the heart to hurt her feelings.

"There aren't words," I said truthfully.

"I *knew* you'd love it. You can wear it to your new friend's house, can't you? Try it on, try it on."

I smiled weakly as I desperately searched for something to say. Hmm? *How* do I get out of this one?

Ten minutes later, I was in the kitchen wearing the dress and still wondering, literally, how to get out of this. Course, that had to be the very moment Scott banged on the back door.

"Evenin' all," he said, letting himself in and stroking Mojo, who jumped up in greeting. Then he saw me. "Yuk. You going to a fancy dress?"

"*Shhh,*" I said. "Mum's upstairs. She bought it for me."

"What, to wear?"

"No. To scare off burglars. *Yes,* to wear."

Scott pulled a face. "You look weird. Like you're in *The Waltons.*"

"Thanks a bunch. So how do I get out of it?"

Scott went round to my back, put his hands on my waist and nuzzled into my neck. "Now *that's* one thing I'm good at, helping girls out of their dresses." He

Cathy Hopkins

started to stroke my hair then play with my zip. "Now, Miss Watts," he whispered. "I really don't think this is your style. Let me help you out of it and into something . . . more . . . comfortable."

I giggled and slapped him, hoping he didn't see me blushing. Him nibbling my neck made me feel all fluttery inside. Nice.

"*Uhyuh yunnawee,*" I started to say, then took a deep breath and made myself remember this was Scott *for heaven's sake*. "Seriously though," I said, turning so he couldn't see my red face. "I'm going to a sleepover tonight at a new mate's house and I can't possibly wear this. She'll think it's so naff."

"What new mate?"

"*Oh,*" I suddenly remembered he fancied Nesta. "Er . . . Nesta Williams new mate."

"You're kidding. *Nesta?* Why didn't you tell me? When did this all happen? I thought you said she was an airhead."

"Well, I was wrong. She's actually very nice."

Scott punched the air. "*Yes.* Will you promise, promise, *promise* to put a word in for me? Or even better, you could bring her here and I could kind of casually drop in and you could introduce us?"

I *could* I suppose, I thought, watching Scott as he went into the hall and checked himself in the mirror. I just wish that a boy would feel that enthusiastic about me one day. And even more to my surprise, I found myself thinking, I wish *Scott* would feel that enthusiastic about me.

By the time I was due to go, I had a plan.

I went down into the kitchen wearing my usual tracksuit and trainers to find Mum chopping peppers and onions on the counter.

"I can't wear the dress tonight, Mum. I'm going via Lucy's house and they've got two huge dogs. Labradors. *Very* hairy. *Always* moulting. The kind of dogs who jump up on you. With *enormous* claws and muddy paws and they like to chew everything. They'd *ruin* my dress. Do you mind if I put it away for a special occasion?" (Special occasion like Bonfire Night and I put it on a guy to be burned, I thought.)

"Sure," said Mum. "And are you *sure* you like it?"

Was she giving me a get out? I was about to open my mouth and say *nooooo*, I hate it . . .

"Because they had it in pink," she said.

Ag. Agh. Agherama.

Later, I thought, as I made for the door. I will sort this later.

"Got your jimjams?" asked Nesta, closing the front door behind us. She looked fab in a lilac cami set with the words *Groovy Chick* across the top.

I nodded as she led me through into a living room with high ceilings, deep-red walls, and plush brown velvet sofas. Impressive, I thought, as I took in the mix of dark wood and Turkish and Moroccan-looking rugs.

Izzie and Lucy were already there, curled up for our telly night, and both gave me a wave. Izzie was wearing red flannel pajamas with fluffy sheep on them, and Lucy had blue ones with stars and moons all over. I waved back and hoped that they couldn't see how nervous I was feeling. Nesta's flat was so glam, I hoped they wouldn't think my house was mega-dull when they came to visit me.

"You can change in there," said Nesta, showing me a cloakroom off the hall. "No one's here. Tony's staying over at a mate's, and Mum and Dad have gone out to eat. Mum said we can order pizza. What's your fave?"

"Four cheese. Please," I said as I closed the cloakroom door behind me.

"Coming up," called Nesta. *"Quattro formaggi."*

My pajamas looked so boring as I got them out of my bag. A pale grey vestie thing for the top and bottoms to match. Ah well. What you see is what you get, I thought, as I pulled them on, then went back into the living room and pulled a cushion onto the floor.

"Let the viewing commence," said Izzie, passing me the Pringles.

After we'd finished watching *South Park* and munching our way through crisps, pizza, chocolate, and ice cream, the real fun began. Nesta put on a DVD of mad Irish dancing. After we'd danced our socks off for fifteen minutes, we all collapsed on the sofa and they talked about *everything*—music, clothes, mags, school gossip, horoscopes, and, finally, boys.

As they chatted, we painted each other's toenails. I did Nesta's dark purple and then she did mine the same color. Izzie did Lucy's pale blue and she did Iz's red. None of them seemed to mind that I didn't say a lot. I was happy to sit back and take it all in.

Nesta was a hoot and seemed to be *very* experienced with boys. She's had loads of boyfriends. At least eight.

Maybe more, I lost count. And she seems to be an expert on snogging.

Izzie is just fab. She's into loads of interesting stuff, not just horoscopes but alternative health, food, nutrition, aromatherapy, crystals, and witchcraft. And she's *also* in a band with her boyfriend. His name's Ben and the band's called King Noz. She sang a song for us that she'd written herself. She has the most amazing voice.

And Lucy. Lucy's sweet. And kind. She kept checking on me to see I had enough to drink and eat. And was I comfortable. Did I need another cushion?

They all made me feel so welcome I suppose it was inevitable that, in the end, they'd turn the spotlight on me.

"So T. J., is there anyone you fancy?"

I shook my head. "Not really."

"So why've you gone red?" asked Nesta.

"Nesta!" said Lucy.

"What? *What?*"

"Let her tell in her own time," said Izzie.

I decided to plunge in. They'd all been so open with me, I felt I should be the same with them.

"Well, I suppose there *is* one boy," I said. "I've known him all my life, but he treats me more like one of the lads than a girl."

"Does he know you fancy him?" asked Lucy.

"*Noooo*. In fact," I said, looking at Nesta, "he fancies you."

"*Me?*"

"Yeah, he's seen you at the Hollywood Bowl and asked if I'd put a word in."

Nesta looked surprised. "What's his name?"

"Scott Harris."

"Don't know him," said Nesta. "And anyway, I have a boyfriend."

"Posh boy," teased Lucy.

"Simon Peddington Lee," said Izzie in a voice like the Queen's.

"He's away at school at the mo," said Nesta, "but we speak or text most days. He'll be back soon for the summer hols. And, *anyway*, I don't steal other girl's boyfriends."

"He's not my boyfriend."

"Not *yet*," said Nesta. "Anyway, you saw him first, so in my book that means he's yours whether he knows it or not."

"Maybe you should let him know you like him," said Iz.

"*Noooo*. Can't. *No*. You don't understand. That would ruin everything. See, he's one of the few boys I can talk to. I have known him so long I don't get all tongue-tied like I do around boys I fancy."

"You got on with my brothers okay," said Lucy.

"Yeah. But that was different."

"Ah, you don't fancy Steve. Is that it?"

"No. Yes. I don't know. I didn't think about it. It felt so natural round your house, I kind of forgot he was a boy. And, well . . . it's just, we got off on the right foot. I won at arm wrestling and we were away."

"Got off on the right arm then," grinned Lucy. "Not foot."

I decided to tell them everything. "See, I can karate-chop a boy to the floor and stand on his neck easy peasy, but the thought of having to kiss one and I'm terrified."

"*Ah . . . ,*" said Lucy. "I get it."

"You have to be like Buffy," said Izzie. "Like, one minute she's snogging Angel, the next, she's out vaporizing vampires. It's a question of balance."

"Right," I said, feeling more confused than ever.

I could see Nesta was bursting to say something.

"What?" I said.

"Nothing," she said, but she was holding her stomach as though keeping something in.

"Spill. I can take it."

"No. Nothing. Well. What if . . . ? No . . . nothing . . ."

"Oh, for God's sake, Nesta. Spit it out," said Izzie.

"Well," said Nesta. "How about you don't tell Scott you fancy him? How about we get him to fancy *you*?"

"Ah," I said. "And how do you propose to do that?"

I knew exactly what she had in mind, but felt like teasing her.

"Er . . . ," she looked anxiously at Lucy. "Dunno really."

I decided to help her out. "You still want to do a makeover, don't you?"

"Er, *no*," she said with a quick glance at Lucy.

"You think I look like a bag lady, don't you?"

"*NO*. I never said *that!*" Now Nesta looked really worried. Lucy may be small in height but she's clearly big in Nesta's books. "No. *No*. I think you look fab. Oh, all right. . . . I think you could look fabber. With a makeover. That's all. And now you're going to hate me. And think I'm mean because I want to help. And Lucy's going to go on about my big gob. And how I never know when to stop. . . ."

I laughed. "I'm only teasing you. No, please, do it. To tell the truth, I took a look at myself in the mirror this evening in the dress from hell that my mum bought me and I thought, T. J., you need help. I'd love it if you gave me a makeover. I'll use it in the magazine. And . . . anyone got a pen? I've had an idea for a feature for the mag. A Sleepover Special Report."

Nesta handed me a pen and paper from the drawer in the desk behind the sofa. Then she took my face in her hands and turned it to profile and back. Then she clapped her hands and went into drama luvvie persona, "A mi-vake over. Oh, *daaahlling*, ve're going to mi-vake you look *faaaabulouse*."

D'oh, I thought. What've I let myself in for?

Sleepover Special Report

Ever wondered what makes the perfect sleepover? For Real asked four teenagers for their top tips and fave ingredients. Here's what they came up with.

Six main ingredients
1) Nosh for the munchies
2) Drinks
3) DVDs
4) Music
5) Makeup for makeovers
6) Mags

Special Spot Report

Izzie Foster. 14. Aquarius. Finchley. London
Fave thing to do at sleepovers? Goss. Listen to music. Nosh.
Fave music for sleepover? Anastacia. Christina Aguilera.
Fave DVD? Austin Powers 2. Yeah baby yeah.
Top nosh? Choc-chip cookies. Doritos.
Top drink? Organic elderflower juice.

Nesta Williams. 14. Leo. Highgate. London
Fave thing to do at sleepovers? Dance. Read problem page in
mags and have a good laugh. Makeovers.
Fave music for sleepover? The latest love ballads compilation.
Fave DVD? *Charlie's Angels* or *Scream*.
Top nosh? Nettuno pizza with extra cheese. Häagen Dazs.
Top drink? Coke.

Lucy Lovering. 14. Gemini. Muswell Hill. London
Fave thing to do at sleepovers? Talk about snogging and boys.
Fave music for sleepover? Robbieeee.
Fave DVD? *Titanic*. I'm King of the Wooooorld.
Top nosh? Chinese take-away. Yum. Pecan nut Häagen Dazs.
Top drink? Hot chocolate made with milk and marshmallows.

T. J. Watts. 14. Sagittarius. Muswell Hill. London
Fave thing to do at sleepovers? Chill. Laugh my head off.
Fave music for sleepover? *The Best Summer Ever*.
Fave DVD? *South Park Christmas Special* starring
   Mr. Hankey the Christmas Poo.
Top nosh? Burger and chips. Toffee popcorn.
Top drink? Banana milk shake with vanilla ice cream on top.

9

American Pie

"So The Plan is," said Nesta, through a mouthful of toast, "we all go to T. J.'s and sift through her wardrobe."

It was Saturday morning and we were still in our jimjams, sitting round in the kitchen, eating toast, and drinking milky coffees.

I wondered if I could get out of The Plan. Not that I was bothered about the makeover anymore, no, I was worried what the girls were going to make of the Wrinklies. Izzie, Lucy, and Nesta's parents were normal ages. And Nesta's are so *glamorous*. I met them this morning while I was waiting for the bathroom. Her mum's a newsreader on cable television and her dad's a film director and both *très* good looking and stylish as far as grown-ups go.

Mainly though, I was worried what the Wrinklies might make of the girls. Dad in particular. He can turn into Scary Dad at the slightest bit of noise or disturbance. Our house was never one to throw its doors open and welcome in the neighborhood. I always used to go to Hannah's house rather than the other way round. Dad likes his privacy, the fewer people he sees when he's not working, the better. Radio 4 and peace and quiet and he's happy. Last thing I wanted was him showing me up in front of new friends by asking them pointed questions like, "What time's your bus home?"

I thought I'd better warn the girls.

"Okay, er, about my parents, well my dad . . . ," I said, and explained the situation.

"Same at our house," said Izzie. "My mum doesn't exactly encourage me to bring my mates back. Some parents are like that. It's easy to hang at Lucy's or here where no one's running round cleaning up after you all the time."

"So, no problemo, T.J.," said Nesta. "We will be the perfect example of quiet refined teenagers."

"Well behaved and demure," said Izzie.

"And *very* mature," said Lucy.

I breathed a sigh of relief. I could trust them to be cool. At that moment, the back door opened and

Leonardo DiCaprio's younger Italian brother walked in. I mean, this boy was *seriously* handsome.

"T. J., Tony. Tony, T. J. My brother," said Nesta as if I hadn't realized.

"Hi, T.J.," said The Vision.

"Hi, Tony," said a friendly voice inside my head. However, what came out of my mouth was, *"uhyuh."* Oh, *noooo*, I thought. Alien Girl from the Planet Zog is back to haunt me.

Tony looked at the croissant I was about to eat, then looked right into my eyes and did a half-smile that made him look even more gorgeous. "So, T. J., what do virgins eat for breakfast?"

"Dunno," I replied, breaking his gaze and staring at the floor.

"Thought so," he said and laughed.

"Take no notice of Tony, he's a dingbat," said Nesta. "So. Aren't you going to ask?"

"Ask what?"

"How come Tony is my brother?"

"No."

"Why not?" asked Nesta. *"Everyone* asks. He's light-skinned, I'm dark-skinned, how come?"

"Obvious," I said. "Same father, different mothers."

"Hmmm," said Nesta. "Smart cookie."

Not really, the voice in my head said. I met your mum and dad this morning. I know she's Jamaican and your dad looks Italian. Tony looks like your dad so I reckon he must have had a different mother. Elementary, my dear Williams. However, Noola the Alien Girl is a person of few words and all that came out was, "*uh.*" Smart cookie indeed. Why did this *always* happen when boys I fancied were around?

"My real mum died before I knew her. I was six months old," explained Tony, coming over and laying his head on my shoulder. "Really, I'm an orphan. An orphan prince who needs *love* and *affection.*"

"*Uhyuh,*" I stuttered, hoping that by some strange quirk of fate, Tony might be fluent in Zoganese.

I could see Lucy giving me a strange look then giving Tony a *filthy* look. Hmm? Something going on there, methinks. Must ask later.

Tony went over to the fridge and opened the door. "What's to eat?" He got out a half-eaten apple pie, put it on the breakfast bar, and cut himself a huge slice.

"Apple pie for breakfast?" said Iz. "Ew. Gross."

He turned and grinned at her. "Would you prefer I did something else with it?"

"Like what?" said Iz.

"You seen that film *American Pie*?"

"Yeah," said Izzie, then pulled a face. "*Ew,* double gross."

"What are you on about?" I asked.

Nesta looked at Tony wearily and sighed. "Sorry about my disgusting brother, T. J. In *American Pie,* a boy asks what it's like to have sex. His mate says it's like putting your thingee in a warm apple pie."

I blushed furiously as Tony watched me closely to see my reaction.

"Apparently some guy in Australia tried it," said Lucy, getting down from her stool at the breakfast bar and refilling the kettle. "Steve read about it in the paper. This guy didn't wait for the pie to cool when it came out of the oven. He was taken to the local hospital and treated for burns."

"*Aggghhh,*" said Tony, putting his hands over his crotch as the rest of us laughed. "I wonder how he explained *that* to the nurse on duty."

Lucy looked at the apple pie and I saw a wicked twinkle appear in her eye. "Would you like me to warm that up for you, Tony?" she asked sweetly. "I could put it in the microwave. On high?"

Tony went over to her and put his arm round her. "And how *is* the love of my life?"

"Dunno. How is she?" said Lucy as she took his arm away from her shoulder.

"You know you want me really," said Tony.

Lucy began to walk out of the kitchen. "Yeah. Right. It's *agony* keeping my hands off you. Not."

"That girl . . ." Tony sighed as he watched her go out of the room. "So what are you lot doing today?"

"Makeover," said Nesta.

"Who's the poor victim this time?"

Nesta looked at me. I looked back at the floor.

Tony got up and started dancing in front of me. "'Don't go changing, tryin' to please me . . .'"

"Go and see Mum, Tony," said Nesta. "It's time for your medication."

"So what was all that about?" I asked Lucy. The four of us were sitting on the bus on our way over to my house later that morning. "You know, Tony?"

Lucy shrugged. "We used to go out. Then we finished. Then we got back together. I don't know where we are now."

"Muswell Hill," teased Nesta as the bus went up the Broadway past Marks & Spencer.

"He adores you," said Izzie.

"That's part of the problem," said Lucy. "See, we're just getting on great, then he starts again"—she caressed the air with her hands—"with wandering hands. I'm not ready for all that yet. I want it to be special when I go further with a boy. I don't want to do it because I feel pressured that if I don't, he'll dump me for someone who puts out more easily. You know?"

I nodded. No, I didn't know. I hadn't even been *snogged* yet.

"And you saw what he's like," said Lucy. "Flirting with you . . ."

"Oh, I never . . . ," I started. "I would never . . . I mean he *is* gorgeous, there's no denying that, but . . ."

"Oh, don't worry, T. J., he's like that with all girls. That's another reason why I don't give in to the wandering hands. I'd never feel as if I could trust him."

"Well, no reason to worry about me. You saw what I was like back there. Always the same when there are decent boys around. I told you, I go *stupid*. You know there's that book *Men are from Mars, Women are from Venus*. Well, I want to write one, *Men are from Mars, Women are from Venus, Teenagers are from Planet Zog*."

"Good idea," said Lucy.

"It's mad," I continued, "because, I want to be a

writer but, well, I told you my problem with finding the right words at the right time. Why do they always come after, like when I'm falling asleep?"

"That's good, it means your subconscious mind is working on it," said Izzie. "I find that with my lyrics. You have to consider the words. Play with them until you've got them right. Let them come to you sometimes. It can happen in the middle of the night. I'd say that is the sign that you *will* be a writer."

"And if you're from Planet Zog," said Lucy, "you can always write science fiction."

I laughed and punched her arm. "I wish I could be more like you, Nesta. I wish I could come out with great one-liners or put-downs."

"*We* all wish she'd be more like *you*," said Lucy with a grin. "Think before she speaks, sometimes."

"It does get me in trouble," said Nesta. "Sometimes."

"So, at last," said Lucy as we got to our gate. "We get to meet the man of the moment."

"Who? Scott?" I said, glancing up at his bedroom window to see if he'd seen us. "He usually goes out Saturday mornings."

"No, silly. Not Scott," said Lucy, pointing at the downstairs window next to our front door where a furry face was looking out. "Mojo."

I laughed as I unlocked the door and was almost knocked over as he leaped up to say hello.

"I've only been away a night," I said as he licked my face then ran round the girls, sniffing then rolling on the floor, his tail wagging madly.

After they'd all made a huge fuss over him, we all trooped up to my bedroom.

"Fab garden," said Nesta, looking out of the window. "It's huge and *wow*, a hammock. How cool. You've got visitors though. On the patio, your gran and grandad are here."

I went over to look out.

"Er, no," I said, pulling back. "That's my mum and dad."

Nesta looked like she wanted to die.

"Mum had me late, when she was in her mid-forties."

"Oh, *très* Cherie Blair," said Izzie, going for a look.

"No," said Nesta. "*Très* Jerry Hall. Much more glam. Now let's look in your wardrobe."

And that was it. No problem. *Très* Jerry Hall and show us your clothes. I needn't have worried at all.

"I hope I didn't offend," said Nesta as she held up

baggy tracksuit bottoms and put them on the reject pile. "You know, calling them your grandparents."

"No prob. I know they're ancient. In fact I call them the Wrinklies."

"I nicknamed my step-father The Lodger when he first arrived," said Izzie, flopping on the bed next to Mojo. "I couldn't relate to him any other way, although we get on better now. But the thought of him sharing a bed with Mum, you know, *eew*. . . ."

"Huh," said Lucy. "You think you've got problem parents? Mine get the prize. Why can't they be normal instead of mad hippies? They're so embarrassing sometimes."

"My brother's a hippie. You know, the one who's abroad. I could introduce him to your mum and dad when he's back."

"Yeah," said Lucy. "They could have a soy bean party or something and talk about vegan shoes."

"Vegan shoes?" I asked.

"Plastic. No leather. Dad sells them at the shop."

"I think your mum and dad are great," said Izzie. "I really like them."

"Well that's because you are a *very* strange person," said Lucy.

Izzie retaliated by throwing a cushion at her.

Not wanting to be left out, Nesta grabbed one of my pillows and bashed both of them over the head with it. "Oh, be*have*," she said in her best Mike Myers voice.

Both of them picked up cushions and began pelting her.

If you can't beat them, join them, I thought as I reached for a second pillow.

It was hysterical. Even Mojo joined in, jumping on whomever he could and barking his head off.

Five minutes later Lucy was face down on the floor with Izzie sitting on her back. Izzie was tickling her under her arms. "Repent, repent. Say I am the most fab fabster in the world, no, the *universe*."

"Never," cried Lucy into the carpet.

Whilst they battled it out on the floor, Nesta and I were using my bed as a trampoline.

"I'm Queen of Wanda, Warrior Princess," cried Nesta as she leaped in the air and whacked me over the head with a pillow.

"And *I'm* Buffy the Vampire Slayer," I yelled as I delivered a nifty whack to her knees. "*Die*, you pathetic imbecile."

Just at that second, my bedroom door opened.

"What in *heaven's* name is that din?" shouted Dad above the racket. "It sounds as if someone's being murdered."

We all froze on the spot as if playing a game of statues.

Dad was definitely in Scary Dad mode and I prayed he wasn't going to make a scene.

"Aren't you a bit old for this tomfoolery?" he asked.

Nesta and I got off the bed and Lucy and Izzie got up off the floor. We stood in line, looking sheepish and not knowing what to do next. Lucy was staring at the floor, Izzie was grinning at my father like an idiot, and Nesta was looking at her nails, trying to pretend that she wasn't there.

Then I noticed Lucy's shoulders going up and down in silent laughter. This set me off. Then Izzie. Then Nesta, as all of us exploded into a fit of laughing.

Dad looked to the heavens in exasperation. "*Fourteen*, T.J. Isn't it about time you started acting like a young woman?"

I nodded furiously, but tears were falling down my cheeks.

"I'm going to my club for a bit of *peace*," said Dad, going out and slamming the door behind him.

"Oops," I said, then started sniggering. "Iz, Lucy, Nesta meet my dad. Oh dear . . ."

"Sorrysorry," said Nesta. Then she picked up one of my bras from a pile of ironing on the desk and put it on over her T-shirt.

"Guess we're going to have to work on our refined and well-behaved bit, huh?" she said, sticking her chest out.

I nodded. "Demure and wotsit," I said, picking a pair of knickers from the pile and putting them on my head.

"And vewee vewee mature," said Lucy in a little girlie voice as she sprang up on my bed and jumped up as high as she could.

e-mail:	Inbox (4)
From:	hannahnutter@fastmail.com
To:	goody2shoes@psnet.co.uk
Date:	22 June
Subject:	Cape Town boy babe

Mambo bandana baby. Bin bisy bee. Fabola barbie last night and I have neeews. I met a boy. I seriously think he may be the One. I may even have to phone you for a yabayaba. He is Drop Dead Divine. A bronzed Adonis. His name is Luke. We had devine tucker and deep talk.

H X

P.S. Luke (swoon swoon) has a book title for you.
  Romantic Fantasies by Everly Night. Heehee. Double arf.

From: hannahnutter@fastmail.com
To: goody2shoes@psnet.co.uk
Date: 22 June
Subject: Scary Dad

Where are you? I phoned and got Scary Dad who said you were at a sleepover. Then he grilled me about whether my mum and dad knew I was phoning. Don't dare phone again. Get thine holy finger out and e-mail me as SOOON as you get in. Loooooooooaaaaaaaaaaads to tell you.

Hx

From: hannahnutter@fastmail.com
To: goody2shoes@psnet.co.uk
Date: 23 June
Subject: Alert alert. Lost T. J. Watts.

Okela. Ista no joke no more. *Ou est* you? *Ou Ou OU?*

Hx

From: paulwatts@worldnet.com
To: goody2shoes@psnet.co.uk
Date: 23 June
Subject: hols

Hey, little sis. Hope it's all going well and Scary Dad not giving you too hard a time. Life here is truly wonderful. Did a day with a holy man, amazing as he is out here in India, but is really from Kilburn. Lots of stuff happening with my third eye. Plus he's re-energized my chakras.

Did two-day meditation session with holy man. Nice group. All gelled well. Fairy-story landscapes and sunsets. Friendly people but Saskia has got amoebic dysentery.

Rock on. Stay true.

Paul

PS Please can you ask Ma to go to the Embassy and get me a new passport. Mine was nicked when I slept on the beach the other night. Ta. Plus some peppermint oil and sulphur and pulsatilla homeopathic stuff for the runs.

---

e-mail: Outbox (1)
From: goody2shoes@psnet.co.uk
To: hannahnutter@fastmail.com
Date: 23 June
Subject: Friday night

Hey H

Glad you met boy. Luke. I want *details*. Height? Weight? Snogged yet? Level of snogging? Marks out of ten for snogging? etc.

↻

Me had fabola time at sleepover with Nesta, Izzie, and Lucy. Nesta's bro is divine, but taken by Lucy. Sort of. He has wandering hands apparently, which Nesta says is a disease a lot of boys in North London suffer from. She's going to do a makeover on me for the magazine. Before/after kind of thing. They all came over to go through my wardrobe but couldn't find anything. *Quelle* surprise. Oh and Mum bought me the dress from hell. Lucy said I had to be honest with Mum so I was and she's given me the receipt so I can change it. Thank de Lord. After we'd been through my wardrobe, we went into the garden as we are having uno heat wave here. It was nice and relaxed as Dad had gone to his club for A BIT OF *PEACE*. (He caught us being *un peu* silly and making a lot of noise and well, you know what he can be like.) Nesta had a go on the hammock under the cherry trees. Scott came running over the minute he spotted her from his bedroom window. He leaped over the fence with a flower, trying to impress her, but he gave her the shock of her life and she fell out of the hammock. Then Mojo jumped all over her. It was very funny. Scott was all over her, all dopey with big cow eyes. I felt a bit jealous, although I know that she has a boyfriend and she said after that Scott wasn't her type. Still. I wish a boy would be all over me. I think I may be the only girl in our class who hasn't been snogged. Maybe I'll never get a boy ever. Maybe I'm just not the sort boys like.

T. J.

e-mail: Inbox (1)
From: hannahnutter@fastmail.com
To: goody2shoes@psnet.co.uk
Date: 23 June
Subject: you don't 'alf talk rubbish sometimes

T. J.

You're not the only girl who's never been snogged in Year Nine. I know for a fact that Joanne Richards and Mo Harrison haven't been and unless Mo sorts out her halitosis, she never will be.

Luke. Height 6ft at least. Blond. Body like a god. Snogged, yes. Level 3. Okay, 4. Well, he is a god. Marks out of ten for snoggability? 9. But practice will make perfect.

I think it's great, those girls doing a makeover. You are gorgeous, but don't make the most of yourself. I've always said this. I like the sound of Nesta, Iz, and Lucy and often thought that if I hadn't been friends with you, I would like to have been friends with them.

   Tata for now,
   Hannah. South African goddess of luurve

Books: Are you still doing this?
   Run to the Loo by Willie Makeit

10

My Fair Lady. Not

"You'll never do it," I said, beginning to feel desperate. "It's hopeless. I am Ugly Git from Uglygit-land."

"Roma wasna builta in a day," said Nesta, tugging her way through my hair.

"The darkest hour is just before dawn," said Lucy, who was kneeling on the floor next to me, retouching my nails.

"Suppose," I said, looking gloomily at my reflection in the mirror in Nesta's bedroom. My hair was a frizzy mess. I had an aloe-vera face mask on that made me look like a ghost and a big spot threatening to erupt on my chin.

"Lack of self-esteem," said Izzie. "That's your problem, T. J. You are a babe, but you don't know it. Look, you have fabulous hair that you always scrape back in a plait, long *long* legs that you never show, a fab figure that you hide in baggy tracksuits, and a great mouth that all those thin-lipped models who have collagen injections would die for."

Always one to accept compliments graciously, I said, "Humphh. And you clearly have the observational skills of a brain-dead gnat."

We'd already done the "before" shot in the morning at Lucy's house. Steve had offered to be photographer with his new camera and it was hysterical. I'd worn the "dress from hell" that Mum had bought me, and Izzie had done my hair in two bunches high on either side of my head. Lucy had stuck dog hair from Ben and Jerry's brush onto my legs with Evostick so that I'd look like I had hairy legs. (I put my foot down when she got carried away and tried to stick some on my upper lip to give me a mustache though.) And Nesta had given me some lessons in bad posture so I looked even more frumpy.

"All beautiful women have great posture," she'd said. "It's one of the first things they teach at modeling school. To stand up straight. So for these shots, stoop, like you have round shoulders."

Lucy raided her mum's jumble sale bargain bags and produced some seriously tasteless jewelry. Big dangly earrings and an Indian necklace.

"But they don't go with the dress," I'd said.

The girls had looked at me as if I was stupid.

"And the object of this exercise *is*?" said Nesta.

By the time they'd finished, I looked like a sack of old potatoes. With hairy legs.

"You look awful," Steve'd said approvingly when I came down the stairs, then walked across the hallway like a duck. A round-shouldered duck.

"Yeah, like Queen of Slobs from Slobville," laughed Lal.

"I want to do the shots round the back garden near the trash cans," said Steve.

"What, like I'm on the scrap heap?" I asked.

Steve gave me a look as if to say "yeah", then he grinned. "You don't look that bad," he said. "It's only that dress that makes you look like a frump."

"But the trash cans in the background give a sort of subliminal message, like I'm a load of rubbish," I said.

"Yeah," said Steve. "Exactly. We've been doing it in film class, all about how surrounding images register with the subconscious and can reinforce what you're trying to say without people realizing."

"What are you on about?" said Lucy. She did an enormous yawn as though bored out of her mind, but I found what he was saying interesting.

We had a great laugh as Steve clicked away and I assumed the most unattractive positions and facial expressions I could.

At one point, Mr. and Mrs. Lovering came out to see what we were up to. They watched for a moment as I cavorted for the camera doing my sumo-wrestler position, then a bit of karate chopping. They looked very puzzled to hear Steve say in a French accent, "And look as miserable as you can. Like your durg 'as just died and gone to durgee 'eaven *avec les autres chiens*. That's it. *Eh bien. Marvelleuse, mon ooglee légume. . . . Diable* mon sooth, chins up, chins down. *Mais oui, bien sûr. Degoûtantamont.*"

Clearly languages were not his thing, I thought, as his parents both shrugged and went back into the house.

The second part of the makeover wasn't a laugh. Oh no-ho, not at all. The girls were taking it seriously. As in *mega*-seriously. They were on a blooming makeover mission.

I was plucked, waxed, massaged, moisturized, conditioned, manicured, pedicured, blow-dried, made up, made over, and dressed.

"Okay, you can look now," said Nesta, removing her dressing gown from the mirror where she'd draped it so I couldn't see.

The reflection of a brunette Barbie doll gazed back at me. I was wearing one of Nesta's dresses, a short pale blue number and her mum's Jimmy Choo gray strappy heels. Nesta had given me "big" hair, loose and flowing over my shoulders, and Lucy had made up my face with a little shadow, blusher, and rusty lipstick.

"You shall go to the ball, Cinders," said Nesta. "You look fab."

"Yeah, a top babe," said Lucy. "Do you like it?"

I wasn't sure. I did look good. And I had to admit that my legs looked really long. But I wasn't sure that looking like such a girlie girl was me. Mind you, I didn't know what *was* me.

"What do you think, Izzie?"

"Watch out boys," she sang. "There's a new kid in town."

* * *

Nesta's mum gave us a lift to Hampstead High Street where we were meeting Steve to do the "after" shots.

She dropped us halfway down Heath Street and as we got out of the car, someone did a long wolf whistle. I looked over to where it was coming from and there was Scott. He was with a bunch of his mates sitting at a table outside Café Nero.

"T. J. Watts. *Cor* bloody cor," he said as he looked me up and down and then up and down again, his eyes finally resting on my legs. "You're a *girl*."

"*Uhyuh,*" I said as I noticed all the other boys round the table also ogling me. I felt exposed standing there in my shorter-than-short dress and I wasn't sure I liked the attention I was getting. Everyone was staring and there was nowhere to hide. Even an old bloke in his forties was gawping as he went by. Served him right, I thought, when he walked smack into a woman with her dog and got all tangled up in the lead.

Scott took my hand and introduced us to his friends. He seemed to be enjoying himself immensely. Then he was all over Nesta and acting like he'd known her for ever. All his mates sniggered when she dismissed him saying, "In your dreams."

He didn't seem to mind though. In fact, I think he took it as a come-on.

Lucy spotted Steve coming down the street and waved. He waved back and, when he saw me, he did a slow whistle under his breath.

"See they've done a number," he said.

"Wow," I said to Izzie as we walked or rather they walked and I tottered. "Is it really this simple? A bit of lipstick, high heels, show your legs and boys turn to jelloid?"

Izzie nodded. "And even more so if you show a bit of cleavage. It's amazing to watch. Hysterical. You see boys' cheekbones twitching with the effort not to look at your chestie bits, but their eyes keep zinging back there as if pulled by an invisible magnet."

"Not a problem I have," said Lucy, "being a thirty-two triple A myself."

"Lucy's bros call her Nancy-No-Tits," confided Nesta.

"We can't all be Dolly Parton like you," laughed Lucy, punching her arm.

We went down to the bottom of Heath Street with Scott and his mates trailing after us and sat at a table outside House on the Hill. Nesta ordered drinks and Steve took some shots as he said he wanted them to look natural rather than posed. This time I didn't have to do much, he did all the work. He was much quieter this time, not acting as loony mad as he had been in the morning. He wasn't as much fun. In fact he seemed to want to get it over with, as though he'd lost interest.

"Why did you choose Hampstead for the 'after' shots?" I asked, in an attempt to get him talking.

"Trendy place. It's glam. Rich," he said, then he clamped up again.

He didn't hang around after he'd got his photos and muttered something about having to get back to finish homework.

Something had clearly upset him since this morning. He was really subdued. I must ask Lucy if she knows.

---

e-mail: Outbox (1)
From: goody2shoes@psnet.co.uk
To: hannahnutter@fastmail.com
Date: 24 June
Subject: The new *moi*

Hey Hannahlooloo

Had brill time today with makeover. Steve took photos on his new camera. Will send copies. Nesta made me look very girlie girl but not sure it's me. Felt uncomfortable for a few reasons. I never realized before that you can be invisible in big baggy clothes and no one takes too much notice. It's kind of safe. But going out in Hampstead today, everyone was staring. I felt exposed. Nesta said to "strut my stuff, girlfriend," but people act differently to you if you do. Girls can be bitchy. Boys disturbed.

Scott went all googly-eyed at me. But mainly people stared. I wasn't sure if I liked it. Talking of which, we bumped into Wendy Roberts coming out of Accessorize. She did a double take when she saw me and almost spat out her Magnum. Then she said that dressed like I was, I should go far, the further the better. I wasn't sure what to make of her reaction.

Spika soon

Love, T. J.

P.S. Yes, yes. More book titles, as I'm definitely going to put some in the mag. *Body Parts* by Anne Atomy

---

e-mail:	Inbox (2)
From:	hannahnutter@fastmail.com
To:	goody2shoes@psnet.co.uk
Date:	24 June
Subject:	The noo *vous*

Ole *le* noodley noodles baby

I think the word to describe Wendy's reaction is *envy*. God, I wish I'd been there to see her. And you. I do miss Hampstead and Highgate and hanging out. I bet you looked the business. Don't worry about looking girlie. You'll find your style. Today was just the beginning of T. J. as Sex Queen of North London. Remember Confucius he say, "Every journey start with first step. That is, unless step going sideways or backward."

Have been to Luke's posh pad *avec* pool this weekend. Some consolation for missing Ingerlandie.

May your flobbalots be mighty

HannahXXXXXXXXXXXXXXXXXXXXXXXXXXXXXX

From: hannahnutter@fastmail.com
To: goody2shoes@psnet.co.uk
Date: 24 June
Subject: d'oh. Steve?????

Er exs*cooth* me?? But I just re-read your e-mail. Have you been holding out on me? More about Steve? Details? Height? Weight? Fanciability? Etc etc.
Immediatetment.

Hannah

---

e-mail: Outbox (1)
From: goody2shoes@psnet.co.uk
To: hannahnutter@fastmail.com
Date: 24 June
Subject: d'oh. Steve?????

Gordy flobbalots. I told you already. *Lucy's* older brother. Fanciability. I guess he's nice-looking, but not in a drop-dead way like Scott, who I think I may be in love with. And at last he's noticed I am a girl. It's different with Steve. He's easy to talk to. I don't go peculiar when he's around. He's a mate.

T. J.

Book: *Strange Breasts* by Won Hung Low

e-mail: Inbox (1)
From: hannahnutter@fastmail.com
To: goody2shoes@psnet.co.uk
Date: 24 June
Subject: d'oh. Steve?????

Zoot allors. Snog him anyway and get in some practice!

   HXXXX

Book: *Drink Problems* by Imorf Mihead

11

Walking the Durg

"Don't go into the woods," said Mum as I got ready to take Mojo for a walk on Wednesday after school. "Stay on the roads where people can see you."

"I'm going to ask if Scott will come," I said. "Then it will be okay, won't it?"

"Yes, fine," said Mum. "But don't be too late back. You've still got homework to do."

I couldn't wait to call on Scott. I'm sure it wasn't my imagination that he'd been so flirty in Hampstead on Saturday. He'd seemed genuinely bowled over by my new look and at one point he'd held my hand and squeezed it. I'd got that lovely fluttery feeling again, like when he'd nuzzled my neck. I couldn't stop thinking about it and what it might be like to hold his hand

again and even kiss him. My insides went all liquidy
and peculiar just imagining it.

I combed my hair loose, put on a bit of lipstick, then
put Mojo on his lead and went next door.

Mrs. Harris answered.

"Is Scott home?" I asked, trying my best not to give
away the fact I was quaking. Mad really, as I'd been over
to his house a million times and thought nothing of it.

She called up to him in his room and he emerged at
the top of the stairs a few minutes later.

"Oh, hi, T. J."

"Er. Hi. Um. I'm taking Mojo for a walk. Do you
want to come?"

He shook his head. "Watching *The Simpsons,*" he said.

"Oh. Okay, cool. Another time," I said, hoping that I
hadn't shown how disappointed I was. He didn't even
come down to say good-bye.

As Mojo and I went up to Muswell Hill Broadway, I
wondered if I'd misread the signals. Had he ever held
my hand before? Or squeezed it? I couldn't remember.
Maybe I was reading too much into it. Maybe he hadn't
liked my new look after all. But he seemed to at the
time. He kept staring at me. I felt so confused.

I decided I'd look in a few shop windows in the hope

of finding an alternative style to Barbie babe. Fat chance, I thought, as I looked at the various tops and skirts on display. I wasn't sure what I wanted to look like, though one thing I was certain about was that I didn't want to wear those high heel things again. Agony. They may have looked good, but there was only so far I was prepared to go in the have-to-suffer-to-be-beautiful game.

Mojo trotted alongside me happily as I pondered the great philosophical question of who was the real T. J. Watts.

Is she Noola the Alien girl?

Or Miss Strop-Bossy Prefect who likes to put boys straight?

Or Arm Wrestling Champion of North London?

Or Miss Goody 2 Shoes who always does her homework?

Or Norma Know-It-All?

Or Barbie's brunette sister?

Or on the other hand, is she a total nutter with loads of different characters living in her head?

"What do you think, Mojo?" I asked as we made our way past the cinema and down Muswell Hill High Road.

"Aha," said a voice behind me. "Talking to yourself, first sign of insanity."

I turned and there was Steve with Ben and Jerry.

"I was talking to Mojo," I said. "But you might be right about the insanity bit. In fact I was just thinking I might well be going bonkers."

He laughed. "You going to Highgate Woods?" he asked as Mojo, Ben, and Jerry got down to the dignified business of sniffing each other's bottoms.

"No," I said. "Mojo would love to, but Mum said I mustn't go on my own."

Steve checked his watch. "Well, we have just been, but I've no doubt these guys wouldn't object to a bit longer. Come on, I'll keep you company."

I gave Mum a quick ring on my mobile and, after giving me the third degree, she finally agreed.

We set off for the woods and once inside, let the dogs off their leads. They raced off excitedly, best of friends already. As they charged about, Steve and I chatted like old mates. It's so weird, I thought. Here's me, all great pals with Steve and nervous with Scott, whereas only a week ago, Scott was my pal and Steve was a complete stranger.

"So, what's with you and that guy?" asked Steve after a while.

"What guy?"

"One outside Café Nero. You seemed to like him."

"God, am I *that* obvious?" I was taken aback that he'd read my thoughts. "I hope he didn't notice."

"I don't think he did. Too busy ogling Nesta."

My heart sank. Maybe that was it. It was really Nesta he was interested in. And he'd been doing the flirty bit to get to her through me.

"I know," I said. "He lives next door to me. Has done for years and we've always been mates. Until lately. It's all changed. I found myself . . . you know, er, well, thinking about him a lot. I don't know what I feel, it's all so weird. And I certainly don't know what he thinks, but I don't think he rates me other than someone to talk to. Oh, I don't know. . . ."

"Any boy who doesn't fancy you must be mad," said Steve. "And I'll tell you one of the biggest secrets about boys. . . ."

I held my breath for the great revelation.

"They're exactly the same as girls in that they also feel shy and awkward that they don't always say the right thing or act the right way."

"Really?"

Steve looked at me closely. "Boys may act confident but can be just as nervous as you underneath. Everyone fears being turned down and looking a fool."

"I just don't think he's interested. . . ."

"How do you know who's interested or not?" said Steve. "Sometimes when a boy is acting disinterested, it's actually more frozen than cool. Frozen with fear as mostly girls call the shots. Boys fear rejection like anyone else."

Me calling the shots? That was a laugh. But boys being nervous too, that was obvious really. I'd never thought about it before. I'd been so caught up in my own ill-ease, I hadn't thought about theirs. Of course boys must feel that way too sometimes.

"For instance," said Steve, "you may think a boy doesn't want to know, but he may be too scared to say anything. I know I am sometimes, you know, if I like someone."

Maybe that's what Scott had been doing just now, I thought. Acting cool. Afraid I'd reject him. No. Not possible. Or was it? I felt more confused than ever.

"In fact . . . ," said Steve.

"How does anyone ever get together then?" I interrupted. "I think I'd need someone to make it *very* clear to me."

"How?"

"Dunno. Cards. Presents. Billboard in Piccadilly? Shout from the top of the rooftops I FANCY T. J. WATTS."

Steve laughed. "I'm sure there are loads of boys after you," he said. "You just don't know it."

"Really?"

"Well you saw the reaction you were getting yesterday."

"Yeah. But I wasn't sure if that girlie-girl look was really my style."

Steve nodded. "Yeah. Don't get me wrong, but I thought Nesta had made you into a Nesta clone. That look suits her, but I see you more as Buffy than Barbie."

"Really?" Cool, I thought. I liked the sound of that. More Buffy than Barbie. I must make a note of what kind of clothes she wears.

"So how's the mag going?"

"Okay. But it's brought out the competitive side of everyone at school. And some of them can be pretty bitchy. Like there's this one girl, the one we saw in Hampstead. She's giving me a really hard time." I continued filling him in on the Dog of the Week stunt that Wendy had pulled. "Wendy Roberts."

Steve slapped his forehead. "The one outside Accessorize? I *knew* I knew her. Now you say the name . . . A mate of mine went out with her." Then he chuckled. "I could tell you some good goss about her."

"What?"

"No front teeth."

"How do you know?"

"My mate found out when he snogged her. One of them came loose. That's how I remember her name. She's waiting for implants, but the dentist won't do them until she's older. So she's got dentures. Real false teeth. Apparently she knocked both of them out in a riding accident. You could print a piece about dentists. And put in a picture of her as an example."

I laughed at the thought of it. "With a caption: All I want for Christmas is my two front teeth."

"Or instead of 'wide-eyed and legless,' you could write, 'wide-eyed and toothless.'"

"Don't tempt me," I said.

The time whizzed by as we chatted on about ideas for the school newspaper and Steve offered to do a piece on photography.

When I looked at my watch, it said eight o'clock.

"God, I'd better go," I said. "Mum'll kill me."

We rounded up the dogs, put them back on their leads, and Steve walked me to the top of our road.

"So, bye," he said as we reached our gate.

"Bye."

He went to go, then turned back.

"Er. Um. Do you . . . would you like to play tennis one day?"

"Sure," I said. I'd enjoyed the time we spent together and was beginning to think we could be good mates. "If you're prepared to be beaten."

---

e-mail:	Outbox (2)
From:	goody2shoes@psnet.co.uk
To:	paulwatts@worldnet.com
Date:	25 June
Subject:	runs

Dear Bro

Sorry to hear about the amoebic dysentery. Have asked Mum to get you another passport and get it sent to you. Haven't told Dad. Be careful.

Love,
T. J.   XXXXXXXXXXXXXXXXXXXXXXXXXXXXXXXXXXXX

From: goody2shoes@psnet.co.uk
To: nestahotbabe@retro.co.uk
Date: 27 June
Subject: movie

Do you fancy the new Julia Roberts movie on Friday? It's on at the Hollywood Bowl. Lucy and Izzie are up for it. Hope you can come.

   T. J.   XXXXXXXXXXXXXXXXXXXXXXXXXXXXXXXXXXXXXXXX

e-mail: Inbox (1)
From: nestahotbabe@retro.co.uk
To: goody2shoes@psnet.co.uk
Date: 27 June
Subject: movie

Cool. I'll be dere.

12

More Buffy Than Barbie

To do:

1. Watch Buffy DVDs to note clothes.
2. Return Dress From Hell and swap for something the Buffster would wear.
3. Go to movie wearing new outfit.

It worked.

"T. J., you look wicked," said Izzie as we walked from the bus stop toward the Hollywood Bowl the following Friday. "Your hair looks so much better now you leave it loose, and I love the combats."

Lucy looked me up and down and nodded her approval. "Yeah. And I'm glad to see you haven't ruined the effect by hiding in a big baggy fleece. The tank top is great."

"Yeah. Bootylicious," said Nesta.

I *think* that means she approves.

We made our way through the car park to the cinema and it felt great. I could see groups of lads ogling us. And not just Nesta this time. Even I was getting a few looks.

When we got to the foyer, Izzie and Lucy went off to get the tickets while Nesta and I went upstairs and queued up for popcorn. As we were standing in line, I noticed Scott standing at the top of the escalator on his own. He kept checking his watch and looking down toward the entrance as if he was waiting for someone.

After we'd gotten our popcorn, Scott was still standing on his own, so we found Lucy and Izzie, then made our way over to him.

"Been stood up?" asked Nesta.

Lucy punched her arm. *"Nesta!"*

"What?" said Nesta. *"What?"*

"Actually," said Scott, his face brightening immediately. "I was waiting for you."

"As *if*," said Nesta, tossing her hair.

Scott checked downstairs then, seeing no one was coming up, he linked his arm through hers. "Looks like my mate has been held up, so the honor of keeping me company is yours."

"Mate or *date* been held up?" asked Nesta. "Admit it. You've been stood up."

Lucy punched her arm again. "Excuse my *rude* friend," she said to Scott. "We don't often let her out at night."

Scott grinned. "So, you coming then?" he said to Nesta before turning to the rest of us. "Sorry, girls. Only got dosh for two tickets."

Nesta took his arm out of hers and came to stand behind us.

"Actually," she said. "I already have plans. With people who actually bother to turn up. Come on, girls. I'm going to the ladies'."

Scott looked taken aback as we walked off leaving him standing there. As I looked over my shoulder, I couldn't help but feel sorry for him. I know him well enough to recognize that what we'd just witnessed was a huge act of bravado. Everything Steve said to me yesterday came flooding back. How hard it is for boys to take rejection even if they don't show it. It still hurts. His date hadn't shown and Nesta had made a fool of him on top of everything else.

As we stood in front of the mirrors doing our hair and lippie and stuff, I made up my mind.

"I'm going to ask if Scott would like me to go with him to a movie."

"*No,*" chorused Izzie, Lucy, and Nesta.

"Why not? He's been let down. He probably feels lousy."

"Who? Scott? Nah, he's well sure of himself," said Nesta. "He thinks he's God's gift and could probably do with being brought down a peg or two."

"No, he's really sweet underneath. It's all an act," I said.

"Ah," sighed Lucy. "Love is blind."

"Well, you don't want to be too easy if you really like him," said Iz. "You need to play hard to get. Boys like the chase."

"But I feel sorry for him," I said. "I'm going to go and ask him."

"How can someone with so many brains be so stupid?" asked Nesta as Lucy sighed in exasperation.

"You can think what you like," I said as I did a last check of my appearance. "But I've known him longer than you and this is something I have to do."

With that, I turned on my heel. As the loo door closed behind me, I could hear Lucy telling Nesta off for being insensitive.

* * *

"Yeah. Okay, then," said Scott when I told him that I'd keep him company. "But I'm not going to see the same movie as your mates."

"But Izzie already got me a ticket."

"I'm not sitting anywhere near that lesbian."

"Lesbian?"

"Nesta."

I laughed. Sour grapes, I thought, but I didn't say anything. He was just lashing out because she'd humiliated him in front of the rest of us.

There were five other films on at the complex so I let him pick what we were going to see. He chose a sci-fi film.

"I'm not mad on sci-fi," I said. "Are you sure you don't want to see the new comedy with Julia Roberts? I've heard it's a real laugh. And we can sit on the other side from the girls."

"No way," said Scott. "The sci-fi or I'm going home."

In the end, I gave in. I didn't mind. What I really wanted was a chance to spend some time with Scott alone and see what happened.

Scott loved the film, but I couldn't concentrate. As the screen filled with manic scenes from intergalactic wars, I was only aware of the proximity of Scott. Our knees and elbows touched a couple of times and I was hoping that he would hold my hand, but he just stuffed his face with popcorn.

Maybe real life isn't like the movies, I thought, as another alien got his three heads ripped off, squirting green blood all over the hero. Maybe in real life romance isn't beautiful sunsets and gentle kisses. Maybe in real life romance is sitting in the dark wondering if the boy you're with is *ever* going to make a move that isn't him merely shifting position in his seat. Maybe romance is all fantasy. For the last few days, that's all I'd done. Every night before I went to sleep, I imagined my first kiss with Scott. First he'd push a lock of hair behind my ear, then look deeply into my eyes, then softly press his lips on mine and . . .

A *phwt* noise beside me disturbed my thoughts.

Scott had farted.

"Oops," he said with a grin. "Popcorn-scented."

After the movie, we made our way out back into the foyer and Scott was a few steps in front of me. Suddenly he spotted a few of his mates who had been with him in Hampstead on the day of the photo shoot.

One of them came over.

"You're the girl who was having her photo taken the other day, aren't you?" he asked.

I nodded.

"You looked really good," he said.

"Thanks."

Suddenly Scott took my hand.

"Yeah, this is T. J.," he said as he introduced the group of boys.

Then he put his arm round me. "Just been to see *Alien Mutants in Cyberspace*," he said, then winked at them. "Didn't get to see much of the film, though, if ya know what I mean. . . ."

The boys sniggered knowingly.

"Anyway, got to go," said Scott and looked at me fondly. "The night is young."

"Yeah, right," said one of the boys as Scott pulled me away.

What was going on? I wondered. Did he fancy me after all and, as Steve said, had been acting cool? Or was this all a big act to make his mates think we were on a date? He still had hold of my hand as we went down the escalator and out the foyer but, unlike the day in Hampstead, I wasn't feeling all fluttery inside. I felt muddled. I didn't want to take my hand away though, as I remembered what he'd said about the night being young. Things could only get better.

When we got outside, I suggested we go and have a cappuccino.

"Got no money left," he said.

"No prob. My treat."

Scott shrugged. "Okay, then. And a hot dog?"

"Fine," I said.

"With onions."

"Fine."

For the next half hour, he talked. I listened.

He talked.

He talked.

I listened.

I was bursting to tell him all about my last few weeks. E-mails from Hannah and Paul. The magazine. My new mates. So much had happened, but I couldn't get a word in edgeways. He talked, I listened. That was the deal and always has been since I'd known him. I'd just never been bothered about it before. As I tried to appear interested, I thought that even Mojo was more interested in what I had to say. And he's a dog.

"So, enough about me. What about you?" he said, finally pausing for breath. "What do you think of me?"

Then he laughed like he'd said the funniest thing ever.

I couldn't help but think how easy Steve had been to talk to. We'd never shut up the other day in the park. But with him, it had been equal. I talked, he listened. He talked, I listened. He'd seemed interested in what I had to say and what my opinions were.

I took a long look at Scott. No doubt he was mucho cute to look at. A lovely curly mouth and deep-brown eyes. But as I stared into them, I thought, Scott Harris, I've never realized this before but you are boring. As in B. O. R. *iiing*.

I had a sudden urge to go home, talk to Mojo, e-mail Hannah, and even maybe catch up with Steve. He had promised to start work on his article for the magazine and I could call to see how it was coming along.

We got the bus home together and when we got to our houses, Scott did a quick check up and down the street, then up at the windows. I was about to go in when he suddenly pushed me against the wall and the next thing I knew I was being snogged.

My first snog.

Ugh. Agh, I thought as his mouth crashed into mine. And erlack, onions. His mouth tasted ukky. It was a really wet, slimy kiss, not how I'd imagined it at all.

When he'd finished cleaning my teeth with his tongue, he stood back, looking really pleased with himself.

"Catcha later," he said, pointing his index finger at me. Then he turned and went inside.

Not if I see you first, I thought as I wiped my mouth on my arm.

A couple of hours later, I was up in my room working on some ideas for the magazine when the phone went.

"T. J., it's Nesta."

"Oh, hi . . . Nes . . ."

"Listen," interrupted Nesta. "I've got something to say to you and I hope you won't take it the wrong way, but, well, that boy Scott . . . he's not the one for you. Don't ask me how I know, I just do. He thinks too much of himself and I know boys like that look pretty, but all they are interested in is themselves. You deserve better. You mustn't be a doormat. You can do better, believe me. It's just you're suffering from low self-esteem, but someone will come along who you'll have a better time with. Who really wants to be with you. Because you are a babe. With brains. Lethal combination as I've said before. And I know you like Scott, and now you're probably going to hate me and not speak to me, but as a friend I felt I had to tell you. T. J., are you there? Do you hate me now? Please say something? Oh, hell bells and poo. Lucy said I shouldn't phone but Izzie said I should. T. J., T. J. . . . ?"

I couldn't say anything because I was too busy laughing and I'd put my hand over the phone so she couldn't hear.

"Nesta. I agree."

"You . . . you *what*?"

"Yeah, you're right. Scott Harris. Cute but dull. Dull as dishwater. And . . . he's a bad snogger."

"He *snogged* you!" exclaimed Nesta. "*Ohmigod*. Details."

We spent the next half-hour yabbering about snogs and Nesta told me all about some of her early disasters.

"It's not always like that," she said in the end.

"Phewww," I said. "So there's hope."

"Mucho mucho," said Nesta. "It can be just how you imagined it and better."

When I put down the phone, I felt really happy. That night, as I fell asleep, a different boy seemed to have taken Scott's place in my snogging fantasy.

e-mail:	Outbox (1)
From:	babewithbrains@psnet.co.uk
To:	nestahotbabe@retro.co.uk
Date:	29 June
Subject:	new e-mail

Note new e-mail address. Whatdoyathink?

T. J.

e-mail:	Inbox (2)
From:	nestahotbabe@retro.co.uk
To:	babewithbrains@psnet.co.uk
Date:	29 June
Subject:	new e-mail

Bootylicious. See you tomorrow P.M. at Lucy's for the magazine finale.

Nesta

From: paulwatts@worldnet.com
To: babewithbrains@psnet.co.uk
Date: 29 June
Subject: hol

Hi T. J.

Holiday really not going as planned. Monsoons have hit the
resort. Torrential rain so impossible to sleep on beach. Am
crashing in a hut with four other travelers, but caught head lice
after I borrowed a sleeping bag (mine was nicked). Oh, and to
top it all, Saskia has run away with the holy man from Kilburn. I
have the runs and mosquito bites as big as golf balls.
   Hope all well your end.

   Love,
   Paul

P.S. Please ask Dad to send very strong medical supplies.
Anything and everything.

13

The Mad House

The next afternoon, I had half of North London employed as my editorial staff.

At home, I'd asked Mum and Dad each to write something.

"We're theming the magazine toward summer," I said to Dad, "so I'd like you to do some handy hints for traveling abroad from a doctor's point of view. Make it relevant. A mini medical cabinet that you could pack in a suitcase. Stuff for sunburn, mosquitoes, the runs, and so on."

"Will do," he said with a grin.

I think he was really chuffed to have been asked.

And Mum was doing an article on how to deal with exam stress.

"Ten handy hints," I said. "It has to be accessible."

I left them listening to Radio 4 and sipping Earl Grey tea as they worked.

Over at Nesta's, Tony was working on a cartoon for a competition. We were going to invite readers to send in captions and print the best in the next edition. If there *was* a next edition.

At Lucy's, Steve and I worked on the computer in his and Lal's bedroom.

Lucy and Nesta were finishing their articles in the living room.

Izzie was on the computer in Lucy's bedroom, working out horoscopes for the coming month.

Mrs. Lovering kept bringing us herbie drinks with ginseng and some icky-tasting stuff called Guryana.

"Keeps you alert," she said.

And Mr. Lovering sat in the kitchen playing his guitar.

"Music to inspire the workers," he said when I went down to ask for a new ink cartridge for the printer. How a rendition of "You Ain't Nothing but a Hound Dog" was supposed to motivate us, I have no idea, but Ben and Jerry seemed to like it as they joined in, howling away with great gusto.

"This place is a *mad* house," said Lal, looking at his dad with disapproval. "I'm off somewhere normal. Where I can *think* in peace!"

"Go to my house, then," I said. "It's like a morgue."

No one's ever happy with their lot, I thought, as I watched him storm off in a huff. I'm sure Mum and Dad would agree with Lal if they came over, but I loved it. Mr. L. (as Izzie calls him) is a real laugh and as opposite to my dad as anyone you could meet. He's an old hippie who's losing his hair, yet has a ponytail. And he wears very bright Hawaiian shirts and Indian sandals. Mrs. L. is hippie-dippie too, today wearing a Peruvian skirt with mirrors round the hem and a rather strange crocheted top.

"You okay, T. J.?" asked Steve when I went back upstairs. "You're kind of quiet today."

"*Yuh, yunewee,*" I muttered.

A *lot* had happened in the last twenty-four hours. Mainly in my head. I'd had my eyes opened to what a user Scott was, and I was experiencing an almighty twinge of conscience that I'd treated Steve the same way. Someone to earbash with my problems. Only last week I'd been on about how much I fancied Scott and how he never noticed me and treated me like a mate and nothing more. That was *exactly* how I'd treated Steve. And he'd been so sweet, reassuring me that I was fanciable and telling me how boys really felt about girls.

As I sat next to him at the desk, I felt the warmth of his arm against mine and caught the scent of soap on his skin. Back came the old fluttery feeling, only this time, I was with Steve, not Scott. How had I not noticed what nice eyes he had? Kind. Hazel-brown with honey flecks around the iris. And good hands, I thought, as he pressed keys on the computer keyboard—long fingers, elegant.

And it was too late. If I said anything, he'd think I was a complete airhead. Fickle and a half. In love with Scott one week, fancying him the next.

"So have you decided what to do about Wendy Roberts and her dentures?" asked Steve, leaning over me to see what I'd written.

"Er, *yu . . . nu . . . wee . . .* Wendy, yes. I've decided I'm not going to stoop to her level. I'll save stuff like that for my secret notebook and use it later when I write novels."

"Good for you," said Steve. "So do you reckon we'll be ready to hand the mag in on Monday?"

"*Nih . . . ing . . . yah . . . ,*" I said, cursing Alien Girl who had taken over my vocal chords. "Umost. I mean, almost."

Steve was looking at me as though I had two heads.

"Gottask Luceand Nestasomething. Backinaminute," I said, jumping up.

I stumbled downstairs to find Lucy and Nesta. I needed help.

I sat on the floor and put my head in my hands. "Ag. Agh. Agherama."

"Hey, it'll be all right. We're almost there," said Nesta. "We'll do it on time."

"Do what?" I said, looking up.

"The mag."

"Oh it's not that. It's . . ." I looked at Lucy. Steve was her brother. What would *she* think if she knew I'd been fantasizing about him? She knew how I felt about Scott. She'd think I was a complete tart for changing my mind so fast.

"So what is it?" asked Lucy.

"Nothing," I said.

"Yeah, looks like it," said Nesta. "Come on, spill."

I sighed. Then looked at the two of them waiting expectantly. Then I sighed again.

Nesta and Lucy started doing big sighs as well. Then really exaggerating them, heaving huge extended breaths until I had to laugh.

"Okay. Lie out on the sofa," said Lucy.

I did as I was told and Lucy sat at the other end.

"So Miss Vatts. Vat seems to be ze problem?"

I couldn't say. Silence. Big silence. It grew and filled the room.

"Ah. Boy trouble," said Lucy.

"But which boy?" said Nesta. "You're over Scott, *n'est-ce pas?*"

I nodded. "It's another boy who I've only just realized I like. Much nicer than Scott. And now I'm all tongue-tied and stupid around him. And I think I've blown it. And it's probably too late."

"Oh, you mean *Steve?*" asked Lucy.

"*How* did you know?"

"Kind of obvious from the start," said Lucy.

"*Obvious?* To *whom? I've* only just realized. And who knows what's going on in his head. If he likes *me.*"

"Er, *hello?*" said Lucy. "What planet are you on exactly?"

"Planet Zog, actually," I said, and explained all about Noola and her ability to take over my head.

"Well, for your information, Steve hasn't stopped talking about you and asking about you ever since he met you," said Lucy. "And he was well miffed with the fact you fancied Scott. Didn't you notice how weirded out he was when we bumped into Scott in Hampstead?"

"Suppose he was kind of quiet that day. I thought I'd done something to upset him."

"D'oh. *Yeah*. You had," said Lucy. "Fancied someone else."

Izzie came down the stairs and flopped on the sofa.

"Whassup?" she asked.

"T. J.," said Nesta. "She turns into Noola the Alien Girl whenever she fancies a boy. Noola only knows three words. Tell her, T.J."

"*Uhyuh. Yunewee.* And *nihingyah.*"

Lucy started giggling and doing an alien robot impersonation like C-3PO in *Star Wars* up and down the room.

"*Uhyuh,*" she squeaked in a high voice. "*Yunewee. Nihingyaaaah.*"

We were laughing so hard that Steve came down to see what was going on. Of course, I went purple.

"So?" said Steve.

"So noth . . . nothing," chuckled Nesta.

"Just something Lucy said," said Izzie.

Steve looked up to the heavens, then turned to me. "You coming back to finish your editorial?"

"Uh . . . *uhyuh*," I said, and Lucy exploded with laughter.

Steve heaved a sigh, which Lucy and Nesta copied.

Steve looked at us all as though we were stupid. "*When* you're ready, T. J.," he said, and went back to his room.

"See, do you *see* now?" I said. "I'm going to blow it. And we were getting on so well and now I'm going to act like an idiot around him and he'll think I'm Dork from Dorkland, Nerd from Nerdville, Airhead from . . ."

"Shut the door, Lucy," said Izzie. "We clearly have work to do."

We spent the next twenty minutes doing a visualization with Izzie. She's well into self-help stuff and had been reading in one of her books about positive thinking.

"It's all in the mind," she said. "You can get over this and put Noola the Alien Girl to rest. But you have to see yourself acting confidently. I've been reading all about it for when I do gigs."

"But I think you're either confident or not," I said.

"Like Nesta. It's not something you can learn."

"Oh, yes it is," said Nesta. "We all have our own tricks. Sometimes I pretend I'm a character out of a film if I feel nervous. Then I act as I think they would. It really works."

"And I used to be hopeless about singing in public," said Izzie. "So bad I couldn't sleep at night. I used to be well terrified of looking a fool and this has really helped."

"So, you think I could learn to talk sense when I meet a boy I like?"

"Definitely," said Izzie. "In fact, my book says, 'We are what we repeatedly do. Confidence is not an act but a habit.' You have to practice."

"Cool," said Lucy. "Sounds good to me. What do we do?"

Izzie made us all sit down and close our eyes. First we had to imagine the situation we felt nervous in, so I thought about being close to Steve upstairs. We had to imagine the room, the surroundings, what we were wearing, all the details.

Then Izzie said, "Imagine yourself being relaxed, calm, and completely in control. Imagine the other person's response to you. In your mind, see them laughing at your jokes, listening with interest to what you say, *liking* you."

She made us imagine the situation over and over again until in my imagination, Steve was gawping at me in open admiration, amazed at my witticisms. In *awe* at my brilliant conversation.

"Okay, open your eyes, everyone."

We did as we were told and looked around at each other.

"How do you feel now, T. J.?"

I stood up and went to the door. "Awesome. Noola. She dead." I put my hands on my hips Arnold Schwarzenegger style and said, "I'll be back. *Hasta la vista,* baby."

Nesta laughed. "Go get him, girlfriend."

I went back up the stairs. As I stood outside Steve's bedroom, my butterfly nerves came back, so I imagined Steve smiling at me and enjoying my company.

I went in, sat down next to him at the computer, did a quick visualization in my head, then turned and gave him a huge smile.

He turned to look at me. "Aaagjjhh. What's the matter with you *now*?"

"Nothing," I beamed, thinking, I am confident, I am great, stunning, brill, dazzling, fantabulous.

Steve looked at me as though I was totally bonkers.

"You're *really* weird, you know that, don't you?" he asked.

Just at that moment, my mobile went.

"'Scuse me, Steve," I said as I put the phone to my ear.

"Hey, T. J.," said Scott's voice. "What you doing?"

"Magazine. Remember, I told you. Deadline Monday."

"Oh, that can wait," said Scott. "Wanna go out to the Heath?"

"Sorry, Scott," I said. "Busy. Later."

Then I hung up.

"That guy?" asked Steve.

"That guy."

"And . . .?"

"And . . . history," I said.

Now Steve had a huge grin across his face.

"What's the matter?" I asked.

"Nothing," he beamed.

"You're *really* weird," I said. "You know that, don't you?"

"Yeah," he nodded. "So that makes two of us."

Cathy Hopkins

For Real
Summer edition

Contents

14

Sabotage

The magazine looked great. We'd done the final layout on Steve's computer, eight full pages that looked fun and interesting.

Steve had found all sorts of visuals on the Internet to liven up the articles, pictures of dogs for the Battersea Dogs' Home article, stars for the horoscope page, herbs and flowers for Izzie's aromatherapy piece. Plus the mad "before" and "after" makeover photographs for the center spread.

It looked good. Very good. I reckoned I was in with a chance.

At assembly on Monday, Mrs. Allen asked that all entries were handed in to our form teacher.

"I know a lot of you have worked very hard on this," she said, "so we won't keep you waiting. We hope to have an announcement about the winner by the end of the week."

Five minutes later we filed into class and I joined the group hovering around Miss Watkins' desk. I put my copy on the small pile of entries from our class.

"Quite a number getting it all finished on time, wasn't it?" I asked Wendy Roberts, who was standing behind me.

"Er, *no*," she said. "Unlike some saddos in this class, I didn't do one. See, I have a life."

"Oh, I thought you were into it."

"You thought wrong. Deadlines are for losers. And, by the way, Mrs. Allen said she wanted to see you. I saw her just now in the corridor. She wanted you to go to her office immediately."

That's strange, I thought as I hurried off down the corridor to Mrs. Allen's office. I hoped nothing was wrong.

"Mrs. Allen wants to see me," I said as her secretary looked up when I knocked on the office door.

"I don't think so, dear," she said. "Mrs. Allen's in with Mr. Parker. She said not to be disturbed. Must be some mistake."

No mistake, I thought as I went back to class. I suppose Wendy thought she was being funny.

Miss Watkins was at her desk flicking through the entries when I walked back into the class. "You're late, T. J.," she said.

"Er, sorry, miss," I said, going to my desk.

Luckily she didn't go on about it, as Wendy Roberts came in just behind me.

"And you, Roberts, what's your excuse?"

"Loo, miss," she said, breathlessly taking her place.

Miss Watkins continued flicking through the entries. "Well done girls, we have six entries from this class." Then she looked at me. "But I thought we'd have had one more. I thought you were going to enter, T. J."

"I *did*, miss," I said. "I put it in the pile after assembly."

"Well, it's not here now," she said.

I looked round at Wendy Roberts. She was gazing out of the window, looking like butter wouldn't melt in her mouth.

"Are you sure, T. J.?" said Miss Watkins. "Check your bag."

I did as I was told, but I was sure I'd put it on the desk. "Not there, miss."

"So where is it?"

Suddenly I didn't know what to say. And I had no proof that Wendy had taken it.

"Maybe it's fallen on the floor?"

Miss Watkins had a quick look around, then faced the class.

"Has anyone taken T. J.'s entry?"

No one spoke.

"This is very serious. If T. J. says she put her entry on the pile then either she's lying or someone's taken it. Is anyone going to enlighten me?"

Again no one spoke.

"She *did* do an entry," said Lucy. "I saw it. Honest, miss."

Miss Watkins looked upset. "This is *very* unfortunate, girls. It's almost the end of term and next year, you'll be going into Year Ten. You're not beginners anymore and, frankly, I'm disappointed in this sort of behavior. However, I'm going to ask you to act like mature adults and sort this out amongst yourselves. Twelve thirty this lunchtime is the deadline for entries, so unless you find it, T. J., or someone owns up, I'm afraid there's not a lot more I'm prepared to do."

"That cow," said Lucy, as we filed out at break-time. "I'm sure it was Wendy Roberts."

"Did anyone see anything?" I asked.

Nesta shook her head. "She must have taken it from Miss Watkins's desk when you went to see Mrs. Allen."

"There was a whole crowd round Miss Watkins' desk," said Izzie. "Anyone could have taken it. You know how competitive everyone's been."

"But Wendy did come in after you, T. J. You know, before lessons started. Remember?" said Izzie.

"To the loos," said Nesta. "Let's go."

We ran down the corridor to the cloakrooms. Lucy looked in the cubicles while Nesta searched in the trash can.

"Er*lack*," said Nesta, as she rummaged around amongst bits of old tissue and paper towels.

"Oh, *noooo*," I heard Lucy say, as she reached the third cubicle.

She came out holding a sopping wet pile of ripped paper. "I'm *so* sorry, T.J., it was in the trash can next to the loo."

Izzie took what was left of the magazine. "It looks like she ran it under the tap first."

"But *why?*" I said. "Why has she got it in for me?"

"Doesn't have to be a reason," sighed Nesta. "Some people are just very *very* sad. They can't stand to see anyone else doing well."

"I reckon she never got over being made to look an idiot

when Sam Denham was here," said Izzie. "You know, when he praised your answer and dismissed hers."

"What are we going to do?" I said, leaning back against one of the sinks. "I can't hand it in like this."

"We could go to Mrs. Allen," said Nesta.

I was gutted. "We could, but what will that achieve? Only make Wendy hate me more. The main thing is, my entry's unreadable. *All* that work, wasted." I was near to tears. "And all your contributions."

Lucy got her mobile out of her bag. "What time is it?" she said.

"Eleven," I said.

She began dialing frantically.

"Who are you phoning?" I asked.

"Steve," she said. "His year's doing exams and stuff, so their schedule's all over the place. He might be at home revising."

"Brill," said Izzie. "He's got the mag on his computer. It will only take a minute to print out."

"That's if he's there," said Nesta.

Lucy listened as the phone rang, then she grimaced. "Voice mail," she said. "He must be doing something."

"Leave a message anyway," said Izzie. "It's our only chance."

We went back into the next lesson, but I couldn't concentrate. And neither could Nesta, Izzie, or Lucy, by the looks of it.

"If you look at your watch one more time, T. J. Watts," said Mr. Dixon, "I'm going to take it off you. And Lucy Lovering, if whatever you're staring at outside the window is so fascinating, I suggest you go and stand there for the rest of the lesson."

I glanced across at Wendy Roberts. She looked up from her book and smiled smugly.

You just wait, Wendy Roberts, I thought. It's not over yet.

We flew out of the classroom at lunchtime and out into the playground toward the gates.

No one there.

Lucy got out her phone again. She dialed, then shook her head. "Still on voice mail."

I checked my watch. Ten past twelve.

Twelve fifteen.

Twelve twenty.

"Did you say what time the deadline was when you left the message?" asked Nesta, looking up and down the street anxiously.

"Yeah," said Lucy. "I said twelve thirty. I'll try ringing again."

She was about to dial when Izzie grabbed my arm.

"Here he is," she cried as Steve came flying round the corner on his bike.

He screeched to a stop and pulled an envelope out of his rucksack.

"Good luck," he said as he handed it over.

"Thanks," I called over my shoulder as I ran back inside.

This time I wasn't taking any chances.

I went straight to the staff room and asked for Miss Watkins. I wanted to put my magazine into her hands myself.

15

Result

"And the new editor will be . . . ," said Mrs. Allen, as we stood in assembly on Friday.

I held my breath as Nesta gave me the thumbs-up.

"Before I announce the winner, I must say it's been very difficult," continued Mrs. Allen. "The standard of entries was exceptionally high and I'm very proud of all of you. Ultimately there are no losers. We've had a very hard time deciding and . . ."

Izzie gave me a look as if to say, "I wish she'd get on with it."

"Finally we narrowed it down to two. We decided on a tie. Two winners. First, Emma Ford from Year Ten. And second, T. J. Watts from Year Nine."

There were cheers from Nesta, Izzie, and Lucy at the back of the class. But, best of all, Wendy Roberts' face was a picture. Her mouth literally dropped open.

I gave her a huge smile as I went up to join Emma on the stage with Mrs. Allen.

After school we all piled back to Lucy's for celebratory ice cream and cake. When the girls were settled chomping away, Steve beckoned me up to his room.

"I . . . I have something for you," he said shyly.

He went to a drawer in the cabinet next to his bed. He pulled out a small package wrapped in silver, with a gold bow and a card and handed them to me. "These are for you."

I opened the card first. On the front it had a black-and-white photograph of a man on a road, with a caption underneath saying, "Life shrinks or expands in proportion to one's courage." Inside he'd written, "Good Luck to the new Editor of *For Real*."

"Thanks. That's really . . ."

"Open the pressie," he said, smiling.

I ripped off the paper and found a beautiful pen inside. It was Indian-looking, shiny turquoise and silver with sequinny things on the side.

"*Yu . . . nu . . . wee,*" I said, slipping back into Zoganese for a moment.

"You're welcome," he said, as if he understood perfectly. "It's for writing your novels."

For a moment, we just stayed looking at each other. It was the most perfect feeling. Like time stopped still and we were somehow melting into each other.

Then Steve grinned. "So next . . . ?"

"Next?" I asked. "What do you mean? Next?"

"That day in the park, when you asked how does anyone ever get together and you said for you, they'd have to make it *really* obvious—pressies, cards, a billboard in Piccadilly . . ."

I looked at my card and my present and smiled. "Oh. But please, no, not a billboard in Piccadilly, I'd *die*. . . ."

Steve laughed, then leaned toward me, pushed a lock of hair away from my face, looked deeply into my eyes and . . .

"We could go and see a movie next," he said.

"Love to," I said. "As long as it's not *Alien Mutants in Cyberspace*. And you don't spend the whole movie eating popcorn."

"Deal. Anyway, I hate popcorn."

We sort of grinned stupidly at each other, then I

remembered what he'd said that day in the park. That he sometimes felt scared when he liked a girl.

No time like the present, I thought, as I leaned in and kissed him softly on the lips.

e-mail:	Inbox (1)
From:	paulwatts@worldnet.com
To:	babewithbrains@psnet.co.uk
Date:	5 July
Subject:	hol

Dear T. J.

New passport received this morning.
  Coming home.

  Paul

e-mail:	Outbox (1)
To:	hannahnutter@fastmail.com
From:	babewithbrains@psnet.co.uk
Date:	5 July
Subject:	mates, dates

Hey Hannahnutter

Whassup? Sorry I haven't been in touch; it's been mad here. So much has been happening. Paul's coming home. Scott is history. ⊃

Got a date with Steve. Realized boys can be mates as well as dates. Der. Took me a while!

Velly happy. Hope you are.

And I won the competition with Emma Ford from Year Ten. I am now the new joint-editor of the school magazine. Hurrah.

T. J. XXXXXXXXXXXXXXXXXXXXXXXXXXXXXXXXXXXXX

---

e-mail: Inbox (1)
From: hannahnutter@fastmail.com
To: babewithbrains@psnet.co.uk
Date: 5 July
Subject: Goody flobbalots

Velly solly me no been in touch either.

Goody flobbalots and hurrah about mag thing. I knew you'd get it.

And coolerooney about Steve. I could tell even from a zillion trillion miles away that something was going to 'appen zere. Hasta la banana and many jolly jollities to him. He soundeth superbio. A mate and a date. Best kind.

Mad here too. Replaced ze Luke with ze Ryan. So many boys, so little time etc, etc. Most excellent fun here. Loadsa big bashes and barbies, though I truly miss you and your strange angle on life and SOH.

Send me photos of your new look. And new boy. And new mag.

At last le T. J. has recognized she is ze babe avec ze brain.

Keep buzy and yabberyabber spoon.

Lurve and keesses

Your friend for ever and ever and ever and ever and ever and ever and . . . (oh, shutup H)

Mates, Dates, and
SOLE SURVIVORS

*Big thanks to Brenda Gardner, Yasemin Uçar
and the team at Piccadilly, for all their support
and feedback. To Rosemary Bromley at Juvenelia.
And Alice Elwes, Becca Crewe, Jenni Herzberg,
Rachel Hopkins, Annie McGrath and Olivia McDonnell,
for all their emails in answer to my questions.*

Summer Hols

"This has to be the best feeling in the world," I said to Nesta as we walked out of the school gates on the last day of term.

"I know," she said. "Six weeks with no Miss Watkins. . . . Six fabola weeks with Simon before he goes off to university."

"And six weeks with Ben for me," said Izzie linking her arm with Nesta's. "We're going to work on loads of new songs for the band now we'll have time."

"And I suppose we'll be seeing *you* round at ours a fair bit," I said to T. J. She's been seeing my elder brother, Steve, over the last few weeks and they're both completely smitten.

"What about you, Lucy?" asked Nesta. "Going to give *my* poor brother a break at last? You've been giving him the runaround for months now. I don't think his ego can stand much more of it."

Six weeks with Tony? The idea was appealing and I reckoned I was finally ready for a "proper" relationship with him. We'd liked each other for ages and we had gone out for a while earlier in the year, but then I broke it off as it felt like it was all happening too fast. After that there was a lot of flirting between us whenever I saw him round at Nesta's and he did ask me out again a few times, but I turned him down. It's not that I didn't want to date him. He is gorgeous and funny and I love his company—it's just that he has A Bit Of A Reputation when it comes to girls. Nesta had warned me that it was a different one every week at one time. She says he likes the chase, then drops them the minute they show they're interested. So I had to play it carefully, or else by now I'd be on his long list of rejects and broken hearts. But it had been almost nine months since I met him and he did keep trying, saying I was the only one for him, the lurve of his life. I thought, I can trust him not to mess me about.

I grinned and pulled an envelope out of my rucksack. "I know," I said. "I've been doing a lot of thinking about him lately. And I've finally come to a decision."

"Which is?" asked Nesta.

"I've written him a card. Saying no more messing him about. I really like him and we're on on ON."

"About time," said T. J. "I don't know how you've been so cool for so long. I think I'd have fallen at his feet the first time he asked me out." Then her face clouded. "Um, that is, er, I don't mean I would steal him or anything. I'm just saying I think he's gorgeous."

I squeezed her arm. "I know what you mean, T. J. But boys like Tony enjoy a challenge."

"Well, what is it?" she said. "Eight . . . nine months you've made him suffer? I reckon that's enough challenge for any boy."

"I can hardly believe it," said Izzie. "Last year, none of us had boyfriends. Now this year, we all have."

"It's not definite yet," I said.

"This time last year, I hadn't even been kissed," said T. J.

"And now there's no stopping you," teased Nesta. "Snog Queen of North London."

This time last year, I hadn't been kissed either. Tony was my first. That's another reason I wanted to take it slow. I didn't want to get tied to the first boy I'd snogged. I wanted to try a few others and see what they were like. There have been a few others now. No one important or serious. In fact, no one who's come close to Tony. He still has the same effect on me every time I see him. My stomach turns over and I get all hot and my face goes pink.

"You're not just doing this because you'd be the odd one out?" asked Izzie, pointing at my letter.

"But I *am* the odd one out," I teased. "You're all tall with dark hair, and I'm small and blond with short hair."

"No. *I'm* the odd one out," insisted Nesta. "I'm the only one with dark skin."

"No, I'm the—," started T. J.

"I *meant* the only one without a boy," interrupted Izzie.

"No, course not," I said. "I think I'm ready now and I want to see where it goes. To tell the truth, I started thinking that maybe I was messing him around and playing him along because I was scared of rejection. You know what he's like. . . ."

Izzie nodded. "Yeah, and you're right. You can't let fear hold you back."

"I've been reading this book," said T. J. "It's by this guy called D. H. Lawrence and it's about a posh lady who falls for her gardener."

"Oh, Mills and Boon?" asked Nesta.

I laughed. Typical Nesta. Her idea of reading is flipping through *Bliss* or *Now* magazine. T. J., on the other hand, T. J. devours books—proper books. That's why she gets on with my brother Steve. He's a bit of a brainbox as well.

"Um, no, not Mills and Boon," said T. J., "but it is a love story. *Lady Chatterley's Lover*, it's called. Anyway, there's one line I really like. Want to hear it?"

We all nodded.

"I can't remember it exactly," she said, "as I didn't write it down, but it's something like: better a life of risk and chance than an old age of vain regret."

"Yeah, cool," said Nesta. "I'll buy that. You don't get anywhere in life unless you go for it."

"Feel the fear and do it anyway," said Izzie, quoting the title of one of the self-help books she loves so much.

"So what did you say in the card?" asked Nesta.

"That's Lucy's private business," said Izzie. "Don't be so nosy."

Nesta looked offended and poked her tongue out at Izzie. "I wasn't. I was feeling the fear and asking my question. You don't find out anything if you don't ask what you want to know. So . . . go on, Lucy, tell us what you said."

I knew the note by heart, because I'd written and rewritten it so many times. I wanted it to sound right— cool but romantic, so he could keep it as a memento to look back on.

"I did it like one of those Japanese poems," I said. "You know, the ones with only three lines that we did in English last term. Haikus."

"Bless you," said Nesta.

"No," I said. "The poems. They're called haikus."

"Whatever," said Nesta. "So what did you write in your hiccup?"

"I'm not changing, I'm just rearranging, my life to be with you."

"Ahh," said T. J. "That's really sweet."

"Yeah," said Izzie. "You should come and help the band with our lyrics. So what else did you put?"

"Then I wrote, 'Sorry for messing you about over the last year, but now I'm ready. I know we have something really special and I want to make a go of it. Call me.' I wanted to keep it light, you know?"

"Sounds perfect," said T. J.

I took a deep breath and, as we passed a post box, I popped the card in. "Me and Lady Chatterley. No old age of vain regret for us. I've put a first class stamp on, so he should get it in the morning. Gulp. No going back now."

"It'll be fine," said T. J. "I think you'll make a fab couple and we can all do loads of things together—play tennis, go to movies. It'll be great."

"Okay," said Izzie, "so that's Lucy sorted. But there's more to life than boys. Let's make some other goals for the summer holidays."

Typical Iz. She's always setting herself goals and targets, then insists that we do as well. She says it's important to think about what you want in life, then visualize it happening. I visualized me with Tony having a great time. My first proper relationship. It would be fab. No worrying about whether you were going to pull or what boys were going to be where. And, did you really like him and did he really like you? Will he phone or should you phone him? It would be good to be settled for a while. All of us. We could all just enjoy being with each other, hanging out as couples and no one having to worry that anyone was on their own.

"*So?*" said Izzie, looking at us all when we reached the bus stop. There's no arguing with Iz when she's off on one of her Let's-improve-ourselves campaigns. "Come on. Resolutions for the summer hols?"

"Resolutions are for New Year," said Nesta, tossing

her hair back. "You make them on January first then give up on them around January tenth."

"Okay, I've got four," I said. "Number One: Hang out with you lot as much as poss. Two: You already know now—Tony *et moi*. Three: Stop blushing."

"I think it's lovely that you blush," said T. J. "It's really sweet."

"Noooo," I said. "It's horrible. I feel so stupid and everyone stares like I'm a kid."

"No one ever really notices," said Izzie. "And Number Four?"

"I'm going to make T-shirts," I said. "Like those ones on sale in Camden Market. You know, the ones with cool slogans on them."

"So what are yours going to say?" asked T. J.

"Don't know yet. I'm going to start collecting good lines over the hols."

Just then the bus came, so all discussion was stopped while we piled on. It felt great to be alive. School was over. The sun was shining. The evenings were light until ten o'clock. I'd finally taken the plunge and mailed my card, and I couldn't wait to get his reaction.

"What's for dinner?" I asked Mum when I got home.

"Tofu burgers, broccoli, and rice," she said, looking

up from the counter where she was chopping onions. "Want to give me a hand?"

Yuck, tofu, I thought as I threw down my rucksack in the hall and went to join her. I wish she'd cook normal stuff sometimes. My dad runs the local health shop, so we always eat what he brings back. I know it's good for you, and you are what you eat, etc., but my secret fantasy is to come home one night and discover it's chicken nuggets, baked beans, and chips. It's funny because the way we eat is *Izzie's* fantasy. She loves health food—tofu and soy and quinoa. Sometimes I think we got the wrong parents. Izzie would love to live here; in fact, she almost does, she comes round so often. Me on the other hand, I like living here, but I'd love to have supper at Nesta's. Her dad's Italian and does the most amazing pasta dishes, and her mum's from the Caribbean and her spicy fish and peas is to die for. Amazingly, Nesta is as thin as a rake. I think if I lived at her house, I'd be enormous, so maybe it's a good thing I have strange parents who make peculiar meals.

Suddenly I thought of a good resolution for the holidays.

"Mum, how about this summer, I cook supper a few nights?"

"Sounds good to me," replied Mum, grinning.

"Can I get the ingredients as well?"

"Sure," said Mum.

Just at that moment, the phone rang. "Whatever I want?" I asked as I went into the hall and picked up the receiver.

It was Tony.

"Hi," he said. "What you doing later?"

"Nothing," I said. "Nothing for six whole weeks. School ended today."

I decided not to say anything about the card. I wanted it to be a surprise when he opened it in the morning.

"Fancy meeting up?" he asked. "I wanted to talk to you about something."

"What?"

"Not on the phone. I'll meet you at Raj's in Highgate, say, in half an hour."

"Hold on, I'll just ask Mum," I said, putting my hand over the receiver. "Can I go out for a bit? Promise I won't be late. I'll wash up when I get back."

"How can I refuse when you put it like that?" Mum called back. "I'll put your supper in the oven for you."

"See you in half an hour," I said to Tony.

I put the phone down feeling a rush of anticipation. I knew what he wanted to say. He feels the same way I do and wants to make it definite, I thought as I dashed upstairs and changed into my jeans and a T-shirt. A slick of lip gloss, a squirt of the Angel perfume the girls got me for my birthday, then I ran out and caught the bus up to Highgate. I felt so excited. As I sat on the bus, I decided that I'd let him say what he wanted to say and I'd be cool about it, like, "Oh, I'll have to think about it." Then tomorrow, he'll get my card and realize that I wanted the same thing as him all along. It was all working out so perfectly.

He was already upstairs at Raj's when I arrived. He was settled in the corner seat reading one of the ancient books they keep stacked on the shelves there. He looked up and smiled as I walked in, and, as always when I see him, my stomach did a double flip.

"Had your hair cut," I said.

"It's called a French crop. Like it?"

I nodded. Not many boys can take their hair that short, I thought. You have to have good features and the right-shaped head. Of course Tony had both. Good looks run in his family. Nesta is easily the best-looking girl in our school and Tony is probably the best-looking at his. Dark, with sleepy brown eyes and long lashes.

"Take a pew." He smiled as I slid in behind the

table. I smiled back. We always said that when we went there, as the chairs are all old church pews.

"Want some tea or something cold?"

"A Coke would be good," I said as I looked around. I was glad he'd chosen this place to meet. It's T. J.'s favorite place as well as mine. She says she always feels as though she's in a novel from another era when she comes here, as the decor is kind of Bohemian. It's different from all the other cafés in the area—it has its own character, with the pews and heavy wooden tables and bookshelves heaving with interesting books.

"What you reading?" I asked.

Tony pointed at the bookshelves. "Oh, some ancient history book. They have a weird collection here, a real mixture, from cookery to Dickens. All the books look about a hundred years old."

I nodded. "Like the nick-nacks," I said, pointing to a chipped statue of an Indian Maharaja on the corner unit above Tony's head. It had been plonked next to a statue of the Buddha. "In fact, it's a bit like our living room at home with all sorts of junk that doesn't really go together."

"Yeah," said Tony, indicating two brass trumpets that were hanging from the ceiling. "It is a bit mad. But I think that's why I like it."

We spent a few minutes chatting about all the strange

ornaments we could see—the Russian dolls and toy ostrich on one shelf, brass flamingos and ceramic elephants on another, the old sepia photographs on the wall mixed in with some framed ink sketches. I felt so comfortable sitting there with him that I thought it would be difficult not to spill the beans about my card and my Decision.

"So, you had something you wanted to say?" I finally asked.

"Er, yeah," said Tony as the boy behind the counter left his computer and came to take our order. "But first, tell me how you are? Out of school, huh?"

I nodded. "Best feeling in the world."

"So what you going to do with the holidays?"

I knew it. He was going to ask if I'd go out with him.

"Oh, no definite plans," I said, looking into his eyes in what I imagined was a meaningful way. "Got any ideas?"

Tony shrugged. "Not really. That is, um, Lucy . . . How can I put this . . . ?"

I longed to reach out and take his hand, tell him that I knew what he wanted to say and that I felt the same. But Nesta had trained me well. Stay cool. Don't be too easy.

Tony took a deep breath. "Thing is, Luce, well, we've been on and off for ages now and I wanted to get things straight between us. It's not fair on you and it's not fair on me. We've got the holidays ahead of us and it's like a new chapter, for both of us, so . . . so, what I think is that, er . . . maybe we should make a clean slate of it."

"Clean slate? What are you saying?" I didn't understand.

"Well, it's not like we're boyfriend and girlfriend, are we? We never really have been."

"No. No, course not." Was he going to ask me if I *would* be now?

"And I was thinking," Tony continued, "what if, say, you meet someone this holiday or I meet someone? It's kind of confusing. Our situation, that is . . . me and you. Well, we're not free and we're not really committed."

"No, we're not."

"So, what do you think?" he asked.

"I'm not sure I understand," I said. "Are you saying you want to be committed or that you want to meet someone else?"

Tony shifted awkwardly. "That I want to be free," he said finally.

"You're dumping me?" I blurted.

"No. No, course not, how can I dump you when we were never going out properly?"

"But . . ."

He reached for my hand, but I snatched it away. I felt hurt. Confused.

"Look, Lucy, it's not as though I haven't asked you out in the past, but you always put me off."

"I didn't know how I felt then," I blustered. "It wasn't that I was putting you off, but . . ."

"I'm not dumping you. I'm getting it straight, so we both know where we are. We can still be friends."

Friends? I knew exactly what the "We can still be friends" line meant. It means, that's it. *Finito.* The end. I didn't want to be *friends* with him. I didn't want to hear about him being *more* than friends with anyone else. I looked across at his wide sensuous mouth. No more snogging that mouth. I felt the back of my eyes sting. I was going to burst into tears, but I didn't want to do it there. For him to see how upset I was. "Got to go," I said, getting up.

"But what about your Coke?" I heard him call as I reached the door and stumbled down the stairs.

"You have it," I muttered over my shoulder. I only had one thought in my head as I rushed home. Got to phone Nesta and get her to catch the postman tomorrow morning before Tony sees that stupid stupid *stupid* card.

All stressed out and no one to choke

2

Gooseberry Fool

I called Nesta the minute I got home.

"She's not here," said Mrs. Williams. "Do you want to leave a message?"

"Um, no thanks," I said. I knew Tony might see it when he got home, so leaving a message was definitely a no-no.

I quickly dialed her mobile. Murphy's Law. Nesta who *always* has it switched on, had it switched off.

I left a message on voice mail. "Nesta this is *urgent*. You *must* intercept that card I sent Tony. Whatever happens, he mustn't get it. Call me ASAP."

Then I texted the same message. Then I e-mailed it. It would be all right as long as he didn't read the card. But if he *did* . . . the thought made me feel queasy. All that stuff about how we had something special. Oh, arrghhhh. And wanting to make a go of it. Double arrrghhh.

I lay on the bed and groaned.

Mum popped her head around the door. "Are you going to come and have your supper, love? I saved some for you."

I shook my head. "Not hungry."

Mum looked at me with concern. "You okay?"

I shook my head then nodded. "I'm fine, just not hungry yet. I'll heat it up later. Promise." I didn't want to talk about it. I was too embarrassed. Dumped. I'd been dumped and we weren't even having a proper relationship. How sad is that? I needed to talk to Izzie. Wise old Izzie, she always knows the right thing to say.

Luckily Mum knew better than to push it. She's good at knowing when to leave me alone. I guess it's partly because she works as a counselor and is used to dealing with people that are freaked out but can't talk about it. She's always saying that you can't force people to open up when they're not ready.

"Come down when you want. No hurry," she said, and shut the door.

When she'd gone, I dialed Izzie's number.

"Isobel is round at Ben's," said the lodger. He's not really the lodger. He's Izzie's stepfather. She didn't get on with him in the beginning, so she nicknamed him "the lodger" to help her cope. They get on better now, but the nickname stuck.

I tried Izzie's mobile. Also switched off. What is the point of having a mobile if you don't keep it turned on? It's so annoying. I keep mine turned on all the time. Except in the cinema, of course. It's maddening when one of them goes off in the middle of a film.

My mobile rang. At last, I thought as I picked it up. Must be Izzie or Nesta.

"Hey, Lucy." It was Tony's voice.

I panicked. I didn't know what to say. He was the last person I wanted to talk to.

"Lucy, are you there?"

I hung up. I felt like someone was strangling me. I didn't want Tony to know how upset I was and I didn't know how to play it. Not until I'd talked to one of the girls.

The phone rang again. I switched it off in case it was Tony calling back. I felt numb and confused and was just wondering what to do next, when I heard a familiar voice in the hall outside my bedroom. Oh, thank God, I thought, as I opened the bedroom door.

"T. J.!" I cried. "Thank God you're here."

"Why, what's the matter?" she said.

I was just about to launch in when I saw that Steve was standing behind her. Of course, I thought, she'd come over to see him.

"Er, nothing," I said. "Just . . . it doesn't matter. . . . You carry on."

T. J. turned to Steve. "Won't be a mo." Then she pushed me back into my bedroom and shut the door. "What's going on?"

I slumped on the bed. "Oh, T. J., you can't imagine," I said, and filled her in on the whole story.

She listened quietly. "I'm so sorry," she said. "You must be gutted."

I nodded.

"I know it may feel awful at the moment," she said, "but you don't know what or who's round the next corner. Remember what happened with me when I had that thing about Scott next door? I felt awful when it wasn't working out, then it turned out to be the best thing ever. He wasn't worth it and I met Steve. Who is worth it. Maybe it just wasn't meant to be with Tony."

I groaned. I knew she meant well, but it wasn't what I wanted to hear. "But it was different with Tony. . . ."

"I know," she said. "Oh, Lucy, I wish I knew what to say."

A knock on the door disturbed any further conversation, and Steve stuck his head in. "Come on, T. J., I've got the Amazon Web site up, I'm waiting for you."

T. J. looked anxiously at me.

"You go," I said. "I'm fine, honest."

"You sure? Because I can stay here with you," she said.

Steve looked at me as though that was the *last* thing he wanted.

"No, honest. Go." I didn't want to ruin everyone's night just because mine was turning out to be crapola.

"Why don't you come and join us?" asked T. J., looking at Steve for agreement. Which he didn't give.

I shook my head. Dumped and a third wheel in one night. No thanks.

"All part of life's rich tapestry," I said, quoting one of Mum's favorite lines. "I'll get over it, and besides, I have loads to do. You go."

I got up and began to tidy away things in my room.

"Don't worry," said T. J. "Nesta will get the card. It will be okay."

"Yeah right," I said. "Me and Bridget Jones. It's cool to be a singleton. Don't worry, one day my D'arcy will come."

As she shut the door, I thought, But Tony's my D'arcy, isn't he? Or is he the bad boy character played by Hugh Grant in *Bridget Jones's Diary*? Oh, I don't know.

Mum always says that things seem better after a good night's sleep and I did wake up the next morning feeling slightly more positive. At least that's what I told myself. It's not as though Tony and I were having a proper relationship. Then I looked at the clock. Ohmigod. It's nine thirty. *Nine thirty*. Ohmigod. *Ohmigod*. Did Nesta get my message? Did she get the card before Tony did? I checked my mobile, and oh no, I'd forgotten to switch it back on after Tony'd called last night. There were three messages. One from Tony asking me to call him. One from Izzie asking me to call her. And one from Nesta asking me to call her.

I quickly found my robe and ran downstairs into the kitchen.

"Why didn't you wake me, Mum?"

She looked up from the table where she was reading the paper. "It's Saturday, Lucy. And you seemed a bit low last night. I thought I'd let you sleep in. . . ."

"Did anyone call?"

"Izzie. She said your mobile's off and she'll try later."

"You should have woken me."

Mum sighed. "I can't win, can I? Usually if I wake you early at the weekend, I'm wrong, and now I *don't* wake you and I'm wrong. I give up."

I ran back upstairs and called Nesta's number then hung up. Tony might answer. I dialed her mobile number.

Phew, I thought when she answered.

"Lucy . . . ," she began.

"Did you get the card?"

There was an ominous silence.

"Oh, Nesta, please say you did."

"Oh, Lucy, I got back late last night and I've only just listened to the messages on my mobile this morning. And . . . and the postman's already been."

"Has he got it?"

"Tony? Yes. I saw him take a card into his room. But what's the problem? Why did you want me to get to it

199

first? Did you change your mind about wanting to see him over the holidays?"

"No. *No.* He's changed *his* mind. We met up in Highgate and he told me he only wants to be friends. . . ."

"I'll kill him."

"No, don't, Nesta. But find out how he reacted to the card. Oh pants. Oh, and Nesta, *try* to do it in a subtle way."

"Yeah, course. But I think we need to meet up. Urgently. I already said I'd meet Izzie later this morning. You phone T. J. Ruby's, eleven thirty?"

"Fab," I said. "Thanks. And tell me everything Tony says."

"Every last detail."

Ruby in the Dust is Nesta's favorite café. It's by the roundabout in Muswell Hill and is even funkier than Raj's. The sofas and tables are so well-worn, they look like they came off a Dumpster, but it gives the place a cozy, lived-in feel. Loads of local teenagers hang out in there, us included, most weekends.

The girls were all there when I arrived and they looked up at me anxiously when I walked through the door.

"You okay, Lucy?" asked Nesta as I sat beside her on a sofa in the window.

It was then that I spotted Ben. He was at the counter ordering drinks. What was he doing here?

"Do you want a cappuccino?" he called.

I nodded.

"Sorry," mouthed Izzie. "I didn't know what it was all about until Nesta told me just now."

"And Simon's coming too," said Nesta, looking sheepish. "I tried to call him to put him off, but he'd already left."

Oh great, I thought. And I suppose my brother's coming too. I looked over at T. J. She shook her head.

"Steve's at football this morning," she said.

"Yeah, course," I said. He played every week. I was bursting to ask if Tony had said anything about the card, so I turned to Nesta quickly before Ben came back.

"So?"

"He didn't say much. Just that he'd gotten your card and that it was private. I didn't let on that I knew what you'd written. He asked me to ask you to call him."

"Is that everything?"

Nesta nodded.

"Honest?" I asked.

"Honest," she answered. "And I didn't hit him or anything. Though I'd have liked to."

"So what should I do?" I asked, looking around.

"Try to stay friends," said Izzie.

"No. You must never speak to him again," said Nesta.

"Maybe I shouldn't have given him such a hard time," I said. "Maybe it's my fault."

"Rubbish," said Nesta. "You were too good for him. You deserve better."

"You'll find someone else," said T. J.

I looked around the café. There were a few boys there and, as always, they were all ogling Nesta. She did look stunning in her denim shorts and a cut-off T-shirt, with her hair loose like silk all the way down her back.

"No. No one will *ever* look at me again," I groaned.

"Rubbish," said Izzie. "You mustn't let this dent your confidence."

"Find someone else, settle down, and have a really committed relationship. That will show him," said T. J.

"No, *no*. Last thing she needs," said Nesta. "Have some fun. Go out with *loads* of boys. Play the field."

"*No*. You need some quiet time," said Izzie. "Time to heal."

"No, no. Fill your diary. Keep busy—you must keep busy," insisted Nesta.

I couldn't help but laugh. "D'oh, thanks, girls. Now I'm really confused."

As Ben came back with the coffees, the café door opened and Simon came in. Some of the boys in the café looked peeved when they saw him make a beeline for Nesta, who smiled and kissed him. Of course the boys being there put an end to any discussion about Tony, so I did my best to act happy and not let Ben or Simon see how freaked out I really was.

After we'd drunk our cappuccinos, Simon suggested that, since the weather wasn't brilliant, we go to the early show of a movie. I wanted to go home and hide under my duvet, but Nesta insisted that I go as well and there's no arguing with her when she's made up her mind about what's best for someone. T. J. will be there, I thought. So it's not as though I'll be the only singleton.

"Um, I said I'd meet Steve after football," said T. J., getting up and looking anxiously at me. "I can cancel if you want to do something."

I shook my head. "Don't be mad. I'll go to the movie."

I didn't like this kid-glove treatment they were giving

me, like I was ill or something. The last thing I wanted was my mates feeling sorry for me. Oh, poor Lucy, she's been dumped. Poor Lucy sent a romantic card to someone who's not interested. I'd show them I was fine. So they've all got boyfriends and I haven't, I thought. No biggie. I'm not going to let it get to me.

At the cinema, Nesta and Izzie insisted that I sit in between them rather than on the end. It was okay at the beginning and I was glad I'd gone with them. No one can see that you're on your own in the dark. We were just five teenagers watching a film.

That is, we were until Ben put his arm round Izzie and they cuddled up and Simon went into a snogathon with Nesta. I felt a right twerp, sitting with a straight back in the middle, giant tub of popcorn on my lap that no one was eating except me. The only one really watching the movie. I tried to focus on the film and forget about Tony and boys and what was happening on either side of me, but the film was a romantic comedy. Oh, arrggghhh, I thought as the screen hero moved in for a snog. Arrrghh, *arrrghh*. Snogging to the left of me, snogging to the right. And snogging in front of me, in glorious magnified technicolor on the screen. No escape.

I'm not doing this again, I thought.

3

Solo Sundays

The next day, I decided I'd hang out with my brothers. It seemed a good idea, since in term time it's like we're just lodgers in the same house. Eat, queue for the bathroom, fight over what's on telly, go to bed, go to school, pass on the stairs. I'd spend what Mum calls "quality time" with them.

"Do you want to do anything after lunch?" I asked at breakfast.

"Busy," said Steve, peering at me over his glasses. "Meeting Mark for tennis. Sorry."

"Harry and Edward are coming over after lunch," said Lal. "We're going to discuss our summer strategy for getting girls."

"Oh, get a life, Lal," I said. "Don't you ever think of anything else?"

"Yeah, food," replied Lal, spreading peanut butter and honey on his toast then ramming it into his mouth. "Need to keep up my strength for all the top totty."

"Dream on, dorkbrain," I said. "Who in their right mind would look at *you*?"

"Get lost, toadbreath," said Lal. "Loads of girls fancy me."

"Quality time with them? Well so much for that plan," I said to Mum as Steve and Lal scoffed down their breakfast, then scampered off.

"Life is what happens to you when you're busy making plans," she said. She's always coming out with stuff like that.

"Yeah, right," I said, thinking about my plan to spend the summer with Tony. "Tell me about it."

I've got three choices, I decided as I went upstairs to my room.

1. Mope and be miserable
2. Find another boyfriend
3. Find an interesting alternative

I decided to go for option three. Moping and being miserable would be a waste of time during the precious holidays. As Mum says, life is not a rehearsal. You only get one shot at it, so make the most of it. And the thought of option two, looking for another boy just to make up the numbers with Nesta, Izzie, and T. J., was too gruesome. I'm not that desperate and I don't need a *boy* to be happy. Having a boyfriend can be exciting and fun, *if* it's the right boy. It can also be heartbreaking, humiliating, and confusing. So, good alternatives?

I tore a sheet of paper out of my notepad and sat on the bed. Right, I thought. Nice things to do when you're single. A list:

1. Eat chocolate.

Good idea. In fact, I'll get some right now.

I took a quick break from the list to go and raid the cupboard downstairs. Only organic in this house of course, but Green & Black's chocolate is pretty good.

2. Shop.

Got no money, so cross that out for the time being.

3. Movies.

I could go on my own, but as I discovered yesterday, all that's on at the moment are romances. Or boys' films, and I'm not in the mood for watching people blow each other up in space.

4. Little treats, like a manicure, pedicure, or facial.

That's a good idea, I decided. I'll have a beauty day.

* * *

I spent the next few hours pampering myself. I painted my nails with my strawberry-scented glitter polish. I did a papaya facial. I took a long foamy soak with passion fruit bath gel and exfoliated my whole body, including elbows and knees, with citrus and ginger exfoliator. Then I washed my hair with Mum's apple shampoo, rinsed with fresh lemon, and then conditioned with peach afterwash.

Then I was done. Beautified. I smelled like a fruit bowl. Now what? It was one o'clock and the day was starting to feel *very* long.

Life is what you make it, I thought. Clearly I needed a hobby.

I went down into the kitchen where Mum and Dad were preparing Sunday lunch.

"I need a hobby," I said. "Any suggestions?"

"But you have your sewing," said Mum. "All those T-shirts you're making."

I nodded. "I suppose, but they don't take long to make." It's true I do like sewing, as ultimately I want to be a fashion designer, but I wanted to try something new.

"You could walk the dogs more often," said Dad, gesturing toward the garden where Lal was having a pre-lunch cavort with Ben and Jerry, our two golden Labradors.

"Could," I said. "But I can't manage both of them on my own."

"Get some goldfish," said Dad. "I'll get you a tank."

"Um, no thanks," I said, sensing he wasn't taking this very seriously. I remembered last time we had fish. No one ever wanted to change the water, so they only lasted a few weeks.

"Take up jogging," said Steve, coming in from the living room.

"Ever seen a happy jogger?" I asked. I certainly hadn't. Loads of people do it and they all look miserable, red in the face, puffing, but with a determined look in their eyes. Not my idea of fun.

"Well, there's all sorts of exercise you could do," said Mum. "Cycling, swimming, dancing, skating, judo, rowing, aerobics . . ."

It was beginning to sound like the extracurricular classes at school. I pulled a face.

"Well, I don't know, Lucy," said Mum. "What do you want to do?"

"Something new," I said. "Something I can do on my own."

"Ah, is this our new independent Lucy?" said Dad. "You could come with me the week after next. I've been invited to a workshop in Devon. It's run by a friend of mine. I'm sure she'd be glad to have you along as well. You wouldn't be on your own, but it might do you some good."

"What sort of workshop?"

"It's a kind of rejuvenation workshop. Yoga, self-help classes, therapy, learn to de-stress, getting to the root of problems."

"Sounds like Izzie's sort of thing, not mine," I said. Izzie was well into anything new age. If ever any of us caught a bug or fell ill, she always had an explanation for it. Like when Nesta got a sore throat, Izzie asked her what wasn't she saying that was blocking her throat. And when T. J. hurt her knee, Izzie said that it was because she wasn't willing to bend. It was hilarious, though, when her mum got a boil on her bum and Izzie told her that it was because she was sitting on her anger. Literally, we all thought. There might be some truth in it, but personally I'm all for taking someone a bunch of daffodils when they're ill and giving some good old-fashioned sympathy.

"How many psychotherapists does it take to change a lightbulb?" asked Mum.

"Dunno," we said.

"One," she said, grinning. "But only if it really wants to change."

Dad laughed out loud. I suppose that's an in-joke for

people that work in counseling and therapy . . . and their husbands.

"How many Spanish people does it take to change a lightbulb?" asked Dad.

"How many?" said Mum.

"Juan."

"Want to know the very first lightbulb joke?" asked Steve.

Mum nodded. Typical, I thought. Trust Steve to know the original joke. He's a mine of useless information from reading all his books. Though I suppose he would be a good person for "Phone a Friend" if you were on *Who Wants to Be a Millionaire.*

"How many Chinese people does it take to change a lightbulb?" he asked.

"How many?"

"Millions. Because Confucius say, many hands make light work."

Steve, Mum, and Dad fell about laughing.

"Look," I said, "we were discussing a hobby for me. Not telling lightbulb jokes. I've got six weeks and *nothing* to do."

"Oh, poor Lucy," said Mum. "Now let's think. There must be something for you."

"Loads of things," said Steve. "Read, learn to cook . . ."

"Excellent," said Mum. "In fact, you were going to cook for us one night."

"Garden," said Dad. "Those beds outside need a turn over and the weeds need pulling out."

"Learn a language," said Steve.

"Learn to play an instrument," said Dad. "Violin or piano. I could teach you guitar."

"Take up photography," said Steve.

"That's *your* hobby," I said.

"Trainspotting," said Lal, coming in from the garden. "Stamp collecting. Are we playing a game? Who can name the most daft hobbies?"

"Something like that," I said as visions of me in an anorak, watching trains or digging up worms in the garden filled my head.

Luckily, I was saved from any more of my family's brilliant suggestions by the phone ringing. It was Nesta.

"Help," I said. "My family wants me to take up gardening."

"I have a better idea," said Nesta. "I've been thinking. There are plenty more fish in the sea besides my ratfink brother. I've been talking to Izzie about it and we have a new mission."

"Which is?"

"Mission Matchmaker. Lucy, *we* are going to find

you a boy. And not just any boy. The perfect boy."

Even though I'd dismissed that from my list earlier that morning, somehow it seemed a more appealing alternative to stamp collecting or taking up knitting.

"You're on," I said.

4

Mission Matchmake

Nesta called first thing the next day.

"Mission *Numero Uno*. Place: Hollywood Bowl," she said, going into sergeant-major mode. "Outside Café Original. Time: Three o'clock."

"Do we need to synchronize our watches?" I asked.

"Yes, good idea," she replied, not realizing that I was joking. "See, the plan is to catch the boys either going in to the movies or coming out, so we need to find out the times of the films. Coming out is probably better as they'll hang out for a while afterward and give us time to assess the situation and the talent."

"Yes, sir," I said.

Just for a joke, I wore my combat trousers and khaki T-shirt, but Nesta didn't pick up on it when I arrived at the cinema.

T. J. did, though, and laughed. "Ready to do battle, Lucy?" she asked.

"Private Lucy reporting for duty," I said, saluting. "Has anyone brought binoculars?"

"Or camouflage gear," Izzie said, laughing, getting into it. "We could smear our faces with mud, then hide in the bushes with a bit of tree stuck on our heads."

Nesta tossed her hair. "You may laugh, but coming here is a good strategy. See, look—there are loads of boys around."

Nesta was right. It was a good place to start, as Hollywood Bowl is a popular haunt for most North London teenagers. Apart from the cinema, there's a bowling alley, a pool, and a variety of assorted cafés all built in a square around the car park. Today, as always, there were groups of teens hanging out in the sunshine in front of the cinema.

"Looks like we're not the only ones on the pull," said Izzie, watching the groups of teens all eyeing each other up.

"I am *not* on the pull," I said. "It sounds desperate when you put it like that. I don't want a boy just for the sake of it."

"Course you don't," said Izzie. "We're only looking."

"How about we say that we're doing research?" said T. J.

"I saw some girls doing it on one of those 'How to get a date' shows on telly. The presenter said that a good way to meet boys was to pretend that you're doing a survey and ask them a list of questions. It's one way of getting talking to them."

"That would be a laugh," I said. "Anyone got any paper?"

The girls all shook their heads.

"I think we'd need a bit more than paper if anyone was to take us seriously," said Nesta, looking at what we all had on. Izzie was wearing a T-shirt and denim mini, T. J. and Nesta had shorts and T-shirts on, and I was in my combats. "Not exactly dressed like professionals, are we?"

"We'll do that another day," I said to T. J. "And we'll dress the part."

"Now, let's see who's here. Don't look as though you're looking," said Nesta, casually glancing round the car park. "We don't want to be too obvious."

"So how am I supposed to check the talent?" I asked.

Nesta turned her back on the groups of boys then got her mirror out of her bag. "Like this," she said. "See, it looks like I'm checking my hair or something but actually I'm looking behind me."

Izzie and I got our mirrors out and lined up with Nesta to try out her technique. T. J. shared mine with me, and I couldn't stop laughing as we watched the people behind us.

Nesta sighed. "I give up," she said. "You lot are just a wind-up."

"Sorry, Nesta," I said, putting away my mirror. "I do appreciate this, honest I do. And I get what you're saying—look kind of casual."

I glanced at the boys, then over to the left, like I was looking for someone in the distance, then back at the boys, then over at the cinema.

"Perfect," said Nesta. "That's the way to do it. Now, check out left, by the pillar, jeans, black T-shirt. Guy with blond spiky hair."

"Not my type," I said. "Too . . . um, too hair-gelly."

"Okay, left, dark, French crop. Wearing all black."

"Yee-uck," I said, looking over at the boy. "Do me a favor. He's picking his nose."

"Okay, I got one," said T. J. "Behind spiky boy, dark."

"Where? . . . Oh yeah," I said, catching sight of him. "Yeah, he's a possibility."

"He's checking you out, Lucy," said Izzie.

I glanced over. "Ohmigod, he's looking at me. I think he knows we're talking about him. Ohmigod, he's coming over."

"Excellent," said Nesta. "Now play it cool, look away, don't let him know you've noticed him."

Of course I went bright red. A dead giveaway, if ever there was one.

The boy came straight up to me. "Hi," he said. "Can I talk to you a minute?"

I glanced at the girls, who were all grinning like idiots and giving me the thumbs-up behind his back. I couldn't believe it. Success so fast. And he was cute. Very cute, very Latino boy babe.

He led me behind the pillar and looked deeply into my eyes.

"That girl you're with . . . ," he began.

He didn't have to finish. I knew what he was going to say immediately. It's not the first time this has happened. Boys always fancy Nesta. And no wonder; she is stunning.

"The dark one?" I asked.

"Yeah. Has she got a boyfriend?"

"Yes," I said. "In fact, all those girls I'm with have got boyfriends."

He looked disappointed. Not as disappointed as I was,

though. He didn't even bother to ask if I was attached.

"Never mind," he said. "Thanks." Then he shuffled off.

I couldn't help feeling a tiny bit jealous. I do love Nesta—she's a great mate—but it's hard sometimes, being the last one that anyone notices. I went back to join the girls, who looked at me expectantly.

"Wanted to know if you were taken or not, Nesta," I said.

Nesta looked over at the boy. "Really?"

Izzie smacked her arm. "We're here for Lucy, not you. Besides, you have Simon."

"I know," she said. "But no harm seeing what I'm missing."

"Let's try somewhere else," I said. "Any ideas, anyone?"

"How about Hampstead?" said Izzie. "There's always loads of boys there."

"Lead the way," said Nesta, heading off towards the bus stop.

"But please, let's just hang out, look in the shops, and forget about the Mission," I said. "I don't think it's going to work. It doesn't feel right. I mean, so there might be a boy who looks okay, but how am I going to approach him? Get a card with 'Hi, I'm Lucy and I'm available' on it? Besides, I'm always reading that the right boy always comes along when you've given up."

"No," said Nesta. "You have to make things happen."

Izzie shrugged. "No, Lucy may be right, Nesta. You can't force destiny."

"Choice, not chance, determines destiny," said Nesta. "You can't leave everything to fate or the stars."

Oh, here we go again with the conflicting advice, I thought. It's amazing Nesta and Izzie get on at all. They both think so differently about things. If Nesta said "hold on," Izzie would say "let go." They never agree on anything. Chalk and cheese. Still, it seems to work on some strange level. Opposites attract and all that.

"What do you think, T. J.?" I asked.

"No harm in looking," she said. "It's like window shopping. Good to see what's on offer, but it doesn't mean that you have to buy."

I liked that perspective. It took the pressure off.

We caught the bus down to Hampstead where everyone was sitting, sipping cappuccinos, and enjoying the sunshine outside the cafés that line the streets.

After trawling the pavement for a while, looking for an empty table, we finally ended up outside the Coffee Cup. All the tables were full except for one that was occupied by a boy sitting on his own and reading. He looked nice and there were three empty chairs next to him.

"Anyone sitting here?" asked Nesta, pointing at the chairs.

The boy smiled and said, "Nope, only me. And Jesus." He then pointed at the book he was reading, which turned out to be the Bible. "Please, sit down. I'd like to tell you how you can be saved."

Izzie was all for it, as there's nothing she likes more than a discussion about religion and why we're here and stuff. But luckily Nesta had a better idea.

"I really fancy ice cream instead of coffee," she said, making a beeline for the ice cream shop next door.

"Good idea," I said, following her. "When the going gets tough, the tough need chocolate-chip fudge."

5

Wish List

I decided I needed to rethink the plan. Mission Matchmaker had left me feeling more aware than ever that I was single. Nesta and Izzie, however, weren't ready to give up. Nesta wanted me to go out boy hunting again in Kensington on Tuesday with her and Simon, but I said I was busy helping Dad out at the shop. I didn't want to hang around with her and Simon, like a spare part. And I didn't want Simon thinking I was desperate. Because I'm really really not. Of course, Izzie heard about my refusal to go out and came over to see me on Wednesday.

"I don't want to pick up any old boy. I want it to be special, like it was with Tony."

"Then what you need to do," said Izzie, "is to send

a message out into the universe about what you want, then you'll attract it to you. You should do a wish list for a boy, then wrap it in tissue, put it in a secret box, and hide it in your bedroom."

"If it's going to go out into the universe, wouldn't a billboard up at Swiss Cottage work better than hiding a piece of paper in my bedroom?" I teased.

She gave me "the look"—the one our teacher Miss Watkins gives when someone hasn't done their homework.

"Trust me," she said. She was always coming up with ways to make things happen or control your destiny and stuff. She's got one of those spell books at home, and when Tony was coming down with a case of the wandering hands last year, she told me to put a photo of him in the freezer to cool him down. I laughed at the time, but maybe it worked after all. He'd certainly gone cold on me now.

I stretched out on my bed while she took her favorite place on the beanbag on the floor. "Okay, mystic Iz. So what's a wish list?" I asked.

"You have to write down all the things that you want in a boy on one side of the paper, then all things that you have to offer on the other side." She got up and found a pen and piece of paper from my desk and handed it to me. "Start with how you want him to look, then go on to personality—like funny, generous, that sort of thing. Then emotionally and spiritually how you'd like him to be. The more detail, the better. Leave nothing out."

Why not? I thought. I had nothing else to do and it was better than being made to go out and trawl North London like a saddo.

"Okay," I said, and began to write.

> My perfect boy:
> Medium height, not too tall. Fit-looking.
> Nice face.

"Blond or dark?" asked Izzie, coming to sit on the bed next to me and looking at what I was writing.

"Um, don't mind really, as long as he's quite nice-looking."

"Oh, go for it," said Izzie. "Write drop dead gorgeous. Cute. Don't settle for just anyone."

> Gorgeous-looking, cute, long eyelashes. With
> nice hands and nails. Clean. Well-dressed, with
> a sense of style. Interested in fashion.

"Now you're getting it," said Izzie. "Now his personality."
I continued writing.

> Reliable, i.e., will phone me when he
> says he will.

"Excellent," said Iz. "But what else? Just reliable could be a bit boring."

> Good fun to be with. Sense of humor. Really
> likes me. Honest. Doesn't play mind games.
> Not afraid to show his feelings about me.
> Intelligent. Ambitious. Kind. Sensitive.
> Spontaneous. Likes animals.

"Good," said Izzie. "Now do you."
I turned over the paper. "Um, don't know what to put," I said.
"Blond, small, slim," dictated Izzie. "Am fab at fashion. Have my own sense of style. Am honest. Have a great sense of humor. Am generous. Sensitive. Spontaneous. Am a great friend to my mates. Am punctual. Sweet."
"Sweet? Eeeww. Boring."
"No, it's not. And you *are* sweet," said Izzie. "When you want to be."

"How about: Have Wonderbra, will travel?" I added.

Izzie laughed. "Have inflatable bra, will travel."

Nesta and Izzie bought me an inflatable bra ages ago when I was fed up about being so flat-chested. It's on the notice board in my bedroom, pinned under a photo of me taken when I was twelve.

"Maybe I should put on his side that he likes girls who have boobs like peanuts," I said.

"Put: Likes petite," said Izzie. "Sounds better."

I added that to his side of the paper, then as Izzie instructed, I wrapped the paper in tissue and put it in my Chinese box in the drawer in the bedside cabinet.

"Excellent," said Izzie. "Now let's see when he turns up. It may even be on Friday. It's Ben's birthday and his parents are letting him have a party at his house. He said to invite you and Nesta and T. J. You will come, won't you?"

"Are Simon and Steve going?" I asked.

"And Lal," Izzie said. "But there'll be loads of other boys there. It'd be amazing if perfect boy turned up."

I laughed. She really believed in her hocus-pocus.

"Course, I'll come," I said. "It might be fun." I had to admit that a part of me was secretly hoping that Izzie's wish list would work. I had nothing to lose by going to find out.

* * *

All the girls looked stunning at the party. Izzie was wearing a white peasant top, a denim ruffle skirt, and cowboy boots; Nesta was in a blue strappy slip dress; and T. J. was in jeans, but she was wearing a fab turquoise halter top.

I wore an outfit I'd made a few weeks before. It was a tight red corset basque that laced down the back and a black taffeta skirt. And I wore bright red lipstick to go with the corset. I felt really good. Really in the mood for flirting.

"You look amazing," said Izzie to me. "Sexy."

"Thought I'd better make an effort in case dreamboy's here," I laughed.

"You look like a character out of *Moulin Rouge*," said T. J. "Really suits you."

"Thanks," I said, doing a quick scan of the room. On first glance dreamboy was nowhere to be seen. There were loads of boys there, but not one who came close to fitting the bill. There was a thin, dark-haired boy in the corner, and I could see he was eyeing me up, but I turned away. Definitely not my type, though it was nice to be noticed.

As the party got going, it soon became clear who

was a couple and who was single. In the front room, someone changed the music to a CD of love ballads and some of the couples got up to drape themselves round each other and smooch-dance. I decided to go and investigate the rest of the house and practice my flirting, but every room I went into seemed to be full of couples snogging. The front room, the hall, the little conservatory at the back of the house, everywhere. The singletons present mooched about from room to room trying to look as though they were having a great time but I could tell that some of them felt like I did. Like we had neon signs over our heads saying SINGLE. The only person there who seemed to be enjoying being single was Lal. So far, I'd seen him snog two different girls, one in the hall and one on the landing.

"It's quality, not quantity," I told him when he came up for air between girls. "Do those two know about each other?"

He grinned. "Course not."

"And don't you ever think about their feelings?"

"Oh, get off my case, Miss Prissy Knickers," he said. "Chill out. You take it all way too seriously. You should be more like me. Enjoy. We're young, we're free, we're single."

"I don't want to be like you. I do actually want to feel something for the people I snog," I said.

"Why? You're missing out, I tell you," he said as he spotted a small dark girl who looked a bit lonely. "Anyway, got to go. So many girls, so little time."

"Seen anyone you like?" asked T. J. when I went into the kitchen to get a drink.

I shook my head.

"There's a few more boys upstairs. Why don't you go and have a look?" she suggested.

I traipsed up the stairs behind her. A crowd of lads were in Ben's bedroom playing a game on his computer. I glanced over at them, then shook my head.

"No thanks," I said, and turned to go back downstairs. "They all look like they're up past their bedtime. Way too young."

It was then that I saw him. He was coming in the front door and he was drop dead *gorgeous*. A tingle went through me. Dreamboy most definitely, I thought.

It was Tony.

I drew back and sat on the top stair so that he couldn't see me, then watched him through the banisters. There was someone with him. A willowy girl with long blond hair. She was very, very pretty. He took her hand and led her into the kitchen. No wonder he wanted to be free for the holidays, I thought. Free to go out with her.

Nesta came racing up the stairs a moment later. "Ohmigod," she said. "I'm sorry, Lucy. I didn't know he was coming. Do you want me to ask him to leave?"

"No. No. Course not. He'd think I was pining after him," I said. "I'll keep out of his way. It'll be fine. How long has he been seeing her?"

Nesta shrugged. "New one to me," she said.

"Well you can't stay up here all night hiding," said T. J. "Look he's gone into the kitchen. Come down and go in the front room, and, Nesta, you go and distract Tony."

I followed them down, but suddenly I wasn't in the party mood anymore. What was the point of practicing my flirting on boys I definitely had no interest in? I could hear Tony talking in the kitchen and laughing. Oh, hell. What was I going to do?

"Get off with one of the boys," said T. J., coming in to the front room to join me. "Act like you don't care, show him that you've moved on as well."

I looked at the assorted gangly boys on offer and shook my head. "Nah, I don't want to get into playing games just to get a reaction from him. Look, T. J., I'm going to go home. I'll just slip out. Tell the others I've gone."

Izzie got up from the sofa where she'd been sitting with Ben.

"You need to sort it out between you and Tony," she said. "Otherwise, it's always going to come back and ruin your peace of mind. Lucy, for your inner happiness, you have to clear up anything unfinished."

"Yeah, right," I said, and headed for the front door.

When I got home, I thought about what Iz had said as I left the party. Something about finishing everything that's left unfinished in your life. She was right. That's exactly what I needed to do. So I finished off a tub of Ben & Jerry's, a packet of Rolos, and a packet of double-chocolate-chip cookies.

Somehow I don't think those were the sort of things she had in mind.

6

Family Advice

Mum brought me a cup of tea in bed the next day.

"You all right, Lucy?" she said, sitting down on the end of the bed.

I nodded. "Sort of."

"Good party last night?"

"Sort of," I said.

"Usual crowd?"

"Yeah, and a load of Ben's mates." I sat up and took a sip of the tea, then decided to fill her in. "*Everyone* has got a boyfriend except me."

"So what happened to Tony? I thought he was your boyfriend. Sort of."

"He's got someone new. He was there with her last night."

"Oh, Lucy, poor you. Was it horrible?"

"Sort of." I felt my face start to crumple. It always

makes me blub when people are nice to me. I'm weird like that.

"Sort of," said Mum. "Makes a change from whatever. Want to talk about it?"

"It's just . . . all week, T. J. and Nesta and Izzie have been on a mission to find me a boy, but . . ."

Mum nodded. "You don't want just any boy?"

"Exactly. Going out looking for one only made me more aware than ever that I don't have one. Then last night Tony turns up with a new girlfriend and now I'm beginning to feel that I'm the only one without anyone and I'll never meet someone new."

Mum put her hand on my arm and gave it a squeeze. "A gorgeous girl like you—course you will."

"No, I won't. I must be doing something to put boys off. What's wrong with me?"

"*Wrong* with you? Nothing."

"Or maybe I shouldn't be so fussy. Maybe I'm aiming too high, for someone who doesn't exist. Maybe I should just go out with whoever's available."

"Never," said Mum. "You just haven't met the right one yet. I remember when I was a teenager, I used to be quite stroppy and say exactly what I thought and that *definitely* seemed to frighten off the boys. A friend of mine said that I had to learn to compromise—that boys liked girls to be cute, like kittens, and that I'd have to learn to shut my mouth. Yuck, I thought. I could never be one of those whimpering girlie girls who don't know their own mind. But there were times when I doubted myself and thought, what's wrong with me? I thought I'd never meet the right boy or one who I could be myself with. It was rubbish. When you meet the right boy, he likes you exactly the way you are and you don't have to put on any act. You hold out until it really feels right. For *you* and not your friends or anyone else."

"So how do you know if it's right?"

"You just do. You can't stop thinking about him. You're happy around him. But mainly because you can be yourself with him. More yourself than with anyone."

I nodded. I knew what she meant. I felt like that when I was with Tony.

"I'm off now," said Mum, getting up. "You have a lie-in, you lucky thing. Holidays. I *wish*. And Dad told me to tell you that the offer's still open for you to go with him next weekend to that workshop if you want. You never know—you might enjoy it."

I shook my head. "No thanks." Being stuck with a load of adults straining to contort themselves into yoga postures wasn't my idea of fun. "But thanks for the tea and sympathy, Mum."

"Anytime." Mum smiled, then began singing as she went out the door. "Someday Lucy's prince will come."

"Mu-*um*," I groaned. "Let the whole house know, why don't you?" Honestly. She could be really lovely and sensitive one minute, then completely blow it the next.

Steve was slumped over a cup of tea at the kitchen table when I got downstairs.

"What's up with you?" I said, looking at his long face.

"T. J.'s off today," he said. "Scotland. She wants you to call her before she goes."

Of course. She was going on holiday with her mum and dad. Poor Steve. He looked really down in the dumps about it.

"It's only for a week," I said. "You'll live."

"Uh," he said, then glanced up at me. "You all right after last night?"

"Uh," I answered, making an effort to speak his language.

That was as close as Steve and I ever got to a heart-to-heart. He's not very good at talking about his feelings, but maybe that's just because he's my brother and he's different with other people. Sometimes I wonder what he talks to T. J. about. Or maybe he doesn't. Maybe she likes the silent types or men of few words, like "uh" or "nah."

Lal, on the other hand, is different altogether. He's like Nesta—says what he thinks, asks what he wants to know.

A thumping on the stairs announced his arrival and he burst into the kitchen and helped himself to a large bowl of Shreddies.

"So, Lucy," he said, sitting opposite me at the table. "I heard you left Ben's party early last night. What was all that about?"

"And who are you?" I asked. "The Spanish Inquisition?"

He took no notice. "You and Tony? Or not you and Tony? Have you broken up? Gone off you, has he?"

Tactful as ever, my brother. "We were never really *together* together," I said. "And no, he hasn't gone off me, he . . ."

"Want me to beat him up?"

I laughed. I knew he didn't mean it. "Yeah. Like you could."

"No one messes with my sister," he said. "Are you upset?"

"I'll live."

"That means you are."

"Leave off her," said Steve.

"Boys are only after one thing," said Lal. "Did he finish with you because you wouldn't . . . you know . . . put out?"

"Lal," said Steve. "It's none of your business."

"He never said anything about that," I said, "but it probably had something to do with it."

"So put out," said Lal. "Then he'll have you back."

"And when did you become the expert on relationships?" I asked.

Lal shrugged. "Boys like girls who put out. Everyone knows that."

I felt myself starting to get really miffed with him. "And what about your treat-'em-mean-to-keep-'em-keen philosophy?" I asked. "Last month that's what you told me. You can't follow two different sets of rules. I can't put out *and* treat 'em mean to keep 'em keen, can I? *Can* I?"

Lal looked confused for a moment.

"And since when did your angle win the girls?" I went on. "I know you might have snogged a lot, but how many of them have hung around to go out on proper dates? You've never even had a proper girlfriend, so you can't talk."

"Don't want a committed girlfriend," said Lal sulkily. "Girls are nothing but trouble when you get to know them properly."

"Not all boys are like Lal," said Steve. "*Some* boys like girls for their company."

"Who are you kidding?" asked Lal. "I'm just being honest here."

"So am I," said Steve. "I want to be with a girl who's got a good personality. Who I like being with. You just want to snog as many as you can so that you can boast to your mates about it."

"And what's wrong with that? No, you take my advice, Lucy. Put out."

"What? So that he can put me on his conquest chart?" I asked. "There's more to relationships than scoring points, you know."

Lal has a chart on the back of his door—the Snog Chart. He and his mate Harry are having a competition to see who can snog the most girls per week. When they get off with one, they come home and mark it on the chart. Like when Lal was at the party, they're not at all choosy about who they kiss or even if they like the girl, only that it's another conquest for the chart. Lal's winning by two this week.

"You should be more like me," said Lal. "Don't get hung up on one person and get your heart broken. Play the field. You need more experience. Snog loads of boys and boost your confidence."

I'd had enough. "I think I'll go and call T. J.," I said, getting up. "Thanks so much for the advice, boys. I'm *so* lucky to have brothers like you. 'Uh' from Steve and 'put out' from you, Lal. Thanks, it's really helped."

I couldn't believe it. Lal looked chuffed. Maybe he actually thought I *meant* it and was genuinely thanking him!

After I'd called T. J. to wish her a happy holiday, Nesta rang to check I was okay after last night.

"I'm fine," I assured her. "It would be no biggie if all of you didn't keep going on about it. So first, I want you to stop trying to find boys for me. And second, don't worry."

"So, don't you want to know about Tony?"

"Um, maybe."

"He says he's tried your mobile a hundred times but you keep it switched off these days so he asked me to ask you to call him."

"I've got nothing to say to him," I said. "Anyway he's got a new girlfriend now, so why does he want to speak to me?"

Part of me was hoping that she'd say because he realized that he'd made a terrible mistake and wanted to go out with me after all.

"He says he still wants to be friends," said Nesta.

"And we all know what that means, don't we?"

"I guess," said Nesta.

"So who is the blonde he was with?"

"Name's Georgia. He met her at the bowling alley."

"Are they going out?"

Nesta was quiet for a few moments. "Looks like it. I *am* sorry, Lucy."

"Did you tell him I was there and left last night?"

"*No.* Course not. His ego's inflated enough as it is. Anyway, the other reason I rang is, do you want to come over?"

"Oh, Nesta, not yet. I'm not ready to face him yet. Give me a few more days or call me when you know he's not going to be there."

"Okay, well, phone me later, okay?"

"Nesta, I'm fine. You don't have to check up on me every five minutes."

"How about every hour, then?"

"Fine," I said. "But don't worry, I've got loads to do."

I put the phone down and wondered, loads of what, exactly? It was only the first week of the holidays and I'm so desperate for stuff to do that even the thought of school seemed appealing. It wasn't meant to be like this, I thought as I gazed out of the window.

Five minutes later, Izzie phoned.

"You'll never guess what," she said.

"What?" I asked, fearing the worst: that she'd found some boy for me and was going to fix me up on a blind date.

"My mum saw this advertisement in your dad's shop. For a workshop in Devon. To get back to basics, aid relaxation, and find balance in this hectic world, it says. Anyway, she wants to go. We're talking about *my* mum here, Lucy! My straighter-than-straight mum. She wants to go and chill out. . . . Your dad's going, isn't he?"

"Yeah," I said. "It's run by a friend of his. He asked me to go, but I said no way."

"But Mum's just booked for both of us, so I'm going to be there," said Izzie. "Oh, please come as well. It'll be brilliant. We'll have a laugh if we both go."

Suddenly, the idea had appeal. A few days hanging out with Izzie and no Ben and no boys. We wouldn't have to do all the classes. It could be fun.

"Well, I suppose . . . ," I began.

"Excellent," said Izzie. "So that's settled then. Pack your things."

7

Workshop Weirdos

The workshop was being held at an old farm-house manor on top of a hill near Bigbury in Devon. Dad and I drove down on Friday afternoon, and Izzie and her mum arrived soon after. The view from the car park was stunning, and in the distance we could see the sea.

A pretty blonde in a pink tracksuit came out to meet us, swiftly followed by a boisterous black Labrador. He made a beeline for Mrs. Foster as soon as she got out of her Jaguar, and stuck his nose straight up her skirt.

"He's clearly in the Lal camp of thinking," I giggled to Izzie as we watched her mum attempt to push the dog down with one hand and struggle with one of her many Louis Vuitton cases with the other.

"Sorry about Digby," said the tracksuit lady, grabbing

his collar and pulling him away. She put her hand out to Mrs. Foster. "Hi, I'm Chris Malloy and, as you've gathered, this is my dog, Digby. He's still young and tends to get a bit overexcited when we have visitors."

"She's not going to like it," whispered Izzie as her mum gave Chris a tight smile. "You know how she feels about dogs. All that hair and muddy paws . . ."

I laughed. I knew *exactly* how she felt about dogs. I was never allowed to take ours into the house if I ever visited Izzie when I was out walking them. Mrs. Foster has a thing about cleanliness. She's impeccable, her house is impeccable, her car is impeccable. Izzie always jokes that she doesn't use perfume, she uses disinfectant instead. This was going to be interesting, I thought as I watched her totter on high heels round to the back of the car.

"How long does she think this workshop is going to last?" I asked as Izzie and I helped her unload the boot. She seemed to have brought enough luggage for three months.

"Oh, you know what Mum's like," said Izzie. "Has to have the right outfit for every occasion."

"I don't think she'll be expected to dress for dinner in a place like this. More like tracksuits and T-shirts. And high heels in country lanes?"

"Try telling Mum that," sighed Izzie, who, like me, was wearing jeans and trainers. "Anyone would think we're going to meet the queen with the clothes she's brought down."

Chris showed us around the farmhouse and where we were to sleep, and I could see at once that Mrs. Foster didn't approve.

"I assumed that we all had our own private room," she said, frowning, as Chris showed us a whitewashed dormitory at the back of the house with bunk beds. "I mean this is supposed to be a weekend of rest and relaxation."

"We think it makes for a better atmosphere." Chris smiled. "Everyone gets to know each other really fast on a course like this. Soon you'll all be getting along like old friends."

"And there's a yeti living in my fridge," I whispered to Izzie as I glanced over at the other ladies who were busy unpacking their weekend cases. There were five of them: two old ladies with glasses and long gray hair who looked like sisters and were dressed in the sort of clothes my mum wears, i.e., charity shop cardigans and long hippie skirts; a younger woman with short spiky hair with pink streaks through it and a nose ring;

a slim blonde who was sitting on the end of her bed in a meditation pose with her eyes closed; and finally, a very plump lady with big teeth who was helping herself to a sandwich and a flask of tea. They glanced up at us when we walked in and the plump one gave us a wave.

"Hi, I'm Moira," she said, then indicated the beds with a sweep of her hand. "You got any preferences about where you want to sleep?"

"As far away from here as possible," whispered Mrs. Foster, turning away. "Izzie, I don't think I can do this."

"Oh, come on, Mum. It'll be fun. Like a sleepover for adults."

"Yes . . . fun," said Mrs. Foster, unconvinced.

Izzie and I bagged the bunk bed in the corner, leaving Mrs. Foster to take the bunk above Moira. It was hysterical. Everyone stared at her as she unpacked and took over the whole wardrobe with her clothes. When that was full, she hung even more on the board at the end of her bed and the one at the end of our beds.

After half an hour, Chris popped her head round the door. "When you've finished, we'll be serving herbal teas in the dining room, then we'll all get together for introductions and to go through the schedule."

"Herbal tea?" said Mrs. Foster, wrinkling her nose

up. "I'd kill for a decent cup of coffee after that drive."

"Caffeine," spat the slim blonde. "It raises the heart rate and *we've* come to relax."

Moira winked at Mrs. Foster. "Hence the flask," she whispered. "Sometimes I have to have a proper cuppa. Anyone want an egg and cress sarnie?"

Poor Mrs. Foster looked as though she'd landed in a prison camp.

"Come on, Mum, let's go and meet the others," said Izzie, leading her out the door.

In the dining room, the men had already gathered and were sitting about sipping mugs of tea.

"Bit bare," said Mrs. Foster, glancing round at the brick walls, long pine tables, and benches. "When the ad said get back to basics, it really did mean it."

"Oh . . . my . . . God . . . ," whispered Izzie, looking round at the men. "Which one do you want?"

There were five men including Dad, who was chatting to Chris by a hatch to the kitchen. One of them was bald and very fat, and was sweating profusely in a lime green shell suit. Another had gray grizzly hair, trousers that were too short, and open-toed sandals. The third man was wearing a T-shirt and a sarong, and had blond dreadlocks down his back. And the fourth was about six-foot-six, very skinny, and was dressed in Lycra cycling shorts to show off his very knobbly knees.

"I'll have one of the wrinklies," I whispered back. "You can have Mr. Dreadlock, so that leaves Cycling Shorts for your mum."

Mrs. Foster overheard. "Thanks a bunch," she said, then giggled. "And, ahem . . . those shorts don't leave much to the imagination, do they?"

"Mum," said Izzie in a stern voice. *"Behave."* But I could see that she was relieved that her mum was beginning to chill out a bit.

As we sat down to drink our chamomile tea, Chris came over to join us. "I know everyone's a bit older than you," she said to Izzie and me, "but my son Daniel will be here tomorrow. He's sixteen, so at least you'll have some company around your own age."

"If he's anything like this lot, I can't wait to meet him. *Not,*" whispered Izzie when Chris had moved on to chat to some of the others. "Wonder if he's an open-toed-sandal type or an anorak?"

"As long as he doesn't wear cycling shorts," I joked. But I didn't really care. I was starting to enjoy myself even though the assorted guests looked like a bunch of weirdos and were all loads older than us. I didn't feel like I was Single here. I was just Lucy. And Izzie was just Izzie again, not Izzie and Ben.

After tea and rye biscuits that tasted like cardboard, Chris asked us all to sit in a circle and then threw a beach ball at my dad.

"Okay," said Chris. "Whoever has the ball, say a little about yourself, why you're here, and what you hope to get out of the weekend. When you've had your say, throw the ball on."

Mrs. Foster looked like she was going to throw up. "I hope we don't all have to hug each other after this," she whispered to Izzie.

"Hi. I'm Peter Lovering," said Dad. "I'm from London and I run a health shop. I'm here for the rest and relaxation."

Everyone murmured their approval as Dad threw the ball at the slim blonde who'd been meditating in the bedroom.

"Hi, I'm Sylvia. I'm striving for a pure mind and body and I'm a colonic irrigation specialist." More murmurs of approval, but I couldn't resist.

"That must be a crap job," I whispered to Izzie, whose shoulders started to shake with suppressed laughter.

"I'm Moira and I've just got divorced so it's all been rather stressful for me of late. . . . I do Swedish massage."

"For when you need to be kneaded," I said to Izzie.

"I'm Priscilla," said one of the gray-haired ladies. "I work as a gardener and I need to find myself."

I didn't have to say anything this time as Izzie turned to me and coughed, "Doesn't need to go far, then. She's right on that chair!"

"I'm Jonathan, but my friends call me Tabula," said Dreadlocks. "My third eye was recently opened on a trip to Goa. I need to close it again as I can't take the inner visions. . . ."

I couldn't look at Izzie for fear of bursting out laughing.

"I'm Nigel," said Cycling Shorts. "I want to get some fresh air."

"Shouldn't wear his shorts so tight, then," was my comment this time.

"Hi, I'm Grace," said Pink Highlights, "and I work as a vegetarian cook and wanted some time out for me."

She threw the ball to Izzie.

"I'm Izzie," she said. "I'm fourteen. I'm into astrology, crystals, feng shui, aromatherapy, and self-help. I've come with an open mind." Murmurs of approval. "Oh, and I'm also into witchcraft." After which the murmurs of approval turned to looks of concern, especially from her mother.

She threw the ball at her mum. "I'm Laura Foster. I work in the financial sector in the city and, as my daughter keeps telling me," she smiled at Izzie, "I need to find some balance in my life."

She threw the ball at me. "I'm Lucy. Um . . . ," I said, turning bright red. I couldn't say that I'd just come along for the ride and wanted an excuse to spend some time hanging out with my mate. "Er, um, I . . . whatever. Open mind, see what happens. Yes . . . um, that's all." I threw the ball at the second gray-haired lady, but I must have thrown it harder than I intended, as it knocked her glasses off. "Ohmigod, sorry, I'm sorry." I leaped up. "Are you all right?"

She adjusted her glasses and gave me a filthy look. "I'm Prudence. I work in a school library and need to get away from all the noisy kids I have to deal with every day."

Oops, I thought. Made a friend for life there, then.

Next was Hubert, the bearded man. He was an osteopath.

"I bet he knows how to have a cracking good time," I said to Izzie.

Then Eric, the bald man, said he was there because his wife said she'd leave him if he didn't learn how to relax.

"Well, you've all come to the right place," said Chris, getting up and handing out a sheet of paper to each of us.

"Okay," she said. "Tonight we're not going to do much—just let you settle in and relax—then tomorrow, we start. The schedule is there on your paper, so take a quick look and do ask if there are any questions."

I glanced at the paper.

> 6.00 A.M.: *yoga salute to the sun, and*
> *meditation*

"Six A.M.," I said to Izzie. "You mean there are two six o'clocks in a day?"

Izzie punched my arm. "And you'll be up, if I have anything to do with it."

"But the weekend's about relaxation. We ought to be having a lie-in." I looked back at the paper.

> 7.00 A.M.: *breakfast*
> 8.00 A.M.: *brisk group walk*
> 10.00 A.M.: *tea*

I got as far as ten thirty and I had to bite my tongue to stop myself from bursting out laughing. It said that there was to be a talk about overcoming dependency and leaning on things that weren't good for you, like cigarettes and alcohol. It was called Kick Your Crutch in Devon. Izzie had also seen it and I could see she was trying to contain herself as well. Her shoulders were heaving up and down as she continued down the schedule.

12.30 P.M.: *lunch*
2.00 P.M.: *massage workshop*
3.30 P.M.: *tea*
4.00 P.M.: *group counseling session*
6.00 P.M.: *group visualization*
7.00 P.M.: *supper*
8.30 P.M.: *"Cookery for Calm" demonstration,*
    then a relaxation game and wind down.

"I like the look of the lunch," I said to Izzie.

"No. It's all going to be brilliant," she said. "Especially when we get to kick our crutch."

That set us both off again and I had to leave the room pretending that I was having a coughing fit.

Don't blame me, I'm from Uranus

Om Mani Padne Bum

Mrs. Foster lasted one night.

While the rest of us were cross-legged in the meditation room the next morning, chanting *"om mani padne hum,"* she was on her mobile, frantically trying to find the nearest five-star hotel with an en-suite bathroom. And Jacuzzi.

"I'm sorry," said Izzie at breakfast. "I think Prudence and Priscilla's synchronized snoring was the last straw. Then when Moira started breaking wind for Britain . . ."

"I know. Must have been last night's soy burgers and cabbage. But no biggie. At least you'll be here most of the time."

Izzie looked sheepish. "We're going straight after breakfast. She wants to make sure we have a decent room. I'll make her come back once we've checked in, though. Probably after lunch."

And so Izzie and Mrs. Foster disappeared down the lane leaving me to kick my crutch on my own.

We started with the walk, which was fine until Chris made us stop on the outskirts of the village to do stretch exercises. There were a bunch of local kids hanging about near a telephone box and they seemed to find the assorted weirdos straining to reach their toes highly amusing. I wanted the ground to give way and swallow me up.

After that, it was the talk about kicking your crutch. It was interesting in the end, but it wasn't half as much fun as it would have been if Izzie was there to sit at the back and giggle with. The lecturer talked about time management then gave all sorts of alternatives to having a gin and tonic and a cigarette after work or stuffing yourself with food when you feel miserable. I suppose chocolate and ice cream are my crutches when I'm low, but I reckon that if you don't overdo it, sometimes a crutch can help, especially if it's made of double pecan fudge.

After an uninspiring lunch of nut roast and lentils,

there was still no sign of Izzie or her mum so I went back to the dorm and rang her on my mobile.

"When are you coming back?" I asked.

"Oh, Lucy, I'm so sorry. Mum loves it here and I have to say it is pretty cool. Huge beds, ginormous bathroom, comfy sofas everywhere with all the latest magazines. You'd love it—all the glossies, *Vogue*, *Tatler*, and *Harpers* and . . ."

"Yes, but when are you coming back to the prison camp?"

"That's just it," said Izzie. "They have a beauty salon here and Mum's booked herself in for a pampering afternoon. She says this is more the kind of weekend she had in mind. Total indulgence and lying about being waited on. I am sorry. You know I'd love to be there with you, but she's booked me in for a manicure this afternoon."

I looked around at our sparse dorm that now smelt of Moira's egg and cress sandwiches. I couldn't help wishing that Mrs. Foster had taken me as well. In fact, I was beginning to wish I hadn't come at all, considering it was Izzie's idea in the first place.

"Look," said Izzie reading my thoughts, "you have to come and see this place. Why don't you skip the session after tea and come down here. It's not far. Just left of the village that you can see at the bottom of the hill. Ask for Montbury Lodge if you get lost. Big old hotel overlooking the bay."

"Fantastic," I said, my spirits starting to rise again. "I'll be there."

Maybe I could have tea and scones and Devonshire clotted cream. Lie back on a big squashy sofa and read the new *Vogue*. The weekend was looking up after all.

I trooped along with all the others into the meditation room for the massage session, thinking that at least this should be enjoyable. Maybe not as luxurious as the hotel, but it would be a massage nonetheless.

After the teacher gave us a demonstration, we put mats out on the floor and I got paired with Prudence. It was my turn to massage first, so I held up the towel so that she could get undressed in privacy. She lay on the mat and I gave her a gentle massage. Nesta would have had a fit if she'd seen her, I thought as I rubbed her legs. She hadn't shaved or waxed in years and her calves were as hairy as a man's.

Then it was her turn to do me. I lay on the mat and closed my eyes, ready for a nice relaxing massage. Unfortunately, however, Prudence clearly saw it as a way to get revenge for me knocking her glasses off last night. Or maybe even revenge on all the kids that had ever annoyed her in the library. She was of the builder's school of massage. Slap, whack, hammer, as hard as she could.

This is *not* my idea of fun, I thought as I lay there with my neck twisted to one side while some mad woman with hairy armpits used me as a way to vent her anger. Dad didn't seem to be enjoying it much either, as he had the bald man massaging him and he appeared to have studied at the same massage school as Prudence.

It seemed that everyone had taken great care to make sure that not too much flesh was exposed and that they were warm and covered in towels. Except Cycling Shorts, that is. He seemed to have no inhibitions at all and was walking about in a pair of faded blue jockey shorts. I quickly closed my eyes and couldn't help but think once again what a laugh we'd have had if Izzie had been there. As Prudence yanked my leg out of my hip, I twisted my neck the other way and looked at my watch. Twenty minutes to go. Argh argh *arrghhh*.

Dad had no objection to my opting out of the group counseling session when I told him I wanted to go to find Izzie.

"I guess you get enough psycho babble round the kitchen table at home, so fine, go," he said. "In fact, I'll give you a lift down there."

When we got down to the village, we asked where the hotel was, and he dropped me in a small square in front of a drive lined with rhododendron bushes that led up to the hotel.

"There it is," he said, pointing at a gate with a brass sign that read MONTBURY LODGE. "Can you make your own way back or ask Mrs. Foster to drop you? Any problems, call me on your mobile. I . . . um . . . have a few things I have to do before I go back."

As I made my way up to the hotel, I turned back to wave him off, but he'd already parked the car and was heading with a determined walk to a building on the left of the square. I had to laugh when I saw what it was. The King's Arms, the local pub.

I felt slightly intimidated as I went into the reception of the hotel as it looked so grand. Then I remembered what Nesta always told me when I felt like this—that people can only ever make you feel inferior if you give them permission. I belong here as much as anyone, I thought as I pulled myself up to my full four-foot-nine. I approached the desk and pressed the bell. I looked around at the enormous marble fireplace, deep sofas, polished furniture, and huge vases of fresh lilies everywhere. A few guests were sitting in a bay window in reception and helping themselves to a cream tea. Excellent, I thought, in anticipation of the one I'd be having in about fifteen minutes.

"Can I help you?" asked a lady with glasses appearing behind the desk.

"Yes, I'm here for Mrs. Foster and her daughter," I said.

"You just missed them," said the lady. "They went out about fifteen minutes ago. Would you like to leave a message?"

"Um, no thanks," I said, and made my way out and down the long drive again.

Why hadn't she phoned me? I wondered as I reached the gates and rooted round in my bag for my mobile. I couldn't find it and realized that I must have left it back in the dorm when I'd called Izzie earlier. I looked to see if Dad's car was still there and saw that he had just got in it and was about to drive away. I darted out of the gate and smack, I crashed right into someone who was walking past talking to someone on a mobile. His phone went flying out of his hand and landed on the pavement.

"*Oi!* Watch where you're going," he cried as he bent down to pick up the phone.

"Oh, sorry," I said. "I'm so sorry. Are you okay?"

"I am, but I'm not sure that my phone is," said the boy, pressing a few keys and putting the mobile to his ear.

"I, er, didn't mean to . . . ," I said as I saw Dad driving away in the distance. "I was . . ."

"Yeah, you were daydreaming."

"I was trying to catch my dad, actually," I said. Then he turned to face me properly and I had to catch my breath. He was *cute*. Actually more than cute, *très* handsome. Blond, with very blue eyes and cheekbones to die for. "Is your phone okay?"

He dialed a number and began to walk away. "Yeah. No thanks to you."

Probably the local village heartthrob, I thought. Probably got a million girls after him. Not this one, though. I made a face at his back. I don't like boys who can't at least make an effort to be nice, no matter how good-looking they are.

9

Big Brother

There were three messages on my mobile from Izzie when I got back to the dorm.

"Mum's bumped into a friend from the city," said the first one. "She was having a facial in the hotel salon. Anyway, she's got a second home down here and has insisted that we go for dinner. So don't come down today. Ring me to let me know you got the message."

"Where are you?" said the second. "Mum says you can come as well, so call me. We're leaving in about half an hour."

"We're on our way," said the third. "I hope you got the messages. Call me as soon as you get this."

I phoned her straight away and explained that I'd been down to the hotel and missed her.

"Oh, I'm so sorry, Lucy. I feel awful, especially as I talked you into doing this course in the first place. Look, Mum's going out with her friend Kay tomorrow and I don't want to hang out with them so I'll be up first thing to spend the day up there. You okay?"

"Yeah," I said. "I'll survive. It's group visualization tonight then wind down or something."

"Sounds fab. I love doing visualizations. I wish I was there."

"And I wish I was there," I said, and told her all about the day's events and classes. "It would have been a hoot if you'd been here."

"I know," she said. "I feel rotten about leaving you there. But I'll make it up to you in the morning, okay?"

"Okay."

After the phone call, I went along to the meditation room where the others were already lying on the floor on mats. Chris had put a few candles about and lit some joss sticks and in the background there was some soft new age music playing. The room was cozy and warm and the mats looked very inviting. This I can do, I thought as I crept in, lay down by the door, and closed my eyes.

Chris's soft voice began to lead us through the visualization. "Feel yourself getting drowsy, safe, and relaxed. Your body is feeling heavy, your limbs feel limp and warm. The only sensation you are aware of is your breath, rising and falling like gentle waves on a shore. You feel at peace, relaxed, warm, heavy. . . ."

I was asleep in seconds. Next thing I knew, the lights were being turned up and the session was over.

"That was brilliant," said Sylvia. "I went somewhere really lovely—a garden and the sea. . . . How was it for you, Lucy?"

"Um, yes, very relaxing," I said, rubbing my eyes. I didn't feel too bad, though, as it looked like I wasn't the only one who had nodded off. Half of the guests were still comatose on the floor, Moira was dribbling onto her mat, and Prudence and Priscilla were doing their synchronized snoring again. As everyone began to get up and shuffle off to the dorms, I became aware of a figure on a mat at the front of the room. He hadn't been there in the day and he was sitting with his back to me. Oh, must be Chris's son, I thought as I got up to leave. Then he turned and looked up. My jaw dropped when I saw who it was. The boy from the village whose phone I'd knocked flying.

"You," he said, getting up and coming over to me.

"*You,*" I said.

"Daniel, this is Lucy. Lucy, this is Daniel," said Chris, joining us.

"Yeah," said Daniel, looking really disinterested, "we met already. Or rather we *bumped* into each other in the village."

I went bright red and made a beeline for the door. Dad followed me out and caught up with me in the hall.

"That wasn't very friendly," he said. "Where are your manners?"

"Where are *his,* more like," I said. "I accidentally bumped into him in the village, and when I apologized, he was really offhand."

"Come on, Lucy," said Dad. "This isn't like you. You have to make some effort."

"Right," I said, thinking, no way I'm making an effort with him, not until he learns to accept an apology with grace.

I went back to the dorm where it appeared that romance was in the air. Grace, Priscilla, and Moira were all sitting on Moira's bunk giggling like schoolgirls. Apparently, Grace had taken a shine to Jonathan—or

Tabula, as he liked to call himself. Moira had swapped numbers with Cycling Shorts and Priscilla had a date with Hubert the osteopath.

"Where's Sylvia?" I asked, thinking that maybe I could have a chat with her or a game of backgammon or something.

"Gone back to London to look after a friend who was having a healing crisis," said Prudence from her bunk, where she was eavesdropping on the others' conversation while pretending to read. She looked put out that Priscilla had got a date and she hadn't.

So it's me and you, pal, I thought. The singletons. I felt lonely there without Izzie to talk to and wondered whether to go over and try to be friendly to Prudence. But she was definitely in a sulk. She put earplugs in and began to read a book. This is like being on *Big Brother*, I thought, and you, dear Prudence, would be the first to be voted off.

In the end, I decided to get an early night. It had been a long day and we had another six A.M. start the next morning.

Izzie was true to her word and turned up straight after breakfast on Sunday. She was flushed with excitement as she slid in beside me at the breakfast table.

"Lucy, I've just met Daniel. Have you seen him? He's drop dead gorgeous. And so sweet. We must find out if he's single for you."

"Oh, Izzie, give me a break. I thought we'd left all that 'Let's-pair-Lucy-off' nonsense back in London. I *have* met him and I don't like him."

At that moment the dining room door opened and Daniel came in. He moved among the guests, chatting, smiling, and fetching them whatever they wanted from the breakfast hutch.

"What's not to like?" asked Izzie as she watched him move round the room. "He seems really friendly and he dresses nicely."

I glanced over at him. He did look cool in his black jeans and black T-shirt. He helped himself to a bowl of muesli, then came over to the end of the table where we were sitting.

"Hi," he said, smiling at both of us. "Anything I can get you?"

I shook my head.

"I've already eaten, thanks," said Izzie. "But please, sit with us."

I made a mental note to kill her later.

He looked over at me. "I guess we got off on the

wrong foot yesterday, didn't we?" Then he grinned. "Or at least *you* did."

Oh, here he goes again, I thought. "I *said* I was sorry."

"I know. And the phone's fine. So let's pretend it never happened and start again. So, hi, I'm Daniel. And my mum runs this course for escaped lunatics."

Izzie burst out laughing and I glanced up and looked at him properly. He was very good-looking and he had made an effort to be friendly. Maybe I should give him another chance.

"And I'm Lucy Lovering," I said. "I'm here with my dad."

"How are you finding the weekend?"

"Um . . ."

Daniel grinned, then whispered. "Slow torture?"

"It's more Izzie's thing," I said diplomatically. "Though I did enjoy the visualization last night."

"So did I," he said. "Great excuse to have a kip. And did you hear all that snoring?"

I was beginning to warm to him.

"So what are you into?" he asked.

"Oh . . ."

"Fashion," said Izzie. "Lucy's a fantastic designer. She makes loads of her own stuff."

"You're kidding," said Daniel. "That's what I want to do

when I leave school. I want to go to the London School of Fashion, then go and work in Milan or Paris."

"Really?" I asked.

After that, we were off. We discovered that we had loads in common and, like me, he knows all the famous designers and places to get offcuts of fabric, and often goes down to Portobello to trawl round the vintage clothes shops.

I decided to test his sense of humor and told him my latest favorite joke. "A man is driving down a country road," I said, "when he spots a farmer standing in the middle of a huge field of grass. He pulls the car over to the side of the road and notices that the farmer is just standing there, doing nothing, looking at nothing. The man gets out of the car, walks all the way out to the farmer and asks him, 'Excuse me, mister, but what are you doing?' The farmer replies, 'I'm trying to win a Nobel Prize.' 'How?' asks the man, puzzled. 'Well, I heard they give the Nobel Prize . . . to people who are out standing in their field.'"

He cracked up laughing. "Okay, I've got one for you," he said.

"What do you call a French man wearing sandals?"

"Dunno," I said.

"Philippe Philope."

I went down my wish list mentally. Sense of humor? Check. Into fashion? Check.

Izzie sat watching us with a sly smile, like she was a satisfied mother whose children were playing happily together.

Absence makes the heart grow fonder *(of somebody else)*

10

Shiatsu Shmiatsu

Izzie was the first to point it out.

"He's exactly the boy on your wish list," she whispered as we sat at the back of an aromatherapy demonstration in the morning. "He's gorgeous, medium build, fit-looking, sense of humor."

"But he may have a girlfriend, for all we know," I said, taking one of the bottles of oils that was being passed round and inhaling deeply.

Izzie grinned. "He hasn't. I asked him when you went to get your fleece after breakfast."

"Izzie," I said. "What will he think?"

"He likes you," she said. "He asked loads of questions about you. And he doesn't live far from us. His mum runs a clinic in Chalk Farm, so they're just down the road."

"Really?" I glanced over at Daniel, who was sitting two rows in front. Could Izzie's wish list really have worked?

After the aromatherapy session, Chris taught us a Chinese form of self-massage called Do-In. It was hilarious, as the technique seemed to consist of us having to beat ourselves up. Sort of.

"Clench your hand into a fist," said Chris, "and with a loose wrist, tap along the top of your shoulder, the side of your neck and as far down your back as you can reach."

We all did as we were told, tapping along our shoulders, then legs and arms and it did seem to wake us all up. Everyone appeared to be in a better mood afterward and the atmosphere had lightened considerably since yesterday. Daniel kept catching my eye and making daft faces as though he was in agony every time he hit himself.

Next we did shiatsu massage on our faces. We learned various points to press on, along the temple, jaw line, and the sinuses, and I started to feel really good.

"This is brilliant, isn't it?" said Izzie, prodding along her eyebrow line. She seemed to be enjoying it all immensely.

I nodded and looked over at Daniel. Maybe the workshop had something to offer after all.

Next on the schedule was reflexology and, as in the massage class the day before, Chris told us to pair off. Great, I thought, this time I'll be with Izzie instead of Heavy Hands. But Izzie saw Daniel glance over at me and she turned to Moira.

"How about I go with you?" she asked her, then called to Daniel. "Hey, Daniel, Lucy needs a partner."

I went scarlet. Sometimes my friends have no shame.

Daniel came straight over. "I'll do you first," he said. "Lie back and take your trainers off."

I lay on the mat and went even redder as he slid my socks off and dusted my feet with talc.

He smiled as he held my feet in his hands. "Little feet."

"I know," I said. "I hate being so small sometimes. All my friends are really tall. I'm the midget."

"Good things come in small packages," he said, still smiling. "Personally, I like small girls."

Ohmigod! I thought as I mentally checked off another thing on the wish list—likes petite.

As he followed his mum's instructions, I closed my eyes and drifted off into seventh heaven. His touch was so different from Prudence's. He was gentle and firm at the same time. I must add this to my list, I thought. Boy who can do a good foot massage.

"You've done this before, haven't you?" I asked.

He nodded. "Mum taught me. It's nice, isn't it?"

I nodded. "Heaven."

After twenty minutes, we swapped places and I was relieved to find that his feet were clean with neat toenails. It would have been such a disappointment if he'd had smelly feet like my brother Lal's. I began the massage and glanced at his face to make sure I wasn't pressing too hard. He was lying back with his eyes wide open, looking up at me. I blushed furiously as a bolt of electricity went straight through me.

"Close your eyes," I said.

"Why?"

"You're making me nervous."

"Good." He smiled, but he did as I asked and closed his eyes for the rest of the session. This is a new one, I thought. It's strange, but massaging someone's feet can be as much fun as snogging. Hope Dad's not watching, I thought as I quickly glanced over to where he was.

Luckily he was busy massaging Prudence's feet and hadn't noticed his daughter flirting with feet only two meters away.

Izzie looked over at me from where she was being massaged by Moira. She made her eyes go cross-eyed and pulled a face. So it wasn't so much the massage, but the person doing it with you. I thought back to the session yesterday and thanked God Daniel hadn't been there then. I think I would have died if I'd had to strip off and have him massage my back. Although, when I thought about it, it made my stomach go funny, but in a nice way.

By lunchtime I was floating on air and I wasn't sure whether it was all the treatments or whether it was Daniel.

"I think I may be in love," I said to Izzie as we tucked into a lentil cheese loaf.

"Thought so," she said. "I saw the way you two were looking at each other in that last session."

"I know," I said. "I'm going to add 'can do foot massage' to my perfect-boy list. A definite requisite from now on."

I was looking forward to the afternoon session and hoped that it would be more nice treatments. Then I'd have another chance to pair off with Daniel.

* * *

I soon realized that wasn't to be.

"This afternoon, we're going to start with an exercise to vent your pent-up emotions," said Chris.

But I feel great, I thought. I haven't got any, so this is going to be a waste of time for me.

"It's a way to release anger or frustration that you can't express," continued Chris. "The sort of feelings that if held in, can gnaw away at your peace of mind. I believe that negativity is better *out* than in, so now is your chance to let it all out."

"Cool," said Izzie, giving me a meaningful look. "Unfinished business."

"You can't yell at your boss," Chris said, then looked at Iz and me and grinned. "Or your teacher or headmistress, maybe. So I'd like you to pick a cushion from the pile in the corner, then project onto it whatever or whoever has made you angry in the past—a lover, a parent, a colleague, a neighbor, a friend, or even God. As it is sometimes not appropriate to let your anger out at the person directly, this is a way to free yourself of it without any repercussions."

"Excellent," said Izzie, heading for the pile.

I reluctantly went to pick a cushion with the others. The idea seemed a bit mad to me.

"Okay," said Chris, "now let rip. You can throw your cushion, kick it, stomp on it, whatever you feel. Let your inhibitions go."

Izzie picked a red cushion and started laying into it with passion.

"Poor cushion," I said. "What's it done to you?"

"I'm imagining it's all the terrorists who have killed innocent people," panted Izzie as she jumped up and down on it. "It makes me so mad sometimes, as I feel so helpless and *angry* that I can't do anything."

Izzie's always thinking about the problems of the world.

"Who are you going to beat up?" she asked, stopping for a moment to catch her breath.

I looked at the cushions. "Someone closer to home." I grinned and picked a brown velvet one—the exact color of Tony's eyes.

At first, everyone was a bit shy, then Moira started getting into it. Then Cycling Shorts joined in. Then Eric and Tabula, and then *my dad*! After ten minutes, the place sounded like a madhouse. Everyone got stuck in. I quickly glanced round to see what Daniel was doing as I didn't want to look an idiot in front of him, but he was going for it like the rest of them. If you can't beat them, join them, I thought, and got down on my knees and pummeled my cushion. I felt stupid to start with, then I began to get into it. That's for dumping me, I thought as I whacked the cushion. And that's for turning up at that party with another girl. . . . *Whack! Thwump!*

At the end of the session I felt brilliant. Like a dam had burst. Everyone looked exhilarated, even Prudence, whose hair had escaped her bun and was sticking out all over the place. We should have done this session before the massage, I thought. It wouldn't have been so painful for me if she'd done this first. Chris was right. I hadn't known all those feelings were stuck inside. I felt much better about Tony. I knew that I'd be able to handle it if I saw him at Nesta's. We could, as he always wanted, be friends.

"I'm so fed up," said Izzie as we filed out of the room when it was over. "I've got to go back to the hotel for the evening and I'll miss the lecture. It's about Bach Flower Remedies and I'm really into those."

"I'll tell you all about it," I said as Daniel caught up with us.

"Maybe we could go for a walk before the lecture," he said, and Izzie gave me the thumbs-up behind his back.

"Maybe after," I said. "But first I'm going to walk Iz back to her hotel."

My feelings about Daniel might have done a complete turnaround, but that didn't mean I'd forgotten everything that Nesta had taught me. Don't be too available. Don't be too easy.

I got back from the village an hour later, and after putting on a little makeup, went into the dining room. There was no sign of Daniel.

All through the lecture afterward, I kept looking at the door, expecting him to come in. But he didn't. Now what? I thought as I tried to concentrate on the talk. Was he peeved because I'd gone down to the hotel with Iz? Maybe he wasn't as nice as I'd thought he was. All my newfound inner peace evaporated like thin air as I watched the door.

"The Bach Flower Remedies are good for correcting any emotional imbalance," said Chris. "A lot of disease is literally that: dis-*ease*." Then she began reading a list of the remedies out and what they were good for. "Agrimony for mental torture behind a carefree mask, chestnut for failure to learn from mistakes, impatiens for frustration, mustard for gloom, scleranthus for mood swings, white chestnut for mental arguments, wild oat for uncertainty."

That's me, and that's me, I was thinking as she went down the list.

"You'll only need one or two of them," she said when she'd finished. "And they're on sale in the dining room."

After the talk, Chris was surrounded by people asking about the remedies, so I didn't get a chance to ask her where Daniel was. I went and found Dad instead.

"Can I have next month's pocket money as I want to buy some remedies?" I asked.

"Sure," he said. "Which ones do you want?"

"*All* of them," I said.

WARNING!
Next mood
swing in
5 minutes

11

Home Sweet Home

Dad wanted to leave at the crack of dawn the next day so that he'd be back in time to open the shop at nine thirty. He dropped me off at home first, and it felt wonderful to be back in the cozy clutter of our kitchen with only Steve and Lal at the breakfast table instead of a bunch of strangers. Mum had already left for work and Steve and Lal soon went off to play tennis, so apart from the dogs, I had the whole house to myself. It felt great to take a long, hot, foamy bath without a queue of people banging on the door. To make a decent cup of tea and toast and strawberry jam. As I wandered round the house, I felt that I was seeing everything in a new light. The telly in the living room I could sit in front of and watch whatever I liked. My lovely bedroom that I didn't have to share. My CD player. And there'd be no more getting up at six A.M. to contort myself into unnatural positions.

My bed was calling me, so I turned off my mobile, switched on the answering machine, and climbed under the duvet for a few hours of divine uninterrupted sleep.

"How was the course?" asked Mum when she popped in at lunchtime.

"Interesting," I said. "Some of it was a bit boring, but some of it was brilliant."

"What were the people like?"

"Mad. But actually by the end of it, they'd sort of grown on me. Even a grumpy old one called Prudence." Prudence had given me a huge hug when I left, as though I was her dearest friend. "It's fantastic to be home, though. It feels so quiet and comfortable and roomy and there's loads I can do here."

Mum smiled. "Did I ever tell you the story about the farmer who felt his house was overcrowded and went to see a wise man?"

I shook my head.

"I use it at work sometimes when I'm talking to people who are unhappy with their lot in life. Want to hear it?"

I nodded.

"A farmer was very unhappy with his home," she started. "He had a wife and two daughters and only one room. He went to a wise man and asked what he could do to improve the situation. The wise man told him to move in three dogs. So he did what he was told. The next day, the wise man told him to bring in the cow from the field and let it sleep with them. The farmer thought it was a bit strange, but again, did as he was told. The next day, the wise man told him to bring in the chickens. The next day, a few goats. By the end of the week, there was a whole farmyard living in the house and it was unbearable. The farmer went back to the wise man and asked him what to do next. First take out the dogs then the cow, said the wiseman. Then the next day, the goats, then the hens. The farmer did what he was told until he was back to the original situation. His wife and his two daughters and himself. He was over the moon. It felt so quiet and spacious and the farmer never felt unhappy again."

"Exactly," I said.

"Well, let's see how long the feeling lasts," Mum laughed. "And your dad called me from the shop. He said that Chris's son was at the course?"

"Yeah, Daniel. Creep."

"Why?"

"We were getting on brilliantly but then he just left, no message, nothing. Honestly, boys—you never know where you are with them."

Mum smiled. "Oh, I think you may hear from him sooner than you think. He phoned the shop today to ask for our number here."

"Really?" I felt my spirits lift in an instant and dashed to check the answering machine. There were two messages flashing.

"Hi, it's Nesta, call me when you get back," said the first.

"Hey, Lucy, it's Daniel," said the second. "Sorry I had to leave last night. I hope Mum gave you the message and told you what happened. . . . Anyway, I'll call again later."

Luckily I didn't have to wait long, as the phone went soon after Mum had returned to work.

"Hey," he said.

"What happened?" I asked. "I never got any message from your mum, but then we did leave first thing this morning, so I didn't see her."

"Flood," said Daniel. "Our neighbor phoned to say that a pipe had burst in his flat and was pouring water into ours. We're on the ground floor. Anyway, Eric was coming up to London at supper time so I cadged a lift. All sorted now, but I think I got here just in time. You must have been mad at me disappearing like that."

"No, not at all," I fibbed. "I had a fabulous evening. To tell you the truth, I didn't realize that you'd gone until after the lecture."

"Oh," he said, sounding a bit disappointed. "I was hoping you'd missed me. I missed you. I felt like we really connected down there and I'd like to see you again, if that's okay with you."

I grinned to myself. I loved the way he came straight out with it. No games, no pretending to be cool. We'd connected, and he wanted to see me again. I decided to be just as honest back.

"I'd like to see you again too. I really liked meeting you."

"I've got a few things to do this afternoon. How about this evening?"

"Fab," I said.

Life couldn't get better, I thought, after I'd put down the phone. I felt like I was floating on air. I was home. I had a date with Daniel. And there were weeks of the holidays left.

12

Truly, Madly, Deeply

The following Friday I met Izzie and Nesta at Ruby in the Dust.

"At last," said Izzie when I walked into the café. "We were going to put out a missing person's alert."

I grinned back at her. "Not missing, just been out a lot." I felt chuffed to be the one who'd been too busy to catch up, for a change.

"So, how's it going with dreamboy?" she asked as we took our favorite sofas at the window.

"Fantastic," I said. "I'm in *lurve*. . . . Truly, madly, deeply."

"What is this thing called *love?*" said Izzie.

"What? Is this thing called love?" I replied, joining in one of our games—seeing how many different ways you can say the same sentence.

"What is this thing called, luv?" said Nesta.

"What is this *thing* called love?" I said.

"But it's great," said Nesta, spooning the froth from her hot chocolate into her mouth. "You deserve a decent boyfriend after my horrible brother."

I'd had an amazing week with Daniel. We'd seen each other every day and decided to be like tourists in London. We went to the IMAX cinema in Waterloo, up on the London Eye, to the Victoria and Albert museum in Kensington to look at the costumes, to a photography exhibition at the Portrait Gallery, and we spent ages cruising all the boutiques in Bond Street and Knightsbridge. He knew so much about fashion and its history, and I felt I was learning loads from him as well as having a good time. The best thing, though, was that I felt safe with Daniel. Secure. He phoned when he said he would, he was never late, and he didn't play games about where I stood with him.

"He's as different from Tony as anyone ever could be," I said. "He's so romantic. And when I'm not with him, he sends me lovely text messages. Every day, sometimes five a day. Then on Wednesday when we were in Covent Garden, he bought me a rose and a little fluffy teddy bear. He said it reminded him of me."

"Aw, sweet," said Izzie. "I wish Ben would do stuff like

that. Knowing him, he'd probably say that kind of thing is all a commercial rip-off and the only people that benefit are the companies that make them for nothing."

"That's what Steve says about Valentine's Day," I said. "But I think it's mainly because he never gets anything. I bet he'll feel differently next year if T. J. sends him something."

Nesta looked sad. "Simon used to be all romantic with me when we first met, but lately, I don't know, it's like he's cooling off or something."

"No, he adores you," said Izzie.

Nesta shook her head. "Nah, I know the signs. Like I phoned him yesterday and he hasn't called back yet. In the beginning, he always called me straight back."

"I don't need to call Daniel," I said. "He always calls exactly when he says he will and sometimes even before. It's so fantastic not having to worry or wonder. You know, does he like me? Does he feel the same? I know he does."

I was about to launch into telling them about what a great kisser he was, but Nesta looked downcast and I thought that maybe I was being a bit insensitive.

"You're probably imagining it," I said. "No one in their right mind would go off you."

"Well, I only saw him once last week," said Nesta, then pouted. "It's been awful, and every time I called to talk to you, you were out with Daniel. And even you didn't return my calls."

"Don't be rotten, Nesta," said Izzie. "I bet that Lucy felt like that enough times when we were off with Ben and Simon, didn't you, Luce?"

"All in the past," I said. All those times when I felt I was billy loner were ancient history. I was so happy now. I felt bowled over by Daniel's attention and the fact that someone wanted to be with me so much.

"I've never been dumped before . . . ," Nesta started.

"Just because he hasn't returned one call doesn't mean he's going to dump you," I said. "He's probably been busy."

"Too busy to talk to me? To return one call? Get real. There's one thing I do know about and that's boys. And when boys want to be with you, you don't have to spend time agonizing over whether he will or won't call. If he wants to, he calls. What shall I do? Finish with him before he finishes with me? What?"

"Just play it cool for a while," said Izzie.

"I have. I only called twice, then I thought, No way I'm doing this. Reject is not a role I want to play."

I didn't know what to say. Usually it's me going to Nesta for advice not the other way around. But she did look fed up.

"It will be okay," I said, remembering something I'd heard my mum say on the phone to one of her clients. "All relationships go through down patches. It's probably just a phase and next week he'll be back banging on your door begging to see you."

"Yeah," said Nesta, making an attempt to brighten up. "Sorry I'm being a downer. So, when am I going to meet Loverboy?"

"Tomorrow, if you like. We're going to Notting Hill. We're going to go down to Portobello Market to look at the vintage clothes stalls. Do you want to come?"

"Yeah," said Nesta, cheering up immediately. "When the going gets tough, the tough go shopping. Anyway, I love it down there. What are you doing, Iz? Are you seeing Ben?"

Izzie shook her head. "Nah. Actually, I need some space from him. All we ever do is band stuff. I've been locked up in his garage all week. An afternoon with the girls sounds great. Shall we call T. J.?"

"No, I spoke to her," I said. "She's on her way back from Scotland and is going round to ours tomorrow to have the great reunion with Steve. Honestly, he's been like limp lettuce while she's been away."

"Right," said Izzie. "Tomorrow. That's settled then."

Daniel was waiting for me outside Ladbroke Grove tube and at first he looked disappointed when he saw that I'd brought the girls. Sweet, I thought. He wants me all to himself. He was all in black and looking gorgeous as usual. I felt proud to introduce him to Nesta as my boyfriend.

"So, Lucy tells us that you want to do fashion when you leave school," she said as we made our way to the market.

Daniel nodded and glanced at himself in a mirror in a window. "I've started already, actually. I did some designs for our end-of-year fashion show at school. Got first prize and the local paper came and did an article."

"Really," said Nesta. "We'd love to see them some time, wouldn't we?" She turned to Izzie, then back to Daniel. "Has Lucy shown you hers?"

But Daniel wasn't listening. He'd seen a shop with an interesting display and had taken my hand and hauled me off. "Sorry. Just got to show Lucy these designs," he called over his shoulder.

When we got to the market, Daniel insisted that he buy us all a drink and took us to a café he knew. He asked the girls what they wanted, then went to order.

"He didn't ask if you wanted anything," said Izzie.

I blushed. "Oh, I trust his choice. He knows so much about everything, even coffee."

Daniel came back a moment later with Cokes for Izzie and Nesta and double espressos for me and him.

"But you don't like espresso," said Izzie as I took a sip.

"It's what everyone drinks in Milan. It's an acquired taste," said Daniel. "She'll get used to it."

I might have been imagining, but I was pretty sure Izzie shot Nesta a "look."

As the afternoon went on, I could see that Nesta was feeling more and more miserable. She kept checking her mobile for messages and I don't think it helped that Daniel kept putting his arm around me and playing with my hair and kissing me at every opportunity. That's one of the things I like about him, it's like he's really proud to be with me.

After about an hour of Daniel and I running into shops and Daniel explaining to me why he thought this outfit worked and that one didn't, Nesta pulled me to one side. "Izzie and I are going for a wander on our own.

We feel that we're a bit in the way, so see you at the tube about four?"

"Yeah, cool," I said. I didn't mind. It meant I had Daniel to myself again.

Daniel walked me to the tube when it was time and gave me a really smoochy snog in front of the girls before letting me go.

As I watched him walk away, he kept turning back and waving until he'd disappeared round a corner. A moment later, my mobile bleeped that I had a text message. "Big hugs, little bear."

I showed it to the girls. "See what I mean? He's so sweet."

This time Nesta gave Izzie the funny look.

They've been talking about me, I thought. You don't hang around with mates as much as I do and not learn to pick up when stuff's not being said.

"Okay, so what's with the secret looks?" I asked as we went to buy our tickets.

"Nothing," said Nesta unconvincingly.

"What do you think of Daniel?"

"Um . . . he's very good-looking," said Izzie. I knew Izzie well enough to know that she was being diplomatic.

"Okay, spill," I said. "What have you been saying about us?"

"Well he is a bit all over you," blurted Nesta.

"Nesta," said Izzie. "They're in love."

"So, didn't you like him?" I asked.

"It's not that I didn't like him," squirmed Nesta. "It's just, well, I thought he was a bit arrogant. And a bit self-obsessed. He talked about himself all afternoon and never once asked anything about Izzie or me. And I lost count of the number of times he checked his appearance in a window."

Trust Nesta to say exactly what she thought. She can never hide her true feelings and sometimes it can sting.

"*Nesta,*" warned Izzie.

"Yeah, well, we could have been invisible for all he cared."

Ah, I thought, not being the center of attention is a new one for her. And she's clearly jealous because I have a boyfriend who's really into me and hers is cooling off.

"Well, I like him," I said. "And it's what I think that's important. It's me that's spending time with him. He's really great, you just need to get to know him better.

He's not like anyone I've ever met before. Um . . . *you* like him, don't you, Izzie?"

She shifted awkwardly. "He seems a bit different from when we were in Devon. But then so are you. You let him monopolize the whole afternoon, like that espresso—you *hate* strong coffee. And you went where he wanted and it was like, well, he was the only expert on fashion. Usually you have so much to say about it all and your designs are awesome. You were as quiet as a mouse all afternoon."

"I talk to him a lot. I do. And I like listening to him. I feel like he knows so much more than I. I'm really learning from him," I said.

"Just don't let him take you over," said Nesta. "Girls are either goddesses or doormats. Don't let him walk all over you."

"I *don't*," I said. "How can you say that?"

Izzie looked awkward again. "Nesta may have a point, Lucy."

"Why? What do you mean?"

"It's about Daniel," she said.

"What?"

"You might not like it."

"Oh, just *tell* me, Izzie."

"Well, remember Mark in the band? Ben's mate?"

I nodded. I'd met him at Ben's birthday.

"Well, he brought his girlfriend, Amy, along to rehearsal last night and she overheard me saying something about the weekend we had down in Devon. Anyway, she asked if I knew Daniel. I said, yes, my friend's going out with him. . . ." Izzie looked at me anxiously.

"And?"

"Well, she said poor you. Apparently she went out with him last year and said he was a real pain. She said it all started out well, then it all got too much. He followed her everywhere, started telling her who she could and couldn't see. . . ."

I was determined to stand up for Daniel. "Well, actually, I already know about her. But he told me that she was the pain, always running off to her friends the minute they beckoned."

"Well, she said to tell you to be careful and not to let him take over," continued Izzie. "She said he gets jealous if you even look at another boy. I hope you don't mind me telling you."

I shrugged. "No, course not. Anyway, she's an ex. Maybe she wasn't the right one for him. And besides, when does anyone ever have anything good to say about an ex-boyfriend? Maybe he dumped her and it's sour grapes."

"Yeah, that's probably it," said Izzie quickly. "It's whether you like him that counts."

"Exactly," I said with a quick glance at Nesta, who had kept very quiet for once.

"Um, yeah," said Nesta. "Sour grapes. You like him. That's what counts."

The tube journey home felt flat as we all sat lost in our own thoughts. It's not fair, I thought. I felt really hurt that they couldn't be happy that I'd met someone who really liked me. It was true that we always went where Daniel said, though. Was it possible I was turning into a mouse or a doormat around him? We *did* always talk about his designs and he still hadn't asked about mine. He was making the rules. But that was okay, I decided. It was my choice to go along with it and I'm not going to let what Izzie and Nesta think ruin it all.

13

Goddesses

Things didn't improve much with Izzie and Nesta the following week, and it felt like an invisible wall had gone up between us. I spoke to them as usual on the phone but we talked about other things—what was on telly, what was happening at home . . . everything except boy stuff. Izzie invited me and Daniel to go to watch her band rehearse, but Daniel said it was his idea of a nightmare, so I didn't want to force him. People are different, I told myself, with different interests. You can't make everyone like everything the same and we did have a good time on our own, hanging out and exploring London again, even if it was him who chose where we were going every day. It felt like I was having a proper grown-up relationship.

However, despite everything I told myself about it not mattering what the girls thought, a seed of doubt had been planted in the back of my mind. Part of me wondered if I was letting him take over and giving in to him too easily.

Thank God for T. J. She came over to see Steve one evening and came into my room to catch up.

"But I think he sounds great," she said after I'd filled her in on the latest. "You don't want some wimp who doesn't know what he wants or leaves it all up to you."

"Nesta says I have to be a goddess and not a doormat," I confided.

"Ah," said T. J., "but which goddess? There are loads of different types. There's Hestia, the goddess of the hearth, Athena, goddess of wisdom, Artemis, the huntress, Aphrodite the goddess of lurve and beauty . . . loads. What type of goddess do you want to be?"

Trust T. J. to know a whole list of them, I thought. She has a different way of looking at everything. Like she sees all the shades of grey in between the black and white.

"I think Nesta meant I should be the one calling the shots and not him," I said.

"I think it should be mutual," said T. J. "Like both of you decide. You do some things he wants and he does some things you want and you compromise on others."

"Well, it's not that I didn't want to do all the things we've been doing. We've had a great time."

"Then there's no problem," said T. J. "But why not try picking some things you'd like to do next and see how he takes it. If he goes along with it, hey, no biggie."

T. J. was right. When she'd gone I had a think about what I'd like to do with him in the coming days. Bring him into my world, I decided. Invite him home and show him my designs. Maybe a walk in Golder's Hill park. I could show him all the lovely flower displays they always have there. Maybe see a movie at Hollywood Bowl. Introduce him to our favorite cafés. I made a list, then called him to see if he wanted to come up to Muswell Hill and meet at Ruby in the Dust on Thursday.

"Love to," he said. "I'll count the hours as I'm missing you already."

Things were going to be fine.

"Bit of a dump, this," he said, looking round as I bagged the best sofa in the window at Ruby's. The girls and I think it's a good spot because it feels private yet you can sit and watch the world go by outside.

"No, it's not," I said. "It's got a lived-in feel. That's why we like it here."

"We?"

"Well, actually it's Nesta's favorite."

"And yours?"

"Um, mine? Er, I like loads of places, but we come here most."

He shook his head. "Sounds to me like you go along with your friends a lot."

"No, not really," I began to object.

"I'll take you somewhere with real style," said Daniel, then looked at me softly and pulled me toward him. "My little bear."

I snuggled into his shoulder, but I wished he'd call me something else. The nickname was beginning to jar. Little bear, it sounded so yucky.

Then my mobile rang. I'd decided that I'd keep my phone on as even though Nesta had put a dampener on Daniel, she was still a mate and going through a bad time. I got up and went to the ladies to take the call.

"Who was that?" he asked when I came back to sit down.

"Nesta," I said.

"What did she want?"

"We're all meeting up tomorrow," I said. Nesta had decided that she needed a consultation with Mystic Iz for a tarot card reading about Simon. Of course I wasn't going to miss that, plus I was interested to know what the cards said about Daniel and me. I didn't tell Daniel that, as some boys are a bit sniffy about fortune-telling.

"But I wanted to take you to see a movie," said Daniel.

"I am sorry. But, well, Nesta's having a bit of . . . er, boyfriend trouble, so . . . ." I didn't want to go into detail, as I thought it might be a bit disloyal to Nesta.

"You mustn't let your friends dump on you," Daniel interrupted. "The others will be there. Don't let her use you at her convenience. Like you're a dustbin for all her problems."

"It's not like that," I said, thinking he was being a bit unfair. I was beginning to get angry. He'd only met Nesta once. How could he possibly think she used me at her convenience? She was my mate and I felt that I ought to be there for her. Maybe his ex-girlfriend had been right. He had objected to her seeing her friends and now he was trying to stop me seeing mine. I was about to tell him how important my friends were when suddenly it occurred to me that he never talked about his friends. Maybe he didn't have any, with his attitude.

Then the phone went again. This time it was Izzie, phoning to check that I was going tomorrow.

"Can't you switch that off?" asked Daniel when I'd finished. "You're with me now and you don't need friends calling you every minute."

I decided not to be a doormat and stand my ground. "These are my best friends, Daniel. I want to be there for them and I'd expect the same from them."

I could see that he didn't like it and it didn't help that the phone went again five minutes later. This time it was T. J. checking in. Even though I took the call, I felt uncomfortable about it, as Daniel was starting to look bored. Maybe it would be easier to turn the phone off and pick up my messages when I got home.

"There, I've turned it off," I said.

"Good girl," said Daniel, putting his arm back around me. "Now, where were we?"

After that, we chatted about our plans for the rest of the holidays and he seemed quite happy to do things that I wanted as well as things he wanted. So Nesta was wrong. He wasn't a total control freak, and I guess it can be a bit annoying when someone's mobile is going off every other minute.

As we sat sipping our drinks and gazing out the window,

a stunning-looking boy with shoulder-length curly hair walked past. He was wearing a cool pair of sunglasses and looked Spanish.

"*Now,* he's got style," I said.

"Why? Do you fancy him?"

"No," I said. "I was only saying I thought he looked good." Last week, Daniel had commented on loads of girls and what they were wearing. It didn't mean anything.

Daniel snuggled up to me and nuzzled my neck. "I don't want you looking at *anyone* except me," he whispered.

Gerroff, said a voice in my head. I ignored it and took Daniel's hand. We were running out of holiday and I was determined to not let my inner arguments spoil our time together. Izzie says I have them because I'm a Gemini, the sign of the twins; hence the split personality. She's so right. Some days the twins get along just fine, but other times one of them is premenstrual and gets a bit stroppy.

But when I invited him to my house later that day, more cracks began to appear in my dreamboy. On opening the door, Ben and Jerry did their usual "Oh my long lost friend" routine, leaping up with their tails wagging and trying to lick Daniel's face. I could see he didn't like it, so I had to take them away and shut them in the kitchen.

They sloped under the table with their tails between their legs. As I closed the door, I glanced back at them and I swear Ben gave me the Nesta/Izzie disapproval look. Like, "Get rid of the killjoy, Lucy." It didn't bode well.

I took him upstairs where I'd laid out my designs on the bed to be ready for him to look at. I'd even dressed the dummy that Mum had found for me in a second-hand shop. I thought it made my work look really professional.

"So, what do you think?" I asked as he picked up the outfits and studied them. I was really proud of some of them, particularly a couple of the tops I'd made from velvet trimmed with lace.

"Yeah, nice," he said. "Very nice. But . . . well, I can't see your voice coming through. You know, like a singer or a writer has a voice. It's the same with designers. Their clothes should make a statement and be instantly recognizable when you see them. Like me—as you know, I only do designs in black or white. And I only wear black. Yours are too varied, not focused enough."

"Oh," I said, feeling gutted. I knew what he meant about designs having a voice or a signature, but I honestly thought that mine did. I always mixed old and new fabrics and my style was romantic but modern.

"You'll get there," he said. "These are very good for a

beginner. Do you mind me being so honest? I feel that it's important in a relationship, and I really want it to work with us. So no lies, no false praise."

"No, no, I'm into honesty. I think it's very important," I said, thinking, that it was one of the things that I'd written on my wish list, after all. But then I'd also written "likes animals" and Daniel had made it very clear downstairs that he didn't. Or maybe it was because he didn't want the dogs' muddy paws ruining his clothes.

Daniel stood back and looked at me. "Okay then, since we're being honest, I think you should grow your hair longer. That urchin style is, well, a bit passé now."

I felt hurt. I liked my hair short. So did everyone. Nesta said it suited my shape of face and made my cheekbones stand out. And no one's ever said anything negative about my designs. But I knew that part of learning is being able to take criticism, so I decided to be open-minded and listen to what he had to say. He had been doing it longer than me, after all.

He moved the clothes off the bed and slung them across the back of a chair. Then he chose a CD from my desk, put it in the player, and sat back on my bed to flick through my latest copy of *Vogue*. I sat on the end of the bed and turned to look at him. I'm not sure if I like you anymore, I thought suddenly. Then another voice said, You're just sulking because he doesn't like your clothes. Then the other voice said, Well, I don't like his. Only black or white. How boring. *Arghh*, I thought. Here we go again with the arguing twins.

"What sign are you, Daniel?"

"Cancer."

"That's the sign of the crab, isn't it?" I said as a voice in my head said, Yes. Crab, crab, crabby.

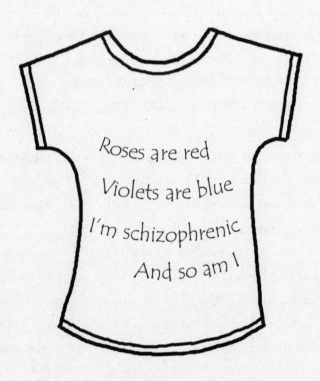

Roses are red
Violets are blue
I'm schizophrenic
And so am I

14

Tarot Readings

"And so gather the Witches of East Finchley," I said as we all sat on the floor in Izzie's bedroom ready to do the tarot cards.

She did Nesta's reading first and they didn't look good, even to me, who doesn't know what they all mean.

"It says there's a bit of a stormy time in love coming up for you," said Izzie, consulting the book, then pointing at a card with a picture of a pierced heart on it.

"Tell me about it," groaned Nesta.

"I am," teased Izzie. "It doesn't necessarily mean bad, though. Just a difficult time. And the last card is the World, and that's always a good one. It means a goal is attained. Success."

"Great," said Nesta. "Either way, I've decided to be

positive. I mean, Simon's the longest I've ever been out with anyone and he is going to university in a couple of weeks. Maybe we do need to cool off a bit so that I can go out with loads of other boys and not feel like I'm cheating."

My mum says that in life there are two types of people. Those who see a glass as half-full and those who see a glass as half-empty. Nesta's definitely a half-full type of girl.

T. J.'s cards were brilliant. Mostly cups, which the book said meant emotional happiness, then the Empress, which Izzie said meant a happy relationship.

"Excellent," said T. J.

Izzie's reading was more complicated. "I think it means that I'm unsure which way to turn," she said as she looked at the layout, then studied her book.

"What did you ask about when you shuffled the cards?" I asked.

"Ben," she said. "It's time to call it a day, but you know, I don't want to hurt his feelings."

"Why do you want to finish with him?" asked T. J.

Izzie shrugged. "Dunno, really. I still really like him, but hey, you know, we're far too young to be tied down."

"You sound like your mum," I said.

"Heaven forbid I ever turn into my mother," said Izzie. "Please, God, no. It's just, all we ever do is band stuff or write lyrics. I do like doing that but not all the time. I want to have a bit of fun as well."

I was dying to tell them about my last meeting with Daniel and ask them what they thought, but I already had a pretty good idea what Izzie and Nesta would say. Izzie would be all protective of me and want to phone him up and give him an earful for criticizing me and Nesta would simply say, "Dump him. Life's too short."

When they went downstairs to get snacks, I told T. J. in private about the day before.

"You're right," she said. "You do have to accept criticism but only if it's constructive. Your designs are fabulous and you have a great eye for color. There's room for everyone. I bet some of the most famous designers hate each other's designs, so it doesn't mean anything that he didn't like yours. Like, oh, I don't know their names but, say, that one who does bright colors?"

"Versace."

"Yeah, him. I bet he doesn't like the subtle ones who do, you know, like simple classical stuff. What's his name? The one that does the aftershave?"

"Armani, and Versace is a she now. Gianni was shot outside his home in 1997 and so his sister took over the business."

"See?" said T. J. "You know loads about the fashion world. I bet he doesn't know that."

"Everyone knows that, T. J."

"Do they? Oh, sorry. I'm not the one to talk to about fashion, am I?"

"Goddesses, yes; fashion, maybe no."

"But I do know that you have your own style and it suits you, Lucy. Remember when Nesta gave me that makeover and made me look like a Barbie doll? It wasn't me at all. It made me realize that you have to trust your own judgment about what suits you and not let others impose their ideas on you."

I laughed. She was right. "T. J., maybe you don't know the names, but I think that you know more than you realize."

T. J. looked at me with concern. "I hope you don't mind me asking, Lucy, but . . . well, it's just, you do seem different since you met Daniel and I wondered if . . . are you having a good time?"

"Yeah. I mean, I know we had a bit of a glitch when I showed him my designs, but apart from that, we've done loads of things together. I feel like I've discovered London. We've been everywhere."

"I know, but . . . you could do all that with anyone—with a teacher or your mum. I mean, do you have a good time, a laugh? Silly times and serious times when you really talk, you know, about what you want and all your plans? About how you feel?"

That made me think. We didn't really. He talked, or rather, lectured. He liked an audience and I did find what he had to say interesting. But no, we didn't talk about personal stuff, not really, and we certainly never got silly. I couldn't imagine Daniel being silly. He's far too busy trying to be sophisticated, I told myself. But that's what I like about him. He's different.

"Okay," said Izzie, coming back in with a huge box of Liquorice Allsorts. "Let's do Lucy's cards next."

Nesta followed her in carrying a tray full of tortilla chips and Pringles and Diet Cokes.

Izzie handed me the cards and told me to shuffle them while thinking about my question.

What's going to happen with Daniel? I thought. What's going to happen with Daniel? Then I laid out the cards as Izzie told me.

"Okay," she started. "Hmmm. The first card is the

Page of Swords." She flicked through her book then read what it said. "This card denotes a young man with a strong will. He's very clever, but can be ruthless and unconcerned about the feelings of others."

T. J. gave me a knowing look. I guess that's true, I thought. He wasn't very sensitive when he looked at my designs.

"And it's crossing the Page of Wands. Another boy. Oh, that's interesting. Hmmm, some kind of conflict coming up, I'm afraid, as there's the Lovers card as well."

"That's good, isn't it?" I said.

"It can be—let me just look it up," said Izzie, turning to her book again. "It says that you have a choice ahead of you, and the other cards are saying that you need to reassess."

Just at that moment, my mobile rang. "Daniel," I said.

"Just checking in," he said. "What are you wearing?"

"Oh, jeans and a T-shirt. It's only us here."

"Ah, but us designers, we're the ambassadors of style. Wherever we are, whatever we're doing."

Oh, get a life, said premenstrual twin in my head. Who does he think he is? The fashion police?

After that, we went downstairs to watch the latest wannabe superstar show. Talk about taking criticism, I thought as we watched some of the judges destroy people's performances. It was funny, though, especially a girl who sang "YMCA" really out of tune. Then Daniel phoned again.

"I miss my little bear," he said. "What are you doing?"

"Watching one of those pop star wannabe programs," I said.

"Oh, that rubbish."

"It's not rubbish," I said. "It's great."

"Well, you're obviously enjoying yourself, so I'll leave you to it," he said huffily. "When am I seeing you next?"

"I have to pick up some business cards for Mum in Hampstead tomorrow morning, so in the afternoon?"

"Great," he said. "We could go round Camden."

"Fine," I said. I wished he'd get off the phone so I could get back to having a laugh with the others as we watched the excruciating performances on DVD.

"Okay, going now. Miss you."

"Yeah," I said, then hung up. Whatever, I thought.

"He's really got it bad, hasn't he?" whispered T. J.

I nodded. The fact that he phoned so often was

starting to bug me. I was beginning to feel suffocated. I decided that next time I saw him, I'd take the bull by the horns and have a word about maybe giving each other a bit more space. After all, Mum's always saying that you have to work on relationships and not give up at the first hiccup. It was still early days for Daniel and me, and maybe it was going to take time to adjust to each other.

15

Page of Wands

The sun was shining with not a cloud in the sky the next day as I walked down Hampstead High Street. Everyone seemed to be enjoying the weather, dressed in light cottons and sitting about outside the cafés. I went and picked up Mum's cards from Rymans and decided to have a mooch in the shops. I still had an hour before I was due to meet Daniel.

Just as I walked past Café Rouge in the High Street, I heard someone call my name. I looked over the road and there was Tony waving at me. He crossed the road and came toward me.

"Hey, Lucy," he said.

"Hi," I said, blushing furiously. "How are you?"

"Good. Are you still speaking to me, then?"

"Yeah, course."

"I tried ringing you. . . ."

"I know. Um, sorry. . . ."

Tony looked around. "So, what you doing?"

"Not much." I showed him the bag with the cards in it. "Just picked these up for Mum, then I was going to have a wander round the shops."

"Let's go and get a drink and catch up, then," he said, linking his arm through mine. "I haven't seen you for ages."

We found a table outside the Coffee Cup and he ordered a Coke, then asked what I'd like.

"Hot black currant," I said, thinking, Thank God I don't have to drink another of those awful espressos.

"You're looking good," he said when the waitress had gone.

"So are you," I said. "Been out in the sun?"

He nodded. "So, Nesta tells me that you have a new boyfriend."

"Sort of. And you have a new girlfriend?"

"Sort of," he said. "Actually, no. That's over. Um, she doesn't know yet, though. I don't know how to tell her, but . . . nah, it's not working."

"Why?"

Tony shivered and pulled a silly face. "You know me,

I'm not really into having the big relationship. You know, the world of coupledom. And she, well, she's getting a bit serious, if you know what I mean. Always wanting to see me, like every day, and always phoning wanting to know what I am doing."

"Too clingy?"

"Yeah, I feel like she's taking over my life."

"Yeah," I said.

"So how's it going with you and what's-his-name?"

"Daniel." I shrugged. "Not sure. I mean, it was great in the beginning, brilliant, but . . . I don't know, still early days. But same thing, really. He wants to do the couple bubble thing, just us in there. I don't know if I like it."

Tony looked at me fondly. "*We* got on, though, didn't we?"

"We did." I smiled back at him. "And I'm sorry I overreacted when you . . . you know, that evening in Highgate. I hope we can be mates."

Tony put his hand on mine. "You bet. Always. I tell you what, we'll be like Hugh Grant and Elizabeth Hurley. They used to go out and they're still best of friends."

"Yeah," I said. "But you can be Liz and I'll be Hugh."

Tony laughed. I'd forgotten how easy he was to be with. Fun. Not like Daniel, I thought. Everything was so intense with him. And so serious.

"So this new bloke is clingy, is he?" said Tony, looking pleased.

"Yeah. Always wanting to know what I'm doing, where I'm going. I feel like he's always checking up on me."

"Like that boy over there," said Tony. "He's staring at you. You've got an admirer."

I glanced over to where Tony was looking and my heart stopped. It was Daniel. And he didn't look happy.

I waved and beckoned him to come over, then introduced Tony. The two boys nodded at each other.

"Sit down," I said. "Join us."

Daniel shifted about on his feet and seemed reluctant.

"Well, I was just off," said Tony, getting up.

He leaned over and gave me a kiss on the cheek. "See you soon, Lucy." Then he left me, but as he walked away, he turned back and gave me a look as if to say, *You're in trouble now, girl.*

He was right. Daniel took his seat and looked at me accusingly.

"So?" he said.

"So what?" I asked.

"Explanation?"

I didn't like his tone. "For what?"

"You said you were doing a job for your mum, then I find you holding hands with some boy."

"We weren't holding hands—well, not exactly. Tony's a mate. I haven't seen him for a while and we were catching up."

"Didn't look like that from where I was," said Daniel sulkily. "It looked like you were really into each other."

"I bumped into him when I came out of Rymans," I said, thinking, Why am I feeling so defensive? "Nothing was going on."

"Yeah, right," said Daniel.

"You know what?" I said, getting up. "You can think what you want."

Daniel caught my hand and pulled me back down. "No, sorry. Don't go, Lucy. It's just, well, it looked like you were having a really good time with him."

"I was," I said. "But we're mates, that's all. Do you think you can't trust me or something?"

"I guess I just want you all to myself," said Daniel, then grinned and said, "and who can blame me? I guess I get jealous."

"Well, there's no need."

"No need, as long as you promise not to see him again."

"*What?* No way. Anyway, he's Nesta's brother. I'll see him whenever I go to her house. Are you going to tell me I can't go there next?"

"No, but maybe I should go with you next time."

I stood up again. "You know what, Daniel? I don't think it's working with us. I don't like people telling me what to do all the time. And I don't like having to explain myself when I'm completely innocent. My friends mean a lot to me. And they include Tony, and if you don't like it, then too bad, because we're finished."

And with that, I left him sitting there with his mouth hanging open. Ha, I thought. Put that in your designer pipe and smoke it.

16

Dumpers and the Dumped

Instead of going home, I called Izzie. She was rehearsing with Ben near Highgate and was only too glad to have an excuse to get out for a break.

"Nesta's just called too. I said I'd see her in Raj's in half an hour," she said.

On the way over to meet her, I began to have second thoughts about Daniel. Had I been too hasty? Mean? Heartless? Just finished with the best boy I would ever find? I hoped that Izzie would make me feel better about it all, as it was my first experience of dumping someone.

As soon as Izzie appeared at Raj's, I filled her in on what had happened in the last week. It was such a relief to be able to talk freely to her again and I told her everything—what he'd been like when he came to my house and what had just gone on in Hampstead.

She looked shocked. "How could he say that about your hair and your designs? You're brilliant. I reckon he's jealous, because he can see you have more talent than he's got in his little finger."

"Anyway, I just finished with him," I said.

"Good," said Izzie. "What a creepoid. He's like an emotional bully. What a control freak. But are you okay?"

I nodded. "I think so. I don't know. I mean, some days we had a really good time. Maybe I shouldn't have been so hard on him. You know, with time, maybe I could have changed him."

Izzie shook her head. "My mum always says that the only time you can change a man is when he's a baby."

I laughed. "I guess. I was starting to feel like I had no space."

"Like that joke," said Izzie. "Boys are like dogs— give them a bit of affection and they follow you everywhere."

"Yeah, right," I said.

Izzie looked thoughtful. "It's never easy being the dumper. You feel rotten."

"Have you told Ben yet?"

"No. But I'm going to do it soon. I've been agonizing over it for days. I don't know what I'm going to say. There's no easy way, is there?"

I thought back to how I'd told Daniel. "Try, 'We're finished.' That says it all."

"I guess," said Izzie sadly. "I hate having to do it."

"Yeah. It's like, I think I made the right decision," I said, "but I feel mean."

"So do I," sighed Izzie, "and I haven't even told him yet."

At that moment, Nesta swept in and flopped down next to me.

"I've just been dumped," she announced. "Simon has dumped me. Me. *Me*."

"Why? What happened?"

"I knew it was coming," she said. "I *told* you I knew it. He said he really liked me, blah blah, and that he hoped we could stay friends, blah blah, but because he was going to go to university, he felt it was a good idea that we make a clean break because it's a new chapter for him, blah blah, and that long distance relationships never work. Blah blah blah blah blah."

"Are you very upset?" I asked.

"Over a boy? Course not. I don't care," she said,

and then she burst into tears, causing a lady on the next table to look over with concern. "I *really* liked him, Lucy."

"I know you did, Nesta. And I am sorry. Can I do anything? Get you anything?"

She shook her head. "I'll be all right. Sorry. Sorry. Just I've never been dumped before."

I went to sit next to her and put my arm around her. "It's a day of firsts for both of us. I've just finished with Daniel."

This seemed to cheer her up. "Really? Good," she said. "I know I only met him once, but I didn't like him. I can say that now, can't I?"

"You can. You can say whatever you like."

She wiped her eyes and attempted a smile. "So here we are, the dumped and the dumper."

"And Izzie's about to join the ranks," I said.

"Ben?" said Nesta.

Izzie nodded. "Boys," she said. "Who needs them?"

"Yeah," said Nesta sadly, "who?"

What is going on today? I thought when I called in at home later. It must be something in the stars. In fact, I'm surprised that Mystic Izzie hasn't picked up on some fight between planets or something which is provoking all our horoscopes. Everyone seems to be changing and rearranging their love life. Even my brother Lal was affected, and it takes a lot for him to change anything, even his socks.

"What's up with you?" I asked when I popped my head in the boys' room and saw him slumped on the bed *à la* tragic hero with his hand over his forehead.

"You wouldn't understand," he said, and turned away toward the wall.

"Try me," I said. It wasn't like him to be low and even though he was a pain mostly, he was still my brother.

"I want to be alone," he muttered.

I went in and sat on the end of his bed. "I just finished with Daniel," I said, in an attempt to perk him up. He usually couldn't resist the latest gossip about my and the other girls' love lives. Says it's good research.

Lal sat up. "See, that's it, isn't it? You finished with Daniel. Another poor boy, subject to the whims and fancies of you girls."

This wasn't the reaction I'd expected. "What do you mean?"

"Girls," he moaned. "Can't live with them, can't shoot them. You can stick that on one of your T-shirts."

"What *is* your problem?" I asked.

"Nothing," he said. "Girls. Or rather not girls. Sometimes it's not fair, you know. You girls call all the shots and us boys just have to take it."

"Hey, what's happened to the snog chart?" I asked, noticing that the back of the door was bare.

"In the bin," he said.

"Why? I thought you were winning."

"I was. But what's the point? All those girls I've snogged and none of them meant anything to me."

"But I thought that was the *point*. No ties, no commitment, just fun. I thought that was your philosophy."

"Shows what *you* know," he said.

"Okay, so what is your philosophy, then?"

Lal sighed. "I can't tell you. You'll laugh or tell your mates."

"Trust me," I said. "I won't tell anyone."

Lal sat up. "Okay. There's this girl. A girl I really fancy. I mean *really* fancy. I think she may be The One."

"Well, that's good, isn't it? You've finally fallen for someone."

"Not finally. I've fancied her for ages, but it's like she doesn't even know I'm on the planet," he said. "She barely even gives me a second glance."

"So, make her notice you."

"You think I haven't tried? No go. She'd never look at someone like me. She's way out of my league."

He looked so sad sitting there, I wished I could do something to cheer him up. "Hey, don't give up. It's not like you. Maybe I could help. Do I know her?"

Lal shook his head. "No. . . . Yes. I mean, no."

"Come on, spill. Who is it?"

Lal shook his head again. "Can't say. See, you lot—you girls—you're *all* so self-assured. You, your mates, all girls, you don't realize how hard it is for us boys. You can destroy us with a look or with a comment that you all think is dead clever or funny and we're supposed to be all, 'Oh, it doesn't matter, ha ha, laugh at me why don't you?'

"But I've had enough. My ego is shattered. My life is over. There is no other girl but her and she'll never give me the time of day. *That's* why I ripped up the snog chart. I've been into this girl for ages. *Ages.* I thought if she saw how popular I was with other girls, she'd be intrigued, fancy me. But I don't think she's even noticed, so what's the point? Snogging a load of girls just to prove something to myself, that I'm fanciable, that girls can't resist me? What's the point when the only one that matters *can* resist me? I may as well be invisible as far as she knows."

Wow, I thought. He's really got it bad. "It can't possibly be that hopeless. I mean, you're a good-looking boy, you're a laugh. Perseverance wins the day. Come on. Who is it?"

He looked at the floor and then glanced up at me hopefully. "Nesta."

Ohmigod, I thought, he's right. No chance. *No* chance. He doesn't stand a hope in hell with her. Oh, poor Lal. It *is* hard being a boy. Poor Lal. Poor Daniel. And poor Ben—he's going to get it soon.

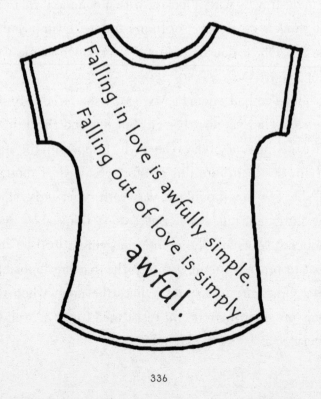

Falling in love is awfully simple. Falling out of love is simply awful.

17

Couple Bubbles

Daniel wasn't about to give up easily.

Monday, he sent the most gorgeous white flowers. Through a proper florist as well.

Tuesday, another toy bear and a card saying, "He's to go with little bear in case she's lonely."

Wednesday, he phoned. "Let's at least meet up, Lucy. Please. We can't just leave it."

In the end, I agreed. I'd have felt mean not to. Nobody had ever sent me flowers before, not even Tony, and I felt at least I should hear him out.

"Okay," I said, "but I'll come down to you."

He was waiting for me at Chalk Farm tube and, as usual, was dressed in his signature black. He was carrying a small bunch of freesias. It was strange seeing him again. Even though it had only been a few days, he looked different. Or I was seeing him differently. No doubt he was good-looking, but this time, I felt the attraction had gone.

"Hi," he said, and took my hand.

"Hi," I said, and took it back.

"Oh, don't be like that, Lucy," he said, and gave me the flowers.

"Daniel, you can't keep giving me stuff. I mean, it's really lovely of you, but . . ."

"I wanted to get flowers for you. I want to be with you. To make you happy. I'm sorry about the other day. I was out of order. Can we give it another try? Start again?"

But I knew that it was over and shook my head. "I'm sorry, Daniel."

"But why? Was it because of the way I reacted to you being with that boy? I'm sorry. I get jealous. Most girls would like that."

How could I let him down gently? "It's not you, it's me. I want . . . that is, I don't want . . . I mean, I'm not . . ." I remembered what Tony had said. "I'm not into having the big relationship. I mean, I think you're really lovely . . ."

Daniel's face clouded over. "I know exactly what

you're saying, Lucy. I'm not stupid. It's your choice. There are loads of other girls who would jump at the chance of going out with me."

Good, I thought. Let them.

He reached for my hand again. "One more try? I really think we've got something special."

I shook my head. "Sorry, Daniel. But . . . but I hope we can stay friends." Argh. I was determined not to come out with that old cliché, but it slipped out.

"Yeah," sighed Daniel. "We all know what *that* means."

"No, I mean it, we could still talk and even see each other sometimes, but as mates."

"Yeah, right," he said.

I felt really uncomfortable as we both stood there staring at the pavement. I couldn't think of anything else to say and he seemed to have gone into a sulk.

"Well, er, um . . . I've got to go," I said finally.

"Sure," he said, and hung his head.

As I walked away, he just stood there looking after me. I felt like the Queen of Mean.

"What's up, Lucy?" Mum asked when I got back home later.

I sat down at the kitchen table and put my head in

my hands. "Relationships," I said. "They stink."

Mum laughed. "What's happened now? I thought it was all going brilliantly. We've hardly seen you for days, weeks."

"Finished. History. *Kaput*."

Mum sat next to me. "Oh, Lucy, I am sorry. You've been dumped."

"No, I dumped *him*."

"Oh," said Mum. "So, what's the problem?"

"It's just not worth it, any of it. Either way, love hurts. I feel mean. Nesta's been dumped and she feels lousy. Izzie wants to finish with Ben, but is worried about hurting him. And even Lal, he's in love with someone who'll never have him."

"Nesta," said Mum.

"How did you know?"

"You mean you've never noticed how he acts when she's around?"

"I thought he acted like that around all girls."

Mum shook her head. "No, he's got it bad for her."

"Poor Lal," I said. "He's just not her type."

"I know," said Mum. "It's hard to watch. I hate to see him pining, but I can't make her fancy him. What can you do?"

"Get a dog like T. J. did," I said.

Mum laughed again. "We've already got Ben and Jerry. I don't know. I guess there's no point in me saying any of this to you, but I'm going to anyway. You *are* young. There will be others for all of you. Plenty more fish in the sea."

"No," I said. "No point."

Mum put her hand over mine. "Life can be hard sometimes, Lucy, no matter what side you're on. It takes a lot of courage to finish with someone. Some people stay in bad relationships long after their sell-by date because they're too frightened to face the repercussions, but it's a good lesson to learn. You have to be cruel to be kind sometimes, especially if it's not working. If it ain't right, it ain't right. So why did you end it with Daniel?"

I shrugged. "Dunno. It's like, I couldn't be myself with him. Like he wanted me to be someone else and was trying to mold me into that person, but it felt a bit like trying to fit a square peg into a round hole, you know? I didn't feel like we really fitted. Remember that day when you said that when the right person came along, you could be yourself with them, be natural?"

Mum nodded. "But you're only fourteen, Lucy. So's Nesta. And Lal is only fifteen. Life goes on, and girls and boys will come and go. Sometimes it will be right, sometimes it will be wrong. Main thing is to stay true to yourself—to what you feel."

"Well, Nesta feels awful. So does Lal."

"Well, as I said, it's not always easy and I know this may sound weird to say, but all of you, *all* of you will be more understanding because of it. Nesta's never been dumped before, has she?"

I shook my head.

"Well, it doesn't hurt to be on that side of things; that is, I know it *does* hurt, but it will give her more perspective and understanding. Boys fall over themselves for her, so perhaps having been dumped will make her a bit gentler on them. It's hard for boys sometimes."

I nodded. "That's what Lal said."

"And Lal. Same with him. Knowing what it's like to have an almighty crush on someone who doesn't reciprocate, maybe he'll go easier on the girls that fancy him in future. He's had his fair share of girls queuing up for him in the past, and I've seen him act a bit ruthless with one or two of them."

"Yeah, me too," I said. "I've seen him give girls the brush-off before and I thought he was being horrible, but now I feel like I misjudged him in a way. I thought he was an unfeeling rat, but really all he was trying to do was prove to himself that he was fanciable, because he felt insecure."

"Exactly," said Mum. "All these experiences, they're all part of life's rich tapestry."

"Yeah," I said. "I guess. But why can't it all be perfect? And everyone be happy. I hate seeing people feeling blue."

Mum squeezed my hand. "And that's what makes you Lucy. You may feel mean that you finished with Daniel, but it shows that you have a heart and that's what's most important. You care about people even if you can't change the situation. You ought to hear some of the stories some of my clients tell me about their relationships. Heartbreaking, some of them, and all I can do is listen and let them know that I'm there for them. That's all you can do with Nesta. And Lal."

"Yeah," I said. "And Lal."

I met T. J., Izzie, and Nesta at Ruby's for dinner later that evening.

"Oh no," said T. J. "Now I'm the odd one out. Izzie's going to finish with Ben and you've finished with Daniel. I'm the only one with a boyfriend."

Nesta grinned. "Give it time."

"Cynic," said Izzie, punching her arm. "Take no notice, T. J. You and Steve are lovely together. And at least he likes doing loads of different things."

"Yeah," said T. J. "And we both have days when we do our own thing. He's not like . . . he has to be with me all the time."

"That's the secret," I said as I looked at the menu. "I mean, I know I haven't had many relationships, but I'm learning already. It's like, all of us did the same thing, except T. J., of course. We all went into couple bubbles and cut ourselves off from each other and the rest of the world like nothing else existed."

Nesta sighed. "Yeah, but you can't help it when you're really into someone."

"But there has to be balance," I said. "You see the boy, but you still see your mates. You do some stuff with the boy, some stuff with your mates and some stuff alone."

"I guess," said Nesta.

"Come on," I said. "Let's be positive. Let's celebrate our newfound freedom and order something to eat. All this dumping and being dumped, I'm starving."

T. J. and I ordered a big bowl of potato wedges with sour cream and chili, Nesta ordered a hot chicken satay baguette, and Izzie had a veg and halioumi kebab.

"Here's to the rest of the holidays," said Nesta after the waitress had taken our orders.

"Yeah and here's to being single." I smiled. "It's so

weird. I used to be, like, Oh it's so rotten because I haven't got a boyfriend, and now I feel good about it. Like I'm free, no one to tell me what to do or who I can or can't see. Never again."

"Oh no," said Nesta, as a particularly good-looking boy came through the door and checked her out. "You must never say never. Not all boys are like Daniel, Lucy. He was very possessive. I'm glad you stood up to him in the end."

"Okay," I laughed. "I'll never say never, then. But I do say, here's to mates. Look how everything's changed since the beginning of the hols, but here we all are, still together. Boys may come into our lives—"

"Oh, I hope so," interrupted Nesta as the boy who'd eyed her up sat at the next table. "Look out, boys— Nesta's back in town."

"As I was saying," I continued. "Boys may come and go in our lives. Sometimes we'll have boyfriends, sometimes we won't, but we'll always have each other. So I say, here's to mates."

"Arr, she's *so* sweet," teased Izzie. "Little bear."

"Little *bear*," chorused T. J. and Nesta, then laughed.

"Naff off, dorkbrains," I said. "But it's true, mates always have each other. I say we celebrate properly. I'll ask my mum if we can have a party on Friday. A no-boyfriends-allowed party. You can only come if you're single."

Nesta's face dropped. "No boys? Are you sure?"

"Yes, Nesta, I'm sure. Everyone's so different when there are boys around. Let's have a night off from them. We can invite some of the girls from school."

"Yeah," said Izzie. "It'll be brilliant to spend some time with just the girls."

"That's settled, then," I said. "I'll ask Mum."

A woman needs
a man like a fish
needs a bicycle

18

Party Time

Mum couldn't believe it when at last I fulfilled my promise to cook for the family. She agreed to let me have the party, so I phoned around and found out everyone's favorite comfort food in times of Relationship Trouble. Then I did a practice run the night before to make sure I had it perfected.

PARTY MENU

Doritos and salsa dips

Oven chips

Pizza

Sausages

Chocolate bars

Ice cream (assorted, loads)

"This cooking lark is quite simple, really," I said as I took the oven chips out of the oven and put them on the table.

"Er," said Mum, "it is when you buy ready-to-serve stuff like this."

"Yeah," said Steve. "For your information, potatoes actually come in their own skin and you have to peel them."

"Ha ha," I said. "But oven chips were big in the popularity stakes and I can't say you seem that bothered, seeing as you've just eaten three at once."

"I think you lot had better get boyfriends again quick," said Dad, helping himself, "or else we're all going to be as fat as pigs."

"Mum, can Lucy cook every night from now on?" asked Lal through a mouthful of chips and ketchup.

"No," said Mum. "All this prepackaged stuff may taste great, but it isn't too healthy. You know what I say—you are what you eat."

"In that case, you're a Nettuno pizza," I laughed as I noticed that she'd cleared her plate and had even gone for a second helping.

The girls and I all got dressed at my house on the night of the party and we took ages doing each other's nails and makeup. We decided to get dressed up even though there weren't going to be boys there. We did it for ourselves, just for the fun of it, as sometimes getting dressed up is the best part of any party. It felt great just to hang out with the girls again and Nesta seemed to be in better spirits, despite her recent dumping. For the first time in weeks I felt myself again. Calm inside, on an even keel instead of on the rollercoaster of emotions. Being single is okay, I decided as I watched Nesta rolling about on the floor, zipping herself into an impossibly tight pair of jeans, especially when you have such good mates.

I'd thought very carefully about what to do on the Big Night. I wanted everyone to have loads of fun with lots to do. I hate those boring parties where everyone stands around in cliques just talking and watching each other. My plan was: a bit of dancing, a DVD to watch while we ate (*Bridget Jones's Diary*, of course), then games and maybe some more dancing.

When everyone was ready, I thought I'd better break a bit of news about the party that I hadn't already told them. I had invited a boy.

"Um, just one thing before we go downstairs," I said. "You know this is a singles' party?"

The girls all nodded.

"Well, single doesn't necessarily mean all female, does it?"

"No," said Nesta, looking at me suspiciously.

"I have invited *one* boy," I said. "Only one."

"Tony," said Nesta. "Oh, Lucy . . ."

"No, not Tony." I grinned.

"Oh, not Daniel," exclaimed Izzie. "I can't believe you've got back with him."

I shook my head. "No . . ."

Just at that moment, there was a knock, and the bedroom door opened. The girls all burst out laughing. A vision of girlie loveliness appeared in the doorway wearing my inflatable bra over his T-shirt and one of Mum's hippie wigs from the dressing-up box.

"Hi," said Lal. "I'm Lalita."

"He's an honorary girl for the night," I explained. I knew it would be a fantasy come true for him to be alone in a house full of girls and I really wanted to cheer him up. I thought it might help him get over his unrequited love for Nesta.

He wiggled into the room, sat on the bed and crossed his legs gracefully. "So," he pouted, splaying out his fingers, "what do you think? Pink nail polish or purple?"

* * *

Half an hour later some of the guests began to arrive. Gabby, Jade, Mo, and Candice from school; Amy, who lives next door to Izzie and has just bust up with her boyfriend; and T. J.'s second cousin who's never had a boyfriend and was very happy to come and celebrate being single.

"Music for singletons," said Amy, showing us her rucksack full of CDs. She put a CD in the player and soon we were all dancing away to "Survivor" by Destiny's Child. Then we sang "All by Myself" by Celine Dion at the top of our voices. After a good bop to more CDs, Izzie, Lal, and I served the food and we all sat on the floor in the living room to watch *Bridget Jones*. I felt so relaxed to be there just with mates. I could tell everyone felt the same. Not having to worry about what was going to happen or how things were going to turn out. What this boy said or didn't say, who that boy was dancing with and who he wanted to snog. No expectations, no disappointments.

"So what games shall we play?" asked Izzie as the credits rolled after the movie.

"We could play spin the bottle, but with dares instead of snogging," I said. "Whoever spins the bottle has to set the dare, and whoever the bottle points at has to do it."

Everyone seemed keen to give it a go, so Nesta found a bottle and got things started. We all sat cross-legged in a circle and began. It was hysterical, as everyone seemed to take it as an opportunity to make their friends act really stupid. Izzie made T. J. do an impersonation of Madonna, so when it was T. J.'s turn, she asked Izzie to do an impression of a drunk snake. Candice asked Nesta to do a cartwheel, and Nesta asked Candice to run out into the garden and sing "God Save the Queen" at the top of her voice.

I already had an idea for when it came to my turn. I spun the bottle slowly to my left, and just as planned, it stopped at Nesta.

"So, Nesta," I said. "All those complaints about no boys at the party. . . . As your friend, I had to listen to what you really wanted, so your dare is . . . to snog my brother Lal in the hall."

Nesta looked over at Lal, who was holding his breath. She raised an eyebrow. "Do you think he could take it?" she asked.

"I'll take the chance," he said.

He looked like all his Christmases had come at once

when she stood up, took his hand, and led him out of the room.

After a few minutes he came back in and had to go and lie down on the sofa to recover. I swear there were stars and planets coming out of his head.

"So what about you and Tony now?" asked T. J. as we cleared some of the dishes back into the kitchen.

I shrugged. He had phoned in the morning, probably hoping to get an invite to our party. It was weird, because at the end of the call, he sounded uncertain, then asked if maybe we could pick up where we left off at the beginning of the holidays. I told T. J. about it.

"So what did you say?"

"I said I couldn't. I mean, to pick up where we were at the beginning of the holidays? All that uncertainty? No thanks. Amazing, huh? A few weeks ago I would have leaped at the chance, but so much has happened since then—since my letter to him, since Daniel. I feel I need some time out to think about things . . . to reassess what I want. To go back to where I was at the beginning of summer, to the ups and downs and wondering what was happening with Tony. If I said, 'Okay, let's get back together,' how long would it last? I know what he's like. He gets bored, and then where would that leave me? Back on the rollercoaster. I'm not sure I want to go through all that again. Not yet."

"Sounds like a very wise decision," said T. J. "No hurry."

"No, no hurry," I said. "We can be friends for sure, but I just don't want a commitment relationship."

"Sounds like you were made for each other."

I laughed and followed her back into the living room where some of the girls from school were urging Izzie to get up and sing. At first she was reluctant, then she smiled. "Actually, I have been working on a new song. . . ."

Everyone started stomping their feet and shouting, "*Izzie, Izzie, Izzie.*"

"Okay," she said. "This one is for all the singletons." She closed her eyes for a few seconds, then began to sing in her lovely, velvety voice.

I was a broken ship with ragged sails
Now calm waters beckon me
Lying out in warming sun, stretching, feeling free
Waiting for a new wind and a wave upon my bow
Wishing on a rainbow, following my star
Welcoming my new world, I'm gonna travel far

Floating in the slipstream, just going with the flow
Booked a passage on tomorrow with no one else in tow
Floating in the slipstream, just going with the flow

I glanced over at T. J. and she smiled back. Going with the flow, I thought. Yeah, now *that* sounds good to me.

THE PERFECT BOY?

One who snogs
for half an hour
then turns into a pizza

Mates, Dates, and
MAD MISTAKES

Thanks as always to Brenda Gardner, Yasemin Uçar, and the team at Piccadilly for making working on these books such a pleasure. To Rosemary Bromley at Juvenelia for all her support. To Steve Lovering for all his help and for being a great sounding board. And to Rachel Hopkins, Georgina Acar, Scott Brenman, Becca Crewe, Alice Elwes, Jenni Herzberg, Olivia McDonnell, and Annie McGrath for keeping in touch with me on e-mail about what's what with teenagers and for answering all my questions.

Chickens

"Sounds *horrible*," said Nesta, pulling a face.

"What?" I asked as Lucy and I came back into her bedroom with sleepover supplies (the usual: Diet Cokes, Salt & Vinegar Pringles, and Liquorice Allsorts). T. J., Nesta, and I were staying over at Lucy's, after she'd held a girls-only party earlier in the evening. We'd finished clearing up after the other girls had left and were ready for some late night nattering before getting into our sleeping bags.

"Yeah, what sounds horrible?" asked Lucy.

T. J. pointed to a book of spells that I'd lent Lucy earlier in the summer. "Becoming blood sisters," said T. J. in a spooky voice. "Says in Izzie's book that if you want to bond with your mates for life, the best way to do it is to each prick your finger with a needle, then press the tiny point of blood on your finger against the prick on your friends' fingers. It makes you sisters for life."

"Yee-*uck*," said Nesta. "Can't we burn our bras instead, like those women in the sixties?"

Lucy laughed. "No, we can't, because seeing as I have no chest to speak of, I haven't got a bra to burn."

"Yes, you have," said Nesta. "I've seen it."

Lucy shook her head. "I chucked it out. No point. It was after something Lal said. He asked, if I had no feet would I still wear shoes? I said no, course not. So then he said, so why do you wear a bra?"

"What a cheek. What does he know?" I said as I put down the Pringles. "That's really mean, even for a brother."

Lucy shrugged. "Nah, he's right. I only wore one because everyone else does. For show. Trouble was, nothing *did* show except an empty wrinkle of lacy fabric under my T-shirt. It's much more comfortable without one."

"Oh, let's do the blood sister thing," said T. J. "It'll be a laugh, and we'll be friends for ever and ever."

I shook my head. "Nah, sounds daft. It's the sort of thing that kids do, junior school stuff. . . ."

"And this coming from Mystic Iz, Queen of Witchiness herself," said T. J. "What's up with you?"

I shrugged. "Nothing. It just sounds childish. I've had that spell book for years. I read it when I was in Year *Seven*."

T. J. looked disappointed. "I think it sounds cool. And there's a nice sentiment behind it—makes a change from all those spells you usually do for getting boys and stuff."

"Yeah, let's try it," said Lucy.

"Well, you have to sterilize the needles, you know," said Nesta.

Lucy rolled her eyes. "You're such a prissy-knickers."

"No, actually she's right," said T. J. "Best be on the safe side."

"Yes, better had, Lucy," I said. "T. J.'s parents are both doctors so if anyone should know about what's safe and what's not, it's them."

"Oh, all right," said Lucy. "I will."

"And as long as it won't hurt . . . ," said Nesta.

"It won't," said Lucy as she began to look for needles in her sewing box. She found a sachet of them and waved them in the air. "Won't be a mo. I'll just put on my nurse's uniform and go and sterilize these."

She was back a few minutes later and handed us a needle each.

"If we're going to do this, let's do it properly," I said. "We should sit in a circle, and, Lucy, can we light a candle?"

"Ah, so Mystic Iz isn't quite dead, then?" said Nesta, grinning.

Lucy found a candle, lit it, then turned off the electric light and we sat in a circle on the floor.

Lucy, T. J., and I did it straight away. A quick jab and we were ready.

Nesta screwed her face up and put the needle close to her thumb, like she was trying to puncture the skin really slowly. "I can't," she moaned. "I really can't. I hate needles, and it's going to *hurt*."

"Just do it quickly," said Lucy. "It just takes a second and only feels like . . . like a quick prick."

"I could answer that with something very rude," laughed Nesta. "But I won't. Are you *sure* these needles are sterilized properly, Luce? We might get some horrible disease. I don't think it's safe to share blood."

"Chicken," I said.

"Oh, come on you big sissy," said T. J., taking the needle from her. "I'll do it for you."

"No, *no*," she cried, rolling over on the floor on top of her hands. "You'll stab me or hit an artery or something."

"Trust me. I'm a doctor," said T. J. "Or at least my parents are."

"No," said Nesta, getting up again. "I'll do it myself." Once again, she softly prodded her thumb with the needle. "No. . . . It's not working. No. Sorry. Can't do it."

"Well, we can't carry on if you don't," said Lucy. "It wouldn't be right. Me, T. J., and Izzie would be bonded for life and you'd be on the outside. It might be awful bad luck."

"Yeah, come on, cowardy custard," I said, massaging my thumb. "My blood's drying up."

"I'm sorry, I can't. I just can't." Nesta leaned back and grabbed the spell book off the bed. "Isn't there some other thing we can do to bond us for life? Something that doesn't involve *pain*?" She reached for the Pringles. "How about we all take a bite of one of these and pass it on. Bond over a Pringle. Same sort of thing—caring sharing, bonding schmonding."

I had to laugh. Nesta never takes anything like doing spells seriously. "Go on, then. Pass us a Pringle," I said.

Nesta selected one from the tub, then we passed it around, each taking a tiny bite of it.

"Okay, by the power vested in me by this salt and vinegar crisp," I said in my best solemn voice, "I hereby decree that these four girls gathered here tonight shall be friends for ever and ever, bound together by the magical force of the Almighty Pringle."

Lucy and Nesta started laughing. "All hail to the Pringle," said Lucy.

"All hail," T. J. and I echoed.

Then I had an idea. "Okay, then how about this? If we really want to have an experience that will bond us, how about doing something that will look good as well?"

"What do you mean?" asked T. J. "Like dressing up to do spells?"

"No. How about we get our belly buttons pierced?"

There was a stunned silence. I don't think they expected anything like that, but I'd been thinking about having it done for a while. Part of a whole new image. We were going into Year Ten at school a week on Monday and somehow I wanted to leave the old Izzie behind with the old year. I felt like I'd grown out of so many of the things I'd been into, including my clothes—

literally with some of them. I seemed to have shot up a few more inches over the last year and some of my jeans were stopping short of my ankles. *Très* uncool. Anyway, I'd told Mum that I was having a midteen crisis and needed some new clothes. She'd laughed and said there was no such thing as a *mid*teen crisis, as when you're a teen, it's crisis all the way through—mainly for her. Poo. I don't think she knows how lucky she is. If she knew what some of the girls at our school get up to behind their parents' backs, she'd have a fit. Relatively, I give her an easy time, although *she* doesn't think so.

"Hmm," said Nesta finally. "Having a stud put in will probably hurt as well, won't it? But . . . I *have* always wanted one." She stroked her impossibly flat tummy. "Yeah, a belly button stud would look neat."

"It won't hurt," I said. "Candice Carter had hers done. She was telling me earlier this evening at the party. She said they put stuff on your tummy that kind of freezes it so you don't feel anything."

"Well, I'm in," said Lucy. "I need all the help I can get, to get boys to notice me. A belly button stud would look really cool and might detract from the fact that I have no basoomas."

"Basoomas?" asked T. J. "What are they?"

Lucy pointed at her chest. "Boobs, you idiot. Lal calls them basoomas or jaloobis."

T. J. pulled a face. "He needs help, your brother does."

"Tell me about it," sighed Lucy.

"We could all have a different color stone on our stud," I said. "Have you got any books on astrology, Lucy?"

"Course," she said, getting up and going to her shelf. "That one you gave me last Christmas."

When she handed me the book, I had a quick flick through and found a section on which stones and colors are right for different signs. "Okay, here it is, our birthstones. It says garnet for those born in January, so that's me."

"What color is a garnet?" asked Lucy.

"Sort of deep wine red," I answered.

Lucy nodded approvingly. "That would look good on you with your dark hair."

"Nesta, you're Leo," I continued, "so it says . . . let me see . . . you were born August eighteen, so yours would be . . . oh, it could be a diamond or a ruby. Wow, that would look fab against your dark skin. Really exotic."

"Nah," said Nesta shaking her head. "I'd look like

some belly dancer. No. I want a diamond if I'm going to have anything. Much classier."

"Fine, whatever," I said. "Lucy. Gemini, born May twenty-four. . . . It says emerald for you."

"An emerald might look better on you, Izzie," said Nesta, "to go with your green eyes."

"Yeah. I'd rather have a sapphire," said Lucy. "You know, blue, to match *my* eyes."

"Yeah, and blue suits blonds," said Nesta.

"Well, we don't *have* to stick to this," I said. "It's just if we wanted our birthstones."

"What's mine?" asked T. J.

I flicked through the book to Sagittarius. "Okay, November to December. It says November, topaz, December, turquoise. You were born November twenty-four, so topaz. It'd be great."

"Topaz? That's yellow, isn't it?" asked T. J. "I don't think that's a good color for a belly button stud at all. You know how some of them go a bit ucky—a yellow stone might look like a lump of solid puss or something."

"Er, *T. J.*, g-*ross*," laughed Nesta. "But I think you're right. I think a turquoise would look better on a brunette like you."

I closed the book, put the back of my hand on my

forehead and sighed my best tragic sigh. "I despair. Sometimes I wonder why I *bother* with you ignoramuses. I just thought we could be the Birthstone Belly Button Gang, that's all."

"You're mad, Izzie," laughed Lucy. "But it would be nice if we all got different colors."

T. J. was looking dubious. "I don't know. You lot have all got really flat tummies, but mine's rounded. I don't think they look as good if your stomach isn't like a washboard. Besides, won't it cost a fortune? I don't think I'll have enough, with the pocket money I get."

"Good point," said Lucy. "Cost—what do you think?"

"I'll find out," I said. "I doubt it will be that much. I mean, it's not like we're buying real diamonds and gold or anything."

T. J. still looked anxious. "I don't think my mum and dad will like it."

"They don't need to see it," said Nesta. "We're going back to school in just over a week. Soon we'll be in winter clothes. No one will see it."

"So what's the point of having one done?" asked T. J.

"When we're out together, stupoid," said Nesta. "When we wear crop tops."

"I guess," said T. J.

"So we all in?" I asked.

The others nodded, T. J. somewhat reluctantly.

"Right then," I said. "Tomorrow morning. I've seen a place in Kentish Town near where the band plays. We'll go there."

Birthstones

January: Garnet (deep wine red)

February: Amethyst (purple/violet)

March: Aquamarine (bluish green)

April: Diamond (clear)

May: Emerald (green)

June: Pearl (off-white)

July: Ruby (red)

August: Peridot (olive green)

September: Sapphire (bright blue)

October: Opal (milk white)

November: Topaz (yellow gold)

December: Turquoise (turquoise)

This can differ to star signs,
and according to what book
or website you use.

2

No Pain, No Gain

T. J. was the first to cop out.

"I can't," she said as we stood in front of a tattoo shop in Kentish Town on Saturday morning, trying to summon up the courage to go in. I had half a mind to agree with her and call the whole thing off. It was one thing having an idea, it was another actually carrying it through, and I was feeling distinctly nervous. It will be okay, I told myself as I glanced at a couple of guys leaning against the shop front smoking cigarettes. Both were a bit hard-looking, dressed in Camden black, and I wondered if they were the ones who did the piercing or just customers hanging out. Either way, both of them were walking advertisements for the shop. Their arms were completely covered in tattoos and they had studs everywhere, in their noses, in their lips . . . and one had little pointy studs on top of his ears that made him look like Mr. Spock in *Star Trek*.

"I'm really sorry," continued T. J., "but Mum and Dad would kill me. I know we agreed not to tell our parents, but . . . I can't risk it. You know what my dad's like."

We all nodded. Everyone calls T. J.'s dad Scary Dad. He's a lot older than the rest of our dads and is very strict and solemn-looking. I'd probably cop out as well if he were my father.

"Plus," said T. J., "we don't know how much it costs yet and I've already spent most of this month's pocket money. Mum and Dad would get suspicious if I asked them for any more, you know. They'd want to know what I'd spent my money on."

"No worries, T. J. Me and Nesta will go in and check it out," I said. "Get the details and find out if it's all cool. If it looks remotely dodgy, we don't do it. Okay?"

"It *will* be okay," said Lucy as Nesta and I headed for the door.

As we approached, one of the guys with a goatee smiled at us. "Can I help you, ladies?" he asked.

"Um, yes," I said. "We wanted to ask about piercings."

"Then come this way," he said, and led us into the shop. Inside, it looked normal enough—very clean, with posters on sale and jewelry on display. At the back were what looked like hairdressing chairs in front of mirrors, and I could see what looked like a dentist's chair in a room off to the right. A shiver went down my spine.

"So what do you want to know?" asked Goatee Man.

"How much is it to have your belly button pierced?" said Nesta.

"Thirty-five pounds," he said. "Is it for you?"

We both nodded.

"How old are you?"

"Sixteen," Nesta lied.

The man shook his head. "Then you'd have to come with your parents. We don't do belly button piercings without parental consent. Sorry."

"But we *do* have our parents' consent," I fibbed. "They're totally cool about it." Ha-ha. Big lie. My mum would hit the roof if she knew where I was, but I didn't think it would be a problem. She wouldn't even notice. She never pays much attention to me these days, except to lecture me about where I've been and what time I get back.

Goatee Man grinned. "That's what they all say, darlin'. Nice try, but sorry, no go."

Nesta and I went back out to join T. J. and Lucy. "No go," said Nesta. "We need our parents' permission."

T. J. looked relieved, but Lucy looked disappointed.

"And it's thirty-five pounds," I said.

"That's me definitely out, then," said T. J. "I've only got fifteen pounds fifty."

"Maybe they'd do a deal and put it halfway in," laughed Lucy.

T. J. punched her arm. "Ha-ha. But have you got enough?"

"I've got forty quid that my gran sent me for my birthday," said Nesta. "I could lend someone five."

"I've got thirty," said Lucy. "That's all my savings."

"I'll lend you the last five," said Nesta. "What about you, Iz?"

"I've just got it. Dad gave me twenty quid a few weeks ago and I saved it. With what's left of my pocket money from Mum, I could just about do it."

T. J. pointed back at the shop. "But they said they wouldn't do it without permission."

"We could go somewhere else," said Nesta, "and blag our way in. You know, slap a bit of makeup on and say we're eighteen."

Lucy's face fell even further. "Yeah right. Like anyone's ever going to believe that I'm eighteen. It's okay for you lot. You're all tall and look older, but me—I'm minuscule and look younger than I am. It's not fair."

"Don't worry, Luce. We'll think of something," said Nesta. "We won't do it without you."

"Let's phone Candice," said Lucy. "No way she had *her* parents' permission, if I know her. I'm going to find out where she got hers done." She punched Candice's number in on her mobile and wandered off down the street to talk to her. A few minutes later, she was back smiling. "Candice says that there are loads of places in Camden that will do them. She says some of them won't and get all snotty about your age, but to keep trying as there are a few where there are no questions asked. She gave me directions to the one she went to."

"Let's go," I said. Now that we had started on Mission Belly Stud, I wanted to get it over with. Although I was brave about the thumb pricking, really I'm a bit like Nesta in that I don't like needles. I'd had a sleepless night thinking about what having the stud might feel like when it was being put in and I'd had weird dreams about giant needles chasing me.

Twenty minutes later, we found the shop that Candice had told Lucy about. Although it sold mainly clothes, belts, and boots, there was a discreet sign on the till saying BODY PIERCING and pointing to the back of the shop. A shop assistant at the counter nodded toward a door when she saw us looking at the sign. So far, so good, I thought. I knocked on the door, but there was no answer.

"Just go on in," said the assistant. "Del's in there somewhere."

I opened the door and we all trooped in. The first thing that hit me was an overpowering smell of antiseptic. There was a small reception room with the usual display of studs and rings and a door to the left, which was ajar. Through it I could see and *hear* a man having a tattoo done on his upper arm. He didn't look like he was enjoying it one bit and looked out at us with thin tight lips.

The man doing the tattoo glanced up at us. "Won't be a mo, girls. Take a seat."

We dutifully sat down and looked around. "This is

like waiting to see the dentist," said Nesta. "It even *sounds* like a dentist's with that tattoo thing buzzing. I feel really nervous."

"It's going to be well worth it," said Lucy. "We're going to look so glam."

"So who's going first?" I said. "We'd better decide."

"I will," said Lucy. "I hate waiting and I want to get it over with."

"Do you want to go next, Nesta?" I asked.

She shook her head. "No hurry. I don't mind waiting. I need to gear myself up mentally."

"I'll go second," I said. "That way you'll know it's all right."

"Okay," said Nesta. "Thanks."

A few minutes later, the tattooist and his "victim" came out. Interesting, I thought, because the tattooist didn't have any tattoos, or at least none that were visible. He looked very ordinary, in fact. He was wearing a normal shirt and trousers—not at all like the typical Camden characters who wear black or Goth clothes. On the other hand, the victim was covered in tattoos. He had a shaved head and swirly patterns all over his arms and up his neck. He looks weird, I thought, like he belongs in the circus or something.

Then I realized that I was staring at him and quickly looked at the floor.

"Right, I'm Del," said the tattooist after Circus Boy had gone. "What is it you're after?"

"Piercing," said Lucy.

"Ears, eyebrows, nose, lips, tongues, belly, or nipples?" asked Del.

Lucy went bright red. "Um, belly buttons."

"All of you?"

Lucy looked back at T. J. "All of us?"

"It'll be thirty pounds each," said the tattooist.

"That means Lucy's got enough," said Nesta, "so I can lend you a ten, T. J. Then I could ask my brother—he always seems to have loads of dosh. I can call him on my mobile and ask if he'll bring the rest if you want. I'm sure he'd come, especially if I tell him Lucy's here."

Predictably Lucy blushed again. She always does when anyone mentions Tony, even though it's him that's running after her these days, not the other way around.

T. J. shook her head. "No. You guys go ahead. I'd be too worried about my dad ever finding out. Anyway, we've bonded over the Almighty Pringle and that's good enough for me."

"All hail," chorused Nesta and Lucy. The tattooist looked amused.

"You sure?" I said to T. J.

T. J. nodded, so I turned back to the tattooist. "Three of us for belly buttons," I said, then I got an attack of the giggles at the thought of us getting our nipples pierced. I imagined going home and flashing my chest at Mum over dinner. Whoa! Look what I've had done, Mater. She'd go *ballistic*. But no worries. I mean, really, who in their right mind would ever want to have a nipple pierced? Yee-*uck*.

"Who's first?" said Del.

Well that was easy, I thought, as Lucy stepped forward and Del ushered her into his work room. We watched from the reception room as she lay on the chair, then I couldn't see any more because Del's back was in my way.

It didn't seem to take long. She was out a short time later and took a huge breath. "Not too bad. Like having your ears done," she said giving me the thumbs-up. "Not as bad as I thought."

"Next," called Del.

I got up and felt my knees go wobbly. Was it too late to do a runner? Whose stupid idea was this? I asked myself. Oh yeah. Mine! No. No, I can do this.

"Can I come in and watch?" asked Nesta as I went in. "I want to know what I'm letting myself in for."

"Sure," said Del. "You can all come in if you want."

"Er, no thanks," said T. J. "I'll stay here with Lucy."

I lay back on the chair and closed my eyes. Then I opened them. Del was coming at me with a pair of weird-looking scissors. They looked distorted like something out of a horror film.

"What are *they* for?" I asked in a panic. "You're not going to cut your way through, are you?"

Del smiled. "Nah, mate. These are to clamp your tummy. They make the skin go nice and tight."

Next thing I knew, he'd fastened the strange-looking scissors to the skin above my belly button and was wiping the area with some kind of lotion. I felt like I was going to pass out, it smelled so like a hospital.

"Is that the stuff to freeze it?" I asked.

"No," said Del. "It's antiseptic. Keeps the area clean. I don't freeze the skin, though my partner does. We've all got our own way, but too risky, I reckon—you might get frostbite. Don't worry. It will only sting for a minute."

I closed my eyes and opened them again. He was taking something out of a small plastic sachet. It looked like a minuscule screwdriver. "That's not the needle, is it?" I asked. "It's *enormous.*"

"Just take a deep breath," he said. "You've got to suffer to be beautiful, right? No pain, no gain."

I closed my eyes again and desperately searched my mind for one of the soothing visualizations I use to take my mind off the discomfort when I go to the dentist's. Sea, waves, nice flowers, I thought as I felt a searing pain rip through my middle. "Whara . . . *arghhhhhhh,*" I cried.

"All done." Del smiled, taking out a plaster and putting it over my belly button. "You can get up now. Now that wasn't so bad, was it?"

"Urg," was all I could say as I stumbled out of the chair.

Nesta had turned pale and backed out of the room. "Er, thanks," she whispered, "but . . . but I think I might wait until another day."

"Nihi—ergh," said T. J., and she ran out the reception door and into the shop with Nesta.

I felt faint. I just wanted to get out of there, but Del insisted on sitting Lucy and me down and giving us a *looong* lecture on how to clean the stud and the importance of being hygienic.

"And don't take the stud out for four to six weeks," he said. "Couple of months, if possible. I'm serious now, as you need to give the area time to heal. I know you girls are always anxious to get the pretty stones in, but start messing about with it before it's completely healed and it can get really ucky." Then he handed us each a bottle of cleansing lotion. "Salt water," he said. "Use it to clean the area three times a day, and mind you don't let the stud catch in your clothes in the early days."

I nodded like I'd understood, but I don't think I took in anything he said. I felt strangely floaty, as though I wasn't quite present any more.

We paid our money, and at last we were out of there. I gulped the air when we got out into the street and Lucy put her arm under mine to steady me. "You okay?" she asked.

"Heh-nuh . . . ," I said.

Lucy grinned. "I didn't think it was bad at all."

I guess she has a higher pain threshold than I do. I thought it was *awful*. And to think, I'd *paid* to have it done.

"Drinks are on me," said Nesta as we headed up to Chalk Farm. "I feel rotten that I chickened out, but . . ."

"Hey, no biggie," I said. "I'd have done the same if I'd known what it entailed."

"Are you okay now?" asked Lucy.

I nodded. "Just needed some fresh air. To get away from the smell of antiseptic. I know it's supposed to be good, but I always associate it with sickness and it makes me feel nauseous."

"So let's head over to Primrose Hill Park. Lots of air up there," said T. J., who up until now had kept very quiet. I guess she was feeling bad about chickening out as well.

When we got to the park, T. J. and Nesta shot off to get drinks from the nearby shops and Lucy and I sat on the grass halfway up the hill.

"How long do you think we can spin this out?" asked Lucy with a wicked grin as she watched them go. "They are both obviously prepared to be our slaves because they feel bad."

I grinned back. "As long as possible, then. Every time we need something done, we can flash our belly buttons at them and groan."

We lay on the grass and practiced our groaning for a while until a man walking his dog stopped and asked if we were all right.

Lucy went bright red. "Um, yeah, just something we ate for lunch."

Luckily he moved on, so I sat up and looked about the park. It felt really calm. The only sound was the hum of distant traffic. There were the usual people out enjoying the late August sun—mums with toddlers, a few joggers, a guy on a bench listening to his iPod, and a number of teens hanging out farther down the hill.

Suddenly the roar of a motorbike shattered the peace as it zoomed down the hill to our left. I glanced through the railings to see who it was—some guy wearing black leather trousers and a tight black T-shirt.

"*Eejit,*" said Lucy. "I *hate* those things. They're so *noisy.*"

"Yeah, but I'd quite like a go on the back of one of them. Wouldn't you?"

Lucy shook her head. "Nah. Think I'll stick with my limo fantasy, thank you very much."

As Nesta and T. J. returned laden with drinks and pastries about ten minutes later, I noticed that the motorbike guy came into the park behind them and went to join the other group of teens down the hill.

"Don't like the look of that lot," said T. J., glancing at them as she sat down.

They didn't look much older than us, maybe sixteen or so. Six of them. I counted. Three boys and three girls. A few of them were smoking, and a few were sharing cans of what looked like beer. One of the boys started acting stupid, throwing things around. It was funny because he was clearly trying to impress Bike Boy. When Bike Boy didn't react, he started throwing bits of sandwich at a jogger who was running past. Still no reaction. Well you can see who's king of the castle there, I thought. Bike Boy got up and went to stand a short distance apart from the rest of them. He leaned back against the railings, lit up a cigarette, and glanced around the park. As he looked up at us, I felt a rush go through me. There was something about him. Tall, dark, slim, and looks like he works out, I thought. He had well-toned arms—not big muscles, just nicely shaped.

"Bad boy, but very cute," said Nesta, casually glancing around the park and noticing that I'd clocked him. I laughed. She doesn't miss a trick.

Lucy looked over to him. "Yeah, handsome, but he looks dangerous."

"Never judge a book by its cover," I said. "Like that guy in the first tattoo shop—he looked hard, but he was a real sweetie when we got talking to him."

"I guess with boys it depends on what you're looking for," said T. J. "I think it's important to find a boy who's dependable."

"Yeah, but fun," I said.

"And a good kisser," said Nesta. "Very important."

Lucy rubbed her forehead. "Hmmm. I know a joke about finding the perfect boy—if only I could remember it. . . ."

"Well, he doesn't look like the perfect boy," said T. J., looking at Bike Boy. "He looks like trouble, and boys that good-looking are usually self-obsessed."

I looked at him again. I wouldn't say that, I thought. I think he looks like he knows how to have a good time. Then I realized that we were all gawping at him. How uncool is that?

"Stop looking, *stop looking*," I whispered to the others. "He can see we're staring."

Too late. He'd already noticed. He raised an eyebrow and gave us a lazy smile before going back to his mates. Then he flopped down next to one of the boys and said something into his ear. They both turned, looked at us, and laughed. He probably thinks we're a bunch of kids, I thought as I sipped on the Ribena Lite that Nesta had bought me. I pretended that I was laughing at something Lucy had said, then I purposefully looked straight at him then in the opposite direction. Two can play at that game, matie, I thought.

Lucy's Joke

It's important to find a boy who is
always willing to help in times of trouble.

It's important to find a boy who makes you laugh
when you're feeling blue.

It's important to find a boy who
is dependable and doesn't lie.

It's important to find a boy who
is a good kisser.

It's important these four boys never meet.

3

Restyle

"How's the stud?" I whispered to Lucy the next morning as I let her in the front door.

"Fine," she said, and followed me up the stairs. "Yours?"

I pulled a face. "Gone a bit crusty, if you must know, and it stings like anything when I put that salt water on it."

"Mine's been okay," said Lucy as we went into my bedroom and I shut the door. "But I showed Mum and Dad, I'm afraid. I couldn't resist."

"And?"

"Dad hit the roof for a while and Mum was miffed that I hadn't asked permission, but they were both cool in the end. In fact Mum came into my room last night and asked where I'd had it done."

"Why? She's not going to go and hassle them, is she? About us being underage?"

"Nah. She said *she* wanted one!"

"No!"

"That's what I said. I said if she dared to have her belly button pierced, I'd leave home."

"Quite right," I said. "Yuck. I can't imagine my mum ever having one done. The thought is too disgusting." And totally unlikely, I thought. She likes the classic look and is always immaculate in beige or black. The only earrings she ever wears are little pearl studs.

Lucy shivered. "Yeah, image overload. Let's change the subject. So . . ." She looked around my room, taking in the piles of clothes I'd thrown on the bed, chair, and floor.

"I know," I said. "I pulled out everything. I want to do a real throw-out. I've found stuff in my drawers that I've had for years."

"Okay," said Lucy, and she began to sort through things. "We'll make two piles: one for the bin, one for keeping." She picked up a pink vest. "Oh, you must keep this. It's really pretty."

"Nooo. It's too . . . boring."

Lucy moved some clothes aside and sat on my bed. "Well what image exactly are you going for?"

I sat next to her. "Dunno. That's why you're here, style queen."

Lucy's been my closest friend for ages, and I really trust her opinion. Not that I don't trust T. J. and Nesta. I do, but I've known Lucy longer—since junior school—and we've shared everything from clothes and CDs to our first day at secondary school. Sometimes we even know what the other is thinking. Also she's great on fashion. She makes loads of her own clothes and wants to study dress design after secondary school. That's why I asked her rather than Nesta or T. J. to help me go through my wardrobe. It's not that Nesta hasn't got style—she has. But if she had her way, she'd dress everyone like her, in girlie clothes, and what suits her doesn't necessarily suit everyone. I'm not a girlie type of girl. And T. J.'s the opposite of Nesta. She's a bit of a tomboy. She does look good in her jeans and trainers, but she's not that bothered about clothes really. She'd rather spend her pocket money on a book than a top.

"All I know is I need a change," I said. "Something more sophisticated, something to make me stand out. Like, I know I'll never be drop-dead gorgeous like Nesta . . ."

"Rubbish," interrupted Lucy. "You have a different

look, that's all, but you're just as good-looking as she is."

Typical Lucy. Always my champion.

"Get real," I said. "I know where I stand in the beauty stakes, and Nesta is a nine and a half out of ten . . . and I'm about a five without any makeup, but can be a seven or eight if I make a bit of an effort. Fact. Reality."

"You're too critical of yourself. I'd give you a nine, easy. You've got a great figure, fabulous eyes, lovely hair . . ."

"Thank you very much, Lucy," I said, "but sorry, I don't share your view. My bum's too big for a start and my nose is too lumpy."

"I saw a program on telly about model school and one of the first things they teach is about confidence. The girls have to do an exercise where they go up to mirrors and tell themselves that they're beautiful. Makes sense, because if you don't believe it, no one else will. If you think you're a five, Izzie, that's what you put out to people. You of all people should know that."

I got up and stood in front of the mirror on my bedroom door. "You are beautiful. You are beeeoootiful," I told myself, then laughed. "No, I'm not. I can look interesting, or maybe attractive, but I know I'll never be beautiful."

Lucy threw a pillow at me. "You're blind, Iz."

"Don't worry," I said. "I'm not major freaked about it. I'm being honest, that's all. I really don't mind if you are too. I think we all should be. Us girls, we're all afraid to say anything critical. In reality, everyone knows exactly what their assets and flaws are."

Lucy sighed. "Okay, you're an ugly old bag."

"I know I'm not that either, but I reckon that if you want to get noticed, there are three ways—you're either drop-dead gorgeous to begin with, like Nesta, who would look fab in a trash bag. Or you develop your own style—one that stands out from the crowd. You know, wild clothes or something. Or third, you wear clothes that are provocative. Cool, alluring. The worst thing is to be boring."

"No one could ever say you're boring, Iz."

I chucked a pair of baggy trousers on the "bin" pile. "Well, that's just it. I seem to go from mad clothes that are definitely different, to boring clothes that make me look invisible. I want to find a new look, one that really suits me."

"Okay then, but it's not just clothes," said Lucy. "Someone can wear the most fab designer labels and still look crapola. Like Linda Parker in Year Eleven. I saw her at the cinema the other week and she was showing off in some Dolce and Gabbana number, but a) just because her stuff was by a posh designer doesn't mean it suited her, and b) her posture is crap. That's the other thing that they teach at model school: Walk tall; don't slouch. And of course we all know that someone can be beautiful on the outside, but boring as anything inside."

I laughed. "You sound like a magazine article."

"Actually T. J. asked me to do one for the school magazine," she admitted. "She's been working on ideas over the holidays for the autumn edition. I've been doing top tips for making the most of yourself, so I've been thinking a lot about it. In the end, though, it's personality that makes you want to be with people. I hang out with Nesta because she's a laugh and big-hearted, not because she looks good."

"True," I said. "But try telling a gorgeous boy all that stuff about how much personality matters. I read in one of my mags that boys are ninety-five percent visual. The first thing they notice is what girls look like—hair, shape, legs, and so on. With girls, looks are important too, but to a lesser degree. You've got to make boys notice you in the first place so that they'll take the time to get to know your personality."

"Ben seemed to like you the way you were."

Ben was my boyfriend until last week. He plays in the band that I sing with and we'll still be mates, I hope.

"Yeah, he liked me the way I was. But I want to change. Finishing with him was part of it. I mean, we got on and everything, but it all started to feel too safe, predictable. All we ever did was band stuff. I feel like I've spent the whole of the holidays stuck in his garage going over songs, and although I know you have to practice if you want to be good, I want a bit more excitement. It's like, I dunno, Ben doesn't have any edge. Not a great challenge anymore."

"So you want a new image to get a new boy?"

"Not necessarily just to get a boy. It's part of it. It's just that, I dunno . . . I feel different lately. I want my clothes to reflect that. I want to do cool, sophisticated, a bit more grown-up, you know?"

Lucy nodded and picked out a black T-shirt. "Here, try this. Black is good for 'sophisticated,' especially if you wear it with the right accessories."

I took off the blue top I was wearing and was just pulling the black T-shirt over my head when the door opened.

"Oh hi, Lucy," said Mum, popping her head round

the door. "I didn't know you were here. Er, Izzie, I'm just popping out to the garden cen— What the . . . ?"

I'd tried to get the T-shirt over my head and down before she noticed, but it was too late. Old eagle eyes had seen it.

"Izzie! Is that a *stud* through your belly button?"

Lucy looked like she wanted to crawl under the bed.

"No." I pulled my T-shirt down as far as it would go.

She entered the room. "Let me see."

"Oh please, Mum, leave it."

"Let. Me. See. It," she demanded.

Reluctantly I lifted my T-shirt and her face turned to stone.

"When did you have that done?"

"Yesterday."

"Where?"

"Camden."

"Did you know about this, Lucy?" asked Mum, turning to Lucy who was staring at the floor. Lucy looked up at me anxiously and I managed to quickly shake my head behind Mum's back. I didn't want her getting in trouble with my mum for something I'd decided to do. Lucy shook her head.

Mum turned back to me. She looked furious. "Take it out, this instant."

"I can't," I said.

"You can and you *will*."

"No, really. You're not supposed to take it out for weeks, otherwise the hole will heal over."

"You take that stud out this instant, young lady. No one gave you permission to have it put in. We never even discussed it."

"Only because I knew you'd say no."

"Exactly," said Mum. "And I'm saying no now."

"You should have knocked," I said, suddenly feeling angry. If she'd knocked, I could have got the T-shirt on and none of this would be happening. "You're always walking in when I'm doing private things. I want a lock on my door."

"Er, got to go," said Lucy, getting up and heading for the door. "Um, er, catch you later, Iz."

And with that, she fled.

Lucy's Top Tips for Making the Most of Yourself

* Stand up straight. Don't slouch or hunch over. Think supermodel and strut your stuff.

* Eat healthy food. Hair and skin glow on a good diet and are dull on a stodgy junk-food diet.

* Have regular pampering sessions, even if they're DIY at home. You'll get the idea that you're worth it, then others will pick up on this.

* Pay attention to detail: nails, hands, feet, eyebrows, skin.

* Keep hair clean and well cut. It's Murphy's Law—the day you put off washing your hair is the day you'll bump into someone you fancy.

* Save up and buy one wonderful item that makes you feel fabulous whenever you put it on.

* Wear underwear that fits properly and looks good.

* Think positively. Of all the things you wear, your expression is the one that people see first. If you are miserable and feel bored with yourself, others will pick up on that.

* Invest in a fab pair of sunglasses for days when you feel tired and not at your best.

* Ninety percent of looking good comes from confidence. Believe in yourself. Everyone has it in them to look wonderful in their own individual way.

* Find out what suits you as an individual. A designer label doesn't guarantee it will look fab on you.

4

Loud Lady

Of course Mum got her way. I begged, I pleaded, I offered to do the washing up for the next month, but there's no arguing with her when she's got a strop on, and this one was major. After a long lecture about infections, looking cheap, going behind her back, blah de blah de blah, she made me take out the stud. She even waited outside the bathroom door while I did it, then demanded that I hand it to her.

"I'll put this in the bin," she said, wrapping it in a tissue like it was dog's doo-doo. "And don't think we've finished, Isobel. You and I are going to sit down later and have words." And with that, she headed down the stairs and out, slamming the front door behind her.

Words, I thought. Huh. Well, it's going to be her saying them all because I'm never going to speak to her again. Ever.

As soon as I heard the car engine start up I rang Lucy, but her mobile was off. I dialed Nesta's number.

"Oh, you poor thing," she sympathized, after I'd filled her in on the latest. "After all you went through as well."

"I know. She's gone to the garden center in a huff. Poor plants, that's all I can say. You know they say that they're sensitive to vibes—well, I bet they all wilt when she walks in."

"What does Angus say about the stud?"

Angus is my stepdad. I nicknamed him The Lodger when he and Mum first got together, as it was the only way I could deal with him and his daughters, Amelia and Claudia. But we get on okay now, so I call him by his proper name. He tends to stay out of it when Mum and I aren't getting on.

"Dunno. Nothing. He's hiding in the greenhouse, feeding geraniums or something equally boring. Is this what Sundays are about when you get old? Plants? I hope it never happens to me, Nesta. Anyway, Mum's being totally unreasonable. Lucy's parents are totally cool about her stud. It's not fair. I mean, it's not like I've got pregnant or become a drug addict or anything. I mean, what is her problem?"

"Maybe you should have told her you *were* pregnant," said Nesta. "You know, gone in with a long face and said, Mum I have something to tell you, then come out with this long list of *really* awful things. All fictitious, of course. Then, when she was totally freaked, you'd say, No, it's not true. But, oh . . . one tiny thing: I *have* had my belly button pierced. By then, she'd have been so relieved, she'd probably even have offered to pay for it."

"D'er, why didn't I think of that?" I laughed. "Look, do you fancy meeting me in Muswell Hill? I've had an idea."

"What?"

"Tell you when I see you," I said. "Meet me in Ruby in the Dust in half an hour."

"Izzie . . . what are you up to?"

"Tell you later."

I raced up to Muswell Hill, and luckily the shop I wanted was open, even though it was Sunday. I went in and headed for the back, where I knew they kept their jewelry displays. The quicker I get a new stud in, the better, I thought.

I found a perfect one. It was really pretty, silver with a square glass stone that reflects all the colors of the rainbow.

I made my purchase then went to Ruby in the Dust café where I headed straight for the ladies. Once inside, I locked the door and unwrapped my new stud. I know Del said you had to wait a few weeks, but I have no choice, I thought as I pulled up my T-shirt. Oh god, I don't think I can do this, I said to myself, as I looked at the tiny hole. It was scabbing over already and the area around it looked red and raw. I poked at the skin. It felt bruised and sore. No pain, no gain, I thought, and I took a deep breath and pushed the stud through in one quick go. "Ow, ow, *OWWW* . . ."

There was a knock on the door. "Are you all right in there?" called a woman with a very loud voice.

"Yes, fine," I said, sitting on the loo for a moment to catch my breath and dab my eyes, which had started watering as the stud went through.

"You going to be long?" the voice boomed again.

"Just a minute." I stood up and quickly wiped my belly button area with some water from the tap, then opened the door.

The lady outside gave me a strange look as I came

out, so I gave her what I hoped was a reassuring smile, headed back into the café, and made for the window seat.

I ordered a large hot chocolate and leaned back, trying to relax. After a while, I began to wonder if I'd done the wrong thing by buying the new stud. I hadn't really thought about it too much in the heat of the moment—only that Mum wasn't going to stop me. I'm not a baby anymore, although she treats me like one sometimes. But maybe I'd gone a bit far by defying her this much. And I also wondered if it was worth it, as my belly button was stinging like anything.

I began to wish Mum was more like Dad. He's really cool. They split up yonks ago and he's remarried now, with a little boy. I don't think Dad would have objected to me getting my belly button pierced for a minute. He married one of his mature students and she has *three* earrings in her right ear. She's pretty cool too.

Just at that moment, I noticed a boy come in and sit on a sofa to my right. He looks familiar, I thought, then a rush of heat flooded through me. It was the guy from the park yesterday, only today he was dressed in jeans and a denim jacket instead of his black leathers. He didn't appear to notice me, and as he sat waiting to be served, he started either playing a game or text messaging on his mobile.

A few seconds later, the woman from the loos came out and sat at the table behind him. The moment she sat down, her mobile rang. I couldn't help but turn to look at her when she answered. She talked *so* loud. You would have thought the person at the other end was deaf. Maybe she's talking to an aging parent or someone, I thought. But then she finished that call and started another. She *still* talked really loud. The whole café could hear what she was saying and she seemed completely oblivious. The guy from the park turned around, glanced at her, then over at me. He raised his eyebrows as if to say, "Some people."

For the next ten minutes, the café customers got to know her life story intimately—she was having chicken for dinner, but cooking fish for Duchess, her cat. She was seeing John, whoever he was, at the weekend, and he had a nasty rash on his ankle, so she thought he should see a doctor. And on and on and *on* at top volume. A few people gave her disapproving looks, but she didn't register them. On one call, she asked whoever she was talking to to ring her back and gave her number. I glanced over at Park Boy and I could swear that he was writing it down. What's he up to? I wondered. He can't possibly fancy her; she must be at least forty. Then at last, at *last,* Loud Lady got up to leave and the café was peaceful again. You could almost hear everyone breathe a sigh of relief.

From where I was sitting, I could see the woman exit the café, walk a few meters down the road, and stand at a bus stop.

And then her mobile rang. As she answered it, I noticed that Park Boy was also on his phone.

"Is that 07485 95539?" he asked. That's definitely Loud Lady's number, I thought as I watched him, intrigued as to what he was up to.

I turned to look out the window at the bus stop where, sure enough, I saw Loud Lady nod her head.

"Well, this is the Mobile Phone Police," said Park Boy. "And it has come to our attention that you have the *loudest* voice ever recorded on our sound monitors. We're going to have to ask you to tone it down or else your phone will be confiscated." Then he put his phone aside.

I burst out laughing and watched as Loud Lady looked around her in bewilderment. Park Boy caught my eye and laughed too. Excellent, I thought, and I hope he comes over. He seems like a real laugh. He didn't come over, though. He just went back to playing on his phone, so I went back to my chocolate and gazed out the window, trying to look cool. After a few minutes, I decided I probably looked more vacant than cool, so I decided to write a song about him.

Nesta arrived about ten minutes later, full of apologies for being late. I glanced over at Park Boy, but he still had his head down, focused on his phone. Weird, I thought. Boys *always* look up when Nesta makes an entrance. They can't help it. She's half Italian, half Jamaican, and that adds up to Stunning with a capital S. With her long silky black hair and dark exotic looks, she's a boy magnet.

As Nesta settled herself down, the boy *finally* got up. Oh, here we go, I thought. I knew it. He won't come over to me, but now he's seen Nesta, suddenly he's interested.

But no, he went straight out of the door. As he walked past the window, he glanced at me and winked. I smiled back. He didn't even glance at Nesta.

Dark Rider

Whenever I see him, I know it's right to be wrong.
I live and breathe him, but I've got to be strong.
Nobody likes him 'cause he thinks it's cool to be bad,
But deep down inside him, I'm sure
there's good to be had.
I should turn away when he's riding down the street,
But a blur of steel and black leather
makes my heart skip a beat.
Dark rider, fly my way and thrill me
with your thunder.
Steely strider, I'm just looking for a smile.
Kick it over and accelerate, take me
with you miles and miles.
Right or wrong, what's going on,
I've got to move on.

5

Peculiar Parents

Mum was in the kitchen chopping peppers when I got back from Muswell Hill. I took a deep breath and prepared myself for the inevitable. Just bite the bullet, I told myself. Let her have her say, look apologetic, then escape to the safety of my room.

"Izzie . . . ," Mum began.

Izzie? I thought. What's going on? She calls me Isobel when she's mad. Was everything okay, then? I was still determined not to speak to her, though, only the requisite, yes, no, sorry, sorry. But as she went on, I began to feel *really* rotten. In her own way, I could see that she was trying to be understanding. I don't get her at all sometimes. I'd mentally prepared myself for the "words," but she was being really nice, a total turnaround since this morning.

Maybe this is some new kind of torture, I thought as she looked at me with concern. Or maybe she's been reading one of those "How to deal with your mad teenage daughter" books. That's probably it. I don't know. Whatever it was, my new mellow mum kind of threw me. She was all, Are you all right? Did you get some lunch? Is there anything you want to talk about? You know I have your best interests at heart, and so on. I felt *awful*. I'd much rather be bawled out, I thought, because now I feel guilty as hell that I've got a new stud in. Hell's bells, and poo. Sometimes I just can't win.

After the "words," she offered to drive me over to Dad's, as I'd arranged to have supper there.

"Er, no thanks, Mum," I said. "I promised I'd drop in at Ben's on the way, just for half an hour to run through some of the songs for the gig next Saturday."

She rolled her eyes. "You're never in these days, Izzie. Look, call me from your dad's later. I'll come and get you."

"Oh, don't worry, Mum," I said. "I'll get Dad to drop me."

"Well, don't be too late," she called after me as I headed for the door.

* * *

The boys were already there when I got to Ben's house in Highgate. There are four of them in the band: Ben, who's the lead vocalist and plays guitar and keyboard, Mark on bass, Elliot, also on keyboard, and Biff on drums. The band's called King Noz and they've made quite a name for themselves locally, playing gigs in pubs and local schools. I'm not officially in the band, but when I started going out with Ben, I sang a few numbers with them and now I've become a regular.

The boys were all out in the garage, going over some of the songs for Saturday. I say garage, but it's really a den/music studio. Ben's dad works as a sound engineer at the BBC and he converted the garage into a studio for Ben to rehearse in. It's totally brilliant in there. At the beginning of summer, Ben and I went down to the East End and bought loads of silk suit lining fabric, which we draped all over the garage, from the ceiling and walls. He put up posters of Krishna, Buddha, and Guru Nanak, and we persuaded his dad to collect this old sofa and chair that we'd spotted on a skip a few streets away. It's a really funky room now—it looks like an Arabian tent and it smells Eastern as well, because he burns the joss sticks I got him for his birthday—

lavender and amber ones. They smell fab. Ben gave me a key to the room when we were going out and he hasn't asked for it back, which is good of him. He said I could go there if ever I want to hang out on my own and get away from home. His parents are really cool and never go in. They're not daft, because I think if the band rehearsed in the house, they'd have gone mad with all the din.

Ben adjusted his glasses and looked up from one of the song sheets. "So, Iz, got any new material?"

"Almost," I said. "I'm cooking a few ideas."

Ben nodded. "Well, let me have a look when you've got something down."

"Will do," I said and I kicked my shoes off and lay on the sofa. The boys started jamming, so I closed my eyes and drifted off. I've no regrets about finishing with Ben, I thought. Everyone said I was mad, as we got on so well, but the excitement had gone. We'd become mates, that's all. I wanted something more. Though I think I'll probably stay friends with Ben for life. He's the type of person that's really easy to be with—laid back, like nothing ever fazes him. Not even me finishing with him. He was like, Whatever you want, babe.

My thoughts turned to the boy in the café this morning and I felt a shiver of anticipation. I wondered who he was, what he was into, and if I'd bump into him again. It was weird seeing him twice in just two days. I'm a great believer in fate and I think that if something's meant to happen it will. I looked at my watch. It was only six. Dad lives in a flat near Chalk Farm, behind the shops on Primrose Hill Road. Maybe I'll get the tube to Camden then walk through the park over to Dad's instead of going up the main road, I thought. See if Park Boy's around.

At that moment, a noise to my right distracted me. I opened my eyes to see Biff over at the tap at the back wall. The others couldn't see what he was doing, but I could. He was filling a plastic bag with water. Biff's a bit of a nutter and likes nothing better than a water fight. I decided to get out while I was still dry. Last week I'd joined in with gusto, hurling water bombs like the best of them, but . . . I don't know. Suddenly it all seemed a bit childish. I wasn't in the mood. I felt restless, so I decided to go off to the park to see if fate had anything more interesting to offer.

On the journey down, my sense of anticipation grew. I really hoped Park Boy would be there. It was a lovely summer's evening and it felt like there was magic in the air. As I walked from Camden to Primrose Hill, there were loads of people around, standing outside the pubs, sitting outside cafés. For some reason, it felt really romantic. I walked up Parkway then right and along and into the park. As I walked through, there was no sign of him and I couldn't help feeling disappointed. Never mind, I told myself, what will be, will be. Anyway, he might have a girlfriend. All the fanciable boys are usually involved, one way or another.

As I got closer to Dad's flat, my thoughts turned to another cute boy: Tom. He's my three-year-old half-brother. One of my favorite things is giving him his nighttime bath, but he was already in bed when I got there.

Dad and Anna were just ordering Indian takeout and they ordered a mixed vegetable one for me, as I've been vegetarian for the last year. When the food arrived, we settled down to a really nice supper. It's always so relaxed at Dad's. The total opposite of Mum's, where there's not a thing out of place and everything is pristine and clean. Here, there are books, magazines, and mess everywhere. It looks lived-in, not like the Ideal Home display at Mum's.

"Got a new book for you, Izzie," said Dad, throwing me a paperback. *"The Catcher in the Rye,* by J. D. Salinger. I think you'll enjoy it."

"Thanks," I said. He's always giving me stuff to read. He lectures in English literature and sometimes I think that he forgets that I'm his daughter and imagines I'm one of his students. Some of the books he gives me are okay, but some of them are heavy going. I try to read them all, though, as I don't want him to think that I don't appreciate it.

Inevitably Dad asked how things were at home, so I told him about the stud incident. I thought that if I could get him on my side, maybe Mum would come around to the idea. I *do* have two parents after all, and even though I live with Mum, she shouldn't have the final say about *everything*.

"So, would you have objected?" I asked.

Dad smiled. "Don't grow up *too* soon, will you, Izzie?"

"No, course not. Anyway, how can you grow up *too* soon? You're meant to grow up and go through changes, aren't you? And I'm going into Year Ten next week, so that's moving on. And *don't* change the subject. . . ." Dad always does this when I try and get him involved with anything that's happening at home. He kind of sidesteps it. "Belly button stud. Would you have objected?"

"Probably not," he said finally. "Not if you really wanted one. It's your decision if you want to mutilate your body."

So I told him I'd put a new stud in after Mum had confiscated the first one.

First he laughed, then he shook his head. "Oh dear. Our Izzie's turning into a rebel. Your mother won't be happy about that, will she?"

"Well, she's not going to find out. And you won't tell her, will you?"

"No, of course not," he said. "But won't she find out? I mean, you *do* live in the same house."

"That's the other thing," I said. "Would you have a word with her about letting me have a lock put on my bedroom door? She keeps walking in on me. I have no privacy at all."

Dad looked at Anna and grimaced.

"Keep me out of it," she said, and started clearing away our dishes. Anna isn't a timid sort of person at all. She's very forthcoming with her opinions about most things, but I've noticed that she never says anything about my mum. Like Angus. He never says anything about Dad.

Dad looked at his hands. "I don't know, Izzie. I don't know if I'm the best one to go laying down the law about how things should be at home. She wouldn't like it."

Poo, I thought. Everyone's scared of my mother. Even my dad. No wonder they split up.

After we'd cleared the kitchen, Anna asked if I wanted to stay and watch a film with them. I looked at my watch. It was half past eight. I'd told Mum I wouldn't be late, so if I left now, I could still stay in her good books.

"Are you sure I can't drop you?" asked Dad as I put on my jacket to go.

I shook my head. "No, you stay and relax. I'll walk up to Camden and get the tube. It's still light and I've got my mobile."

Finally he let me go and I set off for the tube. Once again I chose the scenic route, past the shops at Primrose Hill, through the park, then along Regent's Park Road up to Parkway. Part of me was thinking that if fate had brought me and Park Boy together twice in two days, then it would bring us together again. But another part was thinking that there's no harm in giving fate a hand. That part was definitely winning the argument.

The light was beginning to fade when I reached the park gates, and normally I wouldn't walk through on my own, because I know that there are some dodgy people around and not to take stupid risks. But something inside of me was pushing me to go on. I'll be fine, I told myself, and I have my trusty mobile.

I glanced up the hill to my right as I set off along the path at the bottom of the park. There were a couple of girls sitting near the railings and I was pretty sure they were the ones that Park Boy was with the day before, but no sign of him. Apart from the girls, there weren't many other people about—only an old lady walking her dog and a man jogging.

As I got halfway down the path, I began to wonder if I'd made a mistake taking this route. It was very quiet and even though it wasn't dark yet, it didn't feel as safe as when there were loads of people about. I tried to remember T. J.'s tips for being out on your own at night. She'd been working on a piece for the school mag about being street smart. Not walking in empty places at night, I thought, that was one of them.

I stepped up my pace, then glanced over my shoulder. Someone was on the path behind me. A boy in black. He put his head down when I turned. Was it Park Boy? I glanced again, but he'd left the path and was heading for the trees, so I couldn't see his face. He looked about the same height as Park Boy, but I couldn't be sure that it was him. I could feel my heart beginning to pound as I glanced behind again. No sign of anyone. I don't like this, I thought. I looked across at the trees and could see movement, like someone was darting from tree to tree, trying to stay out of sight. My heart began to beat really fast and I felt my chest tighten with fear. Was it Park Boy playing some daft game? Then it dawned on me that even if it was, I didn't know him at all. Maybe he was some kind of weirdo.

I stopped for a moment to try to locate exactly where the person was. But whoever it was in the trees also stopped. I set off again, walking fast, but not quite breaking into a run yet. What shall I do? I thought. I could feel myself begin to panic and I got my mobile out of my pocket and put my thumb on the keypad, ready to phone Dad if I got into any trouble. He lived nearest and could be there in five minutes if I needed help. I took a *really* quick glance over my shoulder and saw the shape of someone on the path. Yeah, it is Park

Boy, I decided, breathing a sigh of relief. Same denim jacket. Right, I thought. Let's see how *he* likes it when people disappear behind trees! As I turned a corner on the path, I snuck behind a tree and waited. I could hear the sound of footsteps approaching and as the Boy walked by, I leaped out.

"Park Police," I yelled. "What do you think you're playing at?"

A young lad with dark hair almost leaped out of his skin. He took one look at me and began to run as fast as he could away from me toward the gate. Whoever he was, he wasn't the one who had been following me. As I watched him scarper, I heard someone laughing behind me. I swung around and Park Boy stepped out with a huge grin on his face.

"You *creep!*" I yelled. "You really scared me."

"Er, excuse me," he said, and pointed at the young lad in the distance, who was still running. "I think it's *you* who's scaring people. Park Police!"

"I thought he was you. What were *you* doing? You were following me, hiding in the trees."

"I thought you *saw* it was me," he said, pointing back up the path. "Way back there."

"Yeah, but I don't know you."

"From the café, this morning . . ."

"I know. But I don't *know* you. . . ."

"Oh, right," said the boy, then smiled. "Josh Harper." He pointed at the girls I'd passed. "I'm with some mates. Do you want to come and join us?"

I looked behind me to the other side of the park, then toward the gate off to my left. I did a quick calculation. If I walked back over and hung out with them for a while, it would be late and I didn't fancy walking the path again when it was really dark, and I didn't want to act like I was a weed, asking one of them to come with me.

"Er, no thanks," I said.

"Got to be home by curfew time?"

"*No*. Just . . ."

"Then chill," he said, and sat on the grass, smiling a really wicked smile. "I won't bite you . . . least not until I've got to know you better." He pulled out a can of lager from his jacket. "Want a drink?"

I pulled a face. "No, thanks. Lager tastes disgusting."

He laughed and reached into his other pocket and pulled out a small bottle of vodka. "Prefer this?"

I shook my head again. "What are you? A walking bar?"

"No, that's the lot." He lifted his arms and leaned back on the grass, inviting me to go into his pockets. "But you're welcome to go through my things, officer."

I felt myself blushing and was glad that it was beginning to get dark. Hopefully he wouldn't notice.

"No, I believe you," I said.

"So what's your name?"

"Izzie."

"So, no vodka, no lager. What does Izzie like to drink?"

Actually Ribena Lite is my favorite at the moment, but I didn't think it sounded very sophisticated. "Er . . ."

Luckily I was saved from answering as my mobile rang. "S'cuse me a sec." I walked a few paces away to take the call. It was Mum. She sounded harassed.

"Where are you?"

"On my way home."

"Why isn't your dad bringing you? I just called there and he said you were making your own way back."

"I'll be back before it's dark."

"Where exactly are you?"

"Just going into Camden tube station," I fibbed.

"I'll pick you up at East Finchley, then."

I switched off the phone and went back to Josh. He

looked highly amused. "Mum and Dad wondering where their little girl is?"

"*No*. But I've got to go. Er . . . things to do."

"Sure." He shrugged and got up to go back to his friends. "See you around, kid."

Kid, I thought as I walked away. What a cheek. Then I turned to sneak another look at him. He turned back at exactly the same time and laughed when he saw me glancing round. Ha, I thought as I set off for the tube. Caught you looking!

T. J.'s Tips for Being Streetwise

* Always keep a taxi number handy for times of emergency or times you can't reach someone you know. If you have a mobile, save the number in your address book.

* Keep your keys in your pocket in case someone ever steals your bag—that way at least you can get in your front door.

* It's a good idea to have a bag that you can wear diagonally over your body, so it's harder for someone to grab it and run.

* Don't walk in dark secluded places. Use routes home that are well lit and where there are still people about, even if it means walking farther.

* Don't make eye contact with strangers.

* If you ever feel you're being followed, get to a populated area as fast as possible and keep your mobile within reach but out of sight.

* Never hesitate to call and ask someone to pick you up if you've been stranded.

* If a stranger ever asks if you want a lift, always say no and that your dad is on his way and will be there any second. Then immediately phone the person you know who lives nearest.

* If ever traveling on the tube or train, always travel in a compart-ment with people in it. If they get off at a stop, leaving the carriage empty, get off with them and get into a carriage with people in it.

* If ever you are mugged, don't fight. Hand over your phone, watch, or purse, then leg it.

* Walk confidently—head up and briskly.

6

Zombie

"I've got a quiz to try out on you," said Lucy, flopping on the sofa. "It's just your kind of thing, Izzie—sort of a psychological test."

We were all over at Nesta's the following evening. We spent the first twenty minutes swapping news, and I'd filled them in on bumping into Josh again and the ongoing war with Mum. She was back to her usual mad self when she picked me up from the tube station the night before. Apparently when she phoned Dad to ask why I wasn't home yet, he mentioned that he knew about the belly button stud. She wasn't happy. Oh no. She spent the whole journey home going on about how he's too laid back when it comes to disciplining me, he's not the one who has to lay down the rules, the one who worries when I'm out late, wonders where I am and what I'm getting up to. I tried telling her that I could handle myself, but she wasn't really listening. No wonder Dad doesn't want to get involved. She gets so worked up over nothing.

It was good to get out of the house and over to Nesta's to see the girls and have some normal company.

"Okay," I said, sitting on the floor next to the sofa. "Shoot."

"You have to think of your three favorite animals," said Lucy. "Then remember them in order. Tell me when you've got them."

We all sat and thought for a few minutes.

"Okay, ready," I said.

"And me," chorused Nesta and T. J.

"Okay," said Lucy. "Say them out loud and why you picked them. Nesta?"

"Cats because they're elegant and independent. Leopards because they're beautiful, and peacocks because they're stunning when they put their tails up and strut their stuff."

Lucy laughed.

"What?" asked Nesta. "What's so funny?"

"You'll find out in a minute," said Lucy. "Okay, Iz?"

"Um, dolphins because they're friendly and intelligent, orangutans because when you look into their eyes, you can tell they have these really wise old souls, and owls because they're meant to be wise, but if you ever take a good look at them, they're actually hysterically funny—they can turn their heads round almost three hundred and sixty degrees."

Lucy burst out laughing again.

"*What*?" I asked.

"You'll see in a minute. T. J.?"

"Penguins because they're entertaining and have a funny walk, dogs because they're intelligent, loyal, and playful, and meercats because they look after each other—they're really social animals."

"Okay," Lucy said, grinning. "I'll tell you what it all means now. Your first choice was how you see yourself. . . ."

"That's amazing," I said. "T. J. picked penguins because they're entertaining, and you are, T. J. Dunno about the funny walk, though. And Nesta picked cats because they're elegant and independent. It's really true."

"And you said dolphins because they're friendly and intelligent," said Nesta. "That's true as well."

"Okay, what do the other choices mean?" asked Nesta.

"Second one is how others see you and the last one is how you really are."

"We see you as an orangutan. . . ." Nesta laughed, pointing at me.

"Yeah, fat and hairy," I said.

Nesta laughed again. "We're going to have to work on your self-esteem, girl."

"But it's more the reason *why* you picked them that's revealing, not the animal so much," said Lucy. "And Izzie said because when she looks at an orangutan, she sees a wise old soul. That's *exactly* how I see you, Iz."

"And you really are a peacock," said T. J., pointing at Nesta.

Nesta's face clouded. "Proud as a peacock. Oh dear."

"No," said Lucy. "You didn't say that. You said you liked peacocks because they're stunning when they strut their stuff. Nothing could be more true in your case."

"And others do see you as beautiful," said T. J. "You said leopards for your second one because they're beautiful. Second one's how others see you, right, Lucy?"

Lucy nodded.

Nesta started strutting around the room. "Yeah. And you're an owl, Izzie. Why did you say you liked them?"

"Because they can turn their heads three hundred and sixty degrees." I tried to do it, but nope, wouldn't go.

T. J. pulled a face. "And I'm a meercat."

"But all the ones you chose, you said were because they're playful, intelligent, and loyal," said Lucy. "That's exactly how you are, T. J. Don't you see—your choices reveal a lot about your character."

"Kind of like how what you wear reveals who you are as well," I said. "So what did you pick, Luce?"

"Horse, ostrich, dog. Horses because they're gentle, ostriches because they're funny, and dogs because they're faithful and fun."

"Spot on," said T. J.

"Okay," said Nesta. "I'm going to strut my stuff into the kitchen. Who wants what?"

"Diet Coke," said T. J.

"Same," said Lucy.

"Izzie?" asked Nesta.

"How long are your parents out for?" I asked.

"Until about ten thirty, I think," said Nesta. "They've gone to see a movie. Why?"

I eyed the drinks cabinet under the bookshelf behind

the sofa. They had an amazing collection of spirits and liqueur—some I'd never heard of. Nesta saw me looking and went and stood next to them. "What can I get you, madam? Gin and tonic? Vodka and orange? Eggflip and marmite?"

I went and stood next to her and put my finger under my chin. "Hmm, I'm not sure, barman. What do you recommend?"

"Chocolate milkshakes with marshmallows," said Nesta, heading for the door. "How does that sound?"

"Shall we try a *drink* drink?" I asked. "You know, while your parents are out. Just a taste to see what we might like."

"I've tried most of them," said Nesta, "and I can tell you, they're pretty yuck. Whisky is sour, vodka is tasteless, and gin tastes like lighter fluid."

"Since when have you been drinking lighter fluid?" I asked.

Nesta screwed her face up. "You know what I mean. Not very nice."

"I'd like to try one," I said. "See, like what Lucy was saying about people's choices revealing who they are—I don't know what I like to drink."

"But most of them taste awful, honest . . . ," said Nesta.

"I know," I said. "I've tried some of Mum's when she's been out. But you can mix them with other stuff, you know, to take away the taste of alcohol."

"So, what's the point?" asked T. J.

"Well, you can't drink Sprite or Ribena Lite forever. It's looks a bit babyish sometimes."

"Says who?" said T. J. "I don't care. It's what tastes good to *me* that counts. I'm the one drinking it."

"Yeah, but if you're with a load of older boys or something, or at a party, it might be good to ask for something more sophisticated."

I glanced at the bookshelves and spotted a book tucked in with some recipe books. I pulled it out and read the title. "*Cocktails for City Nights*. How about we try one of these?" I flicked through the opening pages. "There are loads here. Barracuda Bite, Moscow Mule . . . Oh, here's one for me. It's called Dirty Mother. What do you think? See what they taste like?"

Lucy came and read the list over my shoulder. "Hey, T. J. How do you fancy trying a Screaming Orgasm?"

"Exs*cooth* me?" she giggled.

"It's made from Irish cream, Kahlua, vodka, and amaretto." I looked at the bottles. "Yeah, your mum has all of those."

Nesta came back over to the drinks cabinet and looked at the bottles. "Shall we?" she asked with a mischievous look on her face.

"Count me out," said T. J. from where she was lying on the floor. "I don't like alcohol. I tried some red wine once and it tasted like ink."

"Yeah, but some of these sound really nice," I said, still reading. "They have juice and liqueurs and some even have cream in them. I'll make you a special one. A T. J. Watts."

"The milkshake sounded good to me," said T. J. "That's what I fancy. Did you know that one glass of spirits has something like three hundred calories in it? I'd rather use my quota up on chocolate."

"Oh, come on," I said. "Where's your spirit of adventure? Let's make a few of them. Just for a taste."

Lucy looked worried and glanced at Nesta. "But won't your parents notice?" she asked. "I mean, if the levels in the bottles have gone down, they'll know it was us."

"We're not going to drink *that* much, Lucy," I said. "Just experiment a bit. Last night when Josh asked what I wanted to drink, I felt stupid. In the future, I want to be able to answer with confidence. I think that's part of being a grown-up, knowing what you like. But I haven't got a clue. I think it's part of finding out who you are—you know, whether you like coffee or tea, spirits or wine, and so on."

T. J. grinned. "Well if you're an orangutan, we'd better get you some banana juice."

"Yeah, right. Very refined. *Not*," I said.

Lucy started laughing. "Drink? Oh, thank you, darling," she said in a posh voice. "I'll have . . ." She glanced at the cocktail book. "Yes, I'll have a Tidal Wave—no, maybe not, sounds pretty lethal. No, make mine"—this time she made her voice go squeaky—"a Coconut Highball."

Nesta read over her shoulder and made her face go stupid. "And I'll have a Zombie."

"That sounds nice," I said. "It's rum, pineapple, lemon, and orange."

"Okay," said Nesta. "Here's the deal. We mix up a few and have a little taste of each other's. Okay?"

"And if the levels are down a bit," said Lucy, "we can fill the bottles up with a bit of water. That's what my brother Lal did when he tried Dad's whisky the other week. Dad never noticed."

We spent a short time picking the ones we liked the

sound of, then checking to see if Nesta's parents had the ingredients.

"They've got most of them," said Nesta. "People always give them weird liqueurs at Christmas and they never get touched unless Mum is making some exotic dessert."

I picked a White Russian as I thought that sounded really cool. Nesta ended up choosing one called a Kamikaze, T. J. went for a Piña Colada, and Lucy decided that she had to try the Screaming Orgasm.

"Just in case I never get off with a boy ever again and never actually get to have sex," she said, laughing. "At least I can say truthfully that I've had a screaming orgasm."

"Yeah. Who needs boys?" I asked, running my finger down the index. "There's one here called Sex with a Shark."

"Think I'll pass on that," said Lucy. "I'm trying to give up sharks. Rats are more my thing. Love rats."

Nesta went and got juices and cream from the fridge and we spent the next ten minutes pouring and stirring. Once our drinks were ready, we took a sip of the one we made, then a sip of each other's. My White Russian tasted fantastic, so after the others had a sip, I drank all of it. It had a load of cream and coffee liqueur in it and tasted really sweet. Fab. Nesta didn't like hers. "Too sour," she said and handed it to me. I took a sip. Yuck. She was right. "Too much lime," I said.

"Stick to the sweet ones," I said. "Here, I'll make you one. A Nesta special." I poured some black currant liqueur, a shot of gin, and some vodka into a glass and swirled it around. It's simple, I thought. You just mix up what you like until it tastes good. Nesta didn't like that either, though. Waste not, want not, I thought, adding a bit of lemonade. Tastes like Ribena. So I slugged it back.

T. J. only took a sip of hers. "I thought we were just trying them," she said. "Not drinking the who e thing. We might get drunk."

"Cowardy custard," I said. I took a taste of Lucy's. Mmmm, I thought. Also quite nice. It tasted really sweet and almondy.

"It's got amaretto in it," she said. "Mum puts it in her cake mix at Christmas."

"Let's try another," I said, raising my glass.

Nesta pulled a face. "Not for me, thanks. I learned my lesson at your first gig with King Noz, remember?"

"All forgotten," I said happily. It was around last Christmas and some plonker had given her a pile of champagne. It was my first performance with King Noz and I was really nervous about it, then Nesta got tiddly and hogged the limelight by dancing madly in front of everyone when they were supposed to be listening to the band. I suppose it was funny, looking back, but at the time, I was really miffed that she'd stolen all the attention.

"I felt quite ill afterwards, if I remember rightly," said Nesta.

"Can't take your drink," I teased her. "Okay. Lucy, do you want to try another one?"

Lucy wrinkled her nose. "Haven't finished this one yet. You're not supposed to slug them back, you know, especially if you want to be more grown-up. You're supposed to sip, like a lady. Like this . . ." She took a mouthful and started gargling it and making her eyes go cross-eyed at the same time.

T. J., Nesta, and I all cracked up and took mouthfuls of ours, then gargled as well.

"Really, though, Izzie," said Nesta when we'd stopped laughing. "I don't think you're supposed to knock them back. And you've had two plus some of ours already."

"I'm fine," I said. "Just one more." I felt like being reckless and daring for a change. Everyone always thinks I'm the sensible one, I thought. Oh, sensible Izzie, she has all the answers. But I don't, not really. I'm just a mad old orangutan. I looked back at the index and picked another cocktail. "I'm going to try one of these Tequila Sunrises. I think that sounds really nice, don't you? And it's mainly orange juice, so it will be okay, won't it?"

Nesta shrugged and started to put the tops back on the bottles. "I guess, but don't blame me if you feel like crapola tomorrow."

I think this will be my drink, I said to myself, as I poured some tequila and orange into a glass. My brain was starting to feel slightly fuzzy, but in a nice way, as I poured in a generous measure. Slightly bitter, I thought when I tasted it. Needs something else. I added a dash of whisky and tried that. Nope, still not nice. So I added a tiny bit of Martini. No, yuck, that one doesn't work at all. I put it to one side.

After that the others sat down and began to watch telly. I was feeling too good to just slob on the sofa, so I started reading through the cocktail book again.

"I'm going to become an expert," I said. "Cocktail queen. When I've got a flat of my own, I'll have *all* these drinks. A whole wall of them, like in a bar. And I'll have the fluorescent ones as well, the ones that make drinks blue or green. Like *really* sopisti . . . no, I mean, soristi . . . no, *sophisticated*. S'a hard word to say, that. Isn't it? Sopis . . . tic . . . ated. Never realized that before."

"Izzie, you're drunk," said T. J. from the sofa.

"No, I'm not," I said. I wasn't. At least I didn't think so. I felt perfectly fine. "Don't be silly. But I do feel good." Then I spotted some crème de menthe. "There's a green one. I bet that tastes nice mixed with Bailey's. My gran always has that, at Christmas. It tastes like it has chocolate in it." I poured a small amount of each into a glass.

Nesta got up, took the glass out of my hand, and took a sip. She almost spat it out. "It tastes of toothpaste mixed with liquified After Eight. *Yee-uck*. Way too sickly."

I took the glass off her and swigged it down. "Mmm. I like it. S'nice. Chocolatey."

"Come and sit down," said Lucy. "We're going to start a film."

"Okay," I said. "Just going to the loo." I started to walk towards the door and that's when I became aware that maybe the drinks were stronger than I'd thought. My legs seemed to have turned to jelly and the room began to sway. Oops, I thought as I reached out to the wall for support. Am okay. Just a bit . . . wobbly. Walk straight.

Lucy, Nesta, and T. J. were half laughing and half looking at me with concern. "S'okay," I said. "I'm fine." I *was* fine. It was *them* who were out of focus.

I made my way out to the corridor and realized I was having a very hard time walking in a straight line. I made it to the bathroom and switched on the light. Very, very bright, I thought as I sat on the loo and tried to pull myself together. Fine, I told myself, feeling fine. But my vision had gone all blurry and I was beginning to feel a tad nauseous.

There was a knock on the door, then Lucy's voice. "Izzie. You still in there?"

"Yeah."

"You've been in there for ages," she said. "You okay?"

I made myself get up, but the room seemed to be spinning. "Yeah. Fine," I said. I opened the door and giggled.

Lucy raised an eyebrow. "Come and sit down."

I followed her back to the sitting room, trying once again to walk in a straight line. Funny feeling, this, I thought. Sort of giggly, but blurry at the same time. As we reached the sitting room door, I was vaguely aware of Nesta's brother, Tony, coming into the house.

This would be a good time to stop and stand still,

I decided. Prop myself up against the wall.

Tony looked at me quizzically. "You all right?" he asked.

"Oops." I laughed as I leaned back on the wall and knocked a picture frame squiff.

He gave me a funny look, then went into the sitting room. I followed, or rather fell, in after him. He took in the bottles and glasses. "You girls have been having fun, I see," he said.

"Izzie's drunk as a skunk," said Nesta from the sofa.

"I am *not* . . . ," I said. I wasn't. I really wasn't. Just felt a bit blurry and in need of a lie-down. On the carpet behind the sofa seemed like a good place, so I knelt down and crawled there. It felt nice and cool, so I curled up and closed my eyes. Euumm. Feel a bit funny, I thought, and opened one eye. All I could see was under the sofa and the skirting board. This is what mice see, I thought. Arrr. Sweet. A mouse's view on life. But fine. Fine. Best have a little sleep.

"Do you want to watch a movie?" asked Lucy, popping her head over the sofa top. "We've got *Titanic*."

I waved my hand at her. "No, you jo astead. Just having a liddle sleep."

After that I was vaguely aware of voices and the telly.

They sounded very distant. "She hasn't had tequila, has she?" I heard Tony say.

Nesta shrugged. "Don't know. Think so."

"Prepare for the hangover from hell, Iz, my old pal," called Tony over the sofa.

"Okeee dokeee," I said without opening my eyes.

"Tequila's lethal," said Tony. I didn't know who he was talking to, though. It was way too much effort to open my eyes. My eyelids seemed to have stuck together somehow. "Even some of the most hardy drinkers can't take it. Very nasty side effects. What else has she had?"

"Black currant liqueur, Bailey's . . ."

I must have drifted off because the next thing I knew there was a bitter smell of coffee. It made me want to retch. Tony was holding a cup next to my nose. "Come on, Iz. Have a sip."

I pulled a face and rolled away from him. "Don't like coffee. I'm vegetarian. Want to sleep."

Tony began to laugh. "Did nobody ever tell you Lesson Number One in drinking, Izzie? Don't mix your drinks."

"Won't," I moaned. "Fact, won't drink again. Been very, very stupid. Kay, go way now, need to sleep."

There was the sound of the front door opening and footsteps in the hall.

"*Ohmigod*," I heard Nesta cry. "Quick, put the glasses under the sofa."

The sitting room door opened and I heard the girls scrabbling about, then another voice. It sounded vaguely familiar. "What in *heaven's* name is going on here?" said Nesta's mum.

"And why is Izzie lying behind the sofa?" asked her dad.

Oops, I thought as I tried to roll into a ball and make myself invisible.

Lucy's Quiz

Name your three favorite animals, birds, or fish in order of preference. Say why you've chosen them.

First choice reveals: how you see yourself.

Second choice reveals: how others see you.

Third choice reveals: how you really are.

It's the adjectives chosen to say why the animal has been picked that are revealing, more than the animal itself.

7

Orangutans in the Mist

Ooooh. Strange dreams. Very strange dreams.
Orangutans in the mist. Snowy forests with penguins
eating black currants. Don't feel very well, I thought
when I woke up the next day and tried to open my eyes.
It appears someone glued my eyelids together in the
night. And my *head*. Oof. Somebody's doing a drum solo
in there. I turned over and looked at the clock. Half past
ten. Oops. I rolled on to my back and looked at the ceiling. How did I get home? I asked myself. I could vaguely
remember Angus turning up. He must have driven me
back. Don't remember seeing Mum. Oh God. Mum. I
pulled the duvet over my head. Think I'll stay under here
from now on. Probably best I never get up again. Ever.

Half an hour later, I was awakened again by my

mobile. I cautiously got out of bed, grappled around for my bag, and found the phone.

"How are you?" asked Lucy.

I rubbed my eyes. "Bit fragile, to tell the truth."

Lucy laughed. "Serves you right. What did your mum say?"

"Haven't seen her yet. I guess she'll be at work now. Don't remember much."

"You were hysterical," said Lucy. "Falling about all over the place when Angus arrived. At one point he tried to pick you up and you told him to bog off."

"Oh *no*, I didn't, did I?" I moaned. "Well, that's it, isn't it? I will never ever *ever* drink again."

"Right. What, not even water?"

"Oh ha-ha, Lucy. I mean alcohol. Not if it makes you feel like this."

"Oh yeah, that reminds me. Tony asked me to pass on his infallible hangover cure."

"Good. What is it?"

"Don't drink the night before," she laughed.

"Oh, very funny. Are the others in trouble?"

"Nesta is. My dad picked me and T. J. up and we just ran out to the car and didn't tell him anything. But Nesta's been grounded today. She's really miffed because it was your idea to try the drinks."

"Oh Go-*od*," I groaned. "I'll phone her and apologize. Got to go and lie down again now, Lucy. Sorry. Call you soon."

"Drink a load of water," said Lucy. "That's what Mum does whenever she's had too much to drink."

After I hung up, I saw that someone had put a glass of water by the bed. Mum probably. I dutifully drank it, then lay down for a while longer. I felt dreadful, like I'd been run over by a bus. After another hour, I finally made it downstairs to get some more water.

Angus works from home some days and this was one of them. He looked up from his desk as I passed his study on the way to the kitchen. I gave him a weak smile and prepared myself for the telling off.

"How are you feeling?" he asked.

"Rotten, if you must know."

He chuckled. "Enough to drive you to drink, isn't it?"

I went to stand in the doorway. "Aren't you mad at me?"

He shook his head. "But your mum is. She said to say that you're grounded and can't go over to Nesta's until school starts again."

"It wasn't Nesta's fault. It was me who started it all.

And I won't be doing it again in a hurry, I can tell you."

Angus chuckled again. "Never say never," he said.

He's clearly never had a hangover like this, I thought as I staggered into the kitchen.

Mum rang early in the afternoon and was true to her word. Grounded, she said. I couldn't go out until she said so, even though there wasn't much of the holidays left. I knew I didn't have a leg to stand on, literally on the night of the cocktails, so I didn't try to argue. I knew I'd blown it with her.

I decided to keep a diary of my imprisonment.

Day One:

First day of prison sentence. Don't mind staying in as feel pretty grotty. Began to feel marginally better after a ton of water.

Cleaned the house. Even though we have a cleaner, thought it was a good way to earn brownie points.

Belly button update. It's healing up nicely at last, phew. It's going to look great in a few weeks. Ha-ha, Mum, you may have grounded me, but I've got a new belly button stud in. You can't control everything.

Worked on lyrics for new songs.

Thought about Josh. Thought a lot about Josh. He said 'See you around.' No chance of that, then—not for a while. Unless Mum relents, and there's not much chance of that. Felt good when I saw him in the park last time. Sort of buzzy. Definitely different from being with Ben. They must be about the same age, but somehow Josh is more exciting. And he's taller.

Practiced doing a new signature. If changing my image, then my handwriting is part of it. Covered about ten pages.

Practiced snogging technique on the back on my hand. Think I may be going mad.

Tried on every stitch of clothing I own and managed to work out some pretty cool combinations. Black and black mainly, with some silver jewelry. Some of the tops I was going to throw out because I thought I'd grown out of them look good on second trying. Used to wear my clothes baggy, but now some of the T-shirts look just right—tight in the right places. Mum won't like it. She doesn't like anything. Mainly me.

T. J. and Lucy came over and brought magazines. Amazingly, even though I was grounded, Angus let them in on the condition that I didn't tell Mum. He can be okay sometimes. Lucy did fantastic makeup on me to go with my new look. Dark eyes and sort of grape glossy lipstick. Definitely makes me look older and will look cool for the gig on Saturday—that is, if Mum lets me go. T. J. asked me to do a piece for her mag on what to do when you're grounded. Don't think I'll include "Practice snogging on the back of your hand," in case people at school think I'm a saddo. But I bet they all do it.

After they left, I practiced my songs for the gig on Saturday. I'm only doing two this time, which is fine by me as I like sitting and listening as well as performing. Please, please, God, let Mum have mellowed by then.

Mum back at seven thirty. Waited for le grando telling off, but it never came. She just looked disappointed, a look she's got down to perfection, if you ask me, but pretty upsetting all the same. Don't really like it when she's seriously mad at me.

Ate a tiny bit of supper. Tummy's still a bit funny. Cleared table, washed up—even the pans. Said sorry a million times. Smiled meekly at Mum and Angus. Am perfect daughter.

Called Nesta. Got her voice mail.

Listened to music. Worked on songs again.

Nothing on telly. Slept like a zombie (not the cocktail).

<u>Day Two</u>:
Called Nesta's mobile as don't want to risk her mum or dad picking up their home phone and giving me another telling-off. Got voice mail. She's obviously screening her calls and is still mad at me.

Feel restless. Surely two days in prison is enough? Called Mum at work to beg forgiveness, but she's in a meeting schmeeting. She'll probably only say that I can't go out until I've learned my lesson, so I don't really know why I'm bothering. Why doesn't she realize that I learned my lesson on Day One? You don't have to tell me twice not to drink alcohol again. Never, never, never. I don't want to go through that again.

Color coordinated my wardrobe. Only took five minutes as it's all black now.

Started reading <u>The Catcher in the Rye</u>. Brilliant. At first couldn't get into it as it's about this boy called Holden Caulfield who's been expelled from boarding school in America. Thought I couldn't relate. But as there was nothing else to do, I got into it and then I couldn't put it down. Even though it was written ages ago, in the nineteen forties, he's just like any normal teenager, and like me, questioning everything. Is it the same for teenagers the world over? Nothing seems to make sense anymore and you don't know who you want to be, what you want to do, and in the meantime, you manage to upset <u>everyone</u>.

Called Nesta. She picked up. Phew. Talked for half an hour. She said I should try calling Mum again as parents do tend to blow steam then calm down. Tried calling Mum again. She said she is prepared to let me go out as long as I let her know where I am and what I'm doing at all times. Felt very tempted to call her five minutes later from the bathroom to tell her I was on the loo, but resisted as that might be pushing my luck a bit.

So, good-bye, diary. Prison sentence cut short. Time off for good behavior. Mum said I can go out, so I'm free! Ha-ha, HEE-HEE, cue maniacal laughter.

I put on my trainers and shorts and decided to go for a jog. It was drizzling but felt really fresh, so I ran and ran and ran. After about twenty minutes, I heard a motorbike approaching. It screeched to a stop next to me.

"Izzie," called Josh as I ran past him.

Murphy's Law, I said to myself as I stopped and turned. I *would* bump into him on the one day I have no makeup on, my hair's dripping with rain, and I'm sweaty from running. Not my most alluring look, I thought as a raindrop fell off my nose. I decided to keep my head down and keep the conversation short.

"Um, hi," I said.

He took off his helmet. "Where have you been? I was hoping to see you in the park again. Didn't scare you off that night, did I? With the tree thing?"

"Um, no, course not," I said to the pavement. "Been busy."

"What you doing tonight?"

"Not sure." Actually I had told Ben I'd go round to go through my songs one last time before the gig, and I'd planned to go to Lucy's after that. But you *do* have to be flexible in life.

"A few of us are getting together later, if you want to meet up. Come and have a drink."

I pulled a face.

"What?" he said.

"Drink."

"What about drink?"

"Bad joojoo," I answered, then decided I would tell him all about it without actually revealing that it was the first time I'd tried alcohol properly. "Had a bit too much on Monday night. Never again."

Josh laughed. "Ah, hangover, eh? You know the best thing for that?"

"Don't drink the night before?"

He laughed and shook his head. "Nah. Hair of the dog. Back on the horse, and so on."

"No thanks," I said. "I've learned my lesson."

"You sound like an old woman."

"Last time you called me a kid," I said. "I can't win."

He smiled. "It's not a competition."

"I wasn't . . ."

"Come on—we're meeting at Pond Square in Highgate. See you there, about five thirty?"

"Maybe," I said. "I'll have to check with my social secretary."

Josh laughed. "Your mum and dad, you mean?"

"*No*," I said. Actually I did mean my mum, but I wasn't going to tell him that. She'd already said that I could go to Ben's, so to do a quick detour to the square wouldn't be going much out of my way. I'd set off early. Mum would never know if I called her before I left, then again from Ben's. It would be worth it. Just for half an hour. "Okay. I'll be there."

"Cool," he said, and with that he roared off again.

Things to Do When You're Grounded

* Catch up on homework.

* Color coordinate your wardrobe.

* Store shoes in boxes. Take a picture/Polaroid of each pair and stick it on the outside of the box for quick identification.

* Do some Feng Shui on your bedroom and get rid of all the clutter. If you haven't worn something for over a year, chuck it.

* Feng Shui your computer. (Tidy your desktop and clear up old files.)

* Update your address book. Then update your diary.

* Start your best-selling novel. If grounded for a loooong time, also finish it.

* Try moving all your furniture around and redecorate your room à la Feng Shui.

* Learn to meditate.

* Do your Christmas card list and plan presents.

* Check out astrology sites on the Web and do friends' horoscopes for them.

* Treat the time as if you're at a health spa: Give yourself a facial, paint your nails, condition your hair, moisturize and exfoliate.

* Exercise.

* Listen to music.

* Write music or lyrics.

* Learn to cook a new recipe (earns good brownie points if it comes out well and may get you time off for good behavior).

* Clean the house and do the garden (also earns brownie points).

* Read. Some books are pretty cool and it's a way to escape from your personal prison into other worlds.

8

Dragon Mother

Josh was already on a bench with his mates at Pond Square when I got there. I felt a bit intimidated as I approached, as I didn't know any of the others, but Josh soon waved me over and introduced me. There were two girls, Chris and Zoë, and a guy called Spider. They looked like they were in Year Eleven. Spider was the one who'd been chucking bread at passing joggers the week before, and I didn't much like the look of him. He had very pale skin and was a bit hard-looking, but the girls seemed okay. They sized me up (girls can be a bit funny sometimes when you're not part of their group) and must have decided I was all right, because Chris rummaged in a carrier bag and pulled out a bottle of Malibu and a paper cup.

"Want some?"

"No thanks," I said. "I've got a band rehearsal later."

"Oh, just have one. One won't hurt you."

I didn't really want any, but I'd only just met them and I didn't want to be a killjoy when they were being friendly. Then I remembered what Tony said on the night of the cocktails. Lesson Number One: Don't mix your drinks. That's probably why I'd felt so lousy. I'd mixed so many. Maybe if I'd just stuck to *one*, I'd have been okay. Then I remembered what Josh said about getting back on the horse after a bad experience. *Then* I remembered Angus saying never say never.

"Okay. Thanks," I said. I took the the cup she offered me.

I resolved not to overdo it, as I could still remember how rotten I felt after the cocktails, so I stuck to my guns and I only had the one, even if Chris did fill the cup full. It tasted quite nice, coconutty, and I imagined it was probably nicer than the cider that Spider was drinking. I tried cider once at my stepsister's wedding and it tasted like apples that had gone off. Foul.

I sipped my Malibu and this time I felt okay. Somehow the drink made me feel more confident about being with strangers. I found myself feeling really talkative and told them all about King Noz and the gig on Saturday. They all seemed impressed and wanted to come along. At one point, my mobile rang, but I quickly switched it off. Probably Mum checking up on me, I thought.

"So do you rehearse often?" asked Chris.

"Yeah, we've done loads over the holidays," I said, checking my watch. It wasn't until then that I realized what time it was. The rehearsal at Ben's was supposed to be at six and already it was a quarter past. "Oh God," I said and got up from the bench. "Better get going."

Josh walked with me to the High Street and just as I was about to dash off, he caught the back of my jacket, pulled me back, and kissed me. Just like that. It took my breath away as it was so out of the blue. After a while, he let me go and we smiled at each other.

"Give me your number," he said.

I scribbled it down on an old tube ticket that I had in my purse, then he gently pushed me down the road. "You'd better get moving if you're going to go and be a rock chick fabster."

"Not that kind of girl . . . or music," I said, laughing, then ran like mad to get to Ben's on the other side of Highgate, down near the tube station. I felt totally exhilarated. He'd *kissed* me. No awkwardness. No build-up. No thinking, Is he going to? Isn't he? Should I kiss him? He'd done it when it was completely unexpected. It felt great. Sometimes getting that first kiss over with can be a bit clumsy.

When I got to Ben's, there was a note taped to the garage door with my name on it. I ripped it open: *Iz. Gone to check out the acoustics at the venue for Saturday. We waited for twenty minutes, then I tried your mobile, but it was switched off. Call me later. Ben.*

Oh poo, I thought. I could have stayed longer in the square with Josh. I wondered if I should go back there, but decided it wouldn't look good. Nesta had drilled into all of us that it was important not to look too keen when you first meet a boy. I looked at my watch again. It was a quarter to seven. No way I felt like going home yet. Nesta's house was closest, but I couldn't go there as that's out of bounds for a while. I quickly called Lucy's. No one there, so I tried her mobile. She was at Nesta's. Oh, double poo, I thought. I can't risk the wrath of Dragon Mother if she finds out. At least T. J. wasn't with them, so I called her. Luckily she was in, so I made my way over there.

* * *

I could see that something was wrong the moment T. J. opened the door. She quickly ushered me upstairs into her bedroom and shut the door.

"Your mum's on the warpath," she said. "She's on her way over."

"What? Why?"

T. J. sat at her desk. "Oh, some mix-up. She's been phoning everywhere. She said you were supposed to have been at Ben's. She rang there and his mum said you hadn't shown up for rehearsal, so the boys had gone off without you. . . ."

I sank on to her bed. "Hell's bells. I *did* go, but I went to Pond Square first." I quickly filled T. J. in on seeing Josh again and how fab it had been. "But I don't believe it. She's checking up on me."

At that moment, we heard a car drawing up outside. T. J. peeked out the window. "She's here. Look, if you had a drink, you'd better go and brush your teeth. She might smell it."

"I only had one and it tasted like it was mainly coconut."

"Breathe on me."

I quickly breathed on T. J. and we got the giggles as she fell back against the wall and feigned passing out.

"Smells slightly of alcohol," she said. "You'd better not risk it. Just rub some toothpaste on your teeth, then I'll give you some gum."

I rushed into the bathroom and did as T. J. had advised.

"Isobel, can you come down," Scary Dad called up the stairs. "Your mother's here."

I had a quick gargle with some mouthwash as well for good measure, then combed my hair. T. J. was waiting for me on the landing outside the bathroom. She looked really sorry for me. "It'll be okay," she said. "Just tell them what happened."

"You don't know my mum," I said. "She'd go ballistic if she knew I'd been hanging out with strangers."

"Izzie." This time it was Mum's voice and I knew I had no choice but to go down and face the firing squad.

Mum was deep in conversation with Scary Dad when we got downstairs. T. J. and I stood there for what felt like hours before they acknowledged us. They seemed to have bonded over shock horror stories about alcohol abuse. I couldn't believe it. So much for keeping what happened at Nesta's private. She'd clearly told him all about it, and now anyone would think I was a regular drinker, the way they were going on and the looks they were giving me. Scary Dad works as a hospital consultant and was telling Mum about his early days when he worked in the emergency room.

"You'd be surprised how many teenagers came in, vomit all over them, out of their minds . . ."

Mum was shaking her head. "I know. Terrible, isn't it?"

I wanted to shout, *"But I'm not one of them!* I'm not *that* stupid," but I just stood there like a lemon instead. T. J.'s dad is so intimidating. I just hoped that I hadn't gotten T. J. in trouble with him, as he was even looking at *her* suspiciously.

Finally Mum turned to me. "Ah, there you are. And where do you think you've been?"

"Upstairs with T. J."

"You told me that you had a rehearsal."

"I did. But by the time I got there, the boys had gone."

"And why were you late getting there?"

Talk about an inquisition, I thought. Why couldn't she wait until later? T. J. and her dad didn't need to hear this.

"I . . . er, walked there."

"Why? Why didn't you get the tube?"

"It was a nice evening. . . ."

"So why did it take so long to walk? You must know how long it takes. You must have known you were going to be late if you walked. So *why* didn't you set off in time? And why didn't you phone when Ben wasn't there?"

"*Mum* . . ." I wished she'd stop. I glanced at T. J. and Scary Dad. She looked uncomfortable and he looked like he was enjoying every minute. "You knew I was going to be out for a while. I didn't think . . ." As I said this, she and Scary Dad exchanged weary, knowing looks. "I . . . I came here instead."

"We had an agreement, young lady. I said I wanted to know exactly where you were at every hour of the day."

"You can always call. I have my mobile. . . ."

She shook her head. "Forget that. For one thing, you can turn it off, and for another, I may phone you, but I still wouldn't really know where you were. You could tell me anything. No, from now on, I want the landline number of where you are so that I can phone and check."

T. J. was looking at me with great sympathy. Her dad was looking at me as though I was a criminal. I wanted to die.

* * *

461

"*Why* couldn't you have waited?" I asked as soon as the car pulled away from T. J.'s. "*Why* did you have to do that in front of everyone?" I'd felt so humiliated, getting a public telling-off, and I hadn't even *done* anything.

"You weren't where you said you were going to be," said Mum through tight lips.

"Then please, I'm asking you from my heart, please, in the future, wait until we're home or at least on our own before you yell at me. And I don't even know why you're so upset. Don't you trust me or something?"

"I don't think your recent behavior has left that open for discussion, Izzie."

"But I haven't *done* anything. It's not fair."

"You don't think, Izzie." Mum turned to look at me. "I'm your mother and I don't know where you are anymore. Or who you're hanging out with."

"Well, I've been upstairs in my room for the last two days. You haven't had to look far. And you *do* know who I hang out with. T. J., Lucy, Nesta. Same as always."

"Well, where were you tonight before Ben's."

"I told you, walking to his house."

"And what were you doing as you walked?"

"Nothing."

"So why do you smell so strongly of toothpaste? Don't think I don't know all the tricks, Izzie."

"T. J. gave me a stick of gum, that's all."

We drove a bit further in silence, then she piped up again. "So who's the boy you were in the park with on Sunday?"

That shut me up for a moment. "What boy?"

Mum hesitated for a moment. "Mrs. Peters next door said she saw you with a boy on Sunday in Primrose Hill park, on the night you were supposed to be coming straight home from your dad's."

"I . . . I don't remember," I said. "Maybe I bumped into one of the boys from the band. I don't remember. And anyway, can't I even talk to people I know now?"

Mum saying Mrs. Peters had seen me threw me for a moment. I didn't remember seeing her around when I was with Josh. The park was empty and she's not someone who's easy to miss as she's about two hundred and fifty pounds. I decided to zip it. At least she hadn't seen me this evening, drinking and snogging.

"And what happened to you and Ben?" she asked. "I thought you liked him."

"I do," I said. "We're mates." Why was she going on about this? I wondered. I hadn't told her that Ben and I had finished, but then I'd never told her that we were going out. It wasn't like we were engaged to be married or anything. It was way more casual. But how did she know we weren't having a relationship anymore? Maybe she's more tuned into my life than I realized.

"So who's this boy in the park?"

She clearly wasn't going to let it go. "Nobody."

"What's his name?"

"Josh."

"What school does he go to?"

"I *don't know!*"

"Don't raise your voice, Isobel. Where did you meet him?"

"Oh, just around."

"And where does he live?"

"Dunno. I'm only just getting to know him."

"Well, I'd like to meet him. Invite him over to the house."

"Whadt!"

"You heard me. I like to know who you're spending time with."

"But, *Mum*, it's not like that. He's not like my *boy*-friend. I *can't* invite him over. I hardly even *know* him." This was appalling. Imagine me inviting Josh back and her giving him the third degree! She must be out of her mind. It was so unfair. She was ruining everything before it even got started.

"Bring him over one night this weekend."

"I *can't*, Mum."

"Why not? If he's a friend, surely he must know you have parents."

"Yes, but . . . *no*. Oh, you don't understand." She didn't. I could *never* in a million squillion years invite the coolest boy I'd ever met back to meet my dragon of a mother. Especially since we hadn't even been on a date. He'd run a mile if I asked him.

"If you don't bring him back, I don't want you to see him."

"But you never met Ben in the early days."

"Yes, but I knew who he was and I know he goes to the same school as Lucy's brothers. And I know where he lives as I've dropped you off there a few times." Then she smiled. "I really think that you're making a fuss about nothing, Izzie. It's no big deal. Just invite him back for half an hour or so. I promise I'll be very nice to him. I just want to meet him, that's all."

Sometimes life really sucks, I thought as we drove on. No big deal? Maybe not if you're living in Jane Austen's times, but it is if you live in North London in the twenty-first century.

Song for Nagging Mothers:
You're So Rotten

You're always telling me to do things like you do.
You're always saying my room looks like a zoo.
Well, I don't care. So there.
You're always telling me that you don't like my mood.
You're always complaining that my friends are rude.
Well, I don't care. So there.

I really hate you, yes I do.
I really hate you, yes I do.
Do I really hate you?
Yes I do.

You never listen to the things I gotta say.
Whenever I need you, you turn and walk away.
Well, I don't care. So there.
I'm so angry, yes I am.
I'm so angry, yes I am.
Am I really angry?
You bet I stinking am.
So there. I don't care.

I really hate you, yes I do.
I really hate you, yes I do.
Do I really hate you?
Yes I do.

9

War

I don't believe it. I *really* don't believe it! Mum has read my diary!

It was obvious as soon as I got back to my bedroom and went to get it out. It had been moved from its place in my underwear drawer. I always kept it under the Calvin Klein pants that my stepsister Amelia gave me. They're a size too big, so I never wear them. Now the diary was under a white T-shirt and I'd never have put it there. How *could* she? I thought as I grabbed it and stormed downstairs.

Mum was sitting in the living room, having a drink with Angus. I could tell that they'd been talking about me by the way they suddenly went silent and looked guilty when I burst in. I stood by Mum's chair and pointed at my diary.

"Mrs. Peters never was in the park, was she?"

For once in her life, Mum looked sheepish.

"How *could* you, Mum?" I asked. "This is really, *really* private."

Angus got up and tiptoed out behind me.

Mum looked at the carpet. "Well, how else am I supposed to know what's going on with you? You never talk to me about your life and I've been worried about you lately."

"But reading my *diary* . . ." I felt near to tears. I wrote *all* sorts of stuff in my diary, mad stuff, thoughts, feelings. It was a way of unloading, and often the way I felt one day was different the next. It wasn't meant to be seen by anyone and it was *horrible* to think that someone had read it. I felt totally exposed, like I was naked.

"Come and sit down, Izzie. Let's talk about this. . . ."

I turned and headed back up the stairs. I had nothing more to say to her. If she's done this, I thought, then she clearly has no idea of who I really am and certainly doesn't trust me. There's only one thing for it, I decided. I'll go to my room, put a chair in front of the door so that no one can get in, and tomorrow first thing, I'm going to go live with Dad.

* * *

"Hello, love," said Dad as he opened the door the next morning and looked at his watch. "You're here early. I was just off to college."

I hauled my bag up the steps to his flat and into the hall. "I wanted to catch you before you left. Can I come and live here with you and Anna? I'll sleep on the sofa bed and I won't be any trouble. I just can't take it at home anymore. It's been awful lately and she's gone too far this time. She's driving me mad."

"Whoa, slow down, slow down," said Dad. "Come into the kitchen and tell me all about it."

I followed him in and blurted out everything that had happened over the last few days. "I really can't stay there any longer," I said finally. "She's a monster. I quite understand why you divorced her."

Dad smiled sadly. "She's not a monster, Izzie, she's just . . . oh dear, Izzie, what are we to do?" He glanced at his watch. "I've got a lecture in half an hour, so I can't get into all this now, but listen . . . I agree your mum should never have read your diary, but, as for walking out on her . . . you know she has your best interests at heart. . . ."

"But she doesn't seem to realize that I'm not a little girl who needs constant looking after anymore. . . ." My voice trailed off. I knew that he was going to tell me to go back. Part of me had been expecting it anyway, as I knew they didn't really have room. I sat at the table and put my head in my hands.

"You have a nice home there," Dad continued, "and your own room. It would drive you mad here, not having your own space. You know that's true."

"Can't I just stay a few days?"

Dad sighed. "You're always welcome, Izzie, but . . . where would we put you? Anna's mum and dad are arriving from Scotland this evening and will be staying for a couple of days. Anna and I are going to give them our bedroom and we're going to camp on the sofa bed in the front room with Tom. So where would we put you? Listen, love, let me call your mum to let her know that you're here, then stay until I get back at lunchtime and we'll talk about it some more. I'll drive you back and I'll have a chat with her and see what we can work out."

"Promise?"

"Promise."

Mum clearly wasn't in the chatting mood. It was horrible. Dad had only been in the house five minutes when they got into a huge argument about responsibility. She was coming out with the same old stuff about it being her who lies awake at night worrying about me. I couldn't bear it, so I slipped into Angus's study to hide until it was all over.

After a few minutes, I heard the front door open. I peeked out and spotted Angus coming back with a sandwich for his lunch. He cocked an ear at the kitchen door, then when he realized what was going on, he turned on his heel and dived into the study, closing the door firmly behind him.

Then he saw me.

"Hiding?"

I nodded.

"Good idea. Don't blame you," he said. "Best to lie low in here until it all blows over." He offered me half of his sandwich. "Cheese and tomato?"

I shook my head and sat on the floor by the bookshelves. I felt miserable. Dad didn't want me at his house and I didn't want to live here. I didn't belong anywhere.

Angus looked at me with concern. "Been having a tough old time lately, haven't you?"

I felt tears prick the back of my eyes. I blinked to make them go away. The last thing I wanted to do was cry in front of Angus. But too late. He'd seen and was handing me a tissue.

"There, there," he said. "Have a good old blow."

I blew my nose into the tissue, but it didn't help. Tears were spilling out of my eyes and down my cheeks. I pointed at the door. We could still hear raised voices in the kitchen. "I didn't mean this to happen. I didn't mean any of it to happen. Just . . . everything seems to be going wrong lately. Everything I touch turns into a disaster. Mum doesn't understand me and now I've caused a row between her and Dad. . . . What's wrong with me?"

Angus chuckled. "Nothing. You're a teenager."

"I bet Claudia and Amelia never did anything wrong," I said. More perfect girls you could never hope to meet. Both polite, both in good jobs, both married to accountants.

Angus laughed out loud and got up and went to one of his shelves. "Those two girls made my life a living hell," he said. "Want to see some pictures of them in their punk days?"

"*Punk* days? Amelia and Claudia? Never!" My stepsisters were straighter than straight—blonde, tidy, the kind of girls who looked like they never had a bad hair day.

Angus passed me the album. Two girls with wild

black hair and a ton of black eye makeup stared defiantly out from the photographs, Amelia with the full spiked-up works, Claudia in a tiny kilt, rubber basque, and chains. Both had green lipstick on. Underneath the photos Angus had written, *Insanity is hereditary. You get it from your kids.*

I burst out laughing. *"Excellent."* That's one for Lucy's slogan collection, I thought. She spent the summer making T-shirts with cool slogans on them and had asked us all to keep our eyes out for good lines.

Angus shook his head. "It got to a point where my wife and I were afraid to go away for fear of what they might get up to in our absence. One time, half the neighborhood came for a party and trashed the place— motorbikes on the lawn, police cars at midnight . . ."

"I'm stunned," I said as I stared at the photos and thought about the girls now. One a lawyer, the other an accountant, neat and demure in their Jasper Conran outfits. Both had homes with matching towels in the bathroom. . . .

"So was I," said Angus. "It took me *years* to recover."

"Looking at these, I can't help but think, so what's Mum's problem, then? I mean, no offense, but I've never been this wild."

Angus sat at his desk. "Your mum cares deeply about you, Izzie. You must know that. I know you've got to grow up and be independent, but you'll always be her little girl, just as Amelia and Claudia will always be my little girls, whatever age they are. Don't forget, a few years ago you were all cuddles and wanting to be with her. It can be hard—suddenly she's being shoved away as you want to be more adult and make your own choices. It's a difficult time of adjustment for parents, as well. I remember when my two didn't want to hug me anymore. If I ever went to embrace them, they'd push me away. And if I ever went to pick them up from anywhere, I was asked to stay out of sight round a corner because they were ashamed of me. They didn't want to be associated with an old fogey like me. I was out of date. Only years before, they were a pair of real daddy's girls. I was their hero; they followed me everywhere. Then suddenly they didn't need or want me anymore. The rejection was tough to take."

I flicked through his album, taking in pictures of the girls as babies, then toddlers, then eight, nine, ten, holding their mum and dad's hands, smiling at the camera. Then they turned into a pair of sulky teenagers with dyed hair and mad clothes.

"I guess," I said. I'd never thought about parents feeling rejected before. To me, Mum was just Mum, always there. But I suppose I had shut her out lately and there was a time when we used to hang out together a lot. And it was true, I couldn't even remember the last time I gave her a hug. "Hmmm." I smiled at Angus. "How about you talk to her? She *can* trust me, you know. Just ask her to chill out a bit."

"I will. Of course I will. Just try to meet her halfway," said Angus. "I bet you'll find that it makes a world of difference. Now, how about half that sarnie while the cast of *EastEnders* finish fighting it out in the kitchen."

I took the sandwich this time. "Thanks, Angus."

He smiled. "You're welcome, Izzie."

After talking to Angus, I went to my room and ripped up the song I'd written about hating Mum so much. In light of what Angus had said, it seemed really harsh, and although I was mad at her at the time, I would have hated for her to ever find it and think that I really meant it. Writing it was just a way of letting off steam. I guess I've got to find a way to express the times when she doesn't wind me up as well, I thought.

As I was ripping the sheet of paper into tiny pieces, I

heard the front door open and close. I looked out the window to see Dad leaving. He looked up at me, smiled, and gave me the thumbs-up. Phew, at least that's over, I thought as minutes later I heard his car drive away.

Moments later, I heard Mum's footsteps on the stairs. I took a deep breath and resolved to be nice to her. It wasn't hard when she came in, as she looked strained after the conversation with Dad. I was sorry I put her through it.

"Er, Izzie . . . ," she began.

"Me first," I said. "I want to say I'm sorry for . . . er, taking off this morning. It's not that I don't appreciate everything you do and I know you worry about me and I'll try harder in future not to upset you."

Mum's face relaxed and she sat on the end of my bed. "Did you really want to leave and live at your dad's?"

"Not really," I lied. I'd love to live at Dad's, if there was room, but I wasn't going to tell her that. "I don't think I'd last a day without my own space. I'm sorry I put you through that."

"Me too. I'm sorry we haven't been getting along lately. I can't help worrying about you, but I'll try not to be too much of an over-anxious mother. So, what are you going to do this afternoon? Oh . . ." She laughed. "I'm not checking up on you, only asking."

I laughed as well. "I may do some homework," I said. "And I may go up to Muswell Hill to get some things from Ryman's that I need for school—if that's okay. Do you want me to call you from Muswell Hill?"

Mum looked up at the ceiling and smiled. "No. I trust you to go to the stationery shop. Honestly. Am I really so bad?" She glanced at the clock. "Oh. . . got to dash. They'll be wondering where I am at work, wandering off in the middle of the day. . . ."

"Sorry about that," I said, looking at the carpet. I did feel a bit ashamed. I'd caused chaos today—Dad having to leave college and Mum having to come home from work on her lunch hour.

Mum looked at me with concern. "So, are we all right now?"

I nodded.

She looked at her watch again. "*Oh.* Got to go. Oh, and . . . I'll be back late tonight. There's a work function I can't avoid. It's such a nuisance, these dinners always come at the most inconvenient times. I'd rather come back and have a proper chat about things, but it's not something I can get out of. Angus will be coming with me, so . . . will you be all right on your own this evening? These things tend to go on a bit. I might not be back until it's gone midnight. I can ask Angus to stay if you like. He doesn't really need to be there."

"No, don't be silly. Go. Have a good time. I don't need baby-sitting."

"Only if you're sure."

"I'm fine, Mum. And we can chat another time," I said, feeling slightly relieved. Then I put on a stern expression. "And if you're going to be in past midnight, I expect a call. I lie awake worrying if you're not in."

Mum raised an eyebrow in surprise. "Don't push it," she said as she went out the door. But she was smiling.

At last everything's back to normal, I thought after she'd gone.

But there are twenty-four hours in a day and Thursday wasn't over yet.

Line for Lucy's T-shirt collection

Insanity is hereditary.
You get it from your kids.

10

Best and Worst

The following day I decided to do the exercise that we'd been set for the holidays. I'd been putting it off all summer, so, with only three days left before school started, I thought I'd better make an effort.

Our teacher, Miss Watkins, had given us the opening lines to the book *A Tale of Two Cities* by Charles Dickens.

I picked up the handout sheet and read:

> *It was the best of times, it was the worst of times, it was the age of wisdom, it was the age of foolishness, it was the epoch of belief, it was the epoch of incredulity, it was the season of Light, it was the season of Darkness, it was the*

*spring of hope, it was the winter of despair, we
had everything before us, we had nothing before
us, we were all going direct to Heaven, we were
all going direct the other way.*

Boy, he sounds confused, I thought, up and down
and round and round. Seems like some things never
change. Then I looked to see what we were meant to
do with the handout. Miss Watkins had written underneath the quote: *"Write a short account of the best and
worst times of your summer."* Forget the *whole* summer,
I thought as I sat at my desk. I could put them all into
one day: yesterday.

I got a few sheets of paper out of my desk drawer and
began to write:

Worst: Being mad with Mum and storming off to Dad's
only to find out that staying with him was a no-go.

Best: My talk with Angus. I'm beginning to really like him.
Then everything being okay between Mum and me again.

Josh phoned an hour after Mum had gone back to her
office. He wanted to meet up, so I suggested Muswell
Hill as I'd already told Mum I was going there.

Worst: Went to meet Josh. It was pouring. Not gentle

summer rain, this was torrential. Arrived looking like a drowned rat. So much for looking cool. I was positively frozen.

<u>Best:</u> Josh was soaked too and looked drop-dead gorgeous with wet hair slicked back and his skin glistening with rain. He put his arm around me as we ran through the downpour, then kissed me under a tree. Possibly the most romantic moment of my whole life, even though water was dripping down the back of my jacket.

<u>Worst:</u> Met up with his weird friend Spider. Don't like him. He is Sullen with a capital S. Josh did ask if I minded hooking up with him. Actually I did mind, as I wanted to get to know Josh better, but then I remembered what happened to Lucy this summer. She went out with this guy who was really clingy and possessive. He started telling her who she could and couldn't see, and in the end, she finished with him because she felt suffocated. Didn't want to do that to Josh.

<u>Worst:</u> Had a cigarette. Spider offered me one and I took it. I don't know why. I guess I wanted to look cool. Hah. I took one puff and blaghh, I gagged on it. Spider cracked up laughing. Won't be trying one of those again

in a hurry, as it tasted disgusting. Josh had one as well and when he kissed me afterwards, it wasn't as nice as before in the rain. He had cigarette breath. But I guess I did too. Should have taken some gum.

Best: Josh held my hand as we walked along in the rain. It made me feel like he was happy to be seen with me.

Worst: Made huge mistake and took Josh and Spider to Ben's garage. I knew it was empty, as Ben had gone to his gran's eightieth birthday in Brighton with his family and wouldn't be back until late. I guess I wanted to impress Josh, but it backfired. I knew it wasn't a good idea the moment we got there. Spider had been drinking and carried on drinking. He was into everything, opening drawers and picking up the guitars. I had to tell him to leave them alone, as the boys are very picky about who handles their instruments and don't like people messing with them. Then he started pulling CDs and things out of Ben's filing cabinet. I know he has everything dated and labeled, so had to tell Spider to get lost. In the end I asked him to leave. He told me not to get my knickers in a twist. Very original. Not. After he'd gone, Josh lay on the sofa, rolling joints. Got a bit worried that Ben would smell marijuana when he got back. Josh said that marijuana is nicer than tobacco, so I had a quick puff. He told me that I had to really inhale it, which I did and it made my head go woozy. Not sure that I liked the sensation.

<u>Best</u>: Listening to music, talking, and snogging Josh on the sofa. I give him nine out of ten on the snogging scale. Minus one because I could taste the tobacco and an aphrodisiac it is definitely not.

<u>Worst</u>: After we left the garage and I locked up, it was ten forty. I knew Mum wouldn't be home until after midnight, so no worries there, but I knew I shouldn't get back any later. Josh said he was off to a party and when I said I couldn't go, he was like, Oh, okay, I'll give you a call, then. Then off he went, leaving me standing there on the pavement. Felt confused, as after all that snogging, I thought he'd at least care about how I got home. Didn't like being out on my own so late at night. Phoned Nesta as she was closest and she and Tony came and escorted me home. Tony was very sniffy about Josh. He said that he thought Josh sounded like a creep and any boy should always make sure a girl gets home safe as there are too many

weirdos about. Nesta thinks I shouldn't see Josh, as he sounds like bad news. Felt very confused. I don't know whether she's right or whether she's jealous because she thought he was cute in the beginning, but he never gave her any attention.

I looked over what I had written for my best and worst, then ripped it up and threw it in the bin. Somehow I don't think Miss Watkins would be too happy if she knew I'd been drinking, smoking, puffing on joints, and snogging boys. I tried to rethink what Dickens had said in the light of what had happened to me.

I wrote:

It was the best of times, it was the worst of times. It was the age of Year Ten, it was the age of growing up. It was a time of discovery. It was a time of being silly. It was an era of fighting with my mum. It was an era of trying to accept her. It was the season of rebellion, then the season of regret. The spring of new love, the winter of disappointment. I had a new boyfriend, I didn't have a new boyfriend. I was going direct to romance, I was going direct home, alone to bed.

Yeah, I thought. Times haven't changed much at all since Dickens lived. Life is still a rollercoaster. Opposites. Good times, bad times, best, and worst. I wondered how the rest of my class was getting on with the exercise and how their summers had been. It would be hysterical if everyone wrote the truth about what we'd got up to, as knowing the girls in our year, they'll have been up to all sorts.

As I tried to get into writing the more socially acceptable version of my best and worst times, Lucy phoned.

"Oh, I've done that homework," she said. "Took two minutes. Best time: breaking up for the summer holidays. Worst time: Well, that will be going back on Monday, won't it?"

I laughed. "I guess. Might be a bit short for what's expected, though."

"I'll tell her I'm going through a minimalist phase with my writing. 'Less is more' sort of thing. Anyway, forget about homework. We'll have enough of that soon when term starts, and if you ever get stuck, Lal has been working on a list of good excuses for handing homework in late. He's hoping T. J. will put it in the magazine, but I don't think she'll dare. He'll e-mail it to you, if you like. But tell me all about Josh. Nesta said you saw him yesterday. What's he really like?"

"Weird," I said, "or maybe not weird. More like mysterious. He's quite unlike anyone I've ever met before. I don't feel I know him at all. Like, I asked him where he lived and he said, 'Planet Earth.' I asked him what school he went to and he said, 'The school of life.' I asked him what birth sign he was, as I thought I could do a horoscope to see if we're compatible. He said, 'Marsupian.'"

Lucy laughed. "Marsupian. At least he didn't say he was from Uranus."

"I even tried your quiz, Lucy. You know, the one about your three favorite animals and why?"

"What did he say?"

"First he went a bit funny and asked if it was one of those girlie magazine quizzes on how to pigeonhole a boy. Then he said, 'Number one: Bugs Bunny because he's got big furry feet. Number two: Shrek from the movie because he's green and rubbery. And number three: a Teletubby because although they're not real animals, they're sure as hell not human.'"

"So he wasn't taking it seriously?"

"He doesn't seem to take anything seriously," I said, and I told her about him leaving me to get home on my own.

"That's sucks," said Lucy. "Bin him."

"Do you think?"

"Definitely. He may be gorgeous and different, but I think it's really uncool for a boy to leave a girl stranded on the street when it's late."

"That's what Tony said."

"Plus, the way he evaded giving you any information about himself," she continued. "It seems like he won't let you get too close. All those jokey answers. I've heard Mum talk about clients who do that. She says people use humor as a block or defense sometimes."

Lucy's mum works as a counselor. She's really cool and has good insight into people. She was certainly right about Josh. It was like he was shielding me off. I knew nothing about him and he knew everything about me, as I'd answered his questions truthfully.

"You deserve better," said Lucy.

"But he *is* a good kisser. . . ."

"So? So are lots of boys."

"You're right. And I did feel crapola standing on the street after he took off last night. Sort of like I'd been discarded when my use ran out. Yeah, from this moment on, Josh is Izzie history."

Excuses for Handing in Homework Late

by Lal Lovering

* My homework is late because I was up all night writing letters demanding better pay for teachers.
* Aliens from the planet Zog took my homework as an example of great Earth literature.
* I can't give in my homework as we had burglars last night and they stole it.
* I couldn't do my homework because I accidentally superglued my teeth together and had to go to the dentist's.
* I can't hand in my homework because the cat had kittens in my schoolbag.
* I've been replaced by an evil robot replica and it doesn't do homework.
* I couldn't do my homework because my contact lenses stuck to my eyes.
* I couldn't do my homework because I was grieving the death of my pet rock.
* I have done my homework, but it's done in invisible ink.
* My homework's late because I have an attention deficient disorder, er . . . what was I saying?
* I didn't do my homework because my inner child didn't feel like it.

11

Turnaround

I was awakened the next day by a frantic phone call from Ben. "Izzie, have you by any chance taken the CD with the songs we're going to do tonight? Remember, I recorded it a few weeks ago when we had that run-through?"

I did remember. It was a good session and everyone was in a really good mood, playing well and in tune. There was a possibility that a talent scout might be at the gig tonight and Ben wanted to be ready with a demo CD to give him.

"I've looked everywhere," Ben continued. "And I've spoken to the other lads. No one's seen it."

I felt my stomach churn. I had a feeling that I knew *exactly* where it was. Spider. He must have taken it last night.

"No, I haven't got it, Ben," I said. "Haven't you got another copy?"

"No. I was going to do some today. Never mind. It's got to be here somewhere. I'll carry on looking."

I felt rotten when I put the phone down, but I just couldn't bring myself to tell him that I'd taken two boys back to the garage. Even though we're not an item anymore, I didn't want to hurt his feelings. I'll kill Spider, I thought. I have to get the CD back, but then I'm not going to see Josh again, am I? So how am I going to see Spider? Luckily the phone went again and this time it was Josh. He asked if I'd meet him in Highgate. My first reaction was to say no, as I still felt bad after being abandoned last night, but I wanted to get the CD back from Spider in time for the gig, plus I wanted to get something for Mum's birthday tomorrow, so in the end, I agreed.

I set off for Highgate, thinking that I'd be really cool with Josh this time. I'd ask how I could get the CD back and I'd let him know that he couldn't just see me when he chose, then abandon me when he had a better offer.

He was waiting for me in Costa on High Street at a table at the back. I sat opposite him and resolved that I wasn't going to gabble away and do all the talking. If he was going to be mysterious, then so was I.

"Hi," he said.

"Hi."

He looked up at me, then down at the floor and shifted uncomfortably. He fumbled in his jacket pocket. "First of all, let me give you this back." He handed me Ben's CD. "I wanted to hear what your band sounded like. I know I should have told you, but I know a few people in bands and it can be so embarrassing if they're rotten and you have to fake what you think. I wanted to listen to you in private. It's good. Genuinely. And you have a great voice, Izzie. Real talent."

"Thanks. I—"

"And second," he interrupted. "I was a real shit last night and I want to apologize. I shouldn't have left you on your own. . . ."

My jaw dropped. This wasn't what I expected.

"So sorry," he continued. "I don't know why I did it. It's weird sometimes with girls. It's like . . . I dunno, like when I really like someone, sometimes it does my head in and I cut off. I know it's mad . . ." He shifted in his seat again. "Plus things have been crap at home, you know, lot going on . . ."

"Tell me about it," I said. "I seem to have been in the

doghouse all summer. So what's happening at home?"

Josh hesitated. "Oh, the usual—parents, school, exams, life," he said finally.

"Yeah. Same ol', same ol'," I said. "Do you have brothers and sisters?"

Josh shook his head. "Just me."

"So what's been the problem?"

Josh hesitated again. "It's my dad, really. . . ." He seemed reluctant to carry on, so I reached over, took his hand, and squeezed it.

"You don't have to tell me if you don't want," I said.

Josh shrugged. "No, it's not that I don't want to tell you, just that a lot of people don't want to know when they find out what my dad does."

"Why? What does he do?"

Josh glanced around him, then sighed. "Let's just put it this way: He spends a lot of his time in police stations."

Even though I tried to look cool about it, I think my face must have registered surprise. Josh scanned my face for a reaction, so I gave him a sympathetic smile as if to say what his dad did wasn't going to put me off him.

"Ever since I was a kid," he continued, "I never really

knew what my dad was up to. Out nights, didn't know where he'd been when he finally did come home. And the stress it causes my mum—the atmosphere at home is rotten. She wants him to get a normal job, live a normal life, but nah, what can you do?"

"Oh, I'm so sorry, Josh. It must be hard having a dad who's been inside . . . ," I began.

"Inside?" Suddenly he grinned as though he found it funny. "Yeah. My dad's a right dodgy geezer, but once someone's turned rotten, you can't change them." Suddenly, his expression changed to sadness. Ah, I thought, so that's it. His devil-may-care attitude is a cover for how he really feels. Poor Josh. It must be awful having a dad who's in and out of prison.

"I try to keep out of his way as much as I can," said Josh. "Not that he's got much time for me. All he cares about is the latest job he's on. That's why I don't like going home much. I don't want to get into it or know what he's up to."

"Where do you live?"

He jerked his thumb north. "Up near Whetstone. But I tell you, I'm off the minute I can leave. I'll find a way to support myself. I mean, who wants to live somewhere where your dad's dodgy and your mum is paranoid that you're going to end up the same way. Like, I didn't get the grades I needed in my GCSEs this summer and now she's convinced I'm going the same way as my dad and won't get off my case. It's hell."

I put my hand over his. "I'm really sorry. I haven't been getting on with my mum lately either."

"Yeah, but I don't think my dad even likes me. He's always picking on me, then mum stands up for me, then they start rowing. I mean, I've no intention of ending up like Dad—no way."

He looked so vulnerable sitting there that I desperately wanted to make him feel better. All my resolve not to get involved went flying out the window. I felt the total opposite of how I felt last night. Then I'd felt used and discarded, now I felt needed. He was confiding in me and I wanted to show him that I was there for him. He lit up a cigarette and offered me one.

I took one and told him I'd have it later.

"Want to hear something funny?" I asked.

He nodded.

"I wrote something about meeting you in my diary and my mum read it. She said she wants to meet you. As if."

He looked chuffed. "You wrote about me in your diary? What did you write?"

"None of your business."

He laughed. "I hope it was flattering."

"Might have been. You'll never know."

He looked at me seriously. "I will come and meet her, if you like."

I shook my head. "No, don't be mad. She's just being overprotective. Worrying that I'm seeing some maniac."

"I'm good with mums," he said. "Honest. I can be very charming when I want to be."

"I'm sure you can, but no, forget it."

"Oh, come on, it'll be a laugh. I can tell her all about how I want to be a doctor when I leave school."

"You never told me that. . . ."

He laughed. "I have no intention of being a doctor, but that's the sort of thing mums like to hear."

"So, you're good at telling women what they like to hear, are you?" I teased.

Josh shrugged, then laughed again. "Yeah. Sometimes all you have to do is feed them a line. They hear what they want to hear and run with it. Anyway, the offer's there and if it gets your mum off your back, then why not? It would also mean we could see each other without her giving you any hassle."

That made sense. "Okay," I said. "But I'm warning you. She can be major inquisitive."

"No problemo. So, you all ready for tonight?"

I nodded. "Sort of, but I always feel a little nervous just before."

"So how about I come over this evening before the gig and help you chill. We could go together."

On the way home, I put the cigarette that Josh had given me in the bin, then quickly called in at Ben's. No one was there, so I posted the CD through the letter box with a note saying, *"Sorry, found this in my bag. Must have picked it up by mistake. Sorry, sorry. See you later."*

Phew, that's sorted, I thought, heading home to meet Lucy. She was coming over to help me put my outfit together for the gig, plus I wanted to look good for Josh. I was glad he was the one who had taken the CD, as I wouldn't have liked a confrontation with Spider, and I felt flattered that Josh had wanted to hear what I sounded like with the band. He was different today, I thought as I walked toward the tube station. All his defenses were down and I realized that he's as insecure as the rest of us. It must be rotten for him. Even though Mum and I have been at war lately, I know that she's there for me in her own uptight way. I decided I'd give her a hug when I got home.

She was in the kitchen making a sandwich when I got in, so I went over to her and put my arm around her waist.

"Hey, Mum," I said. "Had a good morning?"

"You've been smoking," she said pulling back.

"No, I haven't," I said.

Mum sighed. "I can smell it, Izzie. In your hair."

"I've been in a place where people were smoking, but I didn't. I don't even like cigarettes."

"So you *have* tried one, then?"

"*No*. Yes, well only a puff, but never again. They stink."

"What is it with you lately, Izzie? Drinking, smoking. Hanging out with strange boys. What next?"

How can parents switch moods so fast? I wondered. Last night she was being so nice before she went out and now, she's back on my case. It's so unfair. I don't smoke. I *won't* smoke. I try something and make a decision that she'd approve of and still I'm in the doghouse.

"Life is about making choices, Mum. To make choices, you have to know what's on offer. I did try a cigarette and I've decided not to smoke. Everyone my age tries one at some time or other."

"But some choices are dangerous, Izzie. What else are you going to try?"

"Give me a break, Mum. I know what not to mess with."

"Do you? *Do* you? How do I know that?" she said as she took a seat at the table. "You're still young, Izzie. You need my protection."

"Protection, yes. Suffocation, no." I was starting to feel annoyed. Then I remembered what Angus had said about how watching your daughter grow up can be a difficult time of readjustment for parents. Slow down, I told myself. Be patient and meet her halfway.

"Mum, you *can* trust me."

"I hope so, Izzie, because . . ."

"Oh, and that strange boy," I interrupted. "His name's Josh. He lives in Whetstone and he said he'd love to meet you. He's coming over this evening."

Ha. That shut her up.

Line for Lucy's T-shirt collection

As ye smoke,
so shall ye reek

12

The Big Night

True to his word, Josh arrived on my doorstep early evening, carrying a bunch of flowers. I was feeling really good, as Lucy had popped over earlier as promised and we'd put together an amazing outfit for the gig. She'd lent me a black corset-type basque that she'd made. It had crisscross laces at the back, was low at the front, and looked great with my tight black jeans and high boots. Nesta lent me a black beaded choker and I did my makeup darker than normal. When I'd finished, I thought the whole effect looked very rock-chick and cool.

Josh let out a long whistle when I opened the door. "Whoa, you look *amazing*," he said, looking me up and down. Then he laughed and indicated his jeans and fleece. "And look at me, dressed all safe and normal, ready to meet Mummy dearest."

"You look great," I said, then I showed him into the hall. He *did* look good—even out of his usual bike leathers, he still gave off a vibe like he was all coiled up with energy, raring to go. And so sweet, he'd brought me flowers.

"Those for me?" I asked, pointing at the flowers.

He shook his head. "For your mum." Then he whispered, "From the garden on the corner of your road."

At that moment, Mum came out of the kitchen. She looked a bit shocked when she saw me, but didn't say anything. Instead she focused on Josh and shook his hand. "So you're Josh," she said.

He smiled back at her. "And you must be one of Izzie's stepsisters."

"No. I'm Izzie's mother," she replied, and I could swear that her cheeks colored a little.

"No way," he said, handing her the flowers. "You don't look old enough."

Mum raised an eyebrow as though she didn't believe a word of it, then she laughed. "Izzie never told me that you were so charming. Now, what can I get you?"

Cigarette and a can of lager, I thought, knowing

Josh. But he just asked if she had Earl Grey tea.

"That's my favorite too," she said, heading back for the kitchen. "I'll bring it up to you. Izzie, do you want anything?"

"No, no, let me help you," said Josh, following her, then turning back and giving me a conspiratorial wink.

I had to ring Ben to confirm a few last minute arrangements for the gig, so I left them to it in the kitchen. As I dialed Ben's number on the phone in the hall, I heard Mum laughing at something Josh said. Boy, he really is good with mums, I thought.

Over tea, he and Mum got to talking about his career. Anyone would think he's a prospective husband, the way she's sizing him up, I thought as she asked about his aims and ambitions in life. He didn't seem to mind, though, and chatted away happily about plans for college. He even did the "I may study to be a doctor" spiel.

"Come on, Josh," I said after Mum had plied him with cakes and biscuits. "I'll show you my room."

"And you must come and have supper with us one night," said Mum. "I'm sure my husband would like to meet you as well."

"That would be great," said Josh, getting up.

Once we got upstairs, I showed him my room, then quickly went to the bathroom. The pre-gig nerves were beginning to kick in and even though I've performed a number of times before, I still get jittery inside. When I went back into my bedroom, Josh was hanging out of the window, smoking a cigarette.

"*Hey*, don't do that in here," I said, closing the door in a panic. "Mum will kill me."

"She won't smell it," said Josh. "I'm smoking it out the window."

"You don't know my mum. She has the nose of a sniffer dog," I said, and quickly lit a joss stick, then sprayed the room with vanilla room spray. Josh stubbed out his cigarette and threw himself back on my bed. It felt so weird to actually have him there in my room, lying on *my* bed. If I was to choose an animal for how others see him, I thought, it would be a panther. Lean, beautiful, and ready to pounce. Suddenly I felt awkward. I didn't know where to put myself or how to act. I think Josh was well aware off the effect he was having on me, and he caught my hand and pulled me down beside him just as there was a knock at the door.

"Izzie," called Mum. "Can I have a word?"

I sprang away from Josh and gave the room another

spray. Oh poo, I thought. Is it because I closed the door when I've a boy in my room or because she's smelled the smoke? I went out into the corridor and shut the door behind me.

"Yes, Mum?"

She beckoned me into her bedroom.

"Close the door," she said once we'd got inside.

Oh dear, she definitely smelled the cigarette, I thought as I shut the door. What a shame, after it was all going so well.

"I've taken on board what you asked the other night about not saying things to you in front of people, so . . ."

"It wasn't me smoking," I started.

"What do you mean? Smoking?" she asked, looking puzzled.

"Um, er, didn't you . . . I mean . . . Why is it you wanted to see me?"

"*Have* you been smoking in your room?"

"No. *No*. Course not."

"Because I won't tolerate it if you have."

"I told you I don't smoke."

"So what are you talking about, then? Is Josh smoking in there?"

"No," I said. It was the truth. He wasn't smoking in

my room. At least, not anymore. "Mum. What is it you wanted?"

Mum looked at my outfit. "I can't let you go out looking like that," she said. "That basque you've got on is too provocative. It gives out a message to boys, plus you've got far too much makeup on for someone your age."

"But I'm performing, Mum. *Onstage*. Not going shopping in Tesco's. I have to make an effort."

"Just wipe a bit of it off," she said. "Your eyes are too heavy and that lipstick's too strong."

"Fine," I said. "I'll wipe it off. Can I go now?"

"Yes, but please don't be sulky about it. I bet that nice young man of yours would agree with me. Most men prefer girls to look natural."

"Yes, fine. Whatever," I said, heading for the door.

"No, Izzie, I *mean* it. Find something else to wear or you're not going."

"I'll wear my velvet top. Okay?" I said, thinking that the sooner Josh and I get out of here, the better. And I knew I'd better act compliant as I was about to tell her something else. "Oh . . . and Josh said he'll give me a ride on the back of his bike, so you don't need to drop me."

"Bike? What bike?"

"Motorbike."

"No, Izzie. I'm not letting you go on the back of one of those things. They're dangerous. I'll drop you and Mrs. Lovering will pick you up. I spoke to her earlier and it's all arranged. And eat something before you go. I left a sandwich downstairs for you, as you'll miss supper."

"I'm really not hungry, Mum. I can never eat before a gig."

"Then take it with you and have it later."

Poo and stinkbombs, I thought as I went back to my room. She'd have me going to the gig with a Thermos and cucumber sandwiches if she had her way. She really has no idea. And I'd really been looking forward to arriving at the gig on the back of a cool motorbike. The boys in the band would have been well impressed, but no, Mrs. Killjoy had to have her way again. It's not fair. I met her halfway and brought Josh here and yet she still insists on treating me like a little girl who has to do as she says.

As soon as Mum dropped me off, I made a dive for the ladies, where I binned the sandwich she'd made me, reapplied my makeup, and took off the top that I'd put on over the basque. Mum really didn't understand. I couldn't possibly get up onstage in front of everyone, looking like I was dressed for afternoon tea with my grandma.

When I came out, I saw that Spider had turned up and was standing with Josh at the bar, and my heart sank. He gave me his greeting sneer, and for the first time, I started to feel sympathy for the boy that Lucy had dumped for being too possessive. It's hard when you like someone but don't want to hang out with their friends or family, because people come as a package. It's like—like me, accept my mum. Like Josh, accept Spider.

Not long after, all my mates arrived—Nesta and Tony, T. J. with Lucy's brothers, Steve and Lal, and of course, Lucy.

"Bring on the show," Lucy said, grinning. "Your fan club's here."

I grinned back. "Thanks." It felt great to have them all there and made it feel more like a party than a performance in front of a strange audience.

I introduced Josh to everyone and he insisted on buying a round of drinks.

"What would you like, Izzie?" he asked.

"Pineapple," I said. "Need to keep a clear head for the performance."

"A *drink* drink might take the edge off your nerves."

"Maybe later," I said. "In the meantime, I have to remember my lyrics."

The girls asked for Cokes, Josh and Spider ordered lager as usual, and when we'd all got our drinks, we stood at the back of the hall and listened to the first band. They were awful. Most of the time I try to be supportive of fellow musicians, but even Ben caught my eye from the front of the hall and grimaced. Spider, however, wasn't as subtle and started heckling.

"Geddoff! Rubbish," he called from the bar.

Josh laughed and went to get more drinks, but I didn't think it was funny. I thought it was really uncool. I moved away from Spider so that the musicians onstage wouldn't think that I was with him. Josh saw me frowning at Spider and when he brought me another drink, he said, "Lighten up, Iz. They *are* rubbish. Better someone tells them so they don't waste anymore of their time."

"Give them a break. They're probably just starting out," I said. "I'm sure there was a time when even Robbie Williams sounded bad."

"Doubt it," said Josh, then took my chin in his hand, looked into my eyes, and kissed me quickly. "You, my dear Izzie, are far too nice."

By this time Spider had started looning about, doing mad dancing in the middle of the dance floor. Josh went to join him and soon people were looking at them and laughing instead of watching the band. I felt so sorry for them, as I know it takes courage to get up onstage.

"Looks familiar," said Nesta, coming over. "*Please* tell me that I was never that embarrassing."

"Ancient history," I said. "And at least you could dance."

"And what about Josh? I thought he was ancient history."

I shook my head. "Nah. He's all right, really. He's got another side to him, once you get to know him. He's like a little boy who needs a bit of looking after."

Nesta took a sip of my pineapple juice, then looked at me with surprise. "Might be you who needs looking after if you have any more of these. I thought you weren't going to drink again after that night at my house."

"What do you mean? It's only juice."

"Yeah, right," said Nesta. "With a good measure of vodka in it."

"Ohmigod," I said. I'd had two large ones. I was so

thirsty and didn't want my throat to be dry when I sang. No wonder I was feeling light-headed.

"Didn't you know?" asked Nesta.

I shook my head.

"You need to watch it with him," said Nesta. "Slipping you drinks when you don't know isn't on."

"No, really, he's okay. He was probably trying to loosen me up, as I told him how nervous I was."

"That's your problem: You always see the best in people."

"And that's yours: You always see the worst."

Nesta looked at me with concern. "No, seriously, Iz. You take care with him. You might have forgotten that he left you stranded the other night, but I haven't."

"But he apologized for that," I said.

"And that makes it all right, does it?"

I didn't like the way the conversation was going. It felt like the great party atmosphere from earlier had become heavy. "Look, Nesta, he's okay. You should give him a chance and get to know him. There are things going on in his life that you don't know about. Don't be so judgmental."

Nesta looked hurt and I was about to apologize when Ben waved me over to get ready to go onstage.

"Catch you later," said Nesta. "Have a good one up there."

I felt confused as I watched her walk back to Lucy and her brothers. What just happened there? I asked myself as I went for a last minute lipstick check in the ladies. T. J. was in there combing her hair.

"You nervous?" she asked.

"Bit," I said.

"And how's the stud?"

I lifted the basque and showed her. "It's healed up nicely, see? I've been really good about keeping it clean and it seems to have worked okay."

"Oh yeah. Looks great. But what about your mum? Did she ever find out you had another one put in?"

"Sort of," I said. "It's awkward. She read my diary. I know I put something about the new stud in there, but I think she feels bad about having read it—knows she shouldn't have—and it's been kind of unspoken since then. She knows, I know she knows, but neither of us wants to say anything."

"Well, at least she hasn't told you to take it out again."

"No. If she did, it would bring up the whole diary reading thing again and I guess she doesn't want to do that."

"Yeah," said T. J., slicking on some lip gloss, then heading for the door. "Okay. Best of luck up there."

"Thanks. . . . Hey, T. J. What do you think of Josh?"

T. J. hesitated. "Oh, I can't say, Izzie. This is the first time I've met him and we've hardly said two words. I can see why you fancy him, but . . ."

"But what?"

"Well, I know Lucy and Nesta are a bit worried."

"Why?"

T. J. shrugged. "It's probably nothing, but he's, well, he's not like the rest of us, is he? You can see he's got an edge."

"So? I think that's what makes him so attractive."

"I know. Just, Nesta thinks he may be a bad influence."

Suddenly I felt really sad. So they've been talking about me behind my back, I thought. I hate that. I always think if you have anything to say, say it to the person in question. That's what being mates is all about . . . but then maybe I'm growing away from mine. It's felt kind of weird with us all lately.

King Noz did a twenty-minute set and the audience seemed to like it well enough. A few minutes into the first number, they were up and dancing away. I loved it. It's a real buzz being up onstage when the nerves disappear, the lights are on you and the music's rocking.

After I did my two numbers with the band, I went and sat with Josh and Spider.

Josh leaned back and gave me a wide grin. "Impressive," he said. "You're hot."

Spider gave me a kind of grudging smile. I think that meant he liked it as well. At least he didn't get up and heckle us.

As we sat to watch the rest of the set, Spider disappeared outside for a short while, then reappeared with a joint, which he handed to Josh then Josh passed to me. I quickly glanced to check that the barman wasn't looking as I didn't think teenagers smoking dope in the pub would go down too well, but he was busy serving customers. I noticed Nesta staring at me from the other side of the room. I gave her a wave, then purposely took a puff on the joint so she could see, and I inhaled like Josh had told me to do. If you think Josh is a bad influence, then I may as well let him be, I thought as my head began to swim. I saw Nesta glance at T. J. and T. J. looked over at me and said something to Lucy. I took another puff on the joint and gave them a wave too.

I don't remember too much after that. Dancing with Josh. Snogging Josh. Having a laugh with Josh. Falling asleep on his shoulder. The time went so quickly. The next thing I knew T. J. was standing over me. "Izzie. Lucy's mum's here to give you a lift home."

"Oh, not yet," said Josh as I got myself together to go. "It's too early."

"Curfew time," I mumbled. "Dragon Mother will be waiting."

Josh laughed and walked with me to the car park where I could see Lucy talking to her mum, then glancing back at me. My God, I thought, who isn't talking about me? My head felt really thick and dopey and everyone seemed to be looking at me. Want to go home, I thought. Go to bed.

Mrs. Lovering beckoned me over and Lucy squeezed in the back with Steve and Lal, while I took the front passenger seat. I closed my eyes and we drove for a while in silence.

"Tired, Izzie?" said Mrs. Lovering.

"Um," I replied.

"Good gig?"

"Excellent," said Lal from the back. "Izzie was a star."

"So, you kids," continued Mrs. Lovering. "I remember when I was your age . . ."

Ah, I thought, opening my eyes and turning to look at Lucy in the back. It's the "When I was your age" speech. I knew Lucy had put her mum up to this. She shrugged, smiled weakly, and stared out of the window, trying her best to look innocent.

". . . it was quite a time," continued Mrs. Lovering. "Go to a gig like that and everything would be on offer, and I don't mean just alcohol, know what I mean?"

"No," I said, also trying to look innocent. "What do you mean?"

"Oh, drugs. Pot, acid, coke . . ."

I had to laugh to myself. So, is that what everyone thinks now? Izzie's a raving junkie. I've only had a few puffs on a joint and now everyone's on my case.

"It can be hard to say no sometimes," said Mrs. Lovering. "People can pressure you to join in, even when you don't want to. All I'm saying is, be careful, guys. I know you're going to experiment, and ultimately you have to make your own choices, but don't ever feel you have to do something because everyone else is. Right?"

"Right," said Lucy from the back.

I turned around and gave her a cheesy smile. "But Lucy's had Coke tonight, haven't you, Luce?"

"Coca-Cola," said Lucy quickly.

For some reason I thought this was hilarious and started giggling to myself, then I tried to make my face go straight. Boy, I do feel a bit weird, I thought as I gazed out the window. A man at a bus stop gazed back. Not you too, I thought as we whizzed by. I wish everyone would stop *looking* at me.

Parent Speak

Says:

Means:

When I was your age . . .

Prepare for a lecture about how when they were your age, they were a lot better behaved.

What's this lying on the floor?

It's yours. Pick it up immediately.

We need to have a "word."

Prepare for a telling-off.

That TV program doesn't look very interesting.

Turn it off.

It's getting late.

Go to bed.

Your room's a mess.

Tidy it RIGHT NOW.

Are you watching this TV program?

Change it. I want to watch something else.

It's time you learned how to look after yourself, as I won't be around forever.

Wash up.

13

How Embarrassing!

When I was in Year Seven, I used to get a maga-zine that had a section in it with people's most embarrassing moments. People sent in all sorts of anecdotes about being caught naked, or a bee flying down their shorts, or pulling people's wigs off, and so on. I think I now qualify for the star prize.

I'd been home an hour, all snuggled up in my lovely bed after the gig, when my mobile rang. It was Josh.

"Want to live dangerously?" he said.

"Dunurrh . . . ," I said sleepily.

"I'm outside. Meet me at the bottom of your road in five minutes."

That woke me up fast enough. "Out*side*? But it's midnight."

"So? You going to turn into a pumpkin or what? Come on, Iz. You start school again Monday. You can be a good girl then. Come on, come out and play."

I wasn't feeling too good after the spiked pineapple juice and the joint earlier, and the thought of snuggling back down to sleep was very inviting. But so was sneaking out to be with Josh. I'd never done anything like that before. Why not? I thought. Everyone seems to think I'm bad. So why not live up to my reputation for once?

I pulled on my jeans and a fleece, grabbed my mobile, and tiptoed out into the corridor, past Mum's room where I could hear Angus snoring, then down the stairs and into the front garden.

Josh was waiting for me at the gate. "Excellent," he said, putting his arm around me. "Where shall we go?"

"Dunno," I said.

"Okay. I parked my bike at the end of the next road. I'll take us down to Queen's Wood."

Five minutes later, I was clinging to Josh's waist as we roared through the empty streets. It felt totally exhilarating and daring.

When we got to the park, we found a shelter near

one of the gates and Josh produced a bottle of Malibu and a joint. "Picnic," he said.

"I wish," I said. Apart from a piece of toast when I'd got in, I hadn't eaten since lunchtime. I suddenly realized I was starving. I shook my head when he offered me the bottle.

"No thanks. But you haven't by any chance got a cheese sandwich on you, have you?" I said, wishing I hadn't binned the one Mum had made me earlier. My stomach felt really peculiar.

Josh pouted. "But I bought it specially for you," he said, looking at the Malibu. "It's not my thing. It's a chick's drink."

I didn't want him to feel that I didn't appreciate the gesture so I took a swig. Then he offered me the joint.

"No thanks. I don't really like it," I said.

"Give it another go," he said. "I don't want to get stoned on my own." Then he looked away, his expression really sad. "Dad's down at the police station again. Don't know when he'll be back this time. I'm not ready to go home yet and I . . . I don't want to be on my own."

Poor Josh, I thought. It must be awful having to stay out for fear of going home to bad news. I took the joint and had a quick puff, but this time, I tried not to inhale. It didn't seem to make much difference, though, as once again, my head began to feel woozy.

"Hmm . . . it's weird this, isn't it? Makes you feel funny."

Josh smiled and pulled me close to him. "Yeah, but funny in a cool way. You looked great tonight, did I tell you that?" He started kissing me, which felt really nice, then after a few minutes I noticed his hands starting to stray from my back and around to my front.

I pushed him away.

"What's the matter?" he asked.

I felt confused. Ben had never tried this with me, and I didn't know what to do. Suddenly I was aware that I was in a park in the middle of the night and if Josh got annoyed, he could well abandon me again. Josh handed me the Malibu bottle. "Here, have some more drink."

"No, really," I said. "I don't want any." My head was feeling thick again, my stomach was rumbling, I was cold and starting to feel a bit nauseous.

Josh moved in and started the wandering hands act again. Once more, I pushed him off. He sat back and handed me the bottle. "Look, have a drink. Most girls find that it helps loosen them up."

Well, I'm not most girls, I thought. But then I do like Josh, so maybe I should just go along with it and see what happens. I don't want him to think that I'm uptight, plus the drink might take my mind off the fact that I'm starving.

I took the bottle from him and had a good long glug.

"Good girl," said Josh, snuggling up. "It can help you chill out, that's all." He started kissing me again and his hands started roaming around again. I could tell he was getting worked up because his breathing changed. It got heavier and his kisses got more urgent. At one point, he put his hand on my tummy.

"Oh, be careful," I said. "I've got a new stud."

"Really?" he said and lifted up my fleece. "Cool."

And then it happened . . .

I threw up.

"Eeeeww!" he cried in surprise and sprang away.

I was horrified. I leaped up, ran for the gate, and scrabbled around in my pockets for a tissue. I felt awful. My first encounter with a boy that goes a bit further than snogging and I *throw up*. It's never like this in the movies. I'll never live it down. I'm useless, I thought as I ran out on to the pavement. My first drink and I fall asleep behind Nesta's sofa. My first cigarette and I gag on it. My first puff on a joint and I think everyone's watching me. And my first grope with a boy and I *puke!* How grown-up is that? Not at all. I felt close to tears and anything but fourteen. I felt like sitting on the pavement and crying like a baby.

All I wanted to do was get away. I went and stood at the bus stop, praying that a bus would come along so that I could get home, get into bed, wake up in the morning to find out it was all a bad dream.

"A bus has just gone," said a lady going by with her dog.

Oh, now what? I thought as I looked around. The tube would be closed at this time. The streets were empty apart from the occasional car, and the trees seemed alive somehow, shadowy, monstrous, and threatening. I thought about going back to find Josh, but the woods looked so dense and dark. I didn't want to risk it.

A black Golf drove past filled with lads, then it reversed and slowly came back. "Want a lift, darling?" called one.

I shook my head. "My dad's coming to get me," I said. Oh, where's Josh? I thought. Why hasn't he followed me? Oh God. What a disaster. He's probably trying to wipe off puke from his fleece where it splashed him. Luckily the boys in the car drove off and I sighed with relief. This is really, *really* stupid of me, I thought. A mad, *mad* mistake. There are stories every other week about girls my age disappearing, never to be seen again. I'm an idiot to have come out so late. I *never* do stuff like this normally. I'm not thinking straight with everything that's happened and the stupid Malibu and that stupid joint. It all kind of made everything feel unreal for a while, but it *is* real. It's past midnight, very dark, and I'm out on the streets on my own. I wish Lucy was here, I thought. And T. J. And Nesta. They'll all be tucked up in their beds, like I should be, so no way can I call them so late. Dad? No, he'd take too long to get here from Primrose Hill and I don't want to stay out on my own a moment longer than necessary. Then I thought about Mum asleep at home, thinking that I was safe in my room next door to her. I want my mum, I thought. I wish she'd just drive by and pick me up. I don't want to be grown-up any more. I want to be looked after. Should I phone her? I asked myself. No. No way I can call her. I'll be grounded for a decade and never see daylight again. She'd go ballistic and she's got good reason, I said to myself as another car drove by and the male driver looked out at me. What on earth am I doing out here in the middle of the night on my own?

14

Damsel in Distress

There was only one person to turn to and luckily he was still awake when I called. He only lived up the road and said he'd come straight out on his bicycle to get me. While I was waiting for him, Josh phoned my mobile and said that he was looking for me but wasn't sure which way I'd gone when I ran out of the park. I said I was sorry for throwing up and told him to go home as I was all right.

Twenty minutes later I was curled up safely on the sofa in Ben's garage with a cup of tea and three rounds of Marmite toast.

"Thanks," I said as I brushed the crumbs away from my mouth. "I was starving. I missed supper and only had a snack when I got it after the gig."

Ben grinned. "More like a classic case of the munchies. It often happens when people smoke dope."

"Have you smoked it?"

Ben shrugged. "Gave it a go. Not my scene, though, really. I prefer to have a clear head."

I was surprised, as he'd never mentioned it before and I thought I knew all about him. Plus he didn't seem the type.

"I didn't like it very much," I said. "Made my head feel very thick, and back at the gig, it had a weird effect on me, like everyone was watching me. And later, in the park, even the *trees* seemed to be watching me."

"Yeah, well, on an almost empty stomach, the effects would be amplified. No wonder you felt strange. Plus there are different types of dope and they have different effects. Some can be quite hallucinogenic and make you feel like you're seeing things, other types just make you sleepy. Plus it's different for everyone. Some people it disagrees with. Take ecstasy, for example. Some people take just one tablet and it kills them, others seem to be fine. Hell of a risk, though. It's still early days, and researchers are still looking into its long-term effects on the brain. Personally I'd rather stay clear and not take any chances. . . . And drink, that affects people differently as well. Some people get all happy when they've had too much to drink, others depressed and melancholic, others get aggressive and argumentative, others just throw up. I guess it depends on your body chemistry."

"Yeah. My stepmother, Anna, is really funny when she's been drinking. Something seems to happen to the volume control on her voice. She starts talking *really* loud but doesn't realize it."

"So, what's been with you lately, trying all this stuff? I thought you were Miss Straight White and Bright. You know, well into health foods . . ."

"I know. I was. I am. I just wanted to try something different. Part of it was wanting to be more grown-up, more sophisticated."

Ben started laughing. "And doing the technicolor yawn all over Josh was part of that, was it?"

"Not quite all over him, but I think I did get him a bit. I've never been so embarrassed in all my life. I doubt if I'll see him again."

"Maybe you will. Maybe you won't. But throwing up over someone is an interesting seduction tactic. Er, not one I'd try again, though."

Now that I was safe, fed, and warm, I started to see

the funny side. "Well, magazines are always telling us that when starting a new relationship, it's good to let someone see the inside of you that you don't show the rest of the world."

Ben laughed again. "Yeah, but I don't think they meant literally, as in what you ate that day. At least he'll never forget you."

"Yeah. Oh God, Ben. It's been such a weird time lately. All I wanted was for people to take me seriously and treat me like an adult, and I seem to have done nothing but act like a right twerp."

"I don't think that being grown-up means that you have to smoke or drink or anything," said Ben. "I think that being grown-up means finding out what you want as an individual and having the voice to say so, regardless of what anyone else thinks. Loads of fakers at our school drink and smoke because they think it looks cool. To me, that's not what being cool is about. Being cool is being true to yourself."

"It's hard to say no sometimes, though."

"Why?"

"Dunno. It's like you feel pressured to do stuff or try new experiences. Like tonight in the park, I didn't want to seem like a baby, you know, doing stuff for the first time. And I didn't want to refuse Josh's offer of drink for fear of offending him. And then, well, later, I didn't want to come across as uptight."

"You're too nice, Izzie."

"That's what Josh said."

"There will always be people you'll offend. What's that saying? You can't please all the people all of the time. Never go along with a guy just because you're afraid of offending him. You have feelings too. What do *you* want? You can't make everyone like you, Iz. And you shouldn't try to be someone you're not just to please a boy. If you do, you'll lose yourself. Just be who you are. Don't do stuff with a guy unless you really want to and the time is right. If a guy's the one for you, he'll take you at the pace you want to go."

"Ever thought of being an agony aunt, Ben?"

He smiled and put his arm around me. "Auntie Ben. Yeah, if the music doesn't turn out maybe I'll go for a new career."

It felt so comforting to sit there snuggled up to him for a while. No pressure, no stress. If you had to pick an animal to represent how others see you, Ben, I thought, you should pick a big old sheepdog. Cuddly, safe, and warm.

At that moment, we heard a car pull up outside.

Ben looked out of the window. "Taxi's here," he said.

Ben walked me out and saw me into the cab. "Here's a tenner," he said. "Should be enough. Got your keys?"

I nodded. "And hopefully Mum and Angus will still be happily in dreamland." I gave him a hug. "Thanks, Ben. You've been a real mate."

"Talking of which," he said. "Get together with yours. They're a good lot and when you're out, it's important that you all stick together, look after one another, make sure you all get home safe. And never leave each other alone with boys that you don't know well."

I pinched his arm. "Since when did you get so grown-up?"

He smiled back. "Since you started acting like a five-year-old."

Song for Ben:
Knight on a Battered Bicycle

I was distressed,
In a real mess,
Cast down,
Lost my crown,
No more a princess.

I cried out for rescue and look what came my way.

You're my knight in crumpled armor,
My hero for a day.
Forget the milk-white charger,
You just peddle up my way.

I cried for help and look what came my way.

Wheels of fire and thunder
Are okay for the gods,
But a crossbar lift is just the thing
To hold back all my sobs.

Ring your bell and wheel my way,
My knight in crumpled armor.
Ring your bell and wheel my way,
My knight in crumpled armor.

15

Ground Rules

Sunday was Mum's birthday and Angus had insisted that she have a lie-in as a treat. I went down to the kitchen and prepared a tray—a carafe of coffee, orange juice, toast, and the chunky marmalade that she likes. Then I cut a rose from the fence in the back garden and put it in a small vase next to my card and present for her.

Angus was already up and pottering in his study. "That looks nice," he said as I went past.

"It's for Mum."

"Good for you." He smiled. "She's probably ready for a cup of coffee now."

Mum was still dozing when I tiptoed into her room. I watched her sleeping for a few moments and felt really warm toward her. She looked so young and vulnerable somehow, lying there with her hair splayed on the pillow, one arm thrown above her head. *Did you ever stay out at night and misbehave?* I wondered. Somehow I couldn't imagine it. She's always so efficient, organized, and controlled. A typical Virgo, according to my astrology book.

She opened her eyes as I put the tray on the bedside cabinet, then got up and sat on the edge of the bed.

"Is that for me?" she said, rubbing her eyes.

I nodded. "Happy birthday."

"Oh, Izzie, how lovely. Thank you. And a present."

I watched as she opened her card and present.

"Oils for the bath," she said, taking the lid off one of the bottles and sniffing. "Mmm. Lovely."

"It's got lavender and rosewood in it, aromatherapy oils. They're supposed to be good for relaxation."

"It smells divine, Izzie. Thank you so much."

"And . . . and I wanted to say I'm sorry I've been a pain lately and that I really do appreciate you as a mother."

She laughed. "Okay, what have you done now?"

"*Nothing,*" I said. Luckily, I'd managed to sneak back in last night without waking her and Angus. What she doesn't know won't hurt her, I thought. "Mum?"

"What?"

"What were you like when you were my age?"

Mum laughed. "Pretty timid, really."

"Did you ever do anything stupid?"

"What, like you at Nesta's the other night?"

"Yes. No. I mean, didn't you used to experiment with, I don't know, cigarettes? The occasional drink?"

"Not really," she said. "Let me think. I did try a cigarette once, but hated it. As you know, I've never smoked. Drink . . . when did I have my first drink? I didn't really drink until I was at university and then not a lot. Couldn't afford it on my student's grant. Oh dear. Am I a terrible disappointment? Boring? I'm afraid I was never one for experimenting much and there wasn't as much on offer out there, or at least not that I was aware of. My parents were so strict with me, and to tell you the truth, when I did finally leave home and go to college, I thought I'd lived a sheltered life compared to the rest of them. I was a bit of a late developer, really. That's why . . . I look at you and you're *so* different from how I was—I suppose that's why I fear for you. My endlessly curious Izzie. You were always the same, from the moment you were born. Into everything. Restless. Always asking questions. We may be mother and daughter and have some similar features—eyes, the shape of our hands . . . but your spirit is your own and as opposite to mine as it could ever be. And now, so grown-up, still curious, and yet . . . I don't know. I can't help but worry about you and what's out there. For one thing, the streets felt a lot safer when I was young. I thought nothing about walking home on my own at night. These days, I'd never let you do that."

Tell me about it, I thought. Last night is not an experience I want to repeat in a hurry. "Well, it's nice to have someone worry about you," I said.

Mum smiled. "I can't help it. And I know I overreact sometimes, but it's only because I care. I know that there are drugs in school and a lot of teenagers smoke and drink. It's just I want you to enjoy your adolescence, enjoy being young, and yet you're so busy wanting to grow up and leave it all behind you. And boys . . . I . . . I worry that in wanting to grow up, you're going to feel pressured to rush into things before you're ready. Just promise me that you'll be careful, whatever happens."

"I will and I'm okay, Mum. Honest. And I'm learning. Yes, it is mad out there. And yes, you can feel pressured, but I think I know when to say no or yes. Or whatever."

"And . . . um, how's your stud? Has it healed up?"

I laughed. At last, she'd acknowledged that she knew about it. "Yeah, it's good now. But . . . er, how did you know about that?"

She grinned. "You know very well. Your diary, of course. I *am* sorry about that, Izzie. It was wrong of me. I should have respected your privacy. But you know what? No one gives you a rule book on how to be a teenager, and, well, no one gives you a rule book on how to be a mother either. And reading your diary was a mad mistake."

I smiled back at her. "We all make mad mistakes, Mum."

"I know," she said wistfully. "But do you think in the future, we could, well, try to talk about them a bit more? You know, help each other."

"Sure," I said. "I'm game for that. Want to see my stud?"

"If I must," she said, then she pulled a silly face.

"So, does this mean you're back with Ben now?" asked Nesta later that morning.

Straight after I'd taken Mum her breakfast, I'd called T. J., Lucy, and Nesta and asked them to come over. Luckily they were all free, and by twelve o'clock we were all in my bedroom, where I told them about what had happened last night.

I shook my head. "No, I'm not getting back with him, but we are best mates. Like you lot."

Nesta and T. J. looked at each other, while Lucy stared at the carpet.

"Because we *are* best mates, aren't we?" I asked.

"Course," said Lucy. "We have bonded for life over the Almighty Pringle, remember?"

"Maybe we should have done the finger pricking thing," I said. "Done it properly."

"Oh *please*, don't start that again," moaned Nesta.

"Don't worry," I reassured her. "I won't. But I did want to see you all today and say I'm sorry. I guess I've been a bit distant lately and acting a bit out of character. But last night, it made me realize that you guys are the most important people in my life. Besides Mum and Dad, of course . . . and . . . and Angus. It's weird— like, remember how I used to hate him and call him The Lodger? Well, he's been cool lately and I'm starting to really like him. So yeah, Angus is important too."

"Well, we've been worried about you, Iz," said Lucy. "It was like you didn't want to be associated with us anymore. You used to phone or e-mail every day, but this last week, I've hardly heard from you. Like you'd moved on and thought we were too childish for you or something."

"No way," I said.

"Last night, you hardly spent any time with us," said Nesta. "We all thought you were ashamed of us or something, because we didn't want to drink and smoke and be in with your new crowd."

"*Ashamed* of you? I thought *you* didn't want to be with me and you didn't like Josh or Spider."

"Didn't like Spider. He's kind of creepy," said Nesta.

"Maybe that's why his nickname is Spider," said T. J. "Creepy crawly. So what about Josh? Are you going to see him again?"

"Doubt it somehow," I said. "I think throwing up just as he was getting snuggly was probably a bit of a turn-off, don't you think?"

"Dunno," laughed T. J. "But you could probably make it work if you wanted. Phone him up and apologize, and so on."

"Nah. Think I'll give him a break for a while. It's kind of done my head in this last week. Part of me felt sorry for him because he's not happy at home. I thought I could make it better, I guess. I thought I could change him, but . . ."

"As you told me your mum said once, the only time you can change a man is when he's a baby," said Lucy.

"Exactly," I said. "It was exciting being with him, but also exhausting. I didn't feel like I could totally be myself. I was trying to be something different for him."

"So why not go back with Ben?"

"Dunno. It's like, being with Ben was safe and secure and Josh was the total opposite, unpredictable and exciting. Maybe there are some boys who are a bit of both. Do you think?"

"I think my brother's a bit like that," said Nesta. "Don't you think, Lucy?"

Lucy blushed. "Yeah. He's pretty cool. And my brothers are a bit of each. Lal is pretty mad, whereas Steve is pretty sensible."

"Yes, but he's not boring sensible," said T. J. "And he can be mad sometimes."

I looked around at the three of them and sighed with relief. It felt good. We were talking again.

"You know what?" I said. "I really *really* don't want to lose you guys as friends. I'm sorry if I've been acting like a prize prat. I don't know what came over me."

"Maybe it's because we'll all be going into Year Ten tomorrow," said Lucy. "Makes you think about the next chapter. Like where are we going next."

"Yeah. It's going to be weird being back at school," said T. J. "It's like, in the holidays, all the days just flow into each other. No Monday, Tuesday, Wednesday, weekend, and so on. When we're at school, the whole week is punctuated. Sunday night, get ready for school. Monday, go to school. Wait for Friday. Then the weekend."

"I know what you mean," I said. "Back to the old routine after a mad, mad summer."

"How's things with your mum?" asked T. J.

"Better," I said. "I mean, she'll never be cool like your mum, Lucy. She'll always be straight, but that's who she is. We had a good talk this morning and she's even okay about me having my stud now."

"Yeah, but you really started something, Izzie," said Lucy. "I think it was because of last night when Mum drove us home. She was a bit concerned about you, then started asking if I ever smoked or drank. You know, the whole interrogation. This morning at break-fast, she said she wanted to 'have a talk.' It was so embarrassing. One of those 'Let's talk openly about things' type talks. Steve and Lal looked like they wanted to die."

"Have a talk about what?" said T. J.

"First, drink—how when you drink, you're not always in control of your thoughts or actions and must be careful not to be in the wrong place or somewhere unfamiliar. Then how smoking wrecks your skin . . ."

"I think it does," I said. "I've got two aunts—one has smoked all her life, the other never has. The one who smokes is ten years younger than the other one, yet looks ten years older. Her skin is sort of crêpey and dried out."

"Well," continued Lucy, "then we got how drinking can wreck your liver. As if we're going to be drinking bottles of the stuff . . ."

"Yeah," I said. "If I've learned anything these holidays, it's about balance. All things in moderation and not to go overboard like I did at yours that night, Nesta. . . ."

"But the main thing she said about drink and drugs," Lucy said, "is that both can alter your perception. She said her anxiety was that one of us would be out of our heads and not thinking straight and someone would take advantage. A boy or someone, when we didn't know what we were doing. She kept saying that your facility to make proper choices gets impaired, but I think that's only if you drink too much."

I thought back to last night. "That was exactly what Josh wanted," I said. "Me to get drunk so that he could have a jolly old grope."

Nesta shook her head. "Not on," she said. "Not my romantic fantasy, anyway. If you have to get totally plastered to get it on with a boy, then it can't be right, can it? I'd want to be sure that I wanted to do it sober *or* having had a drink. It's like, if you have to get out of your head to do it, maybe you're trying to get out of the situation on some level. It can't be what you really want to do."

"And then Mum started on about drugs," Lucy continued. "She said that one of the biggest risks is that sometimes stuff gets mixed in with them and people don't know what they're actually taking. Unless you know exactly where the drugs have come from, they could be laced with anything."

"Well, at least she didn't give you the sex lecture," I said. "That can be really embarrassing."

"Oh, don't worry, I got that one," said T. J. "Sometimes it's hard having doctors as parents, as they see the downside of everything and think they have to pass it all on. I got a lecture about sexually-transmitted diseases and the number of teenage pregnancies my mum sees. She said everyone thinks it can't happen to them and some of the girls she sees are our age and got pregnant the very first time they had sex."

I remembered what Ben had said last night, about never going along with a boy for fear of hurting his feelings. I wondered if some of the girls who got pregnant simply got into a situation and didn't know how to get out of it—didn't have the courage to say that they weren't ready. Or got so drunk, they didn't realize how far they were going until it was too late, or so drunk that they didn't even care about the risks.

"You know what, girls?" I said. "Back to school tomorrow, and as T. J. said, it's a new start. We don't know what we're going to encounter, and what boys are on the horizon for the next year. Or what any of us are going to go through. I reckon we need to make some ground rules to mark our Pringle bonding. It wasn't enough to eat a bite of it and think we'd be bonded for life. . . ."

"Oh no . . . ," said Nesta. "What are you going to make us do now?"

"Nothing bad. It's just, there are times when maybe we need to watch out for each other. I think we should think about what we really need from each other when there are boys around or drink or drugs, or whatever. How about we all write down a ground rule? Fold it up and put in a hat. I'll do a printout of them on my computer for us all to keep."

"Good idea," said Nesta. "Rule One: No having to prick your thumb in order to be mates."

I punched her arm. "Yeah, that and a few others."

Ground Rules for Mates

* Remember: Trying to change or save a boy is a lost cause. The only time you can change a boy is when he's a baby.

* If you're going to experiment with anything, whatever it is, make sure you know where it's come from. And do it somewhere safe with someone you trust. Drugs and drink can be laced.

* If one of us gets off with a boy the rest of us don't know, the others must keep an eye out for where we are.

* Always make sure all of us have got a lift home or are traveling home together.

* Keep talking to each other, even if one of us has gone a bit weird.

16

Police

Later in the afternoon we went up to Muswell Hill to buy some special card for printing our ground rules on to. Halfway down the Broadway, who should we see standing outside Marks and Spencer, but Josh.

Nesta nudged me. "Eyes right," she said. "Trouble ahead."

Josh hadn't seen me, and for a moment, I felt like turning around and running. But no, I told myself, be grown-up about this. I can't spend my life running away from boys I've had a bad time with.

"Do you want us to come with you?" asked T. J.

I shook my head. "Nah, just give me a minute."

The girls headed into a nicknack shop next to Marks and Spencer and I took a deep breath and walked over to Josh. He looked very surprised to see me, like a rabbit caught in the headlights.

I smiled. "Hey, Josh."

He looked up and down the road as though he wanted to make a getaway.

"I wasn't *that* bad, was I?" I said, trying to make a joke of last night.

"Nah, course not," he said, nervously glancing into Marks and Spencer as though looking for someone.

"Are you all right?" I asked.

Just at that moment, I saw a policeman come out of the shop. He took one look at Josh and headed straight for him. Now Josh really did look uncomfortable. He stared at the pavement, like he was hoping it would open up and swallow him whole. I glanced over at the policeman. No doubt about it, he was definitely coming for Josh. Hell's bells, I thought as my mind began to run riot. Josh is in trouble. Maybe he's been caught smoking dope in the park. Oh God, he's going to be arrested. I started to panic inside. Oh no, what if it gets back to Mum, just when I've made it up with her. It will ruin everything.

The policeman stopped, turned to look at me and smiled a really friendly smile. Uh? I thought. What's going on?

"Well, come on, then, Josh," said the policeman. "Introduce us."

Josh sighed heavily. "Um, this is Izzie," he muttered. "Izzie, this is . . . this is . . . my dad."

Josh's *dad*! I thought. His dad is a *policeman*?

Josh's dad beamed at me. "So you're Izzie? You're the one Josh went to see sing last night. Good to meet you."

My brain went into overdrive. A policeman? Of course. Oh poo. I've been so *stupid*. "Dad spends a lot of time down at the police station," Josh had said. "Never know where he is. . . ." I'd just assumed that his dad was a criminal and he'd let me believe it. I could kick myself. Stupid, stupid, I thought. It was all coming back to me. Josh saying how easy it was to feed girls a line, then they just run with it, hear what they want to hear. Exactly what I'd done, and when he'd seen I'd fallen for it, hook, line, and sinker, he hadn't done anything to disillusion me. Of *course*, a boy like Josh *would* say that he didn't want to end up like his dad. And he never actually said the word "criminal."

"Um, yeah. Izzie," I blustered. Close up, Josh's dad looked really nice. Big and jolly. Nothing like the difficult man who had no time for his son, who Josh had described.

"Josh never lets me or his mum meet his friends," he continued, "so it's good to see one of you at last. Come over to the house one day—that is, if you can get Josh to bring you. He's never at home these days. We never see him. I hope you're not like that with your parents."

I glanced at Josh. He was still staring at the pavement, looking like he wanted to die.

Later we all went back to Lucy's for a farewell-to-the-holiday pizza. The girls thought it was hysterical when I told them what had happened.

"We were watching from inside the shop," said Lucy. "We thought you were going to be arrested."

"I know. So did I for a moment. Even though I haven't done anything wrong, the minute he started walking toward me, I felt so guilty."

"Until he turned out to be Josh's dad," laughed Nesta.

"I know, I could have kicked myself! Talk about gullible, that's me. Just called me stupid."

"No," said T. J. "It could have happened to any of us."

"Well, never again," I said. "I'm older, wiser, smarter."

"Until next time," said Nesta. "Some guy will come along, flutter his eyelashes, and . . ."

"Maybe," I said, "but I don't think I'll be quite as gullible next time."

Once we'd finished the pizza, I got ready to go.

"You're leaving early, Iz," said Lucy.

"Ah well. This is the new sensible Izzie. School tomorrow, so I want to get my things ready, plus I said I'd look in on Mum's dinner party. You know it's her birthday today? Well, she's having some friends over. I'll only pop in for a minute or so, just to show my face as they'll probably all be sitting round, having some boring discussion about mortgages or something. Best show willing."

"Hmm, sounds like a real fun time. Not," said Nesta.

When I opened the front door at home, the strangest sight met my eyes. The kitchen was a total mess, and when I went and stuck my head round the living room door, I saw that all Mum's friends were up hippie dancing. They looked more than a bit merry, especially Angus who waved at me happily from the corner of the room. I stood in the doorway for a moment and watched with amazement. Mum saw me looking and came over. "Do you want to join us, Izzie? Have half a glass of wine?"

"No, thanks," I said, then smiled. "I've just got back from my AA meeting. I've gone teetotal."

One of her friends looked at me oddly. "Only joking," I said, then headed up the stairs. I knew exactly what I was going to do. Bath, bed, and a hot chocolate.

While the adults downstairs danced away, reliving their youth, I was happy to have an early night, tucked up like an old grandmother. Does anyone ever act their age? I wondered as the sounds of the Rolling Stones floated up through the ceiling. I thought about banging on the floor and asking them to turn the music down, then I thought no, Mum's only middle-aged once. I'll let her have her fun.

Song for Aging Parents:
C'mon Let's Dance

My mother is a hippie,
My stepdad is a geek,
My friends all play video games seven days a week.
I'm stuck in the middle, what else can I say?
We're all just little kids, though some of us are gray.
So let's dance, c'mon everybody, let's dance.

You're a short time growing up
And a very long time dead,
Sometimes you gotta shake the serious
Right outta your head.
So let's dance, c'mon everybody, let's dance.

You're a short time growing up
And a very long time dead,
So let's all shake the serious stuff
Right outta our heads.
Let's dance, c'mon everybody, let's dance.

So grab yourself a hippie, hang on to a freak.
Put your loudest music on and get up on your feet.
And let's dance, c'mon everybody, let's dance.
Let's dance, c'mon everybody, let's dance.

For more fab fun with Lucy,
Izzie, Nesta, and T. J., don't miss

Mates, Dates, and
SEQUIN SMILES

by

cathy hopkins

from
simon pulse
published by
simon & schuster

"Pah," I said. "I wouldn't go out with Adrian Cook if he was dipped in gold and covered in fivers."

Izzie gave me a disapproving look. *"Nesta.* Covered in fivers? You mean, if he was loaded. So what? I don't think how rich or poor a boy is should make the slightest bit of difference. It's who he is, if he's interesting, good company that counts."

I pulled a silly face back at her. She can be a real priss queen sometimes. "Yeah, but he has to be *reasonably* cute," I said.

"So what if he's cute," asked Izzie, "if he's boring to be with? Just good looks don't count for much after a few dates. You always judge by externals."

"Do not."

"Do."

"Not."

The four of us were sitting in a line on the edge of the bathtub in the bathroom at Lucy's house. T. J., Izzie, Lucy, and me. We were covered in some home-made facial gloop that Lucy and Izzie had concocted in the kitchen and were discussing the local boy talent in North London. Pretty short on the ground in my opinion. And I *don't* only judge by externals, I thought. Of course I care what a boy's like inside.

"Beauty is only skin deep," said T. J., peering at herself in the mirror opposite.

"Yeah, but not today," I replied, looking at our reflections. "We look like ghastly ghouls. What is in this stuff, Lucy? It feels very sticky. Are you sure you were meant to put so much honey in it?"

Lucy reached for her natural beauty book, which was on the windowsill. "I think so," she said. "Yeah, egg yolk, yeast, and honey."

"Sounds disgusting," I said. "I wish you hadn't told me."

It was Sunday and sometimes there's not a lot to do on a Sunday, especially if it's raining like it was today. Lucy suggested we have an afternoon of beauty treatments round at her house and as none of us were that well off in the pocket-money department, she decided to make DIY face masks. Think I'll stick to nicking Mum's posh ones when she's out from now on,

I thought. Egg on my face? Never a good idea at the best of times.

"Well, if it doesn't work, no problem. You can always eat it," said Lucy, sticking her tongue out and licking her top lip.

"I wouldn't if I were you," said Izzie. "Raw egg can give you that salmonella disease."

"That's quite rare," said T. J. "And I think the egg has to be off."

T. J.'s our resident medical adviser on account of the fact that both her parents are doctors and some of their medical knowledge rubs off on her.

Lucy quickly put her tongue back in her mouth. "Yuck," she said.

Izzie took her trainers off, put a towel in the bath, then got in and lay down with her feet resting up on the taps. "Honestly, the things we girls have to do to look beautiful," she said. "I bet boys never do anything like this."

"Don't you believe it," said Lucy. "Steve and Lal are always slapping moisturizer all over them. And they take an age in the bathroom getting ready. Boys can be just as vain as girls."

"At least we don't have to shave," said T. J.

"Well, not our faces," I said. "But we do our legs and under our arms. Waxing is better than shaving though; it lasts longer."

"My gran does her chin," T. J. added, laughing. "She said it's one of the awful things about getting old. Hair starts sprouting everywhere—from your ears, your nose, your chin."

"Oo, sexy," I said. I took a close look at my nostrils in the mirror. "I hope that never happens to me."

After we'd rinsed off our face masks, we resumed our discussion in Lucy's bedroom about the local boys. What Izzie had said about me judging by externals had irked me. I wasn't so superficial as to only go out with boys because of what they looked like or if they had money or something. My last long-term boyfriend had been very rich, but that wasn't the reason I went out with him. I liked him for who he was. That is until he dumped me because he was going to university in Scotland and wanted to be free to date any new girl that he fancied up there. Maybe the girls think I only dated him because he was loaded. I decided to find out what they really thought about me, but planned to ask them in a really subtle way.

"So, Izzie, about what you said before. Were you saying that you think I'm shallow?" Oops, I thought. I knew before I'd finished the question that it hadn't come out the way I intended. Subtlety was never my best trait.

Izzie laughed. "No, Nesta, not shallow, but image is very important to you."

"Like it isn't to you?" I asked. I looked at my three friends all busy painting each other's toenails. Lucy's petite and blond, T. J. and Iz are tall and dark, and all three of them are gorgeous in their own ways, but they all work at it, forever trying new things and new looks in an attempt to improve on nature. I am *not* the only one. "And Iz, you did a whole makeover on yourself just before term started in September."

"I know. It's important to all of us," she said as she began to paint T. J.'s toenails a purple shade called Vampire. "All I was saying is that there is other stuff that's important as well. Like, what's inside a person."

"I know that. T. J., Lucy, do you think I'm shallow?"

"I never said I thought you were shallow," said Izzie. "You did."

"Yeah, but think about it," I said, looking at T. J. and Lucy.

Lucy looked uncomfortable. She hates confrontation, but I had to know what my friends really thought of me.

"I wouldn't use the word *shallow*," she said after a few minutes, "but I know a certain sense of style and looking good is important to you."

"T. J.?"

"Um. God. I don't know," she said. "You've obviously got a good brain or else you wouldn't do so well at school."

"Yeah, but am I shallow?"

"Depends on what you mean by shallow," blustered T. J. "I mean, I wouldn't say you're deep . . . but you're not shallow either."

"Who wants to be deep," I said, lowering my voice. "*Bor*-ring."

"I think Izzie's deep," said Lucy, "and she's far from boring. She's always thinking about things and asking questions about stuff like why we're here and what it's all about. You're not boring, Izzie."

Oh, here we go. Now I've managed to insult one of my best friends. Me and my big mouth, I thought. I didn't mean to say that Izzie was boring. I'd better try and say something to make it clear what I really meant.

"Yeah, and where does that get you, Izzie?" I asked. "Who knows the answers to questions like that? You could drive yourself mad asking about life, the universe, and everything. Perhaps that's why you are a bit mad. I reckon, we're here, you get on with it. End of story."

Oops, I thought as Izzie's face fell. I don't think that helped. Maybe I should shut up for a while.

"That's it," said T. J. "Pragmatic. That's what you are, Nesta."

Bugger, I thought. I don't know what pragmatic means. But no way am I going to let on or else they really will think that I'm shallow. Whatever it meant, I felt I was being got at. Huh.

"Right, pragmatic. I guess that's okay."

"Yeah," continued T. J., "you just get on with life without questioning it too much. You like to have fun, do girlie things, enjoy life; you're not a complicated person, and you're not that bothered about educating your mind or anything."

"I am too. I read. I keep up with what's happening."

T. J. and Izzie burst out laughing. "Okay, what have you read lately?" asked T. J.

"*CosmoGIRL! Bliss. OK!* magazine."

T. J. and Izzie exchanged glances.

"What's wrong with that?" I asked.

"Nothing," said Izzie. "We all read the mags and they're great. But when did you last read a book?"

"All the time. We read books every day at school. There's a time and a place for everything. And school is the place for books. Out of school is the place for fun."

"But some books *are* fun," said T. J. "They can take you to different places, let you in to different people's experiences, how others think. Don't close your mind to them just because they're not all glossy with photos of celebrities in them."

I was definitely being got at. T. J. is a regular bookworm. She reads everything and anything and Izzie's dad lectures in English at some university in town and is always giving her heavy-looking books to read.

Not my cup of tea at all, I'd rather watch a good soap on telly, but she dutifully reads everything her dad gives her.

"Okay," I said, "so I'm not a bookworm. That doesn't make me shallow. Lucy doesn't read a lot, do you Luce?"

Lucy looked more uncomfortable than ever now. "Actually, Steve passes on some of his books to me and I quite often read late at night."

"Hah! Closet reader," I said. "I never knew that."

"You never asked," said Lucy, blushing furiously. "And I didn't think you'd be interested."

"Hhmmm. So you think I'm too shallow to have a discussion about books."

"No," T. J. and Lucy chorused.

"Well, I didn't know I had such nerdy brainbox friends," I said.

"See, that's just it," said Izzie. "You think that because someone reads that they're a nerd. You couldn't be more wrong."

"Huh," I said.

"I think," said T. J., "you have different people for different parts of yourself. Like, I can talk to Izzie about books, astrology, and stuff like what life is all about; I can talk to Lucy about fashion and design; and I can talk to you about . . . er, makeup and . . . or . . . I know, advice about boys. Nobody knows more about boys than you, Nesta."

Well that's true, I thought. I suppose it helps having an older brother. Boys have never fazed me. I sussed out pretty early that all of them, no matter what age or how cool they act, are little boys underneath. They are as nervous and unsure about girls as girls are about them.

"So," I said. "We have here Izzie the seeker, T. J. the thinker, Lucy the designer *extraordinaire*, and me, the what? The airhead?"

"Course not," said Lucy. "No one said that. What's gotten into you today? You always come in the top ten in exams in school, so how can you think that you're an airhead? You're the one putting yourself down."

"And you are the boy expert," said T. J.

"Okay then," I said, "when it comes to boys. Fact: The cute ones often don't read because they have got a life. Fact: The nerdy ones bury their heads in books because they haven't got a life."

"Noooo," said Izzie. "No way. You couldn't be more wrong. I mean, take Ben. He's cute and reads loads."

Hmm, I thought. Ben is Izzie's ex and although really nice, not someone I'd call a babe magnet. Definitely not my type.

"Well, I think there are two types of boys," I said. "The hot babe magnets who, okay, might be trouble and break your heart, but are fun and great to be seen out with. And there's the other type, not quite as attractive, but cozy and good company and you know where you are with them, because they don't mess you around, basically because they know that if they did, they might not get off with anyone else."

Izzie laughed. "You always see things in black or white. Nothing in between."

"So?"

"You can't always generalize, especially about people," said T. J. "I don't think everything is black or white. I think there are shades of gray as well. Like, take Steve; he's really clever and also attractive."

I kept my mouth shut. Steve is one of Lucy's brothers and he's been dating T. J. for ages now. But once again, like Ben, yes, nice, a laugh, but babe magnet? No way. I didn't want to insult T. J. by saying that her boyfriend wasn't a babe, nor Lucy by saying that I didn't think her brother was attractive. People can be very defensive about their family. It's like they can say the worst possible things themselves about brothers and sisters, but God help anyone else who says anything bad. I guess I'm the same about my brother, Tony. I slag him off something rotten sometimes, but I won't hear a word against him from anyone else. I dutifully kept my mouth zipped about Steve, but sometimes it's difficult holding in what I really think. Sometimes I worry that I might be getting that disease, Tourette's syndrome or something. I read about it in a magazine. Instead of blood leaking out or people being sick, people puke out their thoughts instead and they shout awful things in public or on the tube or somewhere. They can't help it apparently, like the "What not to say and when not to say it" filter is missing from their brain. I'd be forever in trouble if my thoughts leaked out. I wonder if it's possible to have inner Tourette's syndrome. Sometimes I think awful things about people before I can stop myself. Mad things just pop into my head. Sometimes my thoughts shock even me. In school sometimes, I want to shout "knickers" at inappropriate moments like school assembly when our headmistress is droning on. Or if I see someone really unattractive in the street, I think, "Whoa, there goes a fat ugly one," then I feel awful because some people can't help the way they look. Or when Dad is giving me a hard time about something, I think, "Hhmm. Take your advice, Pater, and stick it up your bum." Luckily, most of the time my brain filter works and I manage to keep my thoughts to myself. Maybe I'm secretly insane? It is a worry.

"So you reckon the choices are gorgeous and danger-ous versus safe and secure but not so gorgeous?" asked Lucy.

"Yeah," I said. "That's your choice. One or the other."

"I reckon you can get boys who are both," said Izzie. "Gorgeous and safe and secure. Not all gorgeous boys mess you around."

"They might not at first," I said, thinking about Simon

dumping me, "but they do in the end, basically because they know they can."

T. J. shook her head. "I agree with Izzie," she said.

"Lucy?" I asked.

She's had this on/off thing with my brother, Tony, for over a year. Even though he's my brother, I can see that he's the first type, i.e.: is v. v. attractive even though a little arrogant with it. There's always a queue of girls after him and he never gets serious about any of them. Except Lucy that is. He really likes her, but half the reason that he stays interested is because she doesn't fall over herself wanting to be with him. She keeps him on his toes. I know for a fact that if she wasn't messing him around, he'd be messing her around. It's like they're doing a dance: He steps forward, she steps back. She steps forward, he steps back. Right now, in the dance, Lucy is stepping back and Tony is stepping forward.

"Um, I also agree with Izzie," said Lucy. "Oh, I know Tony's not exactly Mr. Commitment, but at least he's honest about who he is."

"Yeah, course," said Izzie. "There are all sorts of types. There are boys who are deep *and* gorgeous. Cute boys who think about things. Cute boys who will commit and not mess you around. People are different depending on who they're with, so maybe you just haven't brought out the deeper side of the boys you've been with."

"What do you mean?" I asked.

"Well, like, we're different with different people," said Izzie. "You're one way with your parents, another way with your teachers, another way with your friends, another way with boys."

"Yeah. So?"

"Well, like T. J. was saying, she talks to Iz about some things, Lucy about others, and you about others."

"Yeah," said T. J. "Like I go to Iz for advice and I come to you for a laugh."

I had to think about that. Was that a compliment or an insult?

"Are you saying you don't think I can give advice?"

"No . . . yes," said T. J., looking flustered. "I was trying to say something nice about you. Not many people are as much fun as you. Oh, I don't know. I think you're being oversensitive today, Nesta."

"Yes, don't be a drama queen," said Izzie.

I'm not even going to reply to that, I thought. Drama queen! *Moi?* As *if*.

"All I was saying," continued Izzie, "was that we're probably totally different with different boys, too. With some, you don't feel yourself at all and have nothing to say; with others, you can't stop talking. People bring out different sides of you. Maybe you've never brought out what you call the nerdy side of a boy, because you've never talked about anything to bring it out."

"So you *are* saying I'm shallow and I bring out the shallow part of people, boys included. *And* I can't give advice. *And* I'm a drama queen."

"*No,*" said Izzie. "Oh, I don't know. Just maybe, next time you like a boy, try talking about a book you've read or ask him what he feels about the purpose of life or something."

Huh, I thought, not exactly a fun chat-up line in my estimation. I was feeling peeved by what the girls had said. I don't want to be thought of as an airhead-type drama queen bimbo. I'm not. I do well at school. I *do* think about things. Like, what to wear, how to do my hair, which is my favorite boy band, and so on. But maybe I should talk about "deep" stuff. Books. Um. Maybe I'd better read one—a grown-up one, that is. I used to read a lot when I was younger, but I went off it. I don't know why. I'll start again when I get home, I decided. I'll pick a really intellectual, impressive-type book and that will show them, when I start quoting bits off by heart. Then I'll find a boy and knock his socks off with my brainy brain-type brain as well as my looks. I shall show them all that airhead, I am not.

Lucy's DIY Face Masks

Egg and Yeast Mask

1 egg yolk

1 tablespoon of brewer's yeast

1 teaspoon of sunflower oil

Mix into a smooth paste. Apply to face and neck and leave for fifteen minutes, then rinse off.

NB: The yeast can stimulate the skin and draw out impurities, so not the best one to use before a big party in case it brings out any lurking spots.

Nourishing Mask

1 whole egg

1 teaspoon honey

1 teaspoon almond oil

Mix together, then apply. Leave on for fifteen minutes, then rinse off.

About the Author

Cathy Hopkins lives in North London with her handsome husband and three deranged cats. She has published more than twenty-five books, and is currently at work on another. Apart from that, she is looking for answers to why we're here, where we've come from, and what it's all about. She's also looking for the perfect hairdresser. Visit her at www.cathyhopkins.com.